I've travelled the world twice over,
Met the famous: saints and sinners,
Poets and artists, kings and queens,
Old stars and hopeful beginners,
I've been where no-one's been before,
Learned secrets from writers and cooks
All with one library ticket
To the wonderful world of books.

THE VALLEYS BEYOND

Of the many Australian colonists who decided to leave the cities to make a new life for themselves in the valleys beyond, three families moved to the bush country in the shadows of the Australian Alps— the haughty and ruthless "Black" Olivers, the illiterate and despised family of ex-convict Elijah Tregg, and the Martin family of free immigrants. The illicit relationships between Everitt Oliver and a girl from each of the other families climaxes in a bitter fight that underscores the social barriers of their daily lives.

E. V. TIMMS

THE VALLEYS BEYOND

Complete and Unabridged

ULVERSCROFT
Leicester

LARGE TYPE EDITION

First published 1951

First Large Print Edition
published January 1984
by arrangement with
Angus & Robertson (U.K.) Ltd.
London

British Library CIP Data

Timms, E. V.
  The valleys beyond.—Large print ed.
  (Ulverscroft large print series: historical
  romance)
  I. Title
  823[F]   PR9619.3.T48

ISBN 0-7089-1078-5

Published by
F. A. Thorpe (Publishing) Ltd.
Anstey, Leicestershire
Printed and Bound in Great Britain by
T. J. Press (Padstow) Ltd., Padstow, Cornwall

Hither of old queer flotsam drifted,
Borne from afar on an age-old stream—
Men and women, with hope uplifted,
Spurred and stirred by a splendid dream.

They had their triumphs, their gains, their
*   losses,*
Their noons of laughter, their nights of
*   care;*
Back on the hills are some rough crosses—
A name . . . a date . . . and, perchance, a
*   prayer.*

—RODERIC QUINN.

FOREWORD

WITH the abolition of the transportation of condemned persons to New South Wales in 1840, the tide of assisted and unassisted immigration, previously a mere trickle, set in strongly towards the Australian colonies. It was the beginning of the great exodus from the British Isles of those who had influence and money to establish themselves, of unfortunates whom poverty had driven out, and of people who desired a better life for themselves and particularly for their children. The terrible distress of hungry Ireland, the harsh rural and industrial life of England, the inability of thousands in Scotland to find sustenance, the glitter of adventure and the lure of opportunity in a new land, sent a stream of humanity flowing to the antipodes.

These seekers after a new life, these voyagers who looked upon a vision, had heard of the eerie solitudes in the immense Australian distances, those frightening silences of the lonely lands. Stories had been told of ruthless escaped convicts turned bush-rangers; of hardship and peril; of stealthy, treacherous blacks; of thirst and flood; of privation and roaring bushfires; yet they counted these things less terrifying for themselves and their children than the bleak prospects of pauperism and the grim patronage of the parish. The poor of England were further stricken when the Act of Enclosure deprived them of the use of the common lands, and the humble man, the honest and decent man of family, had to sell his few cattle that provided milk, butter and an occasional cask of beef to find money to buy precious daily bread; and industrial workers—tossed by the capricious fluctuations of trade from job to job in the great factories and foundries, in the mines and the shipyards—were in work one month and in the workhouse the next.

And there was the grim background: the fact that a few years earlier, out of England's population one and a half million were paupers; that, although silks and satins shone under the candles and lamps of comfortable manor houses, hungry men and women were still roaming the rural lands and were crowding in jails and workhouses where food was rarely seen and drinking water almost non-existent; and that in such squalid London parishes as St. Giles men and women perforce lay promiscuously in ragged beds costing a penny a night, sacrificing morals to preserve the shivering flesh against the bite of bitter winds in black and stinking streets. The punishment for stealing goods under the value of one shilling was a whipping, and over one shilling, execution—the difference between the whip and the rope being the princely sum of twopence.

All these things were familiar. The people knew their England, their Scotland, their Ireland, and knew that for millions the longed for Reform Act of 1832 was a mockery. They knew when their cries went wailing through the land that if the anaesthetic pomp of a procession did not silence them with its scarlet show of wealth and power the sabres of red-coated guards would. Thousands, tens of thousands, of upright and self-respecting people, as well as the scum of the streets, lifted longing eyes to look towards the land where the Southern Cross shone, determined, if means could be obtained, to emigrate, to get away from poverty or frustration, to venture, to take themselves and their families to a new world and there find a new way of life.

But what did these emigrants, so many of whom could neither read nor write, know of this great country at the very end of the earth? This new civilization born in chains? This continent oldest in time and most recent in settlement where mountains and plains rolled on beyond mysterious horizons, where inland rivers vanished into unknown fastnesses? They knew, of course, of the penal colonies, but who among them could realize that a strange society had fashioned so bizarre a way of life in this land they could not visualize? They could understand that convict and emancipist were despised, but not that immigrants, both assisted and unassisted, were mistrusted, that a haughty gentry of a new landed class looked down upon all. We read in Clark's *Select Documents in Australian History*, a shrewd and searching analysis of this colonial society:

From this time on particularly, a separating wall was raised, perhaps forever, between these two classes of Europeans; between the convict, whose brow bore the mark of infamy, and the merchant, workman or farm labourer who had arrived as a free man with his family; between the emancipated prisoner and the soldier who had been granted the land on which he had with such difficulty forced the lazy convict to work before his emancipation. In this country one finds isolation literally perpetuated from generation to generation, among men of identical origin, language, education, customs; a system of classes which are continually placed side by side, brought together, mingled, and nevertheless always quite distinct and separate. One feels that there is no religion there to inculcate fraternity, love and altruism, to encourage reconciliation, sanctify repentance and break down disdainful pride. The convict's son, when repulsed by his neighbour, bridles and allows his soul to be filled with the worst sort of pride—that of taking pride in the crimes of his forebears. The daughters of convicts cannot be mentioned without a blush; the less said about them the better. The descendant of a free colonist, or the lowest ranking non-commissioned officer, once he has become a landholder, will only mix socially with his family, if he has any, and a small circle of friends; beyond this circle his fellow citizens and other men will be strangers to him, barbarians and almost enemies. These two characteristics, chosen from a thousand others equally authentic, illustrate the mental attitude of the two classes which are still numerous and which predominated during the first phase of colonization.

Of these realities emigrants were in the main ignorant, as they were of the physical characteristics of the land, and the unique populations moulded by the unnatural conditions of life in penal colonies such as New South Wales and Van Diemen's Land. Some of them had heard of the struggles of the first free colonists on the Swan River in Western Australia in 1829; of those free men and women establishing themselves in the swamps of Holdfast Bay; of the primitive village of Adelaide sprawled under the Mount Lofty Range, the new Province of South Australia. The story had been told of Batman and Fawkner and the slab huts of the roaming Van Diemen's Land adventurers, of the settlement named Melbourne by Sir Richard Bourke in 1837 when he went to the Port Phillip district to form an ordered society there; but most people thought of

Australia only as a vast country of black savages and convicts, with here and there a handful of officials, free settlers and military guards. A few were aware that law-breaking and elusive squatters had trespassed beyond the pale, and by their continued expansion and defiance had forced the government of New South Wales to introduce a licence system for granting occupation of the far lands. Those who could read had read that Sydney, now gas-lit, and Hobart, still lamp-lit, were turbulent and rapidly expanding seaports attracting the shipping of the seven seas; and that inland villages were growing with the passing years into towns of permanence and importance. Some even knew that the limit of New South Wales had been extended in 1839 to include New Zealand—that fabulous land where Maori chieftains such as Pomare, grandfather of Hare Pomare for whom Queen Victoria became godmother, kept scores of beautiful slave girls at that Port Royal of the Pacific, the Bay of Islands, for the pleasure of visiting whalemen; where tattooed warriors feasted upon flesh of slain enemies; where in the south snow-capped peaks pierced the cold clouds, and in the north island an almost tropical paradise enclosed grim *pahs* and cooking pots.

Of England at this time it has been proudly said:

Palaces, churches of extraordinary beauty, hospitals, markets, and public buildings for all imaginable purposes, have been erected, and still the grand work of social progress is considered incomplete. Of the great empire over which Queen Victoria sways the British sceptre, it has justly been said that the sun never sets thereon. It exceeds the limit of any other empire, and comprises one fifth of the entire human family. Among this multitudinous population the English language is more or less heard; and to the vast population the small island of Great Britain is the centre of influence and the source of authority. It has been justly remarked, "Not an hour of the twenty-four, not one round of the minute hand is allowed to pass over the dial, in which, on some portion of the globe, the air is not filled with accents that are ours. They are heard in the ordinary transactions of life, or in the administration of law; in the deliberations of the senate-house, or in the council-chamber; in the offices of private devotion, or in the public and private observances of the rites and duties of a common faith." Such is the majesty of England in the 19th century, and, with a noble Queen at its head, rules the world.

But the jewelled cloak of a national pride was carefully drawn over the suffering, the frustration, the impotence, the actual hunger of millions. Crime was rampant, poverty the lot of many sad families, and so the ships of the emigrants began to sail. Emigration agents in the British Isles painted alluring and distorted pictures of what awaited the emigrant in Australia. Eager listeners, so many of them illiterate, were told of unlimited cheap land, of the clamorous demand for labour at unheard of wages. According to these glib agents, Australia was a happy sunlit land, a country where the servant soon became the master, where fortunes awaited everyone: a cunning blend of fact and fantasy.

So these hopeful adventurers ventured across the world, expectations high, their fears, if any, locked deep in their hearts. God-fearing men and women and their children; men of all trades and professions; foreigners from Europe and America, and brown men from the Pacific Isles; soldiers and sailors done with the trade of war; the well-to-do and the ne'er-do-well; single men, and hundreds of unmarried young women from all the counties of the old country hoping to find employment and eventually husbands—all making for the colonies of New South Wales, Van Diemen's Land, Western Australia, and the Province of South Australia, some to settle in the towns and the seaports, others to take the slow-moving covered drays and wagons and coaches and journey on to the valleys beyond. They sailed for this new land to grasp what was denied them in the old—opportunity, the chance to make something of themselves and of their children. And this they did.

E. V. TIMMS.

Sydney
  October, 1951.

1

OCTOBER, 1841.

It was a warm, moonlit night in Sydney Town's street of the wantons, and oil-lamps and gas-lights sent oblique rays through open windows and doorways. Lower Elizabeth Street was turbulent with its customary nocturnal activities, and from where the lamps shone came deep laughter and shrill singing, but where the doors and darkened windows were closed there was a significant silence. Over on the east side Hyde Park stretched darkly away, and hanging on the air were echoes of voices, indistinct, plangent overtones rising above the rattling of town gigs and carriages as they bounced over the rutted roads.

There were many people in Elizabeth Street, for the night was early as yet, and it was still safe to walk in this Alsatia of Sydney Town, this recognized abode of the prostitute and the lawless. Constables in blue jackets and yellow waistcoats twirled twinkling blue batons as they kept a watchful eye on drunken carters and brawling seamen up from the Cove to wench and then wager on vicious dog-fights staged in backyard pits.

Along this street walked a woman, tall, observant, thoughtful. She was good-looking, dignified, and perhaps thirty-three years of age, with dark hair holding a reddish tint, and serious grey eyes that looked at provocatively half-dressed girls lounging in doorways, and at be-feathered doxies strolling arm in arm with the night's prey. She walked slowly on, lamp-light touching now and then her black silk dress with its white collar, and showing momentarily her composed features under her black bonnet. Often, alone and observant, she walked the crooked streets of Sydney Town; the high Rocks area—that "Acropolis of the South"—overlooking Sydney Cove and the Parramatta River winding into the west; the narrow lanes where stone gateways and walls built by convicts sent back the whispers of shadowed shapes; the wharves of Darling Harbour and Sydney Cove where tall ships were fast to the bollards; and the Government Domain and Hyde Park where the unemployed and the unwanted gathered. She was familiar now with the daily and nightly bustle of this lively town of nearly thirty thousand inhabitants; with its sharp contrasts of affluence and poverty; with its harbour-side mansions and back-street hovels; with its bitter political and religious intolerances; with its sober merchants and hard-eyed harlots; with its branded convicts waiting for life to pass; with its daily cavalcade of adventurers going into the far places on rumbling coaches and slow, bullock-drawn wagons and covered drays; with its roaring grog-shops and sedate hotels, its crowded theatre and well-stocked shops. Few knew this town better than she did, for she looked beyond the stones, the rutted streets, the chains, the laden wool-wagons, the ships, the mansions and the hovels, into the hearts of the people. She was horrified by the appalling condition and dire needs of the assisted or "bounty" immigrants, families and single men and women, walking almost daily off ships into this country, the men waiting hopelessly for work, the girls taking to the streets in despair.

Leaving Elizabeth Street, she crossed into Hyde Park in the direction of the Domain. There were lights behind the windows of St. James' Church, and in the Convict Barracks near by a bell struck the hour. The candle-lamps of passing vehicles danced like marsh-lights along King Street and down by the Catholic Church, and from the Hyde Park fountain came the clanging of the pump and high laughter. Her observant eyes saw couples huddled together on the grass; saw men sitting in a circle and passing a bottle; saw ragged urchins flitting here and there in the shadows; saw a group of girls crouched together and not speaking. She walked to the girls and said gently:

"I take you to be immigrants. Have you any money? Have you anywhere to go?"

A girl with a soft Irish voice answered her.

"No, marm—we've no money, marm—we've nowhere to go."

"You *are* immigrant girls?"

"Yis, marm—we be bounty immigrants. There be six of us 'ere, marm."

"How long have you been in Sydney Town?"

"Different toimes, marm. It be a month for some since we left the ship."

"Can you get employment of any kind?"

"No, marm," was said slowly. "No one wants us."

"What will you do?"

There was despondency in the reply. "We don't know, marm. It looks moighty loike

14

starve—or the strate. We've sold most everything we had to git food—except ourselves."

The tall woman stood silent for a moment, then she said, "I am sorry. But don't lose heart. I feel that something will be done for you—"

Another girl said dispiritedly: "Faith, it ud better be quick, marm. We've 'ad no food since yisterday. I got nothin' left to sell. I sold me shoes yisterday. What I'll sell tomorrer . . . I don't want to think about."

"Again I say don't lose heart, and keep off the streets. I am sure something will be done for you."

A third girl, one with a Scottish accent, said sharply, "Aye, they a' tell us tha'. But, losh! here we be, hungry, destitute, unwanted—wi' only ane thing we can do tae live—aye, sell ourselves. It seems tae me they dinna want immigrant lasses at a'—only prostitutes. But they didna tell us tha'—they didna tell us tha'."

The woman who was speaking to them asked, "Would you go into the country if positions could be found for you there?"

"Aye!"

"Yis!"

"No!" said another. "I've 'eard about them blacks an' bushrangers—I ain't agoin' to be speared by one or raped by t'other. I be used to the town—I be afeared of them wild places—but I'll work well for a good mistress 'ere, ma'am. But who be you, ma'am, as be speakin' us so fair?"

Quietly came the reply.

"I am Mrs. Chisholm—Caroline Chisholm. I am hoping to be able to help in some way."

"Och!" said the first girl who had spoken. "No one 'ud listen to ye, marm. Who'd listen to a woman? Faith, I'll wait jist wan day more . . . thin I'll starve no more. More'n two thousan' immigrants 'ave arrived this month. The tents roun' the Immigration Barracks be full—Mr. Merewether, the agent marn, says they can't take no more. There be 'undreds loike us sleepin' in parks an' roun' the waterfront. Lots 'ave gone on the strate arlready—there be no work. They tol' us lies afore we shipped, wicked lies, marm. Th' only work for us, marm, be to warm some marn's bed—an' the marn with it."

Mrs. Chisholm's voice was gentle with sympathy.

"I ask you all to wait one day more. Wait

16

for me here at sunset tomorrow—if you haven't found employment during the day. Will you do that?"

There was a little silence, and in the darkness the sound of someone crying softly. The Scots girl said slowly, "Aye . . . we'll wait till sunset. An' thank ye for speakin' sae kindly tae us."

Caroline Chisholm walked away; she had other girls to talk to in the Domain. Those she had just left watched her go. The Scots girl spoke again.

"Tha' be the first word o' comfort we've had for a lang, lang time. Ah, well—'tisna rainin'—we'll sleep well enough unner the stars."

"Och, yis——" came like a sigh.

"What if she . . . doesn't come back to us tomorrow?" asked one who had not spoken before. "I'm so hungry. I'm sick with it——"

"If she doesn't come back—the strate. An' the good God be kind to us thin."

The girl who said she was hungry stood up.

"I'm not waiting for any sunsets," she said in a cold, flat voice. "I'm eating—tonight."

"No, Becky—no!" came from several.

The toneless voice went on: "I can smell that stinking harbour, the lousy ships, and

the dung in the streets, the lies and the hope-
lessness of the whole miserable town. I want
the smell of food under my nose—good hot
food to choke it all out. So . . . good-bye."

"Becky—no!" it was almost a scream from
the Irish girl. "Wait—wait till tomorrer—jist
wan more day, Becky——"

The voice of the girl named Becky came
out of the shadows as she walked away.

"You said you'd wait one more day,
Mary—I can't wait. What is one more day?
Hell! That's what it is. Good-bye."

"Ah, swate Jasus——" said the Irish girl.
"Did we come arl acrost the world for—this?
No more sunsets, says Becky, but 'tis sunset
for her."

"Aye," said the Scots girl. "Aye . . .'tis
sunset for Becky . . . Aye."

2

CAROLINE CHISHOLM felt the burn of the sun on her shoulders as she walked up Bridge Street towards Government House. The town itself was busy. Carriages and gigs rattled and bumped along; drays, carts, and slow bullock-wagons rumbled over the ruts; some wagons taking heavy guns from the barracks in George Street to the Cove for transfer to Bradley's Head and Pinchgut where Colonel Barney was making preparations to repel a possible French intrusion. Men and women rode on horseback in all the streets; sullen convicts still under sentence swept and repaired flags and stone water-courses; lamp-lighters were adjusting the gas-lights; people entered and left coffee-shops and hotels; wool was lowered into the holds of ships; banks, shops, newspaper offices, foundries, shipyards, slaughter-houses, breweries, coach and carriage works, markets, all were busy; scarlet-coated soldiers, and nondescript seamen of all the seas, passed along; and standing in disconsolate groups were bounty immigrants staring through shop windows at goods they could not buy.

Caroline was conscious of a quick surge of apprehension. How would the Governor receive her? Coldly, no doubt. For a little while she paused beside the public fountain in Macquarie Place and permitted her mind to dwell upon the work she wanted to do in this colony of New South Wales. Two years had passed since she and her husband, Captain Archibald Chisholm, had arrived in Sydney from Madras, but he had recently been recalled to take part in the Opium War, in China, leaving her here, at her own request, with her small sons. She had always been interested in philanthropic work, even when she was Caroline Jones in far away Northampton, where her father had been a yeoman farmer. In Madras, where her husband had been stationed, she had organized and successfully conducted a school for the children of garrison soldiers, and it was her earnest desire now to be of service to the homeless and destitute immigrants in this colony.

But her high intelligence left her under no illusions as to the difficulties of the task she had set for herself. She knew the colony was rent with all the old hatreds of a cruel past, with the bitter strivings of ambitious men, with the terrible indifference of an almost fantastic society towards those damned by the name of "convict" and "emancipist", and towards the bewildered and frustrated immigrants. Her frequent walks and talks in the streets and homes of the town had revealed the distress of the bounty immigrants. This Australia was still a land of punishment where the chains of the convict rattled in the iron-gangs; a land where the free and the freed struggled to win independence and release from the official and social oppression of Downing Street and the local Exclusives; a land of adventuring men and women daily journeying into the unknown; a land of far mountains and plains and hidden valleys where the wounds of old refused to heal. Thinking of all these things, Caroline turned again towards Government House.

When she was shown into the Governor's presence he stood up to receive her. Sir George Gipps, distinguished soldier and administrator, was fifty years of age, with strong features, keen dark eyes and iron-grey hair. He bowed to Caroline. This was not her first visit, and he recalled how, when she was first announced he had expected to see some old crack-pot of a woman, one obsessed with crazy philanthropic ideas. And he remembered his shock on observing the tall and handsome young matron.

As she curtsied he said,

"Please be seated, Mrs. Chisholm."

"Thank you, Your Excellency."

He smiled a little as he sat down at his desk.

"Is it possible I know why you are here—again?" he asked pleasantly.

Then Caroline smiled. Her eyes twinkled, for she liked this Governor and appreciated the difficulties of his high office.

"I am sure you know why I am here, sir."

He nodded, then his eyes became thoughtful.

"I admire your Christian attitude, Mrs. Chisholm, in the matter of these immigrants, but I am not wholly convinced of the wisdom of allowing a woman to deal with such a problem."

Caroline listened intently. He went on:

"I know that you were a Protestant, and that you are now a Roman Catholic, and I fear your personal activities would arouse suspicion as to your motives. And I have heard that many of your own Church are not in sympathy with your scheme."

"That is true, Your Excellency," was said quietly. "But the most important thing, at the moment, is that I *have* a scheme."

Sir George reddened slightly. Then he smiled.

"Yes, that is important, madam, and praiseworthy. I am as well aware as you are of the plight of these people, and Lady Gipps has spoken to me about your wish to engage actively in helping them."

"I am grateful to her ladyship."

"But you are not so grateful to me—eh?" he asked quizzically.

Caroline looked straight at him.

"You have been very kind in receiving me, Sir George, and in listening to my wishes. I believe, with all the faith that is in me, that I can personally do much to help settle these immigrants—especially the unmarried girls—in good positions."

"How, Mrs. Chisholm—how?" he asked.

Caroline drew in a deep breath. It had better be said now and settled.

"First of all, sir, I would like quarters in the present Immigration Barracks at the corner of Bent and Phillip streets——"

The request seemed to astonish Sir George. "Quarters, Mrs. Chisholm? For whom, pray?" he asked.

"For myself, first of all, sir, so that I shall have an office where I can work, and even more important, for accommodation for single girls who have, if I may say it without being indelicate, only the streets left to them. After the ten days' grace allowed them on the ships they are sent ashore to fend for themselves. Hundreds at this moment are in the parks and the Domain unemployed and desperate. It is, Sir George, a sorry and disgraceful state of affairs."

"H'm. And then?" he asked a little gruffly. This Mrs. Chisholm had a disconcerting way of saying what she really thought.

Caroline said slowly and earnestly, "And then, sir, with the help of God, and the sympathy of the people of this colony, I shall begin my work."

"And that work will be, Mrs. Chisholm?"

"I plan to form country centres for the reception of immigrants—depots, in fact, where employers and employees may meet and settle matters. I shall write to suitable people in different parts of the country, and through them let the farmers, and squatters

24

know what labour is availabe. I shall go myself, if I have to, with these girls, and see they are not exploited."

Sir George stared at her. This woman took his breath away with the audacity of her proposals. He looked at her, at the reddish-dark hair under the black bonnet, at the serious grey eyes appraising him, at the determined set of her lips.

"But—but, Mrs. Chisholm——" he began.

Her voice had a ring in it as she interrupted him.

"Please, Sir George. Surely that which I beg of you is a small concession to ask of the government? Just a corner somewhere where I can begin my work. Sydney Town, Parramatta, Windsor, and other centres, have idle and frustrated immigrants not knowing what tomorrow holds for them. Ships are bringing in these people faster than they are being employed. They cannot all be absorbed in the towns I have mentioned—they will have to go out, out to the far places. I do not exaggerate, Sir George, I walk among these people, these girls. I know—I *know*—I can help them if I am permitted to do so. I believe that as a Christian I should help them, and as a woman who has children of her own I want to help them. I am pleading with you, sir, to allow me to try—to try."

"Isn't it likely you will bring only ridicule upon yourself, madam?" he asked somewhat brusquely.

"Upon *myself*, Sir George?" she retorted.

He moved uneasily.

"Mrs. Chisholm, I can see you have great courage. But for a *woman* to attempt to do these things——"

"Who understands a woman better than a woman, sir? I *know* what they want, and what I can do for them. I also know that the government, under the bounty system, has no immediate responsibility in looking after them when they get here. But when they *do* get here—what then? I have been through the streets and the parks, on the wharves and on the ships, and I have seen what confronts them. I cannot make myself content with shrugging away that knowledge. All I ask, sir, is that I be *permitted*, if not encouraged, to do what I can for them. And I want those quarters this afternoon, Sir George."

"Good God——" he said very softly. "Good God! You certainly know your own mind, madam."

"I have very strong reasons——"

"Yes, yes! I have gathered that."

"I am not asking anything for myself. I want no payment——"

He waved a hand.

"The whole thing is . . . most unusual, Mrs. Chisholm. I fear many will consider it fantastic, a meddling in matters of government administration that ought not to be permitted."

"Surely, sir, it cannot be fantastic to help the helpless?"

Sir George leant back in his chair. He was somewhat out of his depth. He was a strong and able Governor, a worthy successor to Sir Richard Bourke, and his problems were very similar to those of his predecessor. He himself had given much thought to the immigration problem. He knew the present era of prosperity in New South Wales was coming to an end; he had to listen to the insistent demands of the Port Phillip settlers for separation from New South Wales; he had the same arduous job of upholding the authority of the Colonial Office in the colony; he had an implacable adversary in William Charles Wentworth whose greedy claim to a big slice of the south island of New Zealand he had disallowed; he knew that the demand

27

for self-government so clamorously upheld by Wentworth and his followers could not much longer be denied by the Imperial authorities; he knew the squatters hated the recent abolition of the transportation system; he had heard of the young radical, Henry Parkes, whose utterances were already attracting attention; and he was aware that the thousands of incoming immigrants, both free and bounty, resented the locking of land for the privileged classes. All these things he could grasp and deal with as an administrator and Governor of the colony, but he was unsure of himself in this small matter, and he feared the giving of any support to this woman might bring ridicule, not upon her so much, as upon his own head. Society frowned upon women who meddled in public affairs, and upon those who permitted them to meddle.

"I—I believe you had some measure of success with your philanthropic activities in Madras, Mrs. Chisholm?" he said.

"Yes, Sir George. I had some success there."

He was watching her intently.

"And you expect the same measure of success in your contemplated undertaking here?"

"I do, sir," came firmly.

"Humph! There is already a private employment agency in the town, you know."

"I know. But it can't find work even for itself, sir," was said quietly.

His eyes twinkled. That was a neat one.

"Well, I—I don't suppose there will be any great threat to the Throne, or to Her Majesty's Government, if I grant you the use of a room somewhere in the Immigration Barracks——"

Caroline's eyes shone. Her voice, always pleasant, was vibrant now.

"Oh, Your Excellency!" she said. "I knew—I *knew* you would help me. May I have your letter now, sir?"

Sir George threw back his head and laughed.

"Gad, madam—I believe you will do something. Very well. I will give you a letter to the superintendent there. You understand, of course, the government must be under absolutely no obligation as to money? If we were to start supporting these people it is certain the majority would cease trying to support themselves."

"Those I help will not be a charge upon the government, sir."

"I am glad of that——"

"But, sir——"

His gaze sharpened.

"Yes, madam?"

"I have seen a number of women almost starving, Sir George. And I know they have no money."

Sir George's tone was a little dry.

"You have a convincing personality, Mrs. Chisholm. I think perhaps . . . some form of subsistence could be arranged from the Commissariat, but only, mind you, for the destitute. Will you excuse me while I confirm all this in writing for you?"

She watched him while he wrote, a high spot of colour glowing in each cheek.

"You have no illusions as to the disappointment, and possible insults, you may encounter, Mrs. Chisholm?" he asked.

"I have no illusions, sir. I expect disappointments—and insults. They shall not deter me."

He stood up, and Caroline rose.

"Well, here you are, Mrs. Chisholm. This letter grants you quarters, and gives you the necessary authority and clears you of interference; it also authorizes you to use your discretion in the matter of rations. I shall watch your kindly, and if I may say so, very courageous, endeavours on behalf of these immigrants."

Caroline's heart beat quickly as she took the letter. She had won. Now—*now* she could really begin to help people; she could meet those girls at sunset and give them more than empty words. Gratitude was like a light in her eyes as she said:

"I thank Your Excellency."

That was all. She curtsied again and turned and walked out of the room. Sir George Gipps stood motionless, a little smile playing about his lips, then one hand came up to rest on the back of his head.

"A remarkable woman," he told himself. "Extraordinary personality! But I trust this won't raise any religious issues. Dunmore Lang, I feel sure, will be at her. But she might do something. Who knows? And if someone else wants to laugh—why, let him laugh. I approve."

3

QUIET was the valley.

Down its grassy, well-watered, well-timbered winding way could be seen, afar off, the white serrated summits of the Australian Alps. It was a pleasant valley, warm under the October sun, fragrant with fresh grasses, flowers, and bronze-tipped gums. Here by creek and lagoon were the kangaroo, the dingo, the black swan, the Cape Barron goose, and, before the sun turned cold, the nomadic Wongals, the black men who had known the valley since time began.

The valley was well south of the Hume and Hovell line, yet still north of the Murray River. It ran for miles between the high spurs of a split range. Hume and Hovell did not see the green valley as they passed on their way from Lake George to the crossing we now know as Albury. Count Strzelecki, had he looked far to the north from the heights of Kosciusko, might have glimpsed it. Joseph Hawdon, overlanding with his dependants and stock from St. Vincent County, missed it. And the peripatetic Commissioners for Lands with their armed escorts never rode into it with a clatter of swords and carbines to disturb its tranquillity.

Yet here, in grim reality, was beginning the human drama of Exclusive, of ex-convict, and of free immigrant, a drama played starkly in these years across all the settled areas of Australia. For on the day that Caroline Chisholm began her work publicly, the Martin family, free immigrants but one year in the colony, came with their slow drays and stock to camp under the gums beside a winding creek. The stock were made up of a bull, and seven cows all heavy in calf, some seventy sheep, a hog and five sows, some cocks and hens, four goats, and ducks and geese in wicker crates. Four bullocks drew the leading covered wagon, a draught-horse the big dray, and a grey horse and a bay mare in foal the small dray. The Martins, on this showing, proved themselves to be a family of substance; that they had overlanded right from Sydney Town revealed they were people of courage, settlers prepared to pit themselves against the soil they now selected. Compared with the Olivers, who were established in the southern end of the valley, who ran a thousand sheep and several hundred cattle, and who claimed, as the first squatters, to own all the valley, the newcomers were insignificant indeed; but when measured against the family of ex-convict Elijah Tregg, whose bark humpy clung to a spur two miles to the south, they were indeed affluent.

When the Martins camped they knew nothing of the existence of either the Olivers or the Treggs who sometimes worked for the Olivers. John Martin and his family had emigrated from Kent, where John had been a yeoman farmer, and while in Sydney he had heard of rich valleys off the main route in the south, and he had decided to find such land for himself. He had done so, and the licence for his location was in his pocket, its boundaries not accurately determined, to be sure, but its position known. He knew his tenure was subject to one month's notice of termination if someone other than himself bought the land, but he thought such risk small where he intended to squat. So his wagon and drays rumbled on day after day until he came to his valley. Martin, ruddy-faced and of medium build, drove the wagon team; the vehicle holding furniture, food, seed, and household goods. His wife, Hetty, quiet, greying, sat beside him. Tilly, a handsome blonde girl of twenty-three, drove the first dray, and her sister, Jeanette, aged twenty-one and a brunette, dangled slim bare legs over the side of the dray as it lurched along. The two sons, Tom and Mark, aged nineteen and seventeen respectively, were in the last dray with the youngest daughter, Nan, a grey-eyed brownette of fifteen. The drays carried farm implements, tools, and more food, for it might be another twelve months before any of them went out for fresh supplies.

Hetty drew in a deep breath as her husband stopped the bullocks.

"Is this it, John?" she asked quietly.

His hand went out to clasp hers. Behind the wagon the drays pulled up.

"This is it wife," he said. "Here, on this slope running down to the stream, and close by that fine lagoon, we will build our home. You're very serious——"

Hetty was looking about her.

"I just thought . . . of the girls, John. It'll be lonely for them, and for Tom and Mark, too. They'll see no one in this valley—we're days away from anywhere."

John laughed as he got down off the wagon. He helped Hetty down.

"One thing at a time, wife. Let's get settled first. And in our hearts thank God for preserving us over all the long miles."

"Yes, John." She turned and called, "Tilly—Jeanette—Nan—Tom—Mark! We're home, children, home! Leave the horses stand a moment and come here."

They came. All were bare-headed and bare-footed. Tilly's yellow hair was a thick mane down over her shoulders, Jeanette's a dark mass. Nan had light-brown hair, and grey eyes like her mother. Tom was swarthy, but Mark was fair, and both boys were tall and muscular, and were dressed, like their father, in check cotton shirts and moleskin trousers. The girls and Hetty put on bonnets as John spoke.

"Before I ask God to give us His blessing and protection I want you to look well around you. We have come to this valley from across the world. The Murray River can't be very far to the south. There is good messmate, red-gum and stringybark here for fencing and building. The stock are already eating the native grasses and liking them, and this soil should grow wheat and corn and root crops in season. Lift your eyes and look into the south. We are close to the shadow of the great mountains. No white man is there. You can see the far glint of snow in the sunlight. Whether we succeed or fail depends on our own efforts and faith in the God above us all. Here is our home, here we shall know the years to come. Our house, at first, will be of slabs and roofed with bark. Just across there, as soon as I have given thanks to the Almighty, I shall plough the first furrow—yes; this very day. Bend your heads——"

He prayed, long and earnestly. There they stood, silent, intent upon his words. All said an earnest "Amen" as he finished the prayer. Their journey was done, their tomorrows were beginning. John spoke again.

"You all know what to do. Tilly and Nan will see to the stock; Jeanette will help mother prepare the midday meal; Tom and Mark will cut poles for a rough yard while I plough. Now to work, then to eat, then to work again till the light goes out of the sky. It is our first day, let us not waste it. When night comes we'll sleep under the drays. Let us be busy."

Tilly said to Jeanette as they went to their

dray, "It's very lonely . . . and empty, Jeanette."

Jeanette nodded. "Why did we have to come here at all?" she asked. "We weren't doing so badly on our farm near Maidstone. We all went to school there, and there was market day with always something of interest——"

Tilly's blue eyes turned to her father.

"Visions. Heavens, it's lonely! We must be a hundred miles from anyone. We'll be old women before we ever see a—a man——"

"Oh, I'm not worrying about *them*," said Jeanette.

"I'm not worrying," retorted Tilly. "There aren't any to worry about."

"Oh, but you always liked being pawed——"

"Oh, don't be a beast, Jeanette," said Tilly a little irritably. "Can I help it if men—well, if they show me some attention?"

Jeanette laughed. "You'll be in no danger of any attention, as you call it, in this place. I like interesting things, and people, but I can't be bothered with silly nonsense."

Tilly looked at her sister. "Don't you *ever* want to be married?" she asked.

Jeanette laughed again. "Of course I

do—when it is time—and when the right man comes along. But I refuse to become heated just because I see a man looking at me——"

"Heated?" retorted Tilly, "You'll be frozen stiff in this valley before you ever do. Oh, well—here we are. Let's get the dray placed and the horse out for a drink. And to think we left England—for this."

"Father's like that. He believes there's a great future here—for all of us."

"Mother's not so sure. She is very quiet at times. I wonder what she really does think?"

"I don't know—except that she places father next to God. It wouldn't matter what he did, it would be right; it wouldn't matter where he went, she would follow him. But I don't know what she thinks about—about any great future, or about leaving England to come here. Move the horse up——"

"It seems all we'll ever do here is slave all day and sit and look at each other at night. Look at it! Nothing but hills and valleys going on and on and on. It's vast, and that doesn't describe it. Father believes we shall become rich, that for every acre we could buy in Kent we shall get a thousand here. His brother left him seventeen hundred pounds. He wanted a new freedom, a new life, a new opportunity in a new land. He had a vision! Well—look around you. Here's the vision."

"And here are you—and here am I. Let's laugh. It'll help." John's voice came to the boys.

"Lift the plough out—I'll use two bullocks——"

Mark said, "Indian corn—that's what he'll plant first. And potatoes, and other things for food. He can't start quickly enough."

Tom grunted.

"Help me lift the plough—careful you don't smash your fingers. There. He'll bring the bullocks. Do you like this place, Mark?"

"Yes. I think it's a grand valley. Do you?"

Tom looked about him.

"There's a lot of valley, and it's pretty enough in a wild way, but . . . I don't know."

"What don't you know?"

Thought was reflected in Tom's dark eyes. "There's something wrong with it——"

Mark stared at his brother. "Wrong? The soil's good—plenty of water and grass—and it's ours—miles of it——"

"I know," said Tom slowly. "It isn't what we can see—it's what we can't see that seems to be impressing me. I seem to feel there is something about this valley."

40

"Blacks?"

"No. But they'll be here."

"What then?"

"Can't tell. Something sent a shiver through me as we stood praying—never felt anything like it before——"

"A cold shiver?"

"Dead cold—like ice slipping down your back." He turned as John came up with the bullocks. "You'd better watch for stumps and roots, father. If you bend that beam——"

"I ploughed before you were born, my boy," said John with a laugh. He looked at them. "What think you of our land?"

"There's a lot of it, father——"

John chuckled. His homely face in its ring of white whiskers beamed at them.

"There is. That's why I brought you here. Here you'll be big men, in time, not little men grubbing turnips as the Martins have been for generations past. In years to come you'll have so much you won't be able to count your sheep—or your acres. This is only a beginning. Hook up the chains——"

"You surely don't expect ever to have more than these five thousand acres, do you, father?" Mark asked.

"As I said, Mark—it's a good beginning, a good beginning."

He drove the bullocks away, skilfully slipping the plough over the ground so that the share wouldn't dip in. Tom turned to Mark.

"Grab an axe. We'll get some sort of a sapling yard up before dark."

Nan had a fire alight. She asked her mother. "Are there savage blacks about here, mother?"

"I—I suppose so, Nan——"

"Will they try to spear us? Is that why we're putting the drays round us?"

"Now! Now! Why would they want to spear us?"

"I heard some folks talking in Sydney Town——"

"Lawks, child! People will talk."

"Are you glad we are here, mother?"

"Wherever you children are, and wherever your father is I am glad to be."

"But you are not answering me——"

"Pish, child! Hammer that cree right into the ground and swing the pot over the flames. But I confess, after all those weeks in a wagon, I'll be glad to have a roof over my head again."

"I liked it. It was fine going on and on, seeing new places, everything seeming to be far away. And crossing the rivers—goodness, we had a few scares! And that dreadful hill at—at——"

"Jugiong, I think they call the place."

"Yes, there. And the——"

"Now stop chattering, do, Nan, and build up the fire."

The sound of axes came to them. A hundred yards away the first cut of the soil turned off the mould-board. John ploughed the furrow a good ten chains before he stopped the bullocks and looked back. Hetty saw him flick sweat from his face.

"He's too old for this," she said. "He should have made Tom break the new ground."

Tilly came to them and squatted on her heels.

"Ninety days at sea," she said tonelessly. "A year in Sydney Town—I liked Sydney Town—and now *this*! After eight weeks in a dray."

"Well, Tilly?" Hetty asked patiently.

"Oh, it will be all right, I suppose. We can always light a bonfire and dance round it if we feel dull——"

Tom called to her.

"Get off your hocks, Tilly, and help carry these poles."

Tilly called over her shoulder, "I'm talking to mother——"

"Go and help the boys, Tilly," said Hetty. "We'll need some sort of a yard to fold the sheep for the night."

Tilly stood up. Her eyes were narrowed, her mouth a little sulky.

"Oh, well, we can always light a bonfire," she said sarcastically.

She walked away. Nan stared after her.

"Tilly's sour today," the girl said. "And she always swings her hips when she's put out about something."

Hetty finished mixing a damper.

"Tilly's twenty-three, and she remembers it, my dear. And I suppose it does look a lonely place for a girl that age. Tilly and Jeanette are different. Tilly's warm, and likes the attentions of men; Jeanette never seems to think about them. She is content to be doing things. But, lassy me! There's time for them both yet, and still more for you."

"Pooh! I don't want to get married," said Nan.

Hetty smiled a little.

44

"Neither did I when I was fifteen, my girl. But at twenty-three things are a bit different."

Nan swung the pot over the flames, then looked about her.

"Everything's different now, mother—very different. It seems like another world."

"It is another world, my dear."

"Goodness, yes! We could always go into Maidstone, there were always people—sometimes a fair, and the old church with its banners and carved stalls, and along the road to Rochester Kit's Coty House—those three huge stones with a flat one across the top——"

"I remember it, Nan. And Leed's Castle on the way to Ashford—built on two islands in a lake—and the ruins of Malling Abbey, and the church with the double heart shrine of a crusader. Oh, dear. There we had our friends . . . oh, dear."

"Mother—you're crying! Oh, mother——"

"No. No—I'm all right, Nan. Get some salt beef out of the cask, dear."

"Why doesn't father kill a bullock and let us have fresh meat?"

"You do talk, dear. But one of these days we'll eat fresh meat—fresh beef, not kangaroo, again. But all in God's good time. We won't go hungry."

As she spoke Tom and Mark were felling and stripping saplings; Tilly was carrying the poles to a slight rise beyond the drays; Jeanette was buckling a saddle on the grey gelding; John walking along behind the plough. Then came the faint report of a gun. The sound seemed to have come from the south, but the bordering hills sent little echoes rolling around the valley. The report brought Tom and Mark and Tilly racing towards the drays; John dropped the plough and came running clumsily.

"A carbine——" panted Tom. "We'd better get ours——"

"We're not alone in this valley," said Mark.

John's face was serious.

"No," he said. "Look—down through the trees—there!"

They looked. Riding towards them were four horsemen, one an old man, bareheaded, whose white hair fell to his shoulders. The others were young men swinging easily to the lope of their horses.

Tom whispered to Mark, "Perhaps *this* is the something I couldn't explain."

No one spoke then until the four armed men rode up to them. The old man sat looking at the Martins for a brief moment. He was a tall man, thin, very erect in the saddle. His manner and his clothes showed that he was a gentleman: his long coat of green, the plum-coloured waistcoat, the grey trousers buckling under spurred boots, were garments of quality. The coal-black stallion he rode had good blood in it. When at last he spoke his voice was high, very cold and contemptuous. His eyes, close together and deep in their sockets beside a high-bridged nose, were like specks of blue ice.

"I am Henry Oliver. These young gentlemen are my sons. I own this valley south from the fence with the turnstile in it. I consider this part of the valley also to be my land. I notice—you have had the audacity to use a plough here. Who are you, and why are you here?"

John's chin came up.

"My name is John Martin. My family is with me. I am here because I have in my pocket a licence to occupy this land. The licence was issued in Sydney Town which controls this southern land district. I also have a map purchased from Mr. Clint, the map-maker of George Street, setting out this location accurately. That is why we are here, why we hold five thousand acres here, and why we will stop here."

Oliver's face flushed.

"You are impudent, my man——"

John's voice deepened.

"I am not your man. I am my own man, a free immigrant knuckling to no man. And instead of being on your land—*you* are on mine."

Oliver's face was empurpled now.

"You damned scoundrel!" he rasped. "You get out of this valley—or take whatever consequences may befall you. Licence! Don't talk to me of licence! I dare say you're an old lag the same as that rascal Tregg who sometimes works for me, but who steals my sheep when he is supposed to be minding them. Tregg told me you had come into the valley. The rogues are everywhere and see everything."

John lifted a hand.

"One moment. And enough of that. I told you who we were, and why we are here. I repeat—I have the right to five thousand acres of this valley—and now I'll run right down to your fence—if you have one. That right has

48

been granted by Her Majesty's Government of New South Wales, and no man may challenge that authority. I bid you good day."

Oliver's voice was shrill. He pointed a bony finger at John.

"I have warned you. I own most of the valley; it is my intention to own all of it."

"Not while my licence holds good. Again I bid you good day."

Oliver's voice seemed to choke in his throat.

"You will find out differently if you don't shift your worthless carcass away from here. I can see insolence in the eyes of your striplings—worse in the eyes of your wenches. Remain at your own risk! I will not bandy words with you——"

John's voice was hard.

"Nor I with you. If you cannot be civil—begone! I—hold—this—land! If you cannot be neighbourly—stay away from us. But this land—is *mine*!"

The Olivers sat motionless. The sons, Everitt, the eldest, Conway, the next, and Elliott, the youngest, were as dark as their father was fair. Their haughty manner equalled his.

Then the old man croaked, "You vile gully-rakers! I'll have you out of this valley! No man—No *man*—takes it from me or mine. Remember it!"

With that he wheeled the black horse and galloped away, his sons riding close behind him. Hetty placed a trembling hand on John's arm.

"We have made a bad enemy, John," she said a little fearfully.

John looked after the departing Olivers.

"Aye," he said slowly. "That we have. It was not of our doing."

Tom asked: "And who is this villain, Tregg, that he spoke of?"

John turned to walk back to the plough.

"That, too, we shall doubtless soon know," he replied. "But what we do now know is that we are not alone in this valley."

4

AT sundown John brought the bullocks back. The boys and Tilly had lashed a rough cockatoo fold for the sheep, and a few logs and poles penned the pigs. The cocks and hens were already scuffling in the trees near the drays, settling down for the night, but the ducks and geese had marched off to the lagoon. Hetty had a hot stew ready, and its savoury odour floated round the little camp. Tomorrow, Tom would get some wild ducks from the swamp, perhaps a swan or wild goose. Grey smoke curled up from the fire, and the boys were stretching sail-cloth for the shelters. On a sledge near by was a cask filled with fresh creek water.

It was a calm evening, cloudless. There would be a moon later. All had been too busy since noon to admire the changing colours of the valley, but as they came in to wash and wait for supper eyes were lifted to look at the far-away summits still glowing in the last of the sunlight. John was careful to bring the plough in behind the bullocks. The visit of the Olivers had been disturbing, and there were the Treggs to be reckoned with. He was not worried about the natives, but the Oliver affair was bad business. Hetty was undoubtedly right in her surmise: the Olivers, cold of countenance and hard of eye, were plainly men of determination, their manner a silent expression of ruthlessness and resolve. But it could not be helped.

Mark took the bullocks to the creek and let them go there; they would not stray from the rest of the cattle. John looked about him cheerfully.

"The first day, mother," he said as he washed himself. "Nearly an acre ploughed. It turned off the board fine."

Tilly gave Jeanette a glance.

"He just can't think of anything else," she whispered.

Jeanette smiled.

"Can you?" she asked. "I noticed you looking hard at the eldest of the Oliver boys—the one with the wide beaver hat and the inquisitive black eyes."

Tilly laughed softly.

"Well—didn't he look at me?" she retorted. "The valley might not be so lonely after all."

"You do get notions, Tilly Martin,"

Jeanette scoffed. "Where's Tom going?"

"Cow," said Tilly shortly. "Calf."

Hetty called to them: "Tilly—Jeanette! Put the tailboards across these logs for a table. Supper's nearly ready."

Tom called as he started to walk back, "It's a heifer. Good omen. Cow's all right. What about the dingoes?"

John answered, "Put the calf in a dray—later will do."

"That wretched cow will bellow all night," said Tilly. "She won't leave the dray."

"Can't be helped, dear," said Hetty.

Mark came from the creek.

"There are fish in those pools."

"Fish!" echoed Nan. "We'll never be hungry here. We'll make a trap tomorrow."

"Sit round," said Hetty. "Help me, Nan. Hungry, John?"

He nodded. "Hungry—and contented. We have fine land, good prospects. That soil cuts like an apple being peeled. I'll soon have ten acres of corn in, although we'll have to leave the trees and stumps in until winter comes."

"What about wheat?" asked Mark.

"Mind that plate—it's hot," said Nan.

"Too late for wheat now, Mark."

"It's time to sow, surely——?"

"This is New South Wales—not Kent. Sow here in March. I kept my ears open at Gubby's inn. And we must fence quickly or the kangaroos and other pests will destroy the crops."

Hetty said, "We were very comfortable at Martha Gubby's new inn in York Street. I never saw such a woman to cheer one up. I do hope we meet her again."

"Gubby wasn't much use," said John with a laugh. "But I'd think twice before saying that to Martha. Yes; she was kind to us."

"Bread, John?"

"Aye."

Hetty went on, "She told me her youngest daughter, Mary Ann, was in some place in Europe learning singing. Where *was* it, Tilly?"

"Milan."

"Yes. And that the older daughter, Penelope, had gone with her husband to the Bay of Islands, in New Zealand. She seemed very disappointed Mrs. Challinor hasn't any children——"

"Probably Challinor is, too," said John. "I think that youngster of Mrs. Gubby's, Albert Ernest, will be a bit of a rip."

"Oh, he's only ten. He's going to be very

like his father." John laughed. "Perhaps that is what is worrying the good woman," he said.

"Perhaps," said Hetty. "But the Gubbys have done well. They came to Sydney from Swan River in '36, and started at the inn of the Cock and Feathers, in Campbell Street. She sold that place. Martha has her own carriage now—*and* a coachman. She's making money fast."

"I liked it there," said Tilly. "The York Inn."

"We all did," said Nan. "More stew, Jeanette?"

"Please."

"Martha likes to drive about the town, and I believe everybody in Sydney Town knows her now—and, what's more, respects her. Be careful of that ladle, Nan."

"Yes, mother. Tilly?"

"Yes."

Everyone ate heartily, and at last John moved back from the boards and felt for his pipe. His homely face reflected his contentment as he looked around him. He was on his own land. This day was the beginning of a wider life. Thirteen thousand miles he and his had come. This valley was their journey's end.

"When we've planted corn, potatoes, turnips, we'll fence all, build our yards—then a house, mother, then a barn, woolshed and wool-washing yards down at the creek. By the time winter comes we must be snug, for those great mountains down there will send a keen wind along this valley. We're on high land here, and it will be cold. I've spent eleven hundred pounds so far in just what we have around us."

"Eleven hundred pounds," echoed Tom. "There isn't much to see for it, father."

"That is why the bounty immigrants have such a hard time here," said John. "They have no money, and must work for years for someone else to enable them to save enough to start for themselves. They are not capitalists as we are, son; they have nothing to start with—but hope. Most of them are tradesmen, servants and labourers, and with hard times looming in the colony I don't know how many of them will fare. Work in Sydney is getting scarcer every day. Here, we can live. We have rations for a whole year. We can get kangaroo, duck, swan, fish—if we are lucky—wild geese, and with our natural increase of sheep and cattle, and what we can grow for food . . . we can live while we build up, live while we work, and live without fear so long as we trust in God and have faith in Him and in ourselves."

"Oh, something will be done for the bounty immigrants, surely," said Hetty. "They can't bring people into this colony and then watch them starve."

"They can—and they are," said John quietly.

"There's the moon!" said Tilly.

"And *that* is a dingo howling," said Mark.

"We haven't seen any blacks," said Tom.

"Don't want to," said Nan emphatically. "Folk in Sydney say they're savage and treacherous."

"They are savages," said John. "But I don't think they will molest us unless we do something to harm them first."

"Better sleep with loaded carbines, anyway," said Tom.

"Don't those mountains look pale and far away," said Jeanette. "I'd hate to be lost in this country."

"Those are the Kosciusko mountains," said John. "Count Strzelecki discovered them last year, but a man named McMillan—

Angus McMillan—found the way for the drays to get from here through to Bass's Straits. That means more to settlers than any tall mountains."

Mark laughed.

"We won't be going up there, anyway," he said. "Throw some more wood on the fire, Tom."

Tom yawned. "What about bed?" he asked sleepily. "Now that we know we have neighbours . . . I wonder who else is in this part of the country?"

"Probably no one within many miles, son," said John. "Explorers, squatters and runaways find new country, settlers follow. Sheep and cattle are always on the move. Smoke rises every day from new huts. I'm not pleased with the Olivers, still less with such as the Treggs. If the Treggs are ex-convicts we'll have nothing to do with them. I won't have my family associating in any way with the felonry. We didn't come to this valley to be browbeaten by such as the Olivers, or to mix with criminals."

"But we don't know these people yet, John," said Hetty. "Perhaps that man Oliver spoke hastily about them."

John nodded. He knocked the ashes out of his pipe.

"True, wife. But what I said . . . what I said . . ." He broke off and slowly stood up.

"What is it, John?" asked Hetty quickly.

"Visitors—again," he replied gruffly. "Look, over there, standing and watching us——"

They all stood, and saw, just within the fireglow, seven people. The Martins stared. Never had they looked upon such an outlandish group: the visitors seemed to be half animal, half human. There were four men and three women. All were barefooted, all wearing opossum-skin caps over long, unkempt hair, and kangaroo-skin jackets laced over ragged dresses and equally ragged shirts and moleskins. They were unarmed, so it could be assumed the visit was a peaceful one. In the fur caps of the two girls were bright parrots' feathers; the tall old woman, obviously the mother of the young people, had the tail of the opossum-skin hanging over one shoulder. The man, Tregg himself, a squat, thick-set fellow, stood next to her. Each of them carried a bundle of kangaroo skins. When they saw the Martins stand they came forward slowly so that the firelight

shone on their faces. Tregg spoke in a hesitant, deep voice.

"We be the Treggs," he said. "I be Elijah
Tregg. This be my ol' woman, Sarah. An'
thar be Johnnie, Rock an' Dick. The gels be
Meg an' Annie. Meg be the one wi' the dark
red 'air. Annie's the one wi' straw-coloured
'air. Mebbe I be tellin' you all this 'cause I
ain't spoke to a white man for a month. An' I
better tell you afore th' Olivers do—thar be
another Tregg, th' eldest son, Royd. 'E's
chained up. We 'as to chain 'im up. 'E goes
wild mad now'n then. We saw you-all come
into the valley today. We brings kang'roo
rugs to trade for flour, tea, salt, beef,
clo'es—anythin' you'll trade. We got no
money—we can't buy. Will you trade?"

John measured him with cold eyes.

"You are a shepherd for the Olivers?" he
asked.

"Aye; sometimes. What of it?" came
harshly. "We mus' live, an' thar be mighty
little to get in this valley."

"You have been a convict?"

Tregg's eyes gleamed in the fire-light.

"Aye," he said slowly. "I sarved time. I be
free now. What of it? Who tol' you I'd bin
lagged?"

"Oliver. He said you told him about us coming into the valley. A moment ago you said you hadn't spoken to a white man for a month. You lied to me."

There was a little silence. The Treggs exchanged slow glances. Then Elijah said, "Will you trade?"

John spoke quietly.

"No."

Tregg, grim-faced, stood looking at him. All the Treggs stared at him, and again came the old man's deep, rasping voice.

"So be it," he said. "The Treggs won't f'git you. The Treggs ain't seed flour or tea or sugar or salt for more'n two munce. You got plenty. The Treggs 've got none. We came fair to trade fair. You said no. Thet word ain't *ever* said in the col'ny when white folks asks for food. But you said no. The Treggs won't f'git you."

He turned and walked away with a peculiar, rolling, bear-like gait, the bundle of furs tucked under his right arm. The others, after a final bleak stare of hostility, followed him. A few paces away, the red-haired girl, Meg, who appeared to be about nineteen years of age, looked back at John.

"You ol' bastud," she said bitterly.

She made a contemptuous backward jerk of her buttocks and then walked on after her people. Hetty sighed as they went out of sight in the moonlight.

"It seems, John, that twice today we have made enemies," she said. "Could you not have done something? They seem to be a tragic family. There was hunger in their eyes—I saw it."

John's face was stern.

"I saw it, too," he said. "But the word had to be said now—or never. If he is Oliver's shepherd Oliver should ration him. We are God-fearing, respectable people. Had I said 'yes' we'd never have seen the last of them. We'll have nothing to do with . . . villains. Now let us all to bed. Tomorrow we take up our task, our new lives. The Olivers and the Treggs have no part in our days to come."

Hetty's voice was gentle.

"You know best, dear."

In an hour the fire had died down. A mist rose to be a silver mantle over the shoulders of the spurs. The Martins slept.

In their hut on the spur the Treggs were also in bed. The Tregg hut—stringy bark roof, slab walls, hard earth floor—was a miserable abode. There was a rough stone hearth, a slab table flanked by poles for benches, and a perpetual odour of stale food, wood-smoke and human bodies. With the exception of the snarling Royd, who was chained to a tree a few paces from the cabin, the family all slept in one wide bunk, Sarah near the door so that she could run out to Royd if his snarl changed to a whimper, then the bear-like Elijah, then Meg, then Annie with Johnnie, Rock and Dick in that order. Moonlight filtered in through cracks in the upright slab walls. Sarah was already asleep: all problems other than her beloved Royd ceased for her at sundown. Elija, dressed except for the fur jacket and cap, as they all were, lay staring up at the dimly-seen roof. He realized now he had spoken hastily to the new man, Martin, and that he had been foolish in trying to deceive him. Oliver would be furious if he knew the Treggs had gone anywhere near the Martins.

The red-haired Meg was also awake, thinking of the newcomers. It was plain the Martins, like the Olivers, considered the Treggs to be no better than beasts—no, not all the Olivers. Everitt had different ideas— well, about her, at any rate. Next to the wide-eyed Meg, Annie, who was seventeen, moved

63

restlessly, and Meg caught her fierce whisper: "Leave me alone, Johnnie, dem you to 'ell!" Then came the sound of Johnnie's suppressed laughter. Johnnie, the second son, was twenty-four, Rock twenty-three, Dick twenty-one. Royd was twenty-six. Every now and then, from outside, came the rattle of a heavy chain, and a low snarling, a savage, unhuman guttural sound like an animal growling deep in its throat. But the Treggs who were awake took no notice of the Tregg chained to the tree outside. Royd—Red Royd—was a giant. It took the combined strength of all the family to hold him down when the fits seized him. They were murderous fits. But the Treggs were used to the rattle of that chain: it was the only way to control Royd; and he did not know he was chained at the time. Only when the fits passed, and they released him, did he look at the chain with horror and loathing, and then Sarah would weep over him and give to him an affection she never gave to the others.

Five miles farther south the Olivers sat in the living-room of the long, shingled, frame house, the timbers of which had been cut in the pit near by. An oil-lamp burned on a wide oak table. It was a comfortable room, carpeted, holding heavy furniture, wall-glasses, specimen glasses, silver and china on a long oak sideboard. Henry Oliver sat in a high-backed, padded chair at the head of the table. Jane Oliver, twenty-five years of age, thin, dark, coldly-composed, sat at the other end of the table. Everitt sat on his father's right, Conway on the left, and Elliott close to Jane on her right side. All the Olivers, except Henry, were very dark, all had the close-set eyes and thin nose. Jane was speaking in her sharp manner.

"Is there *no* way to be rid of these Martins?" she asked her father. "Are we to sit passively and watch this valley being stolen from us? It's Oliver land, isn't it—all of it?"

Henry waved a thin veined hand.

"Something must be done," he said sourly. "Five thousand acres, the fellow said. We have been too sure of ourselves."

Jane's dark eyes were narrowed and angry.

"Five thousand acres! What impudence! What preposterous ambition in such people! They'll not have even five acres in this valley—why, that end of the valley is our only road to the north. Immigrants. Free immigrants! As if that makes them anybody. I think this Martin is no different from Tregg—except that he hasn't been transported. If we *must* have neighbours for heaven's sake let them be gentlefolk. Immigrants! Yeoman farmer! What next, I wonder?"

"Don't make a speech," said Everitt impatiently.

She flashed him a resentful glance. Jane and Everitt never had liked each other.

"It's time someone made a speech," she retorted. "I have taken mama's place now she is gone—I have the right to speak."

"What you need, Jane, is a husband," Everitt drawled. "But——"

Jane's mouth thinned.

"But?" she echoed acidly.

"Who the devil would have you? You'd cut him to pieces with your tongue."

Jane flushed.

"Really, Everitt—at least I don't go looking towards such as the Treggs."

Elliott and Conway grinned at the thrust. Everitt moved uncomfortably and shot a quick glance at his father.

"We're talking about the Martins—not the Treggs," he said brusquely. "And I assure you, my dear sister, I haven't any concern or desire for any Tregg slut."

"That's enough, Everitt," growled Henry.

"Yes, sir—quite enough," Everitt agreed.

Conway's tone was bantering.

"You must remember, Everitt—we are gentlefolk, we are the Olivers. Ask Jane."

Jane stood up.

"I'm going to bed," she announced. "Why you Oliver men permitted this thing to happen I don't know. You'll have to do something——"

"Something, perhaps, short of murder?" suggested Elliott with a snigger. "Would you like to talk to the Martins, Jane?"

"They'd hear something if I did."

"Yes," said Everitt. "They certainly would. You forget, Jane, they hold a licence. And if you want to have a tilt at Her Majesty the Queen, now's your chance."

"You're running away from it," Jane said scornfully.

Henry spoke. "Nothing of the kind. I've been remiss. I should have secured that land. I didn't. But I shall."

They looked at him.

"How?" asked Conway.

"I'll buy it."

Jane smiled.

"Ah! Now we're getting somewhere. You'll have to go to Melbourne."

"Yes. Everitt and I will go. I'll give the matter some thought. This valley belongs to the Olivers. We were the first here."

Jane took up a candle.

"Where will you stay?" she asked.

"At the Lamb Inn, if not there at Lingham's Marine Hotel, at Hobson's Bay. Fawkner, unfortunately, has leased his hotel to the Jockey Club."

Henry stood up and stared at Everitt.

"It might be as well if you do get out of the valley for a week or two, Everitt. You are not, perhaps, as discriminating as an Oliver should be. Good night."

Jane gave her brother a cold smile as she followed her father out of the room. Everitt merely shrugged and smiled back coldly in return.

"She'd cut a man to pieces—just cut him into little pieces," he murmured loud enough for Jane to hear.

"Not if he were a man," was Jane's reply.

5

CLEAR in the moonlight of this same night stood the Immigration Barracks at the corner of Bent and Phillip streets, in Sydney Town. Now and then a late gig or homing carriage came slowly up the hill and turned into Macquarie Street. Right down the moonlit headlands and bays of the harbour, lights in humble dwellings and lordly mansions were going out one by one. The harbour itself, a silver plain under the moon, reflected tall ships creaking at their chains. On the South Head the Macquarie Light sent a pale beam out over the sea. On Pinchgut a red light warned shipping, and sent its red rays down on the heavy guns recently placed on this haunted rock. As the hour grew later the night sounds of Sydney Town became muted. Moon-shadows were sharp and black in narrow lanes. The crowd had left the Victoria Theatre—in later years the "Old Vic"—situated in Pitt Street between King and Market streets; the circus tent of Dalle Casse, in Hunter Street, was empty and dark; the cockpits were deserted; orators, acrobats, pickpockets had all left Hyde Park and the Domain—only the homeless remained under the trees. The time bell of the Convict Barracks sent its strokes down King Street to die away across the town. Gaslamps in silent streets were outshone by the argent moon. The footfalls of constables sounded loudly on the flags. The pulse of the busy town was quiet now, waiting for the sun to come again to renew the urgent life of this lusty focal point of all the colony.

Over all the wide continent the moon revealed much of the land's new story. Nightcoaches filled with road-weary travellers were straining over the Blue Mountains, over Razorback in the south, and along lonely roads towards Bathurst, Goulburn and Yass. Timber ketches hugged scrub-lined banks in the coastal rivers north and south of Sydney Town. Newcastle, still one of the prettiest villages in the colony, slept beside the shining Hunter River, and coal-barges were black at their moorings there. To the north, up on high New England, on the Darling Downs still farther north, out west on the distant warming plains, and south across the far Murrumbidgee and the Murray, flocks and herds moved to water in the deep night stillness. Right round and across this wide arc of more than a thousand miles stately rivergums looked down on lazy rivers; beside winding bush tracks the honey-flowered boxtrees perfumed the air; and on the endless farback levels the mulga, gidgee, salt-bush and wilga kept aloof from glooming forests of dark, dwarf cypress pines. And across all the miles between stations, between those lonely little huts on spur and plain, the tribes of the black people slept, slept where slow rivers wandered, where anvil-topped hills rose to look far across the land.

Yes; here was forming a new civilization in the world's most ancient land. Melbourne Town was growing apace, and its original Van Diemen's Land pioneers rubbed amazed eyes at its progress since Bourke named it in '37. The new Adelaide, the founding town of the Province of South Australia, begun in '36, was divided by the sparkling Torrens, and Mount Lofty near by looked down to see the strange habitations of the new white race. Across the voiceless distances of the Bight, where gallant Eyre had walked, and ill-fated, loyal Baxter met death at the hands of a treacherous savage, the land marched waterless, grim, challenging, defiant, to come at last to the fabulous flats and reefs of gold-towns yet to be, and then on over the Darling Ranges to Perth, Guildford and Fremantle, quiet beside the Swan, small and primitive towns only twelve years old in a vast colony twenty times the size of England, the colony of Western Australia.

And into this almost empty continent, this strange and fascinating country of the south, this land of bewildering contrasts, of deserts, fertile land, snow-capped peaks, parklands and jungles, this Australia where the endless miles were yet to wave under the wheat, where sheep in their millions, and cattle, too, were to graze and multiply, where great cities were to flourish and splendid towns to grow in time, where industry was yet to expand and move across the land like a giant striding, were coming the people who were to accomplish the beginnings of these things: the immigrants sailing across the world in little wooden ships, rich men, poor men, speculators, farmers, artisans, teachers, preachers, labourers, domestic servants, men with families, men with nothing but hope, immigrants coming in month by month, year by year, destined, in time, to break down the old barriers of hate, to heal, over the years, the wounds of punishment, and leave only on stone walls the marks of the convict.

Immigrants, bounty and free! They filled the mind of Caroline Chisholm with deep thoughts as she lay in the room allotted to her in the Immigration Barracks, a room about fifteen feet square, the only room she could use as a bedroom, office and store. That appalling room! Surely no one but a woman of indomitable courage and one holding the most sincere wish to help others would have consented even to enter it. Its furniture was a narrow bed, a rickety table, a large box for a cupboard in which to store food. The walls were slabs, the floor was made of uneven bare blanks. It was draughty: the moonlight filtering through the Treggs' cabin also streaked through this example of government unconcern. This room was to be her head-quarters; here she would work to place un-married men and women, and also families, if she could manage it later, with those in country districts who wanted shepherds, servants, labourers, artisans. She wondered as she lay there if she had permitted the bright-ness of her vision to dim reality. Perhaps she would be a laughing-stock after all. She had already placed a few persons in positions within a few miles of Sydney Town, but not as yet right out in the far country districts; and to do that she must accomplish a miracle of faith and effort and organization. Like every woman of her time and day who dared to challenge a public scandal, she knew she would be suspect: women had no right to encroach upon the sacred domain of masculine control. But she would try, with God's help she would try to do her best to assist these unfortunate girls, and others, whom authority left to rot in the streets. She had gone at sunset to Hyde Park to bring the girls there to this room—but they were not there.

She thought about those girls, the Scots girl's voice still in her ears, when another sound caused her to turn her head sharply to listen. It was a faint scratching at first, then a squeaking and scrabbling of claws, a thumping and running about that chilled her blood and caused her to sit upright in the bed. Hurriedly she lit a candle, then another. Then she recoiled, gasping. Staring at her from the floor, with bold beady eyes, was a huge rat, and even as she looked at it another dropped from the ceiling on to her shoulder. With a cry of horror she shook it off, and was about to rush from the dreadful room when the courage that never forsook her mounted again. Monstrous rats from the waterfront. Sickening. And now there was another on her bed, then another. She knew they might attack her. She must do something—either she must beat the rats or they would beat her. With wildly leaping heart she cut bread and butter and placed it and milk in a saucer on the floor. The rodents rushed to the feast. More than a dozen of them. Big rats. Dangerous. Infested with heaven only knew what diseases. She watched while they ate, and she kept replacing the bread and milk. So, sitting on the bed, feeding the rats, she passed the horrible night.

When night fell again the feast was flavoured with arsenic.

Her public work had begun; she had beaten the rats; she would overcome other trials as they presented themselves. Unknown at that moment even to herself her work was to extend over six years, and make her name acclaimed and blessed in thousands of grateful hearts throughout New South Wales; it was to bring immortality to her name and make future generations of Australians wonder at the spirit and profound humanity of this pious and inspired woman who, in those few years, placed, or caused to be placed, in employment, more than eleven thousand persons.

Sydney Town always awakened early, and soon after seven o'clock in the morning shops opened their doors; labourers began loading and unloading ships and wagons; mobs of sheep and cattle from the Hawkesbury farms, the Camden country, the Illawarra, and the runs beyond the mountains, came under cracking whips to the town's slaughter and sale yards. Bankers and merchants stepped from carriages and gigs into their offices; taverns, hotels, grog-shops and coffee-shops were opened for business; carters sold water in the streets; fires roared in foundries, and the sound of hammers on anvils came with the acrid smell of hooves under hot shoes; gunners in scarlet coats fired practice shots at Bradley's Head to assure the colony it was safe from invasion by the French; and, as the sun mounted, Australia's oldest town roared with the rhythm of another day. The streets filled rapidly with people and vehicles. The central markets were already busy. The day coaches were picking up passengers for the long inland journeys, and the mails were being bagged at the post-office in George Street.

And the convict gangs went out to work.

In her private parlour at the Old York Inn, in York Street, Martha Gubby, the diminutive Henry, and Albert Ernest, a dark-eyed, furtive boy of ten, sat at breakfast. Mr. Gubby was clad in a long blue coat, a wine-coloured waistcoat, and dark trousers clipped under shining black boots. Mr. Gubby hoped he looked a gentleman. Martha, massive in her favourite yellow, had a pile of letters near her hand. She could not read, and presently would pass them to Mr. Gubby. It was two years since they had sold the Cock and Feathers, in Campbell Street, and just over ten since they had landed almost penniless on the empty beach at Fremantle, in Western Australia. The family then consisted of Martha, Henry, Penelope and Mary Ann. The decade had brought both change and prosperity. Penelope, now twenty-eight, was married to the rich but restless gentleman, Simon Lee Challinor; Mary Ann, now twenty-three, was in Milan studying singing. Albert Ernest was at school when he was not dodging his lessons and prowling about the waterfront somewhere.

While she ate, Martha listened to the rumble of traffic out in York Street, and to the sound of voices and movement within the inn itself. The two-storied inn was filled with guests. Compared with the humble Cock and Feathers down in Campbell Street it was a palace. All the corridors and stairs were carpeted, as were the plush and gilt parlours. The best bedrooms had draped four-poster beds and massive furniture; the tap-room, where island curios were banked and criss-crossed above carved shelves backed by gleaming mirrors, was already busy. Capable though Martha was, she readily admitted that the running of the inn would be beyond her without the loyal help of Polly Wedge and Mary Kissane, both now freed-women. Mr. Gubby, of course, did nothing: he just drifted here and there and was known in the inn and throughout Sydney as Martha Gubby's husband. The little man, pathetically dependent on Martha, had never reconciled himself to this new, raw Australia. His heart was always in England where he had idled the days away humbly talking to the quality while Martha and the two girls slaved to keep the family from starvation. His sharp dark eyes, as indirect and furtive as Albert Ernest's, watched his spouse as she gulped down tea and toast and took up the letters.

" 'Ere, 'Arry boy——" came her husky voice. "Read 'em. I knows the writin' but that be all I knows."

"Yes, my dear," said Henry. "One is from Mary Ann, one from Penelope, and one from Simon himself—and one from Yass. Now who could that be from?"

Martha's pale blue eyes lighted with pleasure.

"Them Martins went that way—but start with Mary Ann's, Mr. Gubby. Halbert Hernest! You go an' shine them boots an' be ready for school, me lad!"

Albert Ernest sidled away.

"Yes, mama."

"Read, Mr. Gubby."

Mr. Gubby cleared his throat.

" 'Dear mama, papa and Albert Ernest. Tonight as I write to you the Piazza del Duomo, beyond my apartment, is moonlit. I have written before of Milan, but yesterday I went again to the roof of the wonderful cathedral. I gazed entranced at distant Pavia and the Alps. There were the snow-topped Matterhorn, Mount Blanc, and a dozen other well-known peaks, some in grey shadow, some in the rich and rosy glow of the afternoon sun. And yet I knew I was a stranger, an alien, and the distant peaks stared back at me with cold white eyes as if they also knew it——' "

"Lawks, it mus' be cold there, 'Arry boy——"

"Yes, Martha. She goes on: 'I've been listening to the chatter of my chaperone, Marchoni, who, as I have told you, always calls me by my singing name of Anna Maria. I suppose it sounds better than plain Mary Ann. My teacher, Johann Arndt, says I shall certainly sing in opera some day after someone has succeeded in breaking my heart——' "

"Hey!" said Martha slowly. "I don' like that bit, Mr. Gubby. Hif gettin' into hopera means gettin' a broken 'eart she'd better break 'er neck tryin' to get back 'ome fust——"

"Let me read on, dear. '—by telling me I shall never make a singer——' "

"Oh," said Martha, "be that all. Yus?"

" 'Marchoni, who is like a lively little bird, always twittering and hopping about, hints my ambition is greater than my voice, and that for all the hours with Arndt I shall always be a nobody——' "

"Himpudence!" said Martha coldly. "Our Mary Ann's got a wunnerful voice."

"Yes, dear. It's only a short letter this time. She concludes: 'I do hope *someone* will notice me some day, but there are marvellous voices here in Milan, voices no one will bother to listen to. I often wonder what I shall have to do to get that someone to listen to poor me.' "

"H'm——" came huskily from Martha. "She better not wonder too 'ard. Go on."

" 'I've been in Europe three years now, and can speak Italian, French and German fairly well, but I have much, so much, to learn.' "

"I dunno as I likes a gel o' mine talkin' all them furrin' tongues, Mr. Gubby. Don' seem right, some'ow. We got along with good ol' Hinglish, an' if Hinglish be good 'nough for Hinglind it be good 'nough for anybody."

"It's part of her training, dear. She says, 'I long to see you all, and I think it is wonderful for mama to have her own carriage——' "

"Well, 'tain't bad at that," said Martha. "Not so long ago I was pushin' beef in a dratted barrer from them there markets down to the Cock an' Fevvers. Yus?"

" 'My love to you all, your ever loving daughter, Mary Ann'."

Martha smiled. "Now that do be a nice letter, Mr. Gubby. What do Pagan say?"

Henry opened Penelope's letter.

"It's from Russell, in the Bay of Islands, New Zealand. It's even shorter than Mary Ann's. 'Dear mama, papa, and Albert Ernest. Simon and I are leaving here in about a month. Simon has done good business with the Maoris and the whalers, and has established a depot here. He thinks New Zealand will develop amazingly provided the whites and the Maoris don't clash. The Maoris are a strange people, at times fascinating, at other times ruthless and savage and given to horrible flesh feasts of slain enemies——' "

"Oh, lawks!" said Martha. "I be glad I've 'ad me breakfast."

" '. . . the Bay of Islands, a pretty scene with all the whaleships and traders at anchor, but Simon never leaves me at night. Russell used to be called by the Maoris "Kororareka", and it was here that Mr. Marsden came and started to preach the Christian religion to the natives. Lawks, mama! He must have been a brave man, and very hopeful. I am glad to hear Elizabeth

Collingdale has another son, but every time I hear such good news for others I feel distressed——' "

"Tch, tch!" clicked Martha. "That *do* be a worrit for Pagan——"

" 'but I am glad for Elizabeth. This country has a weird beauty and grandeur all of its own. The land shakes, bubbles and freezes in other parts, and at times there is a horrifying sound deep down, and it is then that everyone, even the Maoris, stands with fear in their eyes. I suppose one might get used to it in time. Now I have an astonishing piece of news for you. You will, of course, remember Edward Challinor, Simon's brother. You will recollect we never knew what became of him after his quarrel with Simon—over me. By some means he came to the Bay of Islands and lived for three years here as a paheka-maori. Simon can't find out how he got here, on what ship, but he came here—and was killed here. Evidently he got into one of his raving fits when drunk, and that is how he ended. A whaleman told Simon. Simon took it badly, blaming himself for his brother's death. But he realizes now that Edward, sooner or later, would have provoked someone into a deadly hostility.

Isn't it dreadful? But dreadful things are done here——' "

Henry paused and looked at Martha.

"Lassy me!" she breathed. "Hedward Challinor! To end that way. Yus; it do be drefful. Read on, 'Arry boy."

" 'When we leave here we are going to Melbourne Town first. There is to be a sale of town lots there at the end of November. Simon is interested. Would you be interested, mama? Simon believes Melbourne will be a big town one day, and that lots will bring fortunes to early buyers. There won't be time to hear from you before we leave here, but we'll look for you on the jetty at William's Town, and if you do come to Melbourne we can all go back to Sydney together. Simon is writing about the sales. All fond love from Simon and me. Your loving daughter, Penelope.' "

"My!" said Martha. "I declare she will be glad to get 'ome again. I'll listen to the Yass letter later, 'Arry boy. Town lots, eh? Now there do be an idea——"

Mr. Gubby looked startled.

"But, Martha—you would have to go there yourself——"

"I knows that, Mr. Gubby."

"Good heavens, my dear—the journey—the, the——"

Martha smiled faintly.

"I ain't like you, 'Arry boy. You sets down an' never goes anywhere or does anythin'. I believes the proper way to get on is to get hup off your bottom an' get busy. I've bin gettin' hup off mine all me life. Yus. The Gubbys mus' 'ave some o' them town lots, Mr. Gubby. There be Halbert Hernest to think of, you know. An' I got the money now—yus."

Henry stared at her.

"But how will you go there?" he asked.

"Us'll go there, Mr. Gubby."

"Me? Me, Martha?" he squeaked. "You know I'm not strong—the voyage——"

"We goes. Now I got to be busy. We'll take the kerridge an' go down to the shippin' hagents in Underwood's Buildin's an' book passages."

Mr. Gubby was pale and upset.

"Martha!" he whined. "You must think well——"

Martha stood up. She towered over the little man as he also rose.

"Pickles!" she said with a laugh.

6

SARAH TREGG took a breakfast of damper and meat scraps out to the chained Royd. Royd stood up, the long chain rattling as he did so. He was a powerful man, barefooted, bare-headed, his shirt and moleskins in rags, his wide-apart, pale blue eyes staring out of a broad, red-whiskered face. As his massive arms, matted with ginger-coloured hair, reached wildly for the food, Sarah's lined face lost its usual expression of indifference. A little colour touched the grey flesh of her sunken cheeks as she spoke to him. "Thar, Royd—don' be 'asty, son—thar it be," she crooned.

The gigantic madman answered with a growl as his fingers stuffed food from the bowl into his mouth. Softly came the old woman's voice.

"Thar, thar, Royd—thar be plenty—no need to wolf it. I think you'll be all right soon. I wish you knowed me, Royd. It be turrible—afore Almighty God, it be turrible—to 'ave to chain you. But you don' know what I be sayin'. . . ."

No. Royd Tregg did not know what she was saying. Not until the darkness lifted from his mind again would he understand or know her, and, curiously enough, the mania could vanish as quickly as it struck. Nevertheless, some instinct told him there was sympathy here, that here was someone who would always speak softly to him, always come with food and drink, always watch him with kindly eye. He did not stand roaring, beating his broad, hair-matted chest with immense fists now, did not hurl himself to the end of the heavy chain with eyes glaring, throat shrieking, teeth bared like an animal's. Only Sarah could approach him when madness broke his mind. If any other member of the family, or a stranger, approached him, he would rave and scream and throw himself towards them in a fiendish fit of homicidal fury. Had the Treggs lived in town he would have been removed by authority, and held in a stout log or stone cell; but here, in this valley, he had to be chained to a tree.

Long ago tall Sarah Tregg had closed her mind to thought. Illiterate herself, hardened years before in Hobart Town's Female Factory for female felons, she had known only the world of the convict with its hopeless outlook and bitter resentments. She was aware that some had shed the brand of the broad arrow and had gained wealth and position, but not many. The Treggs had always been cruelly poor. No one trusted them; they trusted none. No one befriended them; they befriended none. As dependants for years of the Olivers they scraped a living out of life's sorry pot, but they knew the haughty Olivers despised them, and they hated the Olivers.

This valley, deep in the fastnesses of great mountains, hid them, sheltered them from the jibes and sneers of the outer world. Here they could live to themselves, live their own small, frustrated and impotent lives, the wearing down of years, watching the passing of their time.

That there could possibly be such a thing as a future for a Tregg simply did not occur to any of them. Was there a future for the warrigal—the dingo running wild on these high hills? They were human warrigals. To watch them eating at the rough slab table revealed their primitive mental state; they used only knives and nimble fingers and sharp teeth with which to tear their meat, and their trenchers, rough bowls and plates hewn out of the valley timbers, were raised direct to their lips. They had always slept as a family in the one wide bed; they always would so long as they remained together as a family. They had no possessions other than an axe, the chain and straps that held Royd, cast-off clothing thrown at them by the Olivers, their knives and guns, their simple trenchers, the kangaroo-skin jackets and rugs used as garments and bed-coverings. They had no stock, no horses, no saddles, no furniture, no comfort, no money, and certainly no future. They worked occasionally for meagre rations, doing odd jobs for the Olivers—shearing, branding, mustering (the Olivers' horses being used then), fencing, building. But most of their time was spent roaming the valley, shooting kangaroo and wild-fowl for food. Their feet had never known the feel of boots, and were as tough as a blackfellow's. The men grew full whiskers, and the girls and Sarah wore their hair long and falling over their shoulders.

Sarah was aware all at once that her son's eyes were steady. She waited, breathing quickly. His trembling hand gave back the bowl. Then he said slowly:

"Ol' woman—take the curst chain offer me—I can see you straight again. I ain't sick now——"

"Royd——" It was just a whisper, gentle and poignant. "Oh, son, you've come back."

He stood panting a little, looking at her. Then he looked about him.

"Thar be ol' 'Lijah—an' Meg—an' Rock. Yus, I be back again. How long was it—this time?"

"Two weeks, Royd—not long. Mebbe you will grow better soon. It used to be longer—once 'twas more'n a year."

The chain rattled.

"Take it off, ol' woman. Did I—'urt anyone?"

"No, Royd. You was all right." She called to her husband. " 'Lijah—Royd's come back. Take off the chain——"

Elijah grunted and jerked a thumb at Meg who ran into the cabin and got the key. Meg stared at her brother when she was close to him.

" 'Lo, Royd," she said tonelessly.

" 'Lo, Meg," he growled. "Unlock the bleddy chain."

Meg looked at Sarah, who nodded, and a quick turn of the heavy key set him free.

Without speaking again he walked down to the creek, took off his filthy clothes, flung them into the water, and then plunged in himself.

" 'E'll kill someone yet," said Meg sourly. Sarah turned on her furiously.

"Shet y'mouth, you, Meg!" she hissed. "Royd ain't killed no one yet——"

"Yet!" sneered Meg, backing away from the gaunt Sarah. "I reckon 'Lijah'll 'ave to shoot 'im some day—jist like a wild dawg."

"You devil gel," her mother snarled. "No more talk like thet—d'ye 'ear? Or I'll git 'Lijah to put leather roun' you. Now git an' skin thet 'roo Rock shot yesterday—*git*, I say!"

Meg's lips thinned as she walked away. Sarah glared after her with angry eyes. Royd was her first-born; all the affection she was capable of knowing had gone to him. The other children merely marked the years; she had little or no regard for them. They had none for her. Sarah scowled at Meg as the girl went into the hut to get a knife.

"You'll come to a bed end, you, Meg," she muttered. "An' if you torments Royd I'll—I'll——"

Elijah came to her.

"What you growlin' 'bout now?" he asked surlily.

"Meg. She reckoned you'd 'ave to shoot Royd one o' these days."

Elijah shrugged.

"Jist talk. You allus takes on so if anyone even looks at y'precious Royd," he growled.

"They don' unnerstan'——" Sarah began fiercely.

"Ar—shet y'trap, ol' woman," came impatiently. "I wants to talk 'bout them Martins."

She watched him closely.

"What 'bout them Martins? You got y'answer plain 'nough las' night. They don' want nothin' to do with us."

"I didn't know Oliver 'ad spoke to 'im. I bin thinkin'——"

Sarah reached and took the short black pipe from his hand and put it between her teeth.

"Better not meddle, 'Lijah Tregg. No good can come of it. Might lead you back to th' irons."

His hands clenched into hard fists.

"No man'll ever git 'Lijah Tregg back in them irons. Mebbe—mebbe I wasn't smart las' night."

" 'Ere's Royd comin' back——"

"To hell with Royd," he snarled. "I be talkin' to you——"

"No need to take on," she said sullenly.

Royd came and stood beside him. He was naked and carried his washed clothes in his right hand. He gazed at his father with cold eyes. Elijah glanced at him and grunted:

"Royd, you keep away from th' Olivers' place—or one of 'em'll fill your hide with lead. You allus go quar after you've bin near that place."

Royd's pale eyes narrowed.

"I never touched nothin' or no one," he said sullenly.

"Keep away," said Elijah again. "An' I better tell you. Thar be a new fambly come into the valley—they's squatted a coupla miles north. Name o' Martin. An' keep away from them—for Gawd's sake——"

"I ain't a dingo," Royd said harshly.

"Course you ain't, Royd," said Sarah soothingly. " 'Lijah didn't mean nothin' like thet."

Meg came to them. She held out the knife to her brother.

" 'Ere, Royd—*you* skin the bleddy 'roo—I be agoin' somewhar——"

"Whar?" both Sarah and Elijah shot at her.

93

She shrugged.

"Ain't tellin'," she retorted.

"I jist tol' Royd to keep away from them Martins—you do th' same," said Elijah.

"Ain't goin' near the bastuds," came as she turned away.

"She's a bitch," said Sarah. "I'd like to know whar she gits sneakin' off to——"

Royd grinned faintly.

"Better tell 'er to keep 'way from th' Olivers, too," he jeered. "You better——"

"An' you better git some clo'es on," said Elijah. "Git some o' Johnnie's——"

"Nothin' to spare," said Sarah.

"Rock's then. An' what's this 'bout Meg an' th' Olivers?"

"Ain't tellin'," said Royd as he turned away. "Fin' out y'self. Yus, I'll skin the 'roo. Mebbe it'll steady me up a bit. Whar's Rock an' Johnnie an' Dick?"

"Shootin'."

"Whar's Annie?"

"Like Meg—sneaked off somewhars," said Sarah angrily. "One o' these days one o' them black Wongal bucks'll greb them gels. White gels 'as bin took thet way afore. I tol' 'em both."

"Never min' the black Wongals," said Royd. "You watch the black Olivers."

He went into the hut. Elijah spoke harshly.

"Don' b'lieve the fool—no Oliver'd look at a Tregg. I'll go see if thar be any fish in the trap——"

"Thought you wanted to talk 'bout the Martins——"

He shrugged.

"I'll think 'bout it a bit more. Ain't sayin' nothin' yet."

Sarah watched him walk away, then she went to Royd's tree and sat down. The long chain was coiled near her. She moved it away from her. She sat in the sun warming herself. She heard a gunshot far away, then Royd's harsh voice as he talked to himself. She was not in the least concerned about Meg or Annie in spite of what she had said about warning them, or about Johnnie, Rock, Dick—or Elijah. Royd was well again. That was all she cared about; his mind was clear. Yes; some day, some day he would be healed of his sickness . . . some day. Gradually thought drained from her mind. Her eyes closed, and her grey head lolled to one side. With long thin legs stretched out in front of her she slept in the sunlight.

The seventeen-year-old girl, Annie, had turned when away from the spur, and had run easily and fast towards the Martins' camp. When, the evening before, she had stood just within range of their firelight, and had looked and listened in silence, something she herself could not analyse had moved her to unusual thought. All that night she lay thinking, startled deep within herself at the turn of her mind, astonished to know she was somehow pleased these newcomers were in the valley. The Martins were a free family, people who did not peer at others from behind trees. Annie knew she had looked upon something her own family could never be, that she herself could never be like the Martin girls she had seen beside the drays. She and Meg were the daughters of ex-convicts; they must ever seek their own kind, not try to rise or think above that level.

The Martins were free people; so were the Olivers. Annie had always feared the Olivers. Sometimes she had to go to their house, and the cold contempt, the haughty withdrawing, had always frightened her even while it enraged her. But the Martins, she sensed, had no arrogance, no icy contempt for others, although she also knew they would not seek or desire the association or company of such people as the Treggs.

The Treggs. It was two years since Annie had seen any strangers; it was an exciting experience. In that time she had spoken only to her own family and to the Olivers—to Jane Oliver. But here were new people. Neighbours. Even if she never spoke to them they would still be neighbours. Somehow the valley seemed less lonely, but her young face was wistful as she thought about it. No one wanted to be friends with old lags, or the children of old lags. She had never had a friend, and did not expect the newcomers to be friends, but she wanted to see them again—just to see them, to watch them at their work, to listen to their voices, to see for herself how people lived whose ears heard no ghostly echo of the system. So she ran on, her long, straw-coloured hair lifting under her fur cap, her brown eyes eager and watchful. When she topped a rise and saw the camp in the slight hollow she stopped running and sidled behind a tree, then with ease and agility climbed it and sat out on a branch that screened her with its leaves. It was wonderful to sit and look at strange people, to hear them talk. She smiled as she looked down. She

could see Hetty busy near the fire, with Nan
helping her; Tilly and Jeanette at one of the
drays with their father; and close by, quite
close to her, Tom and Mark felling saplings.
All morning she sat very still, just watching.
All afternoon she sat looking at the boys, and
only when evening shadows sent them back
to their camp did she slide down from the
tree and make for her hut. Yes; it was
wonderful to be near other people; the valley
was not lonely now.

Meg, who that morning left the hut after
Annie went towards the Martins, turned
south as she left the spur. Although her
expression was usually defiant and hard she
was a pretty girl, well-formed with strong
body and slender limbs, and she smiled now
as she walked along the valley flats. It was a
warm, sunny morning, redolent of the
fragrance of sun-killed flower and tree, and
she unloosed the kangaroo-skin jacket as she
walked along. A mile farther on, where the
valley began to narrow, she paused to listen.
No sound came to her other than the cries of
birds and the whispering of leaves. She
frowned a little then, and walked on up
another rise to where a two-rail fence
stretched across between close spurs, a fence

in which Henry Oliver had placed a quaint turnstile as well as sliprails. From here she could look down the far south slope of the valley, could see the timbered spurs rising from it up to the ranges, the sheer two-hundred foot cliff of the bluff, a skillion-shaped split hill away to the right, and riding towards her on a bay horse—Everitt Oliver.

"Ev'ritt——" she muttered. "Ev'ritt——"

She had eyes now only for the man coming towards her, and her own blue eyes were narrowed, her full lips parted as she watched him. She did not now see the valley, the spurs, the bluff with its glinting rock face, or the herd of red cattle grazing close to a mob of sheep. She vaulted the fence and ran down the slope towards him. He saw her coming, and brought the bay down to a walk. Meg ran fast, her red hair streaming behind her, and as she came to the horse she leapt, and Everitt's right arm flashed out, held her, lifted her, and swung her with ease to the saddle in front of him.

"I knowed you'd come——" she panted.

He laughed.

"Same place?" he asked.

"Yus—yus!"

A touch of his knee turned the bay towards

a clump of stringybarks. As they went into the screen of the trees Meg's arms rose to clasp themselves round his neck. She drew his face down to hers, and with lips locked they rode slowly. Then he stopped the horse and she slipped to the ground. He followed, throwing the reins over the horse's head.

"Ev'ritt——" she whispered. "Tell me again an' again thet I be your woman—yus?"

She was in his arms again, softly crying his name, trembling as his hands and lips caressed her, pressing wildly to him as the tall grass rose to hide them both. The bay horse did not go far as it cropped sweet grass, nor was it conscious of the passing of time, but the sun was overhead when its master climbed into the saddle again and sat looking at a red-haired girl walking towards the flat leading up to the stile. As she paused there and looked back Everitt raised an arm. But she did not hear him laugh softly as he touched the bay with a spur, did not hear him say:

"My woman—*my* woman! Little idiot. However——"

Meg's eyes were glowing as she watched him ride out of sight.

"Ev'ritt——" she whispered. "Yus, I'll be your woman—again an' again an' again."

Then she turned and walked in the direction of the Tregg hut.

The mutton-fat candle was burning on the slab table as Annie came into the hut, the fire sent a red glow round the walls. Meg, Sarah, Elijah and Royd stared at her as she walked in.

"Whar you bin?" Meg asked curiously.

Annie gave her a slow glance as she took her wooden bowl and went to the hearth for food.

"Whar *you* bin?" she retorted challengingly.

"Nowhar," sneered Meg, not liking Annie's tone.

"Well, I ain't bin the same place as you," said Annie. " 'Lo, Royd."

" 'Lo," came deeply.

As Annie was eating, Johnnie, Rock and Dick came in. They were breathing hard for they had just beaten the rising moon. Annie stopped eating. Johnnie had a small kangaroo over one shoulder, Dick carried the guns, but all eyes were on Rock who stepped forward and dumped a sheep on the table.

Elijah said slowly, "Whar'd you git thet sheep?"

The ruddy light flickered on the fur-capped, fur-jacketed brothers. It seemed to intensify the wildness of these men, to paint them for the outcasts they were. Johnnie's long, ape-like arms hung limply at his sides; Dick's wide mouth was drooping in a flat expressionless face; Rock's blue eyes gleamed, and his freckles made him look pock-marked in the firelight. Rock laughed softly, but there was no mirth in the laughter.

"One o' Martin's," he said. "Us Treggs'll never go without mutton, or pork, or mebbe beef, later on. They'll think a dingo or a Wongal got it. Thar y'are, ol' woman—mutton, an' it ain't one o' the bleddy Olivers'. 'Lo, Royd."

" 'Lo," said Royd. "Th' ol' woman tol' me 'bout the Martins. Good for you, Rock. 'Lo, Johnnie—'lo, Dick——"

" 'Lo——" came without any enthusiasm.

Annie said sharply, "Sheep-stealin'! Gawd—thet can put you in irons, you fool, Rock——"

Rock snarled at her:

"You put them chops in y'belly, Annie Tregg. Didn't thet ol' Martin give us dirt? Did 'e speak us fair? What be *you* flinging at?

102

What did 'e say to 'Lijah? ' 'Ave you bin a convic'?' All right. We can't shove *thet* down 'is preachin' mouth—but we can shove 'is beef an' mutton down ours—an' we will."

Annie got up and went outside as they all roared with laughter.

7

JOHN MARTIN looked round at his family. It was their first Sunday in the valley, a day of worship and of rest. The family prayers had been offered, the Book put away. Annie, perched high in a nearby tree, had wondered as she looked down upon the scene. She sat, clad as usual in print dress, fur jacket and cap, with bare legs dangling from the branch, an arm round the trunk, and with brown eyes wide and intent. She had been astonished when, led by Jeanette, the Martins had sung the Old Hundredth; she had never heard that kind of singing before. Perplexed, she had watched while John read from the Bible, and had observed keenly each member of the family while they stood during the prayer. Now, with John's voice coming faintly to her, she strained to catch every word.

"In the few days we've been here we've done right well," John said. "There are three acres ploughed, and good earth it is. Tilly, Jeanette and Nan have already planted the first seeds. Tom and Mark have split slabs and cut poles. Our stock do not wander as at first I feared they might. We have lost several fowls and a sheep, due, no doubt, to prowling wild dogs——"

Annie's lips pressed together. She knew who were the prowling wild dogs. But she herself had resolutely refused to eat the stolen mutton, much to the astonishment of the Tregg family. For a few moments John's voice was indistinct, then it came to her again.

"None of us believes there will not be great difficulties here, but overcome them we will. And when we have done that our reward shall be great. In but a few years this part of the valley that is ours will have cattle and sheep in goodly numbers. We could not have done this in England: there we could never be more than a small farmer and his family; here we can be, and are, settlers with opportunities ranging even beyond the compass of our eyes. I don't think, in spite of the hard words and looks of the Olivers and the Treggs, we shall have any trouble with those people. We are here lawfully and rightfully, and no more need be said on that score. But it is about those two families I want to say something.

Both your mother and I realize that young folks look for the company of other young folks. We saw young men in the Oliver family, young men and two girls in the Tregg family. There are three girls and two boys in this one. I don't know if Oliver has any girls. But you can't humiliate yourselves by seeking the company of the Olivers, unless they acknowledge and regret their unfriendliness. You can't seek the company of the Treggs without lowering yourselves. You saw them; you know what they are. I don't want to be un-Christian, or uncharitable, but wisdom must prevail there. I think they are a bad lot. But don't let all this dishearten you. In time we shall visit both Sydney and Melbourne, and the villages along those roads; in time, I feel sure, travellers will use this valley as a highway to the south. But that we shall see. This is our first Sunday here, and you are free to roam and look at the valley, but be careful as you do so. Don't forget what I have said to you. The Martins are not greater than any, not less than any, but we do not knuckle to arrogance or countenance the company of criminals, so I bid you remember my words."

Annie did not wait to hear any more. White-faced, and with tears stinging her brown eyes, she came down out of the tree and ran along the valley. John's words hammering at her ears:

"You can't seek the company of the Treggs without lowering yourselves . . . you saw them . . . you know what they are . . . I think they are a bad lot. . . ."

When out of sight of the Martins' camp she stopped running and flung herself down on the grass, and remained there crying, and muttering to herself, for a long time.

"Meg was right—'e's a ol' *bastud*——" she told herself fiercely. "Don' want them to speak to us—even to look at us. We's bad—we's the Treggs—the bleddy Treggs. An' I be a Tregg. Gawd! Why did I 'ave to be a Tregg? What'll I ever be but a Tregg? No good. Bad. Thet ol' preacher wouldn't *let* y'be good. 'E's worser, deep down, than ol' Oliver——"

The sound of hoofbeats interrupted her thoughts. Cautiously she raised her head to see a woman riding side-saddle go cantering by on a grey horse. It was Tilly Martin, dressed gaily in a red dress and red bonnet, riding alone towards the south. Annie stared. The dress and bonnet made her gape, and envy crept into the girl's eyes. Evidently these Martin girls had Sunday dresses. Annie's eyes followed Tilly until the red dress vanished among the far trees.

"She can ride," Annie told herself. "Got yaller 'air, too. Ar—what do I care 'bout the bitch—'bout any of them Martins. I ain't got no red dress—no 'orse to ride—I got nothin'—I be a bleddy Tregg."

She lowered her head to an arm and lay sideways staring into the tall grass. All at once her tattered print dress and kangaroo-skin jacket seemed hideous. Would *she* ever wear such a red dress and bonnet? She thought of old Sarah lolling under Royd's tree; she thought of Meg giving in to Everitt Oliver; she thought of Royd roaring at the end of his chain—of Elijah, of Johnnie, Rock and Dick. A red dress—for her?

The warm smell of earth and grass was in her nostrils, a fragrance familiar to her as far back as she could remember. Remember? What was there to remember? She, with her sister and brothers, had been born in Van Diemen's Land. Elijah was even then Oliver's man. The Olivers had brought them to the village of Bearbrass—Dutergalla, the natives called it—now named Melbourne. Always had there been scraps for food, 'roo skins mostly for clothing, and often just the earth itself for a bed. Then, after some time at Port Phillip, here in this valley. She drew in a breath. There was not much to remember— Royd chained half his time, Johnnie pestering her lately, Meg gone crazy over Everitt Oliver—and *he* had better watch himself, for Meg was vicious when roused to full temper—and Rock and Dick just hanging about like the rest of them. There was no pretty red dress in all that looking back, there would be none, ever, for her.

Then she leapt to her feet as though a whip had struck her when a boy's voice said:

"What are you crying for, girl? Are you hurt?"

It was Mark, and he, too, had on his Sunday clothes to show the standing and respectability of his family. A broad, flat beaver hat sat on his fair hair, his shirt was clean although crumpled, his coat and trousers were neat and dark, and on his feet were black boots. His blue eyes looked inquiringly at Annie as he spoke.

"No—no!" she panted. "I ain't 'urt, boy."

"What are you doing here?" he asked.

"Nothin'—nothin', boy," came sullenly.

"Do you want to see anyone?"

"No," came harshly. "Who in 'ell'd want to see me?"

"You are one of the Tregg girls, aren't you?"

"Yus," was said defiantly. "I ain't doin' no 'arm, boy."

He appraised her critically. She was not pretty—and yet in a way she was. Her straw-coloured hair was long and thick, with bits of grass in it here and there, her brown eyes were large and serious and at the moment red-rimmed with crying. The nose was small, and a little tip-tilted, the mouth wide and well-shaped. Mark smiled at her.

"Well, don't be frightened, girl. I'm Mark Martin."

She nodded.

"I knowed you was a Martin. I—I seed you the night we came to your fire."

He laughed at that.

"I saw you, too. How old are you?"

"Dunno rightly—'bout as old as you, mebbe."

"I'm seventeen. Where do you live?"

She pointed.

"Long thar. Are you mad at me, boy—for bein' 'ere?"

He was silent for a moment, then he said,

110

"No. But I suppose you're mad at me for walking up on you while you were crying."

Annie shook her head.

"No. But you walk soft, boy."

"Why *were* you crying?" he asked curiously.

She looked directly at him. Then her mouth thinned as she said, " 'Cause I 'eard your ol' man say I was a bad lot."

Mark stared at her.

"You *heard* him say——" he began.

Annie's eyes were fierce now.

"Yus—I did—dem 'im! I ain't a bad lot."

"You were spying on us," Mark said indignantly.

"Wasn't spyin'," came in hot denial. "I bin comin' every day to watch you-all workin'——"

Mark's mouth opened then closed. He was vastly surprised.

"Why?" he demanded.

" 'Cause—'cause I got nothin' else to do—'cause I jist wanted to see some other folks—thet's why, Mark Martin. An' I was 'ere in this valley afore you was, don' f'git—I knows every tree an' rock in it—see?"

"Why didn't you come to us and speak to us?" he asked.

Her eyes blazed at him.

"You ask *me* thet?" she retorted. "Would any of you Martins *lower* y'selves atalkin' to me?"

Mark flushed. She certainly had been listening. She went on.

"Mebbe you thinks you be alowerin' y'self atalkin' to me now. Well, you ain't—see? I be as good as any Martin—as any of *your* sisters, Mark Martin——"

He frowned a little.

"The Martins have never been convicts——"

For a moment he thought she would spring at him.

"You be jist like thet ol' preacher—jist a bastud!" she hissed at him. "I wish to Gawd I'd never seed you—you dem-fool boy. I onct 'eard a preacher-man—a diff'rent preacher to your ol' man, say Gawd never flung dirt at no one. 'Ave I ever bin a convic'? No. Then I be jist as good as you, boy—as any of you Martins——" She took a slow step towards him. "You tell thet ol' preacher to stop *flingin'* at us," she panted. "I—I could *fetch* you one, boy, for what you said. You-all stop flingin' at us Treggs—the bleddy lot of you. I never wants to see you again——"

With that she turned and ran from the

startled, red-faced Mark. He stood looking after her, his mouth open a little, perplexity in his eyes.

"There's sauce for you!" he muttered. "Flinging at them, indeed——"

But the perplexity lingered as he, too, walked away. And how she could swear! What strange people the Treggs were; what a strange girl was this Annie Tregg. Flinging at them? Was there truth in that? Mark's young face was set and very thoughtful as he walked along. It seemed there were terrible gulfs, deep bottomless chasms, between the social standing of such as the Olivers, the Treggs—and themselves; gaps no bridge of tolerance or understanding could span. Life had fixed their different levels and ways as God had fixed the stars: they could not meet without clash and disorder, without the heat of contact engendering contempt and hatred and destroying reason. Mark could not forget those bitter words, those angry brown eyes, those quivering lips, as he went on, could not forget that he himself had uttered words that had hurt this girl, words that had seared and roused her to retaliation and fury. "Gawd never flung dirt at no one," she had said, and " 'Ave I ever bin a convic'?" and "I wish I'd never seed you—you dem-fool boy." It was a matter for deep and disturbing thought. And there was something infinitely sad and pathetic in her admission that she had nothing to do, nowhere to go, that she came every day just to be near his family, just to see other people. There was a terrible loneliness, and a wanting, there.

" 'God never flung dirt at no one——' " the boy said softly as he walked on. "At least *she* gave me the truth——"

Tilly Martin was a good horsewoman, and was aware that she made a striking figure cantering along in the red bonnet and dress. The pity of it was, she told herself, there was no one to observe her, to notice how straight she sat in the saddle, how easily she mastered the horse she rode. Except for an old woman asleep under a tree near the hut on a spur the valley seemed to be deserted. The hut, no doubt, would be the Treggs's cabin. But she had no intention of speaking to a Tregg, even if she met one of them; they were a wild lot, and their bedraggled fur jackets and caps suited them.

She brought the horse down to a walk, and presently saw that the valley ahead was closing in. On a rise between two jutting spurs some kind of a fence ran across. That fence would be Olivers' boundary line. The Olivers. Her hand went up to tuck some loose hair firmly under her bonnet; her blue eyes were wide and watchful. She had not seen any blacks, but her father did not think they would be dangerous if left alone.

It was undoubtedly a lovely valley, with park-like flats and gentle rises and the winding creek gleaming under the sun between tall trees. And it was exciting to remember all the land she had ridden over belonged to the Martins—all these grassy miles reaching up to the bordering hills. Her father had not fixed the exact boundaries, but this fence would certainly be one of them. With a sense of anticipation she rode towards it. Would she see the Olivers' house from there? Would she see any of the Olivers?

She came to the fence and saw the turnstile. She looked at it in astonishment, wondering what quirk put it there, then she looked beyond it. To the south was a long vista, a wide, walled valley rich with colour. She saw the Oliver cattle and sheep far away, but not their house. And lifting in the distance were the great mountains, the giants that watched eternally over this land. Down that way was a road to Port Phillip, to Melbourne Town, but she did not want to go there.

And then, along down the valley, she saw something move. Yes, it was someone on horseback, coming in her direction. Her eyes brightened. So intent was she that the running figure of Meg, coming towards the fence behind her, was unobserved. She did not hear the bare feet, did not see the red-haired girl stop all at once, stand staring for a moment, then glide away to a screen of saplings and vanish behind them.

Everitt Oliver's bay cleared the fence easily. Tilly, cool and composed, watched him walk his horse towards her. So, also, did Meg, but Meg was neither cool nor composed. Anger flared in the girl's blue eyes as she watched Everitt take off his wide beaver and give the Martin girl a sweeping bow and flourish. But she was too far away to hear him say:

"You must be my neighbour. I am Everitt Oliver."

Tilly looked at him. He was a handsome fellow, indeed, tall, graceful, wide-shouldered, dark. The dark eyes were a little close to a straight, thin nose, but they were bold and commanding. She spoke quietly.

116

"I am Tilly Martin, sir. The other evening you weren't so quick to call us neighbours."

He smiled. This wench was a beauty. He remembered seeing that yellow hair glinting in the fireglow that night. And she was tall, deep-breasted, and his practised eyes could trace the curving lines of graceful limbs under the folds of the riding-dress.

He said gently, "You must not do me an injustice, Miss Martin. You will remember it was my father who spoke—not I."

"I remember," said Tilly. "And from your present words and manner, sir, I take it you yourself are agreeable to having the Martins for neighbours?"

"My father's quarrels are not mine, Miss Martin," Everitt replied smoothly. "Please believe that. He is getting on in years, and is often irritable about nothing at all. I assure you——" and his eyes took time now in a bold appraisal of her—"I am very pleased, more than pleased, to have you for my neighbour."

There seemed to be just a faint emphasis on the "you". Tilly was thrilled to hear it. She had seen his appraisal of her, and she knew she had attracted him. But her voice was even and cool as she said:

"Thank you, Mr. Oliver. To be enemies—

here on the roof of the world—would be foolish, wouldn't it?"

"Very," he agreed heartily. "For us to be other than . . . friends . . . would be foolish in any place. Do you think you will like living here?"

Tilly breathed deeply, not because she was short of breath, but because she wanted him to see the contours of body and limb. But Everitt had not missed anything.

"I think so, Mr. Oliver. It is lonely, of course; there is no one here——"

He smiled at her.

"I thought we had agreed to be neighbours?"

Tilly laughed softly. Tilly knew how to laugh like that.

"Have you found it lonely here?" she parried.

"Very," he said deeply. "We've been here two years now, and I haven't had the pleasure of speaking to a woman—except my sister, Jane, of course—in that time. From a long way off I saw your red habit—I couldn't get here fast enough."

"How old is your sister?" Tilly asked.

"Twenty-five, I believe—two years younger than I am. You would like Jane—she is so . . . so very charming and agreeable."

"I'm sure she must be, Mr. Oliver. To my surprise I am finding that an Oliver can be agreeable——"

Meg saw the beaver make another sweeping flourish, and her watching eyes were hard and glittering now. How she wished she could hear what they were saying; how she wished *she* had a fine horse and a red dress. But there was one thing she possessed—Everitt Oliver himself, and this red-bonneted Martin girl had better keep away from him.

Everitt was asking politely, "Why did you ride this far, Miss Martin?"

Tilly turned innocent blue eyes on him.

"I wanted to see the valley, Mr. Oliver. It is all so new to me, you know."

"Naturally. I am forgetful, aren't I? It's a vast country, isn't it? I mean compared with—where did you come from?"

"From near Maidstone, in Kent. Yes; distances here are incredible. We travelled for weeks and weeks to get here. And when we did I thought we had arrived at the end of the world."

Everitt laughed.

"And the churlish visit of the Olivers did not improve matters," he said apologetically.

"Scarcely—at that moment."

"You speak well, Miss Martin."

"Thank you. We all do, sir. We were all well schooled. Father was a yeoman farmer of standing, sir. His family have been near Maidstone for generations."

"I am glad I met you today, Miss Martin, to be able, if I can, to improve your opinion of us."

"You are very courteous, sir."

"I confess I did not expect such charm, and may I say it—beauty—in any possible neighbour."

Tilly gave him a side-glance.

"La, sir! That is a pretty compliment. And so soon——"

"Oh, I meant it, I assure you. Can your horse take this fence?"

"Of course," said Tilly lightly.

"Would you consent to ride a little way with me down our part of the valley? I want you to *know* you and I are neighbours."

It was a flattering little request, made with quiet deference. The "our part of the valley" implied that he, at least, recognized that the north side now belonged to the Martins.

"Is there anything to see?" she asked.

"I'll tell you all about it as we ride

along—that high bluff over there—it has a purpose. The Wongals use it for peculiar ceremonies at certain times."

"Very well," Tilly said graciously. "But I must be back before long."

Meg saw Tilly wheel her horse and send it at the fence. Over went the grey, Everitt's bay beside it. Meg saw them no more. She came out from behind the saplings and walked slowly back towards the hut, her face grim and set. She and Annie came to the hut together.

"Whar you bin?" snapped Meg.

"Nowhar," came shortly. "Whar *you* bin?"

"Nowhar!" snarled Meg. "I bin . . . dem nowhar!"

8

JOHN and Hetty Martin walked from the wagon to the ploughed ground. John, in a broad black beaver, black frock coat, trousers and boots, was soberly dressed, and Hetty, for this was a Sunday rule, wore her high-waisted brown gingham dress, and a brown straw bonnet. Nan was with Tom, placing a fish-trap in the creek, and Jeanette, who did not wish to go anywhere, was resting in the wagon. Mark had not returned after his meeting with Annie Tregg, and Tilly was riding towards the bluff with Everitt Oliver.

At the edge of the furrows John and Hetty paused. He stooped and picked up a handful of the brown loamy earth.

"Now don't worry about the children, wife," he said. "They will be safe in this valley."

"I—I hope so, John. You have done well with the ploughing these last few days."

He looked along the furrows.

"A start. And none too soon. By the look of those mountains I'd say there is only a one-crop season here. Winter will be keen, Hetty; we must have the house up before then."

"I do hope so, John. A woman is lost without a house."

"And a man is lost without a woman," John said dryly; "so he builds her a house. Do you regret what we have done?"

"You mean . . . leaving England?" Hetty asked slowly.

He nodded.

"Aye. But it's a pleasant valley, John," was said quietly.

He looked at her for a moment, then put an arm round her shoulders.

"It is. A happy choice, I feel sure. What think you of the other people in it?"

Hetty looked down at her hands as she spoke.

"I think it's a pity we started as we did. We have no friends here, John."

"That was none of our doing," he hastened to say.

"I know, dear. It was all done long ago, done when the first convicts came to this colony. It seems to have gone like this: First of all convicts and their guards; more convicts, more guards. For all the scarlet and buff, for all the arrogance and gleaming swords, they were but prisoners' guards. Then more convicts, more guards, and the first free settlers. Then land was granted free to privileged persons; then to immigrants; then to freed convicts who have served their time. And those three have hated each other ever since."

"That is very true, Hetty," John agreed. "But how else could it be? It is only now this colony—this Australia, indeed—is drawing people in numbers. Didn't we talk long about it all before we took ship? We knew it must be a strange country, a land of tremendous distances and differences. We were prepared for that. Had we gone to any plain or valley in any other place we would have found the same conditions, the same arrogance of the exclusives, the same expectancy of the new immigrants, the same bitter remembrance of the ex-convicts. We have had no part in this colony's cruel past; we take no part in the present bitterness of factions."

His arm left her shoulder, and she put her hand in his.

"I know," she said gently. "But that remembrance is what we have to face here . . . and since we have to face it . . ."

"Yes? Go on, wife."

"I am afraid."

"Of what?" came gruffly.

"Of what could happen to you, to me—to our children. Sometimes I have the feeling we shall be sorely tried in this valley, that terrible things are waiting to confront us. It seemed different while we were in Sydney Town. There all is bustle and getting along. The town is filled with people like ourselves. The privileged keep to themselves and do not seem to be privileged—the emancipists likewise, you do not see the mark on their brows so plainly as we see it here on the Treggs. There people rub shoulders and pass each other quickly in the streets. But here, where these harsh differences *dwell*, and accuse each other daily, it is a matter of terrible reality. I feel we have journeyed into that . . . reality."

"Oh, come now, Hetty," John said reassuringly. "It is the same everywhere. I didn't know you thought so much about things. But we have nothing to fear in this valley. We'll have nothing to do with the Olivers or the Treggs. Forget your fears, and let's go and mark the ground where the house will stand. Where shall it be? I leave it to you, wife."

Hetty nodded.

"Yes; let us do that, John. I'll feel, when the house is up, that we've really started. There is a strange comfort and security in a house. I think—over there beyond where the wagon stands——"

John nodded his approval.

"There it shall be, Hetty," he said heartily. "A pretty site, sheltered by tall trees, looking down to the little waterfall in the stream. It won't be a great house at first—just slabs and stringybark roof; but even at the start we'll have a good-sized living-room and kitchen combined, a room for you and me, one for the boys, one for the girls. Aye—and a store-room running back from the hearth. But, later, wife, when we've split shingles and shaped stone, you shall have a house to be proud of. I *know* we shall succeed here, and that God will bless us."

Mark came round the ploughed ground towards them. John said to him, "Your mother has decided the house will stand over there, Mark. Under those fine trees."

Mark nodded. "Oh, yes," he said quietly.

Hetty and John looked at him.

"Is anything the matter, son?" Hetty asked. "You seem to be very thoughtful."

"No—no, mother," the boy replied. "Where are Tom and Nan?"

"Down at the creek. Did you go far?"

"No, mother."

John eyed him shrewdly.

"Did you meet anyone?" he asked.

"Yes—I did. Annie Tregg."

"Annie Tregg!" echoed John, his eyes widening. "Why would you be meeting this Annie Tregg?"

"She was lying on the ground crying as I came up to her."

"Crying?" inquired Hetty.

"Yes. Not far from here. She heard father say the Treggs were a bad lot——"

"She *heard*?" said John deeply.

Mark nodded.

"It seems the girl is lonely. She has been coming along to watch us at work."

John frowned. There was something in Mark's tone, a faint sympathy, he did not like detecting.

"More likely to attract you two boys," he said gruffly.

"Oh, now, John——" Hetty began.

John's face began to redden with annoyance.

"Well, go on, Mark," he said, interrupting Hetty.

"She was very angry, father. She said you had no right to brand her as an ex-convict——"

"Go on, Mark!" came in an ominous tone.

"She said God never flung dirt at any-one——"

"The blaspheming little baggage!" John exclaimed. "But go on."

"And that the Martins would be better if they stopped flinging—that's what she said—*flinging*—at the Treggs."

John's wrath burst. His usually cheerful countenance was hard with self-righteous indignation.

"I've never heard such impudence!" he said harshly. "Such downright defiance of truth and decency. The minx ought to be whipped——"

"I don't think so, father," said Mark quietly.

John was staggered. Was the boy ill, or bewitched?

"You—what?" he roared.

Hetty was distressed. This had the makings of a very painful scene.

"John—please be calm," she pleaded.

"Mark is only telling us what the girl said——"

"I know what Mark is telling us," came bitterly. "But did you hear him say he supported the wicked little tramp? And why don't *you* think she ought to be whipped, boy?"

Mark was pale, but he went on doggedly:

"Because I believe with her that God is not unkind," he said calmly. "I don't think He would condemn the girl for what her father did years ago."

John was panting. This was an outrageous thing.

"Are you trying to read the mind of the Almighty, Mark Martin?" he thundered.

Mark shook his head.

"Are *you* father?" he asked.

John stared at him. Hetty spoke quickly.

"Mark—go and see how Tom and Nan are getting on with the fish-trap. I want to talk about this matter with your father—and now is the time."

"Yes, mother."

Mark walked away, John's staring and angry eyes following him.

"I never thought a son of mine would ever speak to me like that," he said wrathfully.

"And it's all because of this Tregg girl——"

"Listen to me, John," said Hetty. "Here, sit down, my dear——"

"No!" came emphatically. "I am the head of this household. I expect obedience from my children. I am amazed and alarmed to know that a mere chance meeting with this girl can turn my son into a—a pagan!"

"Oh, John! Mark is a steady, fine boy. He's no pagan——"

"Then what talk was that? Questioning the word of the Lord—questioning *my* authority. But I'll stop it, Hetty. If I don't—God knows what will happen. I *won't* have a son of mine listening to Tregg guile——"

"John," said Hetty quietly. "I suspect you are flinging at the Treggs again."

John's jaw dropped. For a moment he could not believe he had heard aright.

"Hetty!" he said, deep surprise and incredulity in his voice. "You surely don't want our boys to associate with such girls, do you? You must know what they are! Are *they* the kind of women you want our Tom and Mark to take up with?"

"Of course not, John. But, my dear, you can't shake this valley by stamping your feet—you can't expect your sons to shut their eyes and walk blindly at your bidding. I think it well, John, to leave the matter of the Tregg girl to Mark's own good sense—and Mark has good sense. He was not defying you, John. I saw it pained the boy to say what he thought he must tell you. You are a good father, John, and you have good sons and daughters. But they are growing up, my dear man. Do not thunder at them with your tongue, or threaten with your wrath. Look at them for yourself—they are now men and women, no longer children. Remember that, John. They are men and women now."

John took in a deep breath. Hetty could see he was distressed. He stood for a moment without speaking, then he said:

"It needs thinking upon, Hetty. Deeply. And praying about. I feel I can't reverse my thoughts, my Christian faith and principles, simply because a Tregg girl resents the truth of my words. I do not fling at the Treggs— they flung at themselves long ago. But to think of something equally attractive—let us walk to the pen and look at the swine."

"Oh, John!" said Hetty in gentle reproach.

But John's mouth was stubborn, his chin jutting as he walked along.

9

THE sun came south with the passing weeks. Towards the end of November the days were hot, and lifting smoke on many a hill and plain told of raging fires that left black scars on the burnt earth. From dawn to dusk the Martin family toiled. John had said no more to Mark about Annie Tregg; the boy did not mention her name again. All was work while daylight lasted: a rough cockatoo fence of poles enclosed the cultivation paddock; a stockyard of heavy, split slabs stood completed; the pig-pens were floored with slabs and roofed with sheets of stringybark; hen-roosts were built; and a sheep-fold protected the sheep at night.

As his family finished breakfast on a sultry morning just before sunrise John said, "Today we start to build the house."

"That's good news, John," said Hetty. "We'll all be glad to have a roof over our heads."

"Aye. Tilly and Jeanette will help me set the timbers as Tom and Mark trim and drag them to us. Nan will stay with you, wife. Come—let's be busy."

"Yes," said Tilly softly to Jeanette as they walked away from the fire; "It's always 'Let us be busy.' Look at my hands! I'm ashamed to look at them."

Jeanette shrugged.

"Whatever is the matter with you, Tilly? For the past fortnight you've been either silent or grumpy. You don't ever go riding on Sundays now."

"Nothing's the matter," said Tilly shortly. "Except my back is always aching and my hands are as hard and rough as a fence-rail."

"Well," said the practical Jeanette, "There's no one else but us to do the work. And my back aches, and my hands are rough, too."

"Yes," snapped Tilly as they came to the dray where the tools were kept, "but you like this kind of thing. I don't. I think it was unfair of father to drag us all these miles across the world, away from our friends, away from all we had and all the things and people we knew—just to boast he has miles of empty country round him. I don't want to stand on bare feet swinging a hoe for the rest of my life——"

"Better not let father hear you talking like that," Jeanette warned. "Mother told us about Mark upsetting him——"

"Father!" said Tilly sourly. "All he thinks of is himself."

"Oh, Tilly!"

"Well, so he does!" Tilly snapped. "I hate this country—miles and miles of nothing. Of no one! Trees, trees, trees! Mountains! Distance! Nothing! Sky and hill and valley stretching away for ever! And us shut in—buried! A miserable loneliness for young women like me, and you, and even Nan."

"Here's your spade," said Jeanette shortly. "And one for me. I can't understand you. A few weeks ago you'd come back from riding looking happy and well content with this valley. Then all at once you become glum and bitter."

"Oh, never mind about it," said Tilly. An impatient hand tossed her yellow hair back over her shoulders. "Look at mother chopping wood for the fire—one of these days she'll cut a foot off——"

"Nonsense," retorted Jeanette. "Mother's used to the axe—she cut wood before we were born—and ploughed, too, and sowed and reaped and stacked and cured and preserved and baked and made clothes and nursed us when we were ill and helped us with our lessons and taught us to ride and to sing and me to play the fiddle—lawks, Tilly! You're off your head lately. You're as cranky as Jess Walton was when she found she was going to have a baby."

"Well, I'm not going to have a baby—unless I marry a blackfellow——"

"Tilly!"

"Well, there's not much choice, is there?"

"You *are* sharp this morning! The trouble with you is you're good-looking and know it."

"And you have ice in your veins—and *don't* know it," Tilly told her.

Jeanette's dark eyes gave her sister a look of quiet reproof. "Have I? Perhaps, perhaps not. But I hope I have some sense in my head."

"Well," said Tilly bitterly, "I don't like this country. As far as I am concerned the blacks and the convicts may have it. If we *don't* succeed we'll be like the Treggs—running round in animal skins and tossing gnawed bones at one another. I feel this country has cheated me, and that it knows it and mocks me——"

"Oh, you're crazy," said Jeanette impatiently. "It's a beautiful valley, warm and friendly. You ought to have more sense than fret and be miserable just because there aren't a dozen men looking at you."

"Oh, be quiet, Jeanette. You preach like father. Here he comes. Listen——"

John came to them.

"I'll mark where you are to dig, and loosen any hard earth with this bar. Come—let's be busy," he said briskly.

Tilly's lips thinned as she glanced at Jeanette, but Jeanette merely shrugged as she turned to walk beside her father.

"Yes—let's be busy," said Tilly cynically.

John beamed.

"Good girl, Tilly. You're a Martin, to be sure. I like that spirit in my family."

Jeanette laughed.

In the half-darkness of the Tregg hut Annie raised her head to see the dim figure of Royd sneaking out on noiseless bare feet.

"Whar you goin', Royd?" she whispered.

Royd's huge frame stood motionless in the doorway for a moment.

"Olivers——" he growled.

No one moved in the wide bunk. Annie's voice just reached him.

"You bin goin' thar a lot since ol' Oliver an' Ev'ritt rode off to Melbourne a fortnight ago——"

"Olivers——" came again. "Workin'—for Miss Jane."

Annie stared at him, but he seemed to be normal; his speech was not slurred or thick. She edged down the bed and stepped on to the earth floor without waking the others. She followed her gigantic brother outside.

"You—you all right, Royd?" she asked.

He nodded. "Yus, Annie. Miss Jane'll give me summat to eat. Be beck at dark."

"What you workin' at, Royd?" she asked.

But he did not answer. She watched him go striding away through the trees, a tremendous fellow in his skins. She turned as her mother came out of the hut.

"Whar's Royd?" Sarah asked anxiously. "I heered 'is voice——"

"Gone to th' Olivers."

"Freshen the fire," said Sarah. "I don' like it, Annie—I don' like it."

"No," said the girl thoughtfully. "But y'can't stop 'im 'less you chain 'im up. 'E's not goin' to do no work—jist goin' to get a sight o' Jane Oliver. Thet Jane Oliver's all Royd ever thinks 'bout. If 'e can jist get a sight of 'er 'e's 'appy. Better tell 'Lijah an' the boys."

Meg came out, yawning and running her fingers through her red hair.

"Whar's Royd?" she asked.

"Olivers," said Annie.

Sleep vanished from Meg's eyes.

"Gawd!" she breathed. " 'E'll do a mischief thar yet."

"Poor Royd," sighed Sarah. " 'E was a fine little feller onct——"

"Yus," sneered Meg. "Onct. But 'e's not a little feller no more."

"You leave Royd alone," said her mother sharply. "You's allus pickin' on 'im. Royd won't 'urt no one—not my Royd."

"Well," said Meg sullenly, "If 'e does 'e'll git a chain, all right—but roun' 'is neck, not 'is belly."

Rage leapt into Sarah's eyes. She bent down and picked up a heavy stick.

"Out, y'little bitch!" she screamed. "I'll brain you, Meg, if you don' mind your tongue——"

Meg glared at her with fierce blue eyes.

"You 'it me with thet stick, ol' woman—an' mebbe I'll brain *you*," she snarled. "You never thought nothin' of any of us—allus it's

Royd, Royd, Royd! You be jist like a silly ol'
'roo with a joey in 'er pouch. I'll go watch the
fool m'self."

"You better eat," said Annie, edging
between Meg and Sarah.

Elijah, Johnnie, Rock and Dick came out.

"What now?" asked Elijah. "What be the
screechin' *this* time?"

"Whar's Royd?" asked Dick.

"Gone to th' Olivers," said Sarah sulkily.
She threw down the stick.

The men exchanged glances.

"Git us summat to eat, ol' woman," said
Elijah gruffly. "We'll go after 'im. Git the
straps, Johnnie——"

"You be gentle with Royd——" Sarah
began.

"Yus, yus," came harshly. "Git us food."

Mumbling to herself, Sarah went into the
hut.

Johnnie said, "Royd'll break someone yet.
'Ow was 'e?"

"Seemed all right," said Annie. "But 'e
snaps like a stick. Wish 'e'd keep away from
thet Jane Oliver. I don't like it—not
anyways."

Meg looked at her father and brothers.

"Better git 'im quick. She gits 'im all excited. 'E'll rape 'er yet——"

"Huh! Time someone did," growled Rock. "Me—I'd laugh."

Meg gave him a sour look.

"Yus," she retorted. "But when th' Olivers come with their guns—*they* wouldn't be laughin'."

Elijah looked at her with probing eyes.

"What've *you* bin doin' near th' Olivers?" he demanded.

Meg shrugged.

"Keepin' an eye on thet fool Royd," she answered quickly. "Thet be all."

"Better be all," said Elijah. "Now we better eat an' go after 'im. I won't 'ave 'im 'angin round th' Olivers—'im or any other Tregg."

Meg's eyes were low-lidded as she went with the others into the hut, but she did not speak.

Royd had walked with long strides. He came to the fence and vaulted it, ignoring the turnstile. Moving down the slope he turned towards the bluff. His simple mind remembered one thing: he had told Annie he was going to the Olivers, and he knew he would be followed. His pale eyes gleamed with cunning as he made for the west slope of the strange hill, and he laughed deeply as he began to climb to the summit. He knew he could see the Olivers' house plainly from there, and also any movement of man or beast along the valley floor.

Up he went, a gigantic, grotesque, scrambling fellow, panting with the exertion of the pull until he came to the level stretch on top. Here he stood for a moment sucking air deep into his lungs and nodding with satisfaction. There were no blacks. Not that it would matter if there were any; he had been up here before when the Wongals were present, and although they had stood like bronze statues, unmoving with long spears in their hands, they had made no effort to speak to him or to send him away. They knew he was different, that he had a spirit in his head.

He walked to a flat rock-ledge right on the lip of the cliff. Grunting, he lay down on it, his head out over the fearful drop. He could look right down two hundred feet of smooth rock face, could see for miles and miles into the south, right into the towering mountains there, could see the Olivers' red cattle, and the sheep like a small white cloud on the green valley floor. And he could see the

Olivers' house and outbuildings across the winding creek. Chuckling, he waited. Jane would surely come out of doors, and he would see her. That was all he wanted: just to see her.

He did not move as the sun rose, did not move when he saw his brothers and Elijah searching for him, but a snarl twisted his lips when he saw Johnnie's long arms carrying the straps. They were after him, but they would not think to look up on the bluff for him. He looked away from them, and kept his eyes on the house, the woolshed, and the mustering yards. His huge frame quivered with joy when at last Jane came out of the house and walked to the seat encircling the trunk of a lofty stringybark. She sat down and busied herself with some sewing she had with her. Royd could see her plainly for she sat almost facing the bluff. Tiny though her figure was he noted every movement of body and limb, and in his unbalanced brain desire mounted until the hot force of it set his great red hands clawing at the rock under him. Jane. He mouthed the name. He wanted to shout it aloud, but cunning restrained him. He knew Jane Oliver despised him as she did all the Treggs, but perhaps she would not always do that; perhaps some day she would speak kindly to him, look at him as if he were human. Jane. He stared down at the tiny figure. He coud wait . . . yes; he could wait—but some day he would come for her.

He raised his head as she stood up and walked back into the house. She was gone. But he still lay there watching the house and the valley. All day he waited, seemingly untouched by heat or hunger or thirst, and only when the shadows crept out of the western hills did he rise to his feet and go rapidly down the steep slope.

His wide mouth was gaping in a grin when he walked into the hut. He was happy. But Meg was not. The days had dragged since Everitt rode to Melbourne with his father, empty days that robbed her of the excitement of his caresses. She scowled at Royd as he sat down heavily at the slab table. Sarah fawned on him at once.

"Royd—Royd is happy," she crooned as she placed steaming kangaroo-meat stew before him. "Royd'll never 'urt no one—not my Royd."

He laughed out loud then, cunning eyes in a broad face staring round at them all, a hulking fellow with the mind of a child.

"I saw y'all," he jeered at his brothers. "But y'didn't see me—y'never *will* see me if I don't want——" and he roared with laughter again.

Meg tore at her meat with vicious teeth. She hated and resented the way her mother doted on Royd, and, being a primitive herself, she fretted at the frustration imposed by Everitt's absence. She was taut and sullen. Annie, too, looked with cold eyes from one to the other. She had not gone back to watch the Martins, and she wanted to see the fair-haired boy again. So much. Every day was a struggle for her, every night brought long hours of critical and hurtful thought. Her brown eyes came back to Elijah, tilting and draining his wooden bowl with a gulping mouth. Convict. And Sarah. Convict. The ruddy fire-light flickered on them. Because of them the fair-haired boy regarded her as a bad lot; she could not speak to the tall, blue-eyed Martin boy because she was the daughter of convicts; she could not mingle with any respectable people for that same reason. Was she to be scorned, sneered at, spat at, sought as a slut, or avoided, all her years? Was she for ever to walk in shadows, to peer at others from behind trees—was *that* to be her life for ever . . . and

144

for ever? Because of Elijah? And Sarah? Her young face was hard as she ate in silence; hard and drawn in rebellious lines. But she was a Tregg; like the others of her family, she lived little better than an animal; she could not read or write; she was chained to a past as surely as crazy Royd was chained to his tree. Annie was thinking now, thinking long and deeply. She looked at the others mauling the meat with their fingers, and then looked down at her own. Annie, like Meg, but for different reasons, was not happy.

And along the valley, staring into the flames of the Martins' fire, Tilly also was not happy. She knew nothing of Meg's intimacy with Everitt Oliver, knew only that his words, his looks, his presence, were balm to loneliness, a promise of emotional escape from this still and soundless valley.

10

FAR from the valley, the next day, there was a grey sky over Melbourne Town as a schooner came beating up Port Phillip towards Hobson's Bay. On the convict-built stone jetty at Williamstown, a mountain of a woman, with a mouse of a man beside her, stood waiting the arrival of the vessel. The woman was colossal in a loose-fitting blue dress and wide-brimmed blue bonnet; the diminutive man wore a stove-pipe hat, a long brown coat with brass buttons, crumpled black trousers and dusty black boots. Mr. and Mrs. Gubby, down from Sydney Town, were waiting for the *Minerva*, the schooner they hoped would bring Simon and Penelope to Melbourne for the land sales. Martha had not been able to get word to New Zealand that she and Henry would come to Melbourne, and she knew her daughter would not expect a letter before their vessel left the Bay of Islands. Martha, and Henry, too, longed for a sight of their lovely Penelope, and they would be glad to see Simon Lee Challinor also. But Martha chuckled inwardly as she recalled Mr. Gubby's futile efforts to dodge the sea trip. Henry detested a sea voyage. They had left the York Inn in their carriage, and had driven down George Street to their ship in grand style, Sam Pink, the coachman, cracking his whip to attract attention. But the moment they had walked up the plank at the Queen's Wharf Henry's troubles had begun. He had paused on the deck to sniff; he had turned pale; he had looked as if he would turn tail and bolt from the vessel; he knew he was going to be very sick. And he was. The moment the brig cleared the Heads and began sliding down into the troughs, then climbing to the crests with a shuddering roll, Henry took to the cabin for the remainder of the voyage. Martha could still hear his plaintive, "Oh, God—Martha! I must get off this ship——" and her own sarcastic, "Now, now, Mr. Gubby! You jus' can't walk off ships hout in the middle of the hocean. Don' try to 'old on to it, you silly little weasel—let it go an' you'll be better." Mr. Gubby did let it go, and was a very weak and washed-out little man when the ship anchored in quiet Hobson's Bay, and they were rowed to the jetty of the Marine Hotel on the north side.

And now, after several days, they were waiting for Penelope and Simon on the Williamstown jetty. Williamstown—William's Town at this time—boasted a store, a modest but comfortable inn, a blacksmith's forge, a new Mechanics' Institute, a number of dwellings, and about four hundred people. The jetty itself, known as "The Anchorage", close to the new stationary light on Point Gellibrand, and guarded by several small cannon, greeted all comers with a notice board displaying warnings and information.

As they came to it Martha said, "What's them?"

"Public notices, my dear, and one or two advertisements——"

"Ho! Read 'em, Mr. Gubby. I likes to know."

"Yes, my dear. The first are instructions to people using the jetty, no one can use it after sundown, and no wheeled vehicles are allowed on it. It's signed W. Lonsdale, Police Magistrate, and by Thomas Wills, a Justice of the Peace."

"Ho. An' the nex', Mr. Gubby?"

"It is a sheet giving the population of Port Phillip up to last quarter."

"Hindeed. Go on—spit it out, Mr. Gubby——"

"Well, the total population of the Province of Port Phillip is now twenty thousand——"

"You don' say! 'Ow many in Melbourne Town?"

"These are official figures——"

"Jus' tell me."

"Melbourne has eleven thousand in the town and suburbs——"

"Well, now! Lawks they be comin' in fast—jus' as the town be growin' fast. I was real s'prised 'ow big it be. Go on."

"Geelong has nine hundred; Portland three hundred; William's Town four hundred; County of Bourke three thousand, four hundred; County of Grant five hundred; County of Normanby four hundred; Commissioner's district of Western Port one thousand, six hundred; Commissioner's district of Portland Bay one thousand five hundred; making a total for the Province of twenty thousand."

"Lawks! An' all in jus' seven years."

"Yes. That one tells the wages offering to male and female workers in the Province. Good tradesmen get ten shillings a day, some less, craftsmen such as tailors and compositors three pounds a week, pastoral and agricultural workers from twenty-five pounds up to forty pounds per annum with rations. Of the females only a governess gets forty pounds a year, the others—cooks, dressmakers, needlewomen, farm and general servants, housemaids, nursemaids, get from eighteen pounds down to eleven pounds a year with rations."

"Lassy me! They be good wages, Mr. Gubby. Better'n Hingland. What's that one say?"

"A Mr. C. J. Tyers Esquire, R.N., tells that Matthew Flinders made a mistake in charting the position of a rock called the Devil's Tower—Flinders put it over two miles too far north, and more than two miles to the east——"

" 'E should 'a bin more careful. Could be a shipwreck."

"This notice offers ten shillings for information about absconding convicts and up to five pounds reward for capturing armed bushrangers."

"They's villains. They ought to be 'unged——"

"They usually are, my dear. Here is a list of amounts paid as bounties for immigrants—

thirty-eight pounds for a married man and his wife not over fifty years of age; nineteen pounds for unmarried women and men; and from five pounds up to fifteen for children between seven and fifteen years of age."

"H'm. There be some fine swindlin' agoin' on over them bounties. Now the last, Mr. Gubby——"

The last notice on the board, a faded, weather-stained document, read:

ON SALE AT THE STORE OF
MR. J. BATMAN
AT *LOW PRICES* FOR CASH

Taylor's Brown Stout in hhds

Dunbar and Son's bottled ale in 3 dozen cases

Marsella wine in hhds

Superior cognac brandy

Geneva

Jamaica rum

Maritius sugar

Hyson skin tea

Flour

Paint oil

Turpentine

White lead

Black and green paint

Cannister gunpowder FFF

Shot all sizes

Flat, square and round iron assorted

Yacht shirts

Scotch caps

Moleskin trowsers

Cord and olive
  velveteen do.
Swansdown and
  plush waistcoats
Striped shirts
Duck frocks
Velveteen shooting
  jackets
Fustian do.
Superior whitney
  blankets

Pocket knives
Wool bagging
Windsor glass
Superior cavendish
  tobacco
Colonial do.
Also beef, mutton
  and lamb at 5
  pence per pound
Potatoes, etc., etc.

Melbourne, February 16, 1838.

Martha turned to Mr. Gubby when he finished reading.

"My, 'Arry boy—I dunno 'ow you does it—areadin' all them words so easy like."

Mr. Gubby's small chest swelled a little.

"It's quite simple, my dear—quite simple," he said.

Martha nodded.

"Yus—when you knows 'ow. I dunno 'ow. Well, 'ere's the schooner—I 'opes she's from the Bay of Islands, an' that Simon an' Pagan be aboard."

"Yes, dear. I hope they had a better passage coming across from New Zealand than we did coming from Sydney."

"Oh, 'twasn't that bad, Mr. Gubby," said Martha with a laugh. "The ship tossed a bit——"

"*Tossed?*" bleated Mr. Gubby. "I vow there were times it was right out of the water—and other times when it was right under. And the stink! Sealskins, foul whale-oil, rotting whalebone—good heavens! No wonder I was sick."

"You never was a good sailor, Mr. Gubby. But never mind. 'Ere we be in Melbourne Town, safe an' sound, an' if all be well Pagan an' Simon'll be on that ship."

"I wish——" Mr. Gubby began plaintively.

She looked down at him as they walked along the jetty.

"What does you wish, Mr. Gubby?"

"That we could go back some other way."

"You means—hoverland? Lawks, 'Arry boy, an' chance all them blacks an' bush-rangers? I knows they got that villain Jacky-Jacky, what robbed folks on the Goulburn Road—but there's alwus others. What 'bout that woman as was comin' hover the Blue Mountings—she was 'eld up, stripped naked, robbed an' lef bleedin' from knife cuts where they'd cut off 'er stays. Wouldn't I look a sight like *that*? An' I suspec's you wouldn't be much 'elp——"

Mr. Gubby drew himself up.

"I would do what I could to protect you——"

Martha gave him a gentle slap that almost knocked him off the jetty.

"Ah! I likes to 'ear you say that, 'Arry boy. But you wasn't made for resistin' such villains."

"I—I suppose not."

"I've 'eard hoverlanders talk 'bout the long roads atween Melbourne an' Sydney, long an' lonely an' sometimes dangerous. You can get a coach through Liv'pool, Campbelltown, Berrima, Goulburn an' Yass, an' get accommodation in them places, but after Yass you goes either on 'orseback or by dray or your own kerridge—an' that's another three 'undred miles to Melbourne Town. An' that's a dratted long way, Mr. Gubby. In the new village o' Gundagai there be only a blacksmith's forge an' a grog-shop store. Nex' comes Albury, on the 'Ume—the Murray, some calls it now—there be a police barracks there, an' two or three dwellin's an' a 'otel kep' by a Mr. Brown who 'ires out a punt to cross the river in. Lawks! I wouldn't go in

154

them punts—I ain't that silly. Then after passin' through Violet Town there be another punt on the Goulburn where a feller named Clarke keeps an inn. The las' place on the road comin' this way, so they says, be Butler's inn, a few miles out on the Sydney Road. Go back all *that* way, Mr. Gubby? Not me when I can. eat an' sleep on a good ship agoin' back. Five 'undred miles in a dratted dray—I'd wear me bottom off abumpin' it on a board all that way."

"Yes, but——"

"Pickles!"

"Oh, very well, very well," said Henry petulantly. "But you enjoy the sea—I hate it."

Martha chuckled.

"You 'ates anythin' that stirs you up or moves you roun' a bit," she said dryly. "An' don' tell me again you ain't strong. I knows you, 'Arry Gubby. I almost 'ad to *drag* you 'ere to Melbourne Town."

"Well—I think you are foolish to buy town lots here. Melbourne will never be a big town, certainly never a city——"

"Ho? You forgets that jus' six years ago there wasn't no one 'ere at all, an' now look at the town. Anyway, I ain't bought none yet, Mr. Gubby."

"But you're thinking of doing so——"

Martha laughed.

"That's why I come 'ere, ain't it? Mebbe I can't read an' write like you, Mr. Gubby, but I listens well, an' I don' forget what I listens to. Jus' five year ago, in '36, there was only 'bout two 'undred folks—white folks—in all this 'ere Port Phillip distric'. Now we knows there be twenty thousan'—'leven thousan' in Melbourne Town——"

"Yes, yes, yes. I know——"

"You don' know heverythin', Mr. Gubby. Four year ago they sent away a 'undred an' fifty thousan' pounds weight o' wool—today it is jus' on two million pounds weight. In December o' '36 Joseph Hawdon, John Hepburn an' John Gardiner hoverlanded cattle from the Murrumbidgee down to Melbourne, the very fust ever to do that. In '38 the same Hawdon took cattle to Adelaide along the Murray, an' a week later Hedward John Eyre done the same thing—'im that walked all that way roun' the Bight to West Hostralia this very year. Did you know *that*, Mr. Gubby? An' they got good growin' soil 'ere, an' farms raise maize, 'taters, melons, turnips, cabbage an' all vege'bles an' good fruit-trees. We've seen the town for ourselves, the folks lookin' prosperous, all busy, although there be talk o' bad times. You keep rememberin' that, Mr. Gubby! Melbourne be bigger now than Parramatta, built on slopes up from a valley, a pleasant town though a bit dusty when the wind blows. There be good shops already, plenty 'otels, furniture shops, jewellers, music shops, drapers, schools, an' three banks—th' Hostralasia, in Collins Street, the Union Bank o' Hostralia, in Queen Street, an' the Port Phillip Bank, in Collins Street. The streets is wide due to that Mr. Hoddle, the surveyor man, with big trees shadin' the walks. An' *that's* somethin' they f'got to do in Sydney Town, Mr. Gubby. There be kerridges an' wagons agoin' an' acomin'. You can buy mos' things, although right now money's gettin' scarce. An' we's comfor'ble in Mr. Lingham's Marine 'Otel on 'Obson's Bay acrost there. It be a good place—private sittin' an' bedrooms for fam'lies, a conveyance to Melbourne Town, boats for 'ire, plenty good food an' liquor, an' three good wells near th' 'otel jetty. Don' tell me, Mr. Gubby, the place won't go ahead. But, lawks! I be all out o' breath atalkin' so much——"

"In spite of all that, I don't know what all these foolish immigrants will do when they get here," said Mr. Gubby stubbornly. "Mr. Fawkner—we met him at the *Patriot* office, remember? He was in from his residence 'Pascoeville'. He told me all they think of is getting land somewhere—miles of it. You look out over that bay——"

"I be alookin', Mr. Gubby——"

"You can count only ten big ships at anchor. There are smaller ships coming up from Geelong, as they call it, or from Launceston across the straits, but really, Martha, this end of New South Wales will never be more than a back door to Sydney."

"That's what *you* thinks, Mr. Gubby, an' I keeps tellin' you you never thinks. What was Sydney a few years ago but a stinkin' convic' camp? An' that was all. But it be different now——"

"Yes, yes, yes! But Mr. Fawkner says the immigrants——"

"Oh, drat Mr. Fawkner, Mr. Gubby. You'd think that man owned Melbourne Town."

"Well, he started it——"

"Batman started it."

"Really, Martha. Batman was a pastoralist, nothing more——"

"Nothin' more me backside, 'Arry Gubby. Ain't we jus' read Batman's list o' things to sell on that there notice board?"

"He had a store, but John Pascoe Fawkner was the first——"

" 'E was *not*, Mr. Gubby! John Batman was the fust—'im an' Gellibrand an' Wedge an' them others. They were 'ere munce afore Fawkner come 'ere, an' if it 'adn't bin for Batman that Fawkner would never 'ave come at all. Fawkner follered 'im."

"Martha, John Fawkner, the Launceston hotel-keeper, lawyer and newspaper proprietor, must be regarded as the *founder* of Melbourne——"

"I won' 'ave it, Mr. Gubby!"

Mr. Gubby sighed.

"Let's get things in their proper order, my dear."

"They is—Batman was fust!"

Mr. Gubby drew in a breath. He knew how stubborn Martha could be.

"Let's go right back to the beginning of everything," he said. "Captain Cook was the first white navigator to sight the coast of the present Province of Port Phillip——"

"Lawks, Mr. Gubby—Cook never come 'ere——"

"No, dear—I know. He sailed on up the east coast. No one entered this great bay until Lieutenant Murray came in the *Lady Nelson* and named Nepean Point and Arthur's Seat. That was in February 1802. In April of the same year Matthew Flinders came and surveyed the waters of the bay. He called the hills near Geelong Station Peak and named Indented Head. Then early the following year a Mr. Grimes was sent by the then Governor of New South Wales—Captain Philip Gidley King, after whom this bay was named—to report on his part of the colony. Grimes discovered the Yarra Yarra River, although J. H. Wedge, of Batman's party, named it. After him came, in the same year, Colonel Collins, from England, in H.M.S. *Calcutta* with the transport *Ocean*. Collins brought three hundred and sixty-seven convicts. His attempt to form a settlement failed, and he and his convicts went to Van Diemen's Land. After him, for more than twenty years, the land saw no white man—except Buckley, the giant convict who ran

160

away from Collins—who lived with the blacks and in '35 made himself known to Batman's party at Indented Head——"

"More'n twenty years, I do declare," said Martha. "Who come next?"

"Two overlanders—squatters who started from near Lake George, in New South Wales. Hume and Hovell, in '24. They were explorers and didn't stay. They discovered the Murray River—called it the Hume. They came right down to Geelong, although one of them thought they were at Western Port. So favourably did they report on their return that the government sent a Mr. Wright—a captain, I think he was—with soldiers and convicts to form a settlement. But *that* also fell through. Now we come to closer days. In '34 the Henty brothers—the same that failed at Swan River when we were there—came from Van Diemen's Land to Portland Bay. They were the first real settlers in the Port Phillip district. On the twenty-ninth of May, '35, John Batman came over from Van Diemen's Land in the thirty-ton craft *Rebecca* and made his camp at Indented Head."

"There *y'are*! I said 'e was fust, didn't I?"

"Yes, yes. That was in May. Some months later John Pascoe Fawkner's party went up the Yarra in Fawkner's *Enterprise*. They came to the basin, and moored to the bank where the end of William Street now is. Batman had treated with the blacks for six hundred thousand acres, but that was disallowed. The very moment Fawkner's *Enterprise* put its plank on the Yarra bank Melbourne began. Then Governor Bourke sent Captain Lonsdale here as the first magistrate, and now Mr. Latrobe is here as Superintendent, and Lonsdale is Treasurer. Latrobe lives in that fine house called Jolimont. We saw it. Batman's associates wanted pastoral land; Fawkner wanted to make a town. He has done so. He says so himself, and Mr. Henry Oliver, who knows him, supports him."

Martha laughed.

"Lawks, 'Arry boy—'ow we do be atalkin'. Oh well—you be eddicated, I'm not. An' to think all this 'as 'appened in seven short years. My! Seven year ago not a white man south of the Murray River, except that runaway convic' Buckley, an' now thousan's o' people, an' sheep, an' cattle, an' farms growin' things, an' big runs grazin' flocks an' 'erds, an' ships acomin' in, an' towns growin'. My, it do take your breath away when you thinks of it. 'Owever! Batman was 'ere *fust*. Mebbe both 'im an' Fawkner's done it in different ways. An' you've bin atalkin' to that Mr. Holiver, 'ave you?"

Henry permitted his small stature to assume an air of importance.

"I always speak with gentlemen, as you know," he said offhandedly.

"An' did you knuckle to the gen'l'man, Mr. Gubby?" came sarcastically. "Hi don' like the look o' that ol' Holiver—I thinks 'e's a ol' toad——"

"Really, Martha!" Henry protested. "I—I merely raised my hat to him, and we got into conversation. He is a very interesting old gentleman."

"An' be that thin-beaked young 'awk with 'im also hinterestin'?"

"I have scarcely spoken to young Mr. Everitt Oliver, my dear."

"A foxy pair if hever I seen a fox," said Martha. "Funny 'ow all folks an' beastses of the same kind alwus gets together."

Henry gave her a quick, suspicious glance.

"Martha, are you inferring that—that I am foxy? Really, my dear——"

"I ain't hinferrin', Mr. Gubby," came evenly. "I *knows* you can be foxy. But we

163

mustn't 'ave words 'ere in Melbourne Town—or whatever this place is where we be now."

"William's Town——"

"Well, 'ere. I don't want Pagan an' Simon to walk into a Gubby hargyment. The ship's comin' closer."

"I don't know——" complained Henry. "But you never seem to want me to have an opinion of my own."

A little smile touched Martha's lips.

"That's jus' what I've wanted ever since we's bin married, Mr. Gubby. But your opinion be alwus jus' someone else's—not your own, me man. But never mind, 'Arry boy. Hus Gubby's 'ave come a long way since you an' me fust met in ol' Lunnon all them years ago. Lawks! nigh on thirty year ago, when you was a clurk in th' Heast Hindia Comp'ny, an' I was a flower gel houtside Drury Lane Theatre. Ah! I was tol' many an' many a time—afore I met you, o' course—I was th' 'andsomest gel in Lunnon—tall, with yaller 'air an' blue heyes, an' a bottom that used to fetch th' heyes o' the bucks. Lassy me . . . look at me now! But we's come a long, long way, 'Arry boy. You can't be young for ever. An' hif there be some things you ain't

164

got—there be some you 'ave. An' you be my Mr. Gubby. The Gubbys be comin' hup in the world, Mr. Gubby. We's got money now."

"Yes," said Henry slowly. "I know what you've done for us all, Martha. I couldn't have done it—it was never in me."

Martha's huge arm went protectingly round his narrow shoulders.

"You're all right, 'Arry boy. You taught Pagan an' Mary Ann to read an' write an' figure, which I never could do. Without what you've done for 'em the two gels wouldn't *never* 'ave got where they 'ave. I done somethin'—you done somethin'. That's the way it be. The gels be set up fine. Pagan's got a fine man, a gen'l'man, an' rich. There ain't many like Simon Challinor, although mebbe 'e's a bit restless 'avin' bin a wanderer for all them years. Mary Ann's goin' to be a great singer. Halbert Hernest? Well—I dunno. 'E's very like you, 'Arry boy."

Henry was glad when the massive arm was lifted from his shoulders.

"Oh, I—I'm sure he will be all right, Martha," he hastened to say.

"We'll see. So long as 'e don' turn hout to be bone lazy, an' cunnin', an' a dodger——"

Henry looked uncomfortable.

"I think he will be a credit to us," he said. "He has a very sharp intelligence."

"H'm," said Martha. "I've noticed that, Mr. Gubby. But, look! The ship's comin' roun'. They'll drop hanchor in a minute— yus, there it goes. I seen the splash."

"There's a boat with two men in it being lowered. The captain and a seaman, I suppose."

Anxiously Martha and Henry watched the boat pull from the schooner to the jetty. As the two men climbed out and came towards them, Martha stepped forward.

"Hexcuse me, gen'l'men—be there a Mr. an' Mrs. Challinor aboard?"

The taller man, whose jacket and cap proclaimed him to be the master, shook his head as he faced her.

"No, ma'am. Would you be Mrs. Gubby?"

"Yus, I be—I be Martha Gubby——"

The man smiled.

"I am the master of the schooner, ma'am. just in from the Bay of Islands, New Zealand. Mrs. Challinor asked me to look for you here, and if you were here to give you this letter. Here it is, ma'am."

Martha began to tremble.

"Lawks—I do 'ope heverythin' be all right. Was my gel all right, sir?"

"In good health and spirits, ma'am—as was Mr. Challinor," was the reply.

Martha handed the letter to Henry, then thanked the captain. "Thank you, sir. I be mos' obliged. Hif ever you be in Sydney Town, an' come to the York Inn, you'll be made right welcome."

The captain touched his cap.

"Thank you, Mrs. Gubby. We'll be returning to the Bay of Islands on Saturday, the twenty-seventh. I shall be happy to inform Mrs. Challinor I met you, ma'am."

He and his companion touched their caps and walked off. Martha said to Henry:

"Read that letter, 'Arry boy."

Henry opened it and read: " 'Dear mama, All our plans have been changed. Simon, of course, has changed them. And this will be something of a shock to you. We are not leaving New Zealand; indeed, we are going to live here permanently. Simon believes there is a tremendous future for this country. I don't know what to think—he said that about Western Australia, about New South Wales, and now New Zealand has gripped him. But, of course, where he goes I go. He will not be buying lots in Melbourne Town, but will represent Collingdale and Challinor permanently here . . .' "

Martha interrupted Henry. "That do be a shock," she said. "That restless Simon. But go on——"

" '. . . it is possible Simon will be more satisfied with living here than anywhere else, it seems to suit his adventurous spirit. He has decided to sell our house at Vaucluse, and so, mama, New Zealand is to be our home. I am sending this by Mr. Reid, the captain of the schooner. If you get it forgive me if I have put you out in any way, although, of course, I don't know if you are in Melbourne Town. I'll write you fully later on. Your ever-loving daughter, Penelope.' "

Martha filled her lungs with a deep breath as they began walking towards the hired dray that was waiting for them.

"Well——" came at last. "So they's goin' to stay an' live in New Zealand. All I 'opes is they don't get massacreed by them wild Maoris."

"No, no, Martha. New Zealand is now British Territory."

"I wonders. A 'undred whites, an' a million Maoris, an' you calls it British Territory."

"That's what it is."

"H'm. I bet there's not a red-coat in the place. But let's get back to the Marine 'Otel acrost 'Obson's Bay there. We'll take the steamer, the *Sea Horse*, the steamer that took Gov'nor Gipps back to Sydney las' month, an' get back to Sydney ourselves. It sails on the fourth o' December; the bookin' hoffice be hopposite the Club 'Ouse in Collins Street."

"Very well, but I still can't see why we can't travel overland—a stinking steamer with its thrashing paddles——"

"I tol' you why. Get in the dray, Mr. Gubby."

"Very well, very well——"

"Anyways, we's 'ad a good look at Melbourne Town. I don' care what you says or thinks, Mr. Gubby, I b'lieve 'twill be a great town some day. 'Twas only yesterday Batman's sheep was agrazin' in the valley what's now Elizabeth Street, or it mus' seem only yesterday to them that come 'ere fust. Anyway—what's that ol' Holiver adoin' in Melbourne Town? 'E can't be livin' 'ere or 'e wouldn't be staying at the same 'otel as us."

The dray lurched forward on its journey back to the Marine Hotel.

"Mr. Oliver is here to purchase more land up where he is," said Henry with the air of one in the confidence of the great. "He wants a special survey—that's an area of five thousand, one hundred and twenty acres. Blocks are sold in those dimensions. It seems those Martins who stayed with us in Sydney——"

"I remembers 'em. They wrote to us from Yass. They was nice folks."

"Yes. Well, it appears they have squatted under an annual licence on a part of his valley."

" 'Ow could it be 'is valley if they got a gov'ment licence for it?"

"Mr. Oliver didn't explain that, my dear. But apparently he regards them as intruders, 'impertinent intruders', he calls them——"

"Do 'e now!"

"If after a month's notice from someone else they can't themselves *buy* the land they have to get off. He wants to get rid of them, and is sure they haven't the money."

Martha's eyes narrowed.

"I knowed 'e was a toad. So this Holiver be tryin' to down them Martins by a dirty trick, eh?"

"It did strike me as being somewhat

callous, but that is the way men are acquiring huge areas of land."

"Hindeed!" said Martha thoughtfully. "They was good people, the Martins—honest, hearnest, hupright folks. What would they do hif this Holiver did buy their land?"

"I—I suppose they'd be ruined——"

"The schemin' ol' weasel! I knowed 'e stunk as soon's I looked at 'im. Roonin' folks be nothin' to 'im, I s'pose, so long as 'e gets what 'e wants. You *does* get mixed hup with some queer folks, Mr. Gubby, an' you never could tell a rat if it wore a long coat."

"Mr. Oliver is a gentleman, my dear——"

"So's me fat foot. That be a crool trick to play on honest folks."

"I don't see it concerns us, Martha, or that we can do anything about it."

Martha grunted. "There be lots o' things you can't see, Mr. Gubby."

He looked at her, something like alarm coming into his sharp little face.

"But—but——" he stammered. "You're not thinking of interfering, surely?"

Martha's small mouth had that hard set line about it Mr. Gubby knew so well.

"I be thinkin', Mr. Gubby—jus' thinkin'," she said quietly. "Mebbe—mebbe we'll buy that land afore ol' Holiver—if 'e ain't done so already—an' sell it back to the Martins."

"Martha—for heaven's sake!" Henry gasped.

She went on. "I remembers *my* name was Martin afore I married you—an' I 'ad many a dirty trick played on me, an' I couldn't do nothin' about it. But I ain't forgot."

"Martha!" Henry almost squealed. "It's—it's impossible. Mr. Oliver would be furious——"

"Pickles," said Martha. "Lawks, these dratted drays do bang your bottom don' they?"

11

WHILE Martha and Henry were still at the Marine Hotel, and while the first days of December saw the Treggs, with the exception of Annie, feasting on stolen mutton, a strange sight was to be seen on the main road leading out of Sydney Town. Three large drays filled with young women, their luggage piled in beside them, and with more young women trudging beside the slow vehicles, formed an unusual cavalcade. Caroline Chisholm was taking female immigrants into the country and the drays belonged to the inland settlers who drove them.

Although it was still grey in Melbourne, and there was a hint of coming rain in the far valley where the Martins were building, a clear dawn saw the drays leaving the Immigration Barracks, turn into empty George Street, pass silent and close-shuttered shops, and then the white stone toll-gate where the Parramatta Road began.

It was a morning changing swiftly from the

silver-mist of first light to the rose-gold flush of the rising sun, and the first rays touched the drays as they passed the swamp near Grose's Farm—where the Sydney University stands today. Some people were abroad on this highroad to the west, this historic Parramatta Road, this first of all Australian roads, and here and there one stood staring wide-eyed at the strange procession. Drayloads of young women? Not female felons going to Parramatta, surely? No; not these singing, laughing wenches who waved hands and bonnets and shawls and chattered merrily as they went by. Ahead of them went their song; it trailed behind them, rising over the plodding hooves of the bullocks, above the knocking of high wheels. . . .

"I'm lonesome since I crossed the hill
    And o'er the moor and valley,
    Such heavy thoughts my heart do fill
    Since parting with my Sally . . ."

Then laughter high and hearty broke the song, and voices called from dray to dray. Those on the roadside who watched them remembered Mrs. Chisholm and her scheme to settle female immigrants in the country, remembered the *Sydney Herald*'s generous support for and encouragement of her efforts. And the novelty and courage of it held them motionless until the drays creaked on, and the voices of the girls died away along the road.

In Caroline Chisholm's day the "country" was entered the moment one passed through the toll-gate, which stood where Railway Square is in present-day George Street, and it reached north to Brisbane Town, west to the Darling River, and south to Melbourne Town itself. As yet Caroline had gone only a few miles from Sydney. The long journeys to Yass, via Goulburn in the south, by ship to Wollongong, by horseback through Maitland and Scone and up the New England Ranges to Tamworth, and by ship to Brisbane Town, were yet to come; but on this bright December morning she knew a start had been made. There was now a Registry Office at the Female Immigrants' Home, also a school for the children of married immigrants. Hard suspicion of her motives was being replaced by a recognition of the worth of her sentiments and endeavours. In the school the Reverend Francis Murphy, who succeeded Dr. Ullathorne, also the Anglican minister of St. James's Church, the Reverend R. All-wood, looked after the religious instruction of Roman Catholics and Anglicans respectively, while the schoolmistress saw to it that the Presbyterians and Wesleyans were not forgotten. The seed of hope was slowly growing into the tree of accomplishment. People were gradually responding with money, food, applications for immigrants, and vehicles to carry the immigrants inland. Caroline remembered the grim occasion when she gathered together just over sixty female immigrants from Hyde Park, the Rocks and the Domain; and how, when they were mustered at the Home, all the money they had between them was only fourteen shillings and a few pence.

She realized as few did what immigration meant in this country that, until the previous year, had been a convict colony since Phillip brought the first fleet to Sydney Cove fifty-three years before. Indeed, although transportation had now ceased, there were still convicts in New South Wales, men and women who, when they finished their sentences, would become emancipists, and take their places as best they could in a hard and insensitive society that still trooped to Gallows Hill to see men hanged in batches.

And immigrants, bounty and free, were coming in by shiploads to take their places in the changing pattern of the growing colony.

Miles were long in the days of the slow drays. And those who lived in the towns, and those who dwelt inland, close or far, in the year 1841—the fifth year of the reign of Queen Victoria—knew themselves only as colonists. No one thought, as yet, of himself as an Australian. Each colony was separate; ruled, above its local government, by the Imperial authorities of Downing Street; it was a country apart from any other. New South Wales, which stretched from Cape Town to Melbourne, Van Diemen's Land (now Tasmania), Western Australia, and the Province of South Australia, were separate entities, and no one in that day envisaged a nation rising out of the sentimental or political fusion of these territories and their peoples. The only Australian was the blackfellow, the aboriginal; the white man was the colonial.

Caroline hoped to camp that night near Irish Town, a small settlement a few miles on the Sydney side of the village of Liverpool. As the drays went on, the mail coaches for the south and west and for Windsor rattled past, passengers and guards cheering the girls and waving gaily to them. Horsemen and horse-women rode with them a little way, some singing with them, others asking questions before spurring away. Children goggled at them, women waved shawls and aprons from wayside cottages, drovers laughed as their mobs held up the drays, and answering laughter and many a sally came back from the girls. On, with a rest every hour, when the girls in the drays gave their places to those who had been walking, on past the tall trees of Annandale, past the low-roofed, lime-washed Speed the Plough Inn, where they were given warm welcome and a parting cheer, and where the road turned south to Liverpool, on with thought always under the chatter and the song. Where were they going—and to whom? As they plodded along the bush track towards Irish Town none knew just where night would find them: that was left to the remarkable woman who accompanied them, who sang with them, who cheered them, who talked about their problems with them, and who comforted them when sometimes sad tears followed a song that used to be sung in a different land.

But smiles soon banished tears. One and all knew that sore hearts and sore feet were a penniless immigrant's lot in the first days. Then they would sing again. . . .

"Twas on a Monday morning when I beheld
   my darling;
She looked so neat and charming in every
   high degree;
She looked so neat and nimble, O, a-wash-
   ing of her linen, O.
Dashing away with a smoothing iron,
Dashing away with a smoothing iron,
She stole my heart away . . . away. . . ."

So they smiled again, these girls adventuring forth, and sang again, and walked the miles with the drays, and their voices went echoing down many a long, long road.

About the time the drays turned south from the Speed the Plough Inn, Martha and Henry, just before breakfast, were enjoying the morning air on the grassy slope running down from the Marine Hotel to the bay. Lingham's hotel, a rambling, one-storey structure, was well patronized and well liked for its situation on the north side of Hobson's Bay. The hotel jetty, with boats tied to it, stood above shining water as still as glass. Here and there on the sward, between the hotel and the jetty, children played under the watchful eyes of mamas in decorous bonnets, bright shawls, and dresses that swept the grass, mamas who chatted to bewhiskered papas in tall hats, fancy waistcoats, buckled trousers under long coats with large and shining buttons, or to less ornate gentlemen in beaver hats, short jackets and moleskins. Voices were subdued, but heads turned when a woman called shrilly to a child:

"Sophie, you come back here or Buckley will get you!"

Looking to the south, Martha and Henry could see, about two miles away, the tiny settlement at Williamstown, its stone jetty and lighthouse. The grey clouds had gone; it was a fine morning; and Martha was dressed in her favourite yellow bonnet and gown. She was rosy-cheeked and smiling as she walked beside her little husband.

"No town lots for us now, 'Arry boy," she said. "That valley land will cost me plenty. But it be a good investment both ways, that valley."

"I—I hope so, Martha. You've certainly done the Olivers in the eye. But supposing the Martins won't buy from you? That they just walk off? What will you do?"

Martha shrugged.

"Them Martins won't walk off. Where would they go? An' Martha Gubby ain't th' one to push 'em off. I'll fix it."

"Well, it's done," said Henry. "I only wish we were away from here——"

Martha chuckled.

"Now, now, 'Arry boy—don' get your tripes in a knot. No 'arm never come o' doin' someone a good turn. An' supposin' the Martins does walk off—which they won't—the Gubbys'd stock the land with sheep an' mebbe *you* could manage the new station."

Mr. Gubby's jaw dropped. For a moment everything round him became blurred.

"Me?" he squeaked. "Me go out to such a place? Good heavens, Martha—I wouldn't know what to do——"

She smiled down at him.

"I knows that, Mr. Gubby. But don' get all hexcited. You ain't even able to put a crupper unner a 'orse's tail."

"It isn't I'm not able," he defended himself. "It always seems to me to be so indelicate."

"Pickles!" came with a husky laugh. "But it'll be all right, 'Arry boy. I've drawed the sting outer them Holiver wasps—*they* don'

181

get that land. They waited too long; my happlication was in afore theirs. Dunno why they dilly-dallied. They was 'ere fust. Read me that bit Fawkner wrote in 'is paper—the fust newspaper that ever was 'ere."

"Oh, yes—I have it. I found it lying beside some old books on one of the tables. It's faded and crumpled but I can read it. Mr. Fawkner wrote it with pen and ink; it is dated January the first, 1838. Why do you want me to read it to you? It has nothing to do with the Olivers——"

"Mr. Gubby, I seen you readin' it. I likes to know things. I saw you put it in your pocket."

"I wanted to read it again myself. Well, here it is:

We do opine that Melbourne cannot reasonably remain longer marked on the chart of advancing civilization without its Advertiser.

Such being *our* Imperial Fiat We do intend therefore by means of this *our* Advertiser to throw the resplendent light of Publicity upon the affairs of this New Colony, Whether of Commerce, of Agriculture, or the arts and Mysteries of the Grazier. All these patent roads to wealth are thrown open to the adventurous Port Phillipians. All these sources of riches are about to (or already are) becoming accessable to each adventurous colonist of NOUS. The future fortunes of rising Melbournians will be much accelerated by the dissemination of intelligence consequent upon the Press being thrown open here. But until the arrival of the printing Materials *we* will by means of the Humble pen diffuse such intelligence as may be found expedient or as may arise.

The energies of the present population of this rapidly rising district have never been exceeded in any of the colonies of Britain.

It's giant like strides have filled with astonishment the minds of all the neighbouring states. The Sons of Britain languish when debarred the use of that Mighty Engine the Press. A very small degree of Support timely afforded will establish a Newspaper here, but until some further arrangements are made it will be merely an advertising sheet and will be given away to Householders.

"Well," said Martha as Henry finished reading, "there be no doubt Mr. Fawkner be a progressive feller. Mebbe 'e'll see many newspapers in a much bigger town than what's 'ere now. But it be a pity that Mr. Batman died, an' so young. I wonder what them Holivers'll think when they finds out what's bin done to *them*?"

Mr. Gubby trembled inwardly when he thought of Mr. Henry Oliver. Martha went on:

"We start for 'ome tomorrer, 'Arry boy. We ain't never travelled on one o' them steamers afore."

"Horrible things!" said Mr. Gubby. "What if it blows up?"

"I s'pecs we blows hup with it," came dryly.

"I think it's a frightful risk, my dear—frightful. I don't know what the world is coming to."

"No one ever does, Mr. Gubby. Well, it be nice an' peaceful 'ere this mornin'. Today we goes by th' 'otel drag into Melbourne Town—I wants some o' them Morison's pills. What do they call 'em?"

" 'The vegetable universal medicine of the British College of Health. An unfailing remedy for all diseases as tested by upwards of five hundred thousand cases of cures.' "

"Yus—them. I can get 'em at Mr. Fawkner's *Patriot* newspaper hoffice. An' I wants to go to the Bank of Hostralasia again to see that Mr. McArthur, the manager. 'E tol' me t'other day when I fixed hup 'bout the Martin land that the bank 'ad branches in Sydney, Bathurst, Maitland, 'Obart Town an' Launceston, an' Adelaide an' Perth. . . . Lawks! I got that dratted wind again—I *mus'* get them pills. An' I want to go to the post-hoffice an' send that letter you wrote to Pagan. Mr. Kelsh, the new postmaster, tol' me 'e'd get it away all right."

"We can eat at the Lamb Inn—we had a good dinner there the other day."

"Yus. An' we'll take a peep in that Mr. Holmes's book an' stationery ware'ouse, in Collins Street. They got all sorts o' things— Tunbridge ware, Russia leather, rosewood an' mahogany tea-caddies, an' good jewellery—gold an' silver watches—mebbe I'll get you a watch, 'Arry boy, to remember Melbourne by—an' silver snuff-boxes, gold cable neck chains, hair bracelets set with pearls, turquoises, rubies an' hemeralds. An' maybe I'll take back blankets from that Cashmore an' company at the corner o' Great Collins Street an' Elizabeth Street. Might get 'em cheaper 'ere, an' we'll look in at Mr. Crook's furniture ware'ouse in Collins Street.

You never knows what you can pick up, 'Arry boy."

"I always leave these things to you, my dear. And—and I do believe I would like to have a watch——"

Martha beamed at him.

"Bless your 'eart, so you shall, 'Arry boy. An' a gold one, too. Tomorrer we goes back on th' *Sea Horse*—now don' shudder like that!"

"I—I'm never at home on the sea, my dear."

"Well, we got to get back, Mr. Gubby—an' I ain't walkin', or sittin' on a bumpin' board for five 'undred miles. I ain't got no corns on me feet an' I ain't goin' to get none nowhere else. 'Ullo! *'Ullo!* 'ere's that ol' Holiver acomin' this way——"

"And young Mr. Everitt——" muttered Henry. "Perhaps—perhaps we should retire indoors, my dear."

"Mr. Gubby," came gruffly, "you stan' your ground like a man!"

"Yes—yes, but——" Henry quavered. "Mr. Oliver doesn't look pleased . . . about something. . . ."

"Don' 'e now," said Martha calmly. "That *do* be s'prisin'. Yus 'e do look black. I 'opes, for heverybody's sake, 'e don' forget 'is manners."

"He—he looks as if he could kill us!"

"Do 'e? Hi'll talk to th' ol' toad, Mr. Gubby. You leave Mr. Holiver to me."

"Yes, dear—yes, dear——" panted Henry.

"Hif 'e speaks me fair—I'll speak 'im fair. Hif 'e don't—well, you jus' listen, Mr. Gubby."

"Yes, Martha—I do hope there won't be a scene."

Oliver, with Everitt beside him, came striding up to Martha and Henry. Both men wore tall hats, long coats and tight trousers that buckled under their boots. Oliver's close-set blue eyes were as cold as death, his long white hair quivered on his shoulders. He paused in front of Martha, deliberately looking her up and down with an offensively contemptuous appraisal. A common woman, he told himself; an overfed slut who had dared to thwart an Oliver; an overdressed slattern spawned in some narrow and noise-some London warren; a monstrous offence to a gentleman's eyes.

His shrill high voice had a razor-edge to it as he said, "You're the Gubby woman, I understand——"

And then he looked into pale blue eyes even colder than his own.

"An' you be that schemin' ol' skunk of a Holiver, I unnerstan's——" was fired back at him. "Well, you ol' toad—I be Martha Gubby, an' I ain't pleased to be spoke to by you. What want you?"

Henry Gubby's thin little legs were shaking. Henry Oliver rocked on his heels. He went white, then red, than all colour drained from his face again.

He turned to Everitt and said scathingly, "Right out of the cess-pit, Everitt. We might have known it——"

Martha did not allow him to finish.

"I ain't interested to know where you come from," she rasped at him. "An' hif I 'ave any more sauce from you, you fevverless ol' buzzard, I'll fetch you one you won't forget. Don' you loose your tongue on me, me man, or you'll *really* 'ear somethin'. You foun' out in Melbourne I was afore you. You've come hup to us jus' to let fly. But you picked the wrong woman, me man. An' hif I 'ave any more himperance from you Holivers Hi'll take you by your skinny necks an' bang your wretched 'eads together. An' don' think I couldn't do it. You was sayin'?"

Mr. Gubby could scarcely stand. This promised to be a dreadful scene, and he hoped Martha would control herself and not allow her temper to rise. If that happened the very heavens would fall upon them all.

As Henry Oliver seemed unable to get his breath Everitt said acidly. "We understand that yesterday you made application to purchase certain land now under annual licence to people named Martin?"

Martha's eyes turned slowly to him.

"Be that any of *your* business, me young cock?" she asked. "But that be so. Th' happlication be made, an' hall arrangements made for payment through the Bank o' Hostralasia. The lan' now licensed to the Martins be mine—Martha Gubby's—unless them Martins buys it from me. Well?"

Henry Oliver was shaking with rage. She had called him "skunk", and "toad" and a "featherless buzzard". This was monstrous. He had come to give this common, interfering woman the edge of his tongue, and give it to her—*and* to this miserable little wart she called a husband. He pointed a long finger at Mr. Gubby.

"So that little rat was pumping me. That

insignificant, undersized, spindle-shanked, needle-nosed little pimp was——"

That was where Henry Oliver made his great mistake. Martha's massive arm went up like a giant flail, and the next moment Henry Oliver's furious face had vanished inside his top-hat.

"That be my Mr. Gubby you be hinsultin'!" came with a roar.

Oliver, with his hat squashed down to his chin, made only muffled sounds, and began to lurch and stagger about as he wrenched at it. People, attracted by the scene, began to stand and stare. Everitt's dark eyes blazed. He made a vicious step towards Mr. Gubby, but Martha's swinging right hand, as hard and heavy as a cured ham, caught him across his left ear. He dropped as though a cliff had fallen on him, and lay blinking up at the Amazon who seemed to fill all the sky.

"My God—my God—my God——" he panted. "My neck's broken——"

"No, 'tain't," Martha assured him. "Hi jus' tapped you, me crowin' cockerel. But you mind yourself or mebbe 'twill get broke. An' the same to ol' Rattleribs there. Hus Gubbys' as our hethics. We be 'umble folks, but Gawd 'elp them as tries to wipe their noses on us. We don' like rogues, rascals, an' sich reptiles as you be. I bin very gentle with you both, but hany more of your Lord Tiddleypom hattitude with us, an' I'll 'ave words with you. Good day to you both."

Everitt got dazedly to his feet as Martha and Henry walked away. He tore the hat off his father's head and, furious and panting, the two enraged and speechless men stood watching. Long-haired Henry Oliver's gelid soul seemed to be stripped of all emotion, his equally cold mind of all thought. Dark Everitt, his head ringing like a bell, was incapable of movement. They had challenged this giantess, and the result of the impact left them shaken and drained of resolution. Neither had ever before met such a woman; each had the feeling he had rushed blindly into a wall of granite. They saw Mr. Gubby pause at the hotel door and look back disdainfully at them, then the little man walked haughtily in after his huge spouse.

"Now for breakfast," said Martha. "An' the funny part is them Martins don' know what's 'appened yet. But some'ow . . . I feels better."

"You—you don't think they will make trouble, do you?" Henry asked.

"Them? Pickles! But I'm glad I kep' me temper. Let's 'ave breakfast."

12

IT was early morning, a few days before Christmas, when Annie's scream tore through the silence of the Tregg hut. She had awakened to hear Royd growling deep in his throat. Instantly the family rose up, sleep gone in a flash, and Elijah, Rock, Johnnie and Dick flung themselves on the red giant. But they could not have pinned him but for the added weight and strength of Sarah, Meg and Annie. Raving now, Royd thrashed about in a paroxysm of madness.

"For Gawd's sake 'old the bastud——" gasped Elijah. "Smash 'im down or 'e'll tear someone's throat out——"

Meg stunned him with a heavy piece of firewood, and the panting men carried him out to the tree and fastened the thick chain on him.

"Lucky you was awake, Annie," said her father.

Annie's eyes blazed at Johnnie.

"Sometimes I got to keep awake," she replied.

Johnnie shrugged and looked away. Sarah was whimpering.

"Royd—poor Royd. You made 'im bleed——"

Meg sneered at her.

"Poor Royd—hell!" she said harshly. "I keep tellin' you 'e'll do one of us in yet."

Sarah's voice seemed to crackle.

"Oh, you red devil gel," she snarled. "You never did like my poor Royd——"

"Ar—enough," said Rock. "An' git breakfast. Lookit me arm—the loon sank 'is teeth in it."

"Git bilin' watter on to it," said Annie. "Teeth's dead pison sometimes—teeth an' other things——"

Johnnie, with his long arms dangling by his sides, merely lifted a derisive lip as he turned and shuffled back into the hut.

"Yus," growled Elijah. "Breakfast, ol' woman. Johnnie, me an' Rock's got to go over to th' Olivers." He gave Meg a hard stare. "An' thet don' mean *you*. Dick can git us a 'roo."

"Ain't goin' near the Olivers," said Meg sulkily.

Dick's flat face was expressionless as he said, "Th' Olivers be as sour as lemons since they come back from Melbourne. But thet don' stop Ev'ritt makin' up to the Martin gel—I seen 'em ridin' again las' Sunday. Dunno what else they was up to——"

Meg trembled. Her face was pale as she turned away.

"Mebbe somethin' else'll stop 'im," she muttered to herself.

Sarah was looking at Royd.

" 'E's comin' round," she said. "Clear out—all of you! An' don' stand gawpin' at my poor Royd—it makes 'im worser. Annie, stir up the fire an' we'll eat summat. Thar's some mutton."

"Not for me," said Annie harshly. "I ain't touchin' thet mutton—not for any of you."

"Perticlar all of a suddent," said Rock, his blue eyes sardonic in his reckless face. "After what them Martins said 'bout us Treggs you need care!"

Annie threw back her hair with a quick hand.

"Well—I care," she said bitterly. "I got a good mind to clear out o' this valley an' never come back."

They all stared at her. Then the sudden rattle and snap of metal made them turn. Royd was on his feet, crazy, eyes rolling in his huge face, bare feet stamping, hands tearing at the unyielding chain. Sarah was crying openly as she turned and walked into the hut. In silence the others followed her. Royd was uttering choked incoherent sounds as he fought with the chain. Then he started to scream, and Sarah's thin, veined hands went up to cover her ears. There was nothing anyone could do. Royd could not be put away, there was nowhere for him to go, nothing for his own protection and theirs but the long, heavy chain and the tree.

"Better git fresh rations from th' Olivers," said Meg, who was scraping flour from the bottom of a shallow cask.

Elijah grunted as he threw himself down on a bench.

"Las' time I asked, thet Jane near spat at me," he grumbled. "Reckoned we mus' waste what she gives us."

"She's a saucy bitch," said Rock gruffly. "I'd like to draw me fist acrost thet thin mouth of 'ers."

"You won't," said Annie. "She's a Oliver—you're only a Tregg—an' don' you f'git it. The Treggs, everyone says, is jus' dirt. Dirt! An' I'm sick of 'em sayin' it, an' lookin' it, an' thinkin' it. An' I don' want to spend all *my* life 'oppin' round this valley like a 'roo slut."

Johnnie laughed.

"What *do* y'want?" he jeered.

"I don' want other folks to 'old their noses when I come near 'em," the girl flashed back at him. "Ain't we *ever* goin' to git a chanct to be——"

"To be what?" Elijah asked deeply as she paused.

"Anythin'—somethin'! Other folks 'ave things—clo'es, boots, dresses, respect. What've we got? 'Roo skins, no boots, dresses no one else'd wear. An' a bleddy kennel to live in like a pack o' dawgs. Ain't it *ever* goin' to be diff'rent?"

"What gives *you* notions all at onct?" demanded Meg. "How come we ain't good 'nough for *you* all of a suddent?"

"She never said thet," said Dick stolidly. "An' what she did say ain't fur wrong. Thar's them Martins puttin' up a good place—near finished it, too. An' th' Olivers live like real folks. But us Treggs keep livin' like trash, doin' nothin', gittin' nothin', goin' nowhar."

"Well I'll go to 'ell!" breathed Rock. "We've never bin no different—never will. Wouldn't know 'ow to be—an' for me I

197

wouldn't want to. What's comin' over every-body?"

"An' 'ow can we ever be different while we got Royd?" Meg sneered.

Sarah said sharply, "Thar you go again, Meg. Allus pickin' on poor Royd."

"Ain't pickin' on Royd," Meg retorted hotly. "But ain't it true? It's nothin' but Royd, Royd, Royd with you—allus 'as bin. I *ain't* pickin' on the poor bastud—but what can the Treggs ever be but the Treggs? I ain't complainin'—I ain't got fancy notions like Annie thar—I don' hanker to be no nob. But we's what we be—what we'll allus be. So shet up—everybody. All this silly talk don' make sense."

"You be right thar, gel," said her father. "We done time—th' ol' woman an' me—an' it sticks, jist like a skin. Folks thinks nothin' of us—we thinks nothin' of folks. It evens up. Everyone's agen the Treggs—the Treggs be agen everyone. Thar it be."

"Well, I ain't done time," said Annie rebelliously. "An' I don' want it to stick to me——"

"I'll fetch you one in a minute," said Elijah warningly.

"Fetchin' me one won't alter it," Annie

retorted. "Thar ain't a single one of us can read or write; we own no ground; we plant no corn; we *steal* the mutton an' beef we eat. All we can do is slunk away in this valley an' depend on th' Olivers for a crust an' clo'es. If we keep on livin' like this we'll *all* be chained to bleddy trees——"

Sarah's hand flashed out and the blow sent Annie staggering back.

"I'll stop you——" Sarah hissed.

Elijah's bull-like roar seemed to shake the hut.

"Enough! *Enough!* 'Ere we are an' 'ere we be! An' we got to make the best of it. Enough, I say, or I'll lay about me!"

Johnnie laughed again.

"Flatten 'em, 'Lijah," he sneered. "Little Annie's mebbe got 'er eye on one o' them Martin boys—thinks she ain't good enough for 'im, mebbe——"

Annie flushed hotly.

"You *would* say somethin' like thet," she flung back. "Well, you're wrong, Johnnie Tregg. I ain't trackin' after no Martin boy—or any other boy——"

"Better not," growled Elijah. "You was all got lawful—thet's the way it got to be with

199

you an' Meg when the time comes. No more, now."

Meg made a batter and fried thick strips of mutton in it. Annie did not speak again. Presently all except the girl were eating the mutton. Johnnie watched her and laughed silently. Sarah went to the door and looked at Royd. He was stamping round and round the tree, winding himself up to it.

"No use takin' anythin' out to Royd," she muttered. "Ain't never seen 'im so bad. Poor Royd . . . Poor Royd. . . ."

"You keep away from 'im," said Rock. "If 'e gits them great 'ands of 'is on you 'e'll break you like a stick."

"Royd wouldn't 'urt me," said Sarah. "Not my Royd."

Meg drew in a breath, but said nothing. The fried mutton was washed down with black unsweetened tea, and then the men left the hut. Dick took a gun and went loping away down the valley; the others walked in the direction of the Olivers' house. Sarah sat down and, letting her grey head fall on her arms, began crying again. Meg washed the trenchers and left the hut; she did not say where she was going. Annie followed. There was no housekeeping to be done; the bed was never made; and presently, except for old Sarah who still wept, the hut was deserted.

The sun was still not high when, a mile from the hut, Annie came up on soundless feet behind tall, fair-haired Mark Martin.

" 'Lo, boy," she said. "You be along the valley early."

Mark turned quickly. For a moment he stood looking at the slender, bare-legged, brown eyed girl in the tattered print dress and kangaroo-skin jacket. She stood watching him warily, her straw-coloured hair tumbling out from under the opossum-skin cap.

"Hullo," he said. "I didn't hear you."

Annie nodded.

"Didn't want you to," she replied. "Lost somethin', boy?"

Mark looked about him. He felt uncomfortable.

"Can't find a calf. It's planted some-where."

"I knows whar it be," she told him. "I'll show you, boy."

"Far?"

"No. Close. You come with me—'less you be too stuck-up to walk a-ways beside me."

"I'm not stuck-up," said Mark defensively.

A faint smile touched Annie's lips.

"Neither be I, boy. I be sorry I tol' you I'd fetch you one thet day."

Mark coloured a little.

"I'd forgotten about it. I wasn't very kind to you myself," he said awkwardly. "How do you know where the calf is?"

"I know mos' things thet goes on in this valley. Cows is cunnin' thing when they gits a calf. Better take it in afore the dingoes kill it."

"That's what I want to do. We've been losing some sheep lately—they just disappear."

"This a-way, boy," said Annie quickly.

They walked away together, Mark wishing she had not spoken to him, yet grateful for her help.

"Goin' to be 'ot," said Annie, giving him a side glance.

"Yes."

"Near finished your new 'ouse?"

"Yes."

"Ain't you got a tongue, boy? You don' talk much."

"That's right. I don' talk much."

"Your name's Mark."

He looked round at her.

"How did you know?"

She smiled at him.

"You f'git things easy. You tol' me las' time I spoke to you."

"Yes—so I did. Your name's Annie."

She nodded.

"Yus. Mebbe . . . you don' f'git easy. Can you read an' write?"

"Yes. Can you?"

"No. Never 'ad no larnin'. Can you truly read books?"

"Yes."

"Lawks! I wish I could. You mus' be terrible clever, boy."

Mark did not answer. She said:

"Your corn an' vege'bles be doin' fine."

"Yes. How do you know?"

She seemed surprised at the question.

"I got eyes—ain't I? I wanders all 'bout the valley—nothin' else to do—jist wander about an' talk to the cockatoos all bleddy day long by m'self."

"Don't you do any work?" he asked.

"Ain't no work."

"Don't the—don't your folks work?"

"The men do now an' then for ol' Oliver. Meg an' me don't. 'Ave all your folks 'ad larnin?"

"Yes."

"None of us 'ave—narry a one. I s'pose it

203

don' matter. You like it 'ere in this valley?"

"Yes. It's a bit lonely, and a long way from anywhere, but I like it. Do you?"

She hesitated, then: "Yus. I didn't. I does now."

"Why only now?"

"I—I—it seems diff'rent. Mebbe jist talkin' to you makes it diff'rent. Never talked to a boy afore—not this a-way—nor anyone else, neither."

Mark said slowly, "You must have been lonely, Annie."

Her brown eyes flashed with pleasure at the use of her name.

"Yus, mebbe I 'ave, Mark. You don' mind . . . jist a-talkin' to me sometimes . . . does you?"

"No," came quietly. "But my father wouldn't approve."

" 'Cause I'm a Tregg, I s'pose, darter of a convic'?"

"Yes."

"An' jist dirt?"

"I don't think that."

Her voice was husky with surprise and relief.

"You—don't? You truly don't, Mark?"

"No," came evenly again. "Why should I?"

She drew in a deep breath.

"Oh——" she said a little tremulously. "Thet *do* be good to 'ear. No; I ain't dirt—I ain't never done no wrong. I ain't never done . . . nothin' 'cept talk to m'self an' the bleddy 'roos an' cockatoos an' the rocks an' the trees. Sometimes I pertend they's real folks, an' I talks to 'em; then when I sees 'em jist starin' at me I feels jist a fool, an' I don' talk no more."

"Why do you swear?" he asked.

Her eyes opened wide.

"Swear? I don' swear—never 'ave."

Mark smothered a laugh.

"I see. Where do you come from?"

"Borned in Van Diemen's Land—we all was—an' *lawful*. On the Tamar near Launceston. Oliver 'ad a place thar afore 'e follered Fawkner to Port Phillip. 'Lijah 'as allus worked for Oliver. Then we come 'ere. Thar's your calf—in thet long grass thar——"

Mark walked to the calf, Annie beside him.

"You watch for snakes, Mark," she warned. "They's about. Be careful whar you walk in long grass an' put your 'ands down—never f'git it."

"Thanks, Annie. We killed a couple near the wagon. Mother got a bad fright when a big grey-brown one reared its head and hissed at her."

"Yus. But y' gits used to 'em. But don' git bit. They's deadly. A red heifer, eh?"

"Yes. I'll have to carry it."

"Careful—it be gettin' up. Whar's the cow?"

"In the stockyard."

"Good. She won' come chargin' us."

"Thanks for helping me, Annie. I'd never have found the calf myself. You haven't seen any stray sheep of ours, have you?"

Annie gulped.

"Can't say," she said. Then she pointed. "Look!"

Mark looked in the direction indicated. About half a mile away Tilly was riding south.

"That's my sister, Tilly. She's out looking for the stray sheep I spoke about. We've lost seven or eight now."

Annie could scarcely reply.

"They—they's awful 'ard to find sometimes," she stammered. "Does y'sister look for the sheep much?"

"Every day. But I'll get back. Thanks, Annie."

The girl was breathing quickly.

" 'Taint nothin', Mark. An' thanks for talkin' to me. G'day."

"Good day, Annie."

"Put the calf over y'shoulder—the forelaigs over—makes it easier."

Mark did so and walked away. Annie stood watching him. When he was out of sight she threw up her arms and gave a triumphant little cry.

"I ain't dirt—not to 'im," she told herself. "An' I can talk to 'im." Then a thought sobered her and brought a troubled look into her eyes. "Them sheep——" she breathed. "Them bleddy sheep. I could *kill* Johnnie an' Rock. If Mark ever finds out—Gawd! I'll be dirt then—jist plain dirt."

She turned and walked away, a strange elation surging up in her. She was not lonely now. Mark Martin would talk to her; he did not regard her as an outcast because she was the daughter of a convict. It was a great day. Overhead a flight of black cockatoos wheeled. She looked up and wrinkled her nose at them. "Go to 'ell——" she told them. Then she laughed and began to run. She ran until out of breath, until the Tregg hut came in sight.

And then she stopped dead in her tracks. Royd was not beside his tree. Her mouth opened; her eyes widened with sudden premonition; and then she was running again. Up the slope she ran. There was no sign of Royd. She looked at the tree. The chain, broken, hung from it. Panting and terrified she forced herself to go to the hut door. She looked in, and then recoiled, crying shrilly her mother's name.

"Sarah—Sarah—Sarah! Oh, Gawd—oh, Gawd——"

Sarah Tregg lay in a pool of blood before the hearth, her head smashed to pulp. For a moment sight left Annie's horrified eyes, then the blurred outlines came back, and with a scream of terror she turned and raced from the hut.

" 'Lijah—Johnnie—Rock—Dick! Oh, for Christ's sake——" she screamed. " 'Lijah— 'Lijah—'Lijah——"

She knew where they were. She ran as she had never run before along the valley. She saw Tilly on the grey horse near the fence. She cried out to her:

"Git 'ome—git 'ome! Royd's broke loose— 'e's mad—'e'll kill you—git 'ome——"

Tilly caught the frantic words.

"Where are you going?" she called.

"To Olivers to tell 'Lijah—Royd's killed Sarah in th' 'ut——"

"I'll get there before you," Tilly called again.

Annie watched the grey take the fence and race down the slope. So did someone else. High up on the bluff Royd lay peering down into the valley. In his hand was a long length of blood-stained chain, one end of it still fastened round his middle. He lay very still. He saw Tilly; he saw Annie; and he snarled deep in his throat. Annie, fearful for herself, and wondering where Meg was, ran after Tilly. Meg came out of a gully, giving Everitt time to ride out at the other end. She called to Annie as the girl was running past:

"Whar you goin'? What's wrong?"

Annie came to her.

"Royd——" the girl gasped. "Killed Sarah—bashed 'er 'ead in—she's lyin' dead in th' 'ut. 'E snapped the chain some'ow——"

"Sarah——" said Meg faintly. "I knowed it would come. Whar is he?"

"Dunno. Better come to th' Olivers. 'Tain't safe to meet 'im. Seen Dick?"

"Dick's all right—e's got a gun. Oh,

Gawd . . . I knowed Royd would do it one day. 'My poor Royd . . .' she whimpers. 'My poor Royd.' An' *she* was the one 'e smashed. An' now 'e'll kill an' kill! Thet's if someone don' shoot 'im fust. Goddlemighty! An' whar's thet Tilly Martin gone?"

"To warn 'Lijah—I tol' 'er——"

" 'Tain't nothin' to do with 'er——" Meg began.

Annie almost collapsed. Nothing to do with the Martins?

"Meg—you run on to th' Olivers—I'll git back an' tell the Martins——"

"No, Annie—no!"

"I must—I will! Royd'll never catch you—or me. Someone mus' warn them Martins—they got gels thar——"

"Annie!" screamed Meg. "Come back y'bleddy fool—come back——"

But Annie was running as fast as she could back towards the fence. Meg ran towards the Olivers' house.

"Tilly Martin——" she panted. "What's Royd—or Sarah—or any Tregg got to do with 'er? Royd . . . oh, Gawd. . . ."

13

ANNIE could scarcely stand when she came to the Martins' camp. She stumbled towards John who was working on the new house. He frowned when he saw her.

"What want you, girl?" he asked curtly.

"I come—to warn you——" she jerked out.

"Warn us?" John's eyebrows shot up. "About what?"

"Royd—me brother. 'E's broke loose from 'is tree—an' killed ol' Sarah—bashed 'er 'ead in. 'E's ravin' mad—an' loose somewhar in the valley. I ran to tell you—to warn you——"

John went pale with the shock of it. But his voice had a gentler note in it as he said, "Sit down, girl—on that log there. I can see you are badly shaken. I'll call the others."

He went to the bell hung on a pole as an alarm bell and rang it. Its metallic peal went along the valley. Nan and Jeanette came running from the corn paddock; Tom and Mark from the stockyard; Hetty, surprised and agitated, came quickly from the wagon.

"What is it?" Hetty asked anxiously. "Why the alarm bell, John? Is there trouble with the blacks?"

John turned to Annie. "You tell them, girl—just what you told me," he said.

Annie tried to get to her feet, but strength had gone from her legs. She fell back on the log.

"Me brother, Royd. 'E's mad. 'E broke 'is chain. 'E's killed our ol' woman—Sarah. I—I was walkin' in the valley. I went back to th' 'ut. She was sprawled on the floor. I seen 'er brains—all red an' squashed. Oh, Jesus . . . I feel sick. . . ."

"Don't blaspheme, girl!" said John sternly.

Annie's eyes blazed at him.

"I ain't blasphemin', you ol' goat——" she screamed. "An' don' preach at me! I didn't come 'ere to be preached at. I come to warn you 'bout Royd! 'E's loose—*loose*, you ol' fool—*loose*! Can't y'unnedstan'? 'E'll *kill* if 'e catches you. I run miles to tell you—an' you preach at me, dem you——"

John's homely face flushed at the shrill words. It was not pleasant to be so spoken to in front of his family. Hetty, with horror and shock and pity all blending in her grey eyes, said quickly:

212

"There, there, my dear. How terrible for you. Your own mother. And it was good and brave of you to come to warn us. Jeanette, make tea. This poor girl must rest and stay with us until her menfolk come for her. Oh, what a terrible thing!"

"Yes, mother," said Jeanette. "Oh, dear . . . how horrible . . . yes; I'll make tea."

"I'll get the guns," said Tom. "Mark, gather all tools—bars, axes, hoes, anything a madman might use as a weapon. I think this girl has done the Martins a fine service."

"So do I," said Mark.

"And I," said the trembling Nan.

John bit his lip, but he was a just man.

"Aye; so do I," he said. "You're welcome to stay with us awhile, girl. I thank you for coming."

Hetty cried suddenly, "Tilly! Oh, heavens—where's Tilly?"

Annie told her.

"She went on to th' Olivers, Mrs. Martin. She'll be all right. She'll be safe——"

"You're sure?"

"Yus. I warned 'er same's I 'ave you folks. Everyone's now at the Olivers—'cept me brother, Dick—but 'e's got a gun, an' it'll be Gawd 'elp Royd if Dick sees 'im. Thet *bleddy*

Royd! But, o' course, the poor bastud's ravin' mad—don' know what 'e's doin'——"

John opened his mouth to say something, then shut it again. He nodded to Nan.

"Stay with the girl, Nan. It's been a frightful ordeal for her. Hetty, come with me——"

"I don' want no one to stay with me if they don' want," said Annie quickly. "I can go as I come——"

"I want to," said Nan gently. "I think you are very brave—and very considerate to us. I am sorry about your mother. It's an awful thing to happen—awful."

And then Annie broke. She sobbed with the shock and terror of her dreadful experience, wept also because for the first time in her life people were being kind to her. There were tears in Nan's young eyes, too. She sat down beside Annie, but did not speak. Presently Jeanette brought tea and scones.

"Drink the tea and eat something," she said. "And try not to think of it just now. Help her, Nan——"

"If only I 'adn't seen 'er," Annie gasped out. "She was never no mother to Meg or me . . . but I wish . . . I 'adn't seen 'er like thet. Meg tol' 'er—we all tol' 'er, but she wouldn't listen. She loved Royd . . . thought 'e would never arm 'er . . . but she f'got 'e was mad. All she ever did was for 'im . . . an' see what she got. I feel all tight an' sick inside me."

"Drink the hot tea," said Jeanette gently. "We want you to stay with us for a while."

Annie shook the tears from her eyes.

"*Stay* with you?" she echoed.

Jeanette nodded.

"Yes. You can't go back to—that place. You can never go back there."

"No," said Annie harshly. "I c'd never go in thar again. But I—I dunno 'bout stayin' miss——"

"I'm Jeanette——"

"I'm Nan."

Annie's lips quivered, but she steadied herself.

"I be Annie. I thenks you-all, an' I be sorry I miscalled your ol' man. But—I dunno, Jeanette. Your ol' man don' like us Treggs—don' like me. I'd be a worrit to 'im, astayin' with you."

"He asked me to tell you as I was bringing the tea," said Jeanette.

Annie showed her surprise.

" 'E *did*? Then 'e ain't a ol' devil—I mean—oh, lawks——"

Jeanette's dark eyes were soft with sympathy for this forlorn and unwanted girl.

"No; father is a good man, Annie. A little stern at times, perhaps, but kindly. He is very upset about what has happened, and wants to help in every way he can. Would you like to stay with us?"

Annie nodded slowly as she drew a furry sleeve across her eyes.

"Yus. I would. I . . . ain't never bin with decent folks . . . in all me born days. Yus; I would. I won' do nothin' wrong."

"Neither shall we, I hope," said Jeanette. "What about your sister? I remember seeing her that first night."

"Meg? No . . . she wouldn't come 'ere. Meg's wild—wilder even than Johnnie an' Rock. Mebbe th' Olivers'll look after 'er— thet Jane could make 'er work at somethin'. But, I dunno. Meg's fierce when she's up—no; not looney like Royd, but she's got a devil in 'er when she cuts loose. Ol' Sarah never took no notice of 'er, or me, an' it's biled an' biled in 'er like scaldin' watter all her life. I dunno 'bout Meg. I reckon th' Olivers c'd 'andle 'er better'n you folks."

"She's there now, isn't she?" asked Nan.

"Yus."

"You don't know where your brother is?" asked Jeanette.

Annie drank some more tea. She was not trembling so much.

"No. Prowlin' somewhar in the valley."

"How long do—do these fits of madness stay on your brother Royd?" Nan asked.

"Mebbe a week—mebbe more. Mebbe this time 'e'll stay like thet. I woke up early this mornin'—'eard 'im growlin' in is throat like a wild bull. We jist got 'im down in time or 'e might 'ave killed more'n ol' Sarah. 'E was chained to the tree again. Everybody lef' th' 'ut, an' some'ow 'e broke loose. But I tol' you 'ow I went back. . . ."

"We won't talk any more about it," said Jeanette. "I hope Tilly's all right——"

At the other end of the valley Tilly had ridden through a mob of sheep up to the Olivers' house. Jane, hearing the galloping hooves, had come out on to the veranda. Her features were hard as she looked at Tilly.

"Yes?" she snapped, her dark eyes narrowed and watchful.

Tilly sat in the saddle looking at her, aware

instantly of the hostility in Jane's speech and manner.

"I am Tilly Martin," Tilly said pleasantly.

"Indeed?" came icily.

At that, Tilly, whose blood was of good yeoman stock, bridled somewhat.

"Yes—indeed! Are you one of the Olivers—or a servant?" she replied sharply.

Jane was stung by the question. Her dark eyes glinted angrily.

"I am Jane Oliver. Did you come here merely to be impertinent?"

Tilly's voice was as brittle as Jane's.

"I did not come here of my own free will," she retorted. "And as for impertinence, I commend you to a study of civility and good manners——"

Jane flushed hotly, but before she could speak Tilly went on:

"I came to tell you that while riding looking for some sheep of ours one of the Tregg girls called to me that her brother, Royd, broke loose from a chain, or something, and murdered his mother. He is raving mad and loose in the valley somewhere."

Jane blanched.

"Royd——" she said in a harsh whisper. "So it's happened——"

As she spoke, Henry Oliver, followed by Conway and Elliott, came out on to the veranda.

"Who is this?" the old man demanded sharply.

"The Martin girl," said Jane, an inflexion of contempt in her tone.

"And what is *she* doing here?" he rasped. "The Martins are not welcome here."

Tilly spoke quietly.

"The Martins have no wish to be welcome here—they still like to choose their company."

Tilly saw Jane's lips tighten, and anger flared in the eyes of the Oliver men.

Conway said, "A saucy one, eh? Well, what does she want, Jane?"

Jane was shaking. The full import of Tilly's information was making itself felt.

"Royd has killed old Sarah. He broke loose. One of the Tregg girls told her and she rode to warn us. Royd's still loose."

There was silence for a moment, then Henry said, "Elliott, tell Tregg. It was bound to happen."

Elliott walked away.

"Here's Everitt——" said Conway.

Everitt came cantering leisurely up. His surprise at seeing Tilly was well feigned. He had heard her horse coming down the valley while he was in the gully with Meg, but he knew Tilly had not seen him.

"What is the conference?" he asked as he swung out of the saddle.

"Where the devil have you been, Everitt?" Henry demanded irascibly.

"Just riding," came smoothly. "It's a lovely day, you know——"

"Damn the day," growled Henry. "This Martin girl has just informed us Royd has killed Sarah. He's prowling about somewhere."

Everitt gave a low whistle. His dark face was bland.

"Thanks for coming to warn us, Miss Martin," he said.

"Here's Meg," said Jane. "The way she runs that girl must have feet as tough as a blackfellow's."

They watched Meg running towards them, red hair flying, kangaroo-skin jacket open and flapping. She was breathless when she came to the veranda.

"Did—did she tell you?" she panted, jerking her head at Tilly.

"Yes. She told us," said Jane.

Meg's blue eyes were bitter as she stared up at Tilly.

"It ain't got nothin' to do with 'er—she didn't 'ave to come 'an she don't 'ave to stay 'ere, do she?" she said.

Tilly looked down with eyes as hard and blue and challenging as Meg's.

Her lips curled as she said, "It has nothing to do with me, and to stop here is the *last* thing I wish to do——" her voice was cold and cutting. "But before I ride back I want to tell you, as coming from the Martins, who were never cheats, liars, imposters, or convicts, that I have never seen a poorer lot of trash than you upstart Olivers—not even the Treggs."

With that she wheeled the grey and cantered away.

"I'll go with her," said Everitt as he climbed back into the saddle.

"She don' want you," said Meg furiously. "Let the bitch go——"

"If I did, with Royd loose, there'd be something in what she has just said, wouldn't there?" came evenly.

Henry grunted angrily as Everitt galloped after Tilly. Jane was silent and sombre. Meg's glittering eyes watched Everitt ride away.

"Come inside," said Henry curtly. To Meg he said, "Not you, girl. You may wait on the veranda."

"Don't want to come into your 'ouse, Oliver," Meg shrilled at him. "Wouldn't be found dead in it."

"Don't be impertinent, girl," came coldly. "Send Tregg in to me when he comes."

The Olivers walked inside. Meg turned and watched Everitt ride over a rise.

"Thar's somethin' thar," she muttered. " 'E didn't foller 'er just acause of Royd. But thar'd better be no gully-trackin' with that Tilly Martin—Gawd, thar'd better not be——"

Then she looked searching across the valley, this way and that.

"Royd!" she whispered. "Royd——"

In the living-room Conway looked from the thin-lipped Jane to his father.

"What are you going to do about the Tregg girls?" he asked.

Henry sat down in his high-backed chair.

"Nothing," he said sourly. "Why should I do anything?"

"But they can't go back to live in that hut," Conway persisted.

"Let Tregg build another."

"On Martins' land? That's where they are now—or on ours?"

Henry's pale eyes gleamed as he looked at Conway.

"It may be our chance to get rid of the Treggs. They may be . . . induced to quit the valley. They're useless creatures, anyway. We could get bounty immigrants."

"We don't seem to be very successful at getting rid of anyone," said Jane pointedly. "I'm laughing yet at what happened in Melbourne. You ride all that way to let some fat old slut outwit you. It seems to me the Oliver men have gone to seed—they're mere acorns again instead of oaks, dead twigs instead of iron-barks. La! What a gutless lot you are! Even the Martin woman can rake us with her insolence."

With that she walked out of the room.

Conway sat down; neither he nor his father spoke.

Everitt took care not to overtake Tilly until

both were out of sight of the house. Then he spurred up to her.

"Tilly——" he said deeply.

She did not look at him.

"Well?" she asked coldly.

"I apologize for the attitude of the Olivers," he said earnestly. "Slow down——"

Tilly brought her horse down to a walk.

"I am not interested in the Olivers," she told him. "What's the matter with this country that everybody despises everybody else, resents everybody else, and seems to want to injure everybody else? What title have the Olivers to their lordly airs and their spurious condescension? I see no reason to be interested in you Olivers."

Everitt gave her a keen glance. From the first meeting he knew she would be difficult to handle.

"Please don't say that, Tilly. You know I am interested—more than interested—in you. Or you should know that by now."

"I could be mistaken——"

"But you know you are not."

She turned to him, her gaze sharp.

"Are you fooling with that Tregg girl?" she demanded. "You both came to the house pretty much together."

His astonishment was admirable.

"Tilly! I? A *Tregg* girl? The daughter of an old lag? Oh, come, now!"

"Well—by the way the jade looked at you, and the possessive way she spoke, one could think that."

He laughed easily.

"Oh, you can't mean that. You can't think me as stupid or as careless as that, surely. I have already made bold to tell you I have eyes only for you, all my thoughts are for you. I am never happy except when I am with you."

The cold gleam began to leave Tilly's eyes.

"Perhaps you shouldn't say such things to me, Everitt. We certainly met a few times——"

"And we'll continue to meet, Tilly—many times. I assure you I never give the Tregg girl a thought. How could I? A *Tregg* girl——"

"Oh, well," Tilly said a little breathlessly, "perhaps I was wrong. I thought I saw . . . something . . . between you and that red-haired trollop. And that's all she is."

"You might be right, Tilly—I don't know. Or care. But there is nothing between us. And you had better not come riding alone while this madman is loose. We'll soon have him, or destroy him, and then we'll meet again. Agreed?"

She looked into the dark eyes regarding her so intently, anger melting from her mind, desire for this man rising above resentment and better judgment. She nodded slowly, and a smile touched her lips. She would hold him, but on her own terms, and in her own time.

"Yes, Everitt," she said softly. "Agreed——"

14

LATE that afternoon Sarah Tregg was buried under the tree to which Royd had been chained.

Elijah said, "Thet's whar she'd like to be. Some'ow . . . I knows thet."

John Martin read the burial service and, when it was over, Elijah, with his family grouped round him, spoke again.

"Thenks, Mr. Martin. You be a good man. Us Treggs can't pray—dunno 'ow. An' we wouldn't ask th' Olivers to pray for th' ol' woman. They ain't fit to pray neither—they never 'ad nothin' but scorn for 'er—or for us. We thenks you."

John looked at him, at them all. They stood beside the mound, unmoving in their kangaroo-skins and rags, the men with guns in their hands. Elijah seemed to have shrunk in stature, and his face was drawn and all at once very old. Meg was staring at the grave with tearless eyes. Annie, white-faced, trembled as she stood. The Tregg brothers were tight-lipped and silent. And John saw then the pathos of their lives, and compassion rose up in him, and an uncomfortable sense of guilt and shame. He listened carefully as Elijah went on.

" 'Tain't the place or the time, mebbe, to talk 'bout ourselves, Mr. Martin, but Oliver won't let us build again on 'is land. Tol' me this mornin'. In fac' 'e tol' me 'e didn't want the Treggs no more, an' that there'd be no more rations now us Treggs 'as sheared 'is sheep an' pressed the wool ready for the wagons to take it to Melbourne. We wasn't wanted—never no more. It didn't seem the time to say them things—but 'e said 'em. We don' doubt 'twas Jane Oliver goaded 'im—she's as 'ard an' proud as Satan. An' we's decided to burn this 'ut. Can we build on your land? We won't come close, an' you'll never suffer for lettin' us stay."

John asked, "Do you want to stay here?"

Elijah looked at the mound.

"Yus," he said slowly. "I wouldn't want to go 'way now. Th' ol' woman an' me's never bin much, never done much, never 'ad much, but for long years we kep' together. An' all lawful. I was workin' for Oliver near Launceston, in Van Diemen's Land, when she come to 'im as a assigned sarvint from th'

Female Fact'ry, in 'Obart Town. We was married. Seems . . . a long, long time ago."

"You may build on my land," said John, "providing you decide to help yourselves. You may build where there is good soil, and use up to twenty acres of it for growing food and crops. I would not want you to stay if you will not do so. I ask no rent. But you must build well, and grow well—for yourselves. What do you say?"

Elijah spread his arms expressively.

"We got no tools, no seed, no money—no nothin'."

"I will lend you what you want."

Elijah looked round at his family. Dick nodded several times as though pleased at the offer. No one else moved or spoke.

"All right," said Elijah at last. "The Treggs'll do thet. No one else 'as ever said thet to us. We thenks you again, Mr. Martin."

John went on: "Mrs. Martin will care for Annie until you send for her. What about this other girl?"

"Ain't leavin' the Treggs," said Meg briefly. "I can sleep unner a tree."

Elijah looked at Annie.

"You want to stay with Mrs. Martin?" he asked.

She nodded.

"Yus . . . for a while. . . ."

Her father said, "I'd be gled for you to, Annie. Don' do nothin' wrong—*nothin'*!"

"I won't do nothin' wrong," the girl said.

Elijah turned to John.

"We come for you, Mr. Martin, an' we'll see you an' Annie safe back. Rock an' Dick—you go with 'em. Johnnie an' Meg'll stay with me. An' now, for your kindness to us Treggs, Mr. Martin, I'll tell y' somethin'. Don' s'pose I would 'ave if Oliver an' the rest of 'em 'adn't throwed us down. Jus' after 'e an' young Ev'ritt come back from Melbourne I chanced to walk up to their 'ouse when they was inside 'avin breakfast. I walks on bare feet—I makes no sound. I 'eard 'em talkin'—'bout you. An' they was savage. Seems they went to Melbourne to git you kicked off y' land——"

"But I hold a licence for it," John interrupted him.

Elijah nodded.

"Yus. But anyone can buy it an' give you a month's notice to quit—if *you* don' buy it. Thet be the law. Oliver reckoned you

230

couldn't buy it. 'E was goin' to buy it an' kick you off. Well—'e was done in th' eye. Seems a woman from Sydney Town, who knows you, got to 'ear what 'e was up to—an' *she* bought the land."

John stared at him, astonishment and perturbation in his eyes.

"A woman? From Sydney Town? What woman?" he asked.

"I 'eard the name, all right—'twas a Martha Gubby, an' th' Olivers won't f'git *thet* name in a 'urry."

"Martha Gubby? *Martha—Gubby*!" exclaimed John. "Why—we stayed at her inn in Sydney Town. But I don't understand. Why should she buy this land? She's an innkeeper—she has no interest in land——"

"Thet's what's got th' Olivers as savage as stirred-up wasps. Oh, they be wild 'bout it. They knowed *she* didn't want the land for 'erself, an' thet she bought it to stop their little game. She musta took quite a likin' to you an' yours."

"It seems—it seems I have much to thank her for," said John.

"She tol' Oliver you c'd buy it from 'er, an' take your own time to do it. As I sees it, Mr. Martin, this woman stuck to you. I dunno why, but she did thet, an' she tol' Oliver she'd never push you off your own land. Th' Olivers was ragin' 'bout it—'specially Jane. She *was* in a tantrum. But they can't do nothin' to you—not now. No doubt you'll 'ear from this Martha Gubby some time.''

John stood breathing deeply; he seemed unable to grasp the full significance of it.

At last he said, "I'm glad you told me, Tregg. But I won't discuss any more matters now. It isn't the time, or the place. I'll get back, for it will be dark soon. Come to me for tools and seed when you are ready."

When John was out of earshot Johnnie said surlily, "What's the matter with you, 'Lijah. We ain't farmers."

Elijah turned to him.

"We ain't farmers, boy—but mebbe we ain't fools neither. I listened to what Annie said only this mornin', too. She was right. She said, 'Other folks 'ave things—clo'es, boots, dresses, respect. What've we got? 'Roo skins, no boots, dresses no one else'd wear. An' a bleddy kennel to live in like a pack o' dawgs.' Thet's what she said. I c'd never make it different. 'Twas allus 'Thar's Tregg, the convic'.' Now, mebbe, we got a chanct to git somethin'—a chance to git respect, if not for me for you-all. Yus! A *chanct*! It be Olivers thet's kep' us down, made us nothin', wanted us to keep on jist bein'—convic's. We's takin' this chanct—we be *takin'* it. Now git what's worth gittin' out of th' 'ut—then we'll burn it down—an' mebbe all the bad years with it."

He walked towards the hut.

Meg said to Johnnie, "Everybody's gone mad. I wonder what ol' Sarah'd think of all this?"

Johnnie shrugged. "If she'd done a bit more thinkin' times she wouldn't be whar she is. Farmin'. *Farmin'*! Ain't thar plenty 'roos to shoot? An' duck an' goose an' swan?"

"Yus——" said Meg thoughtfully. "Thar be plenty. But whar you goin' to git the bullets? Oliver won' give us no more."

Johnnie spat between his bare feet. "Ar—farmin'——" he said in disgust.

Meg looked towards the hut. "I never thought 'Lijah cared a rap for the ol' woman—but y'never knows, y'never knows——"

"Y'never knows *what*?" asked Johnnie irritably.

"Nothin'—jist nothin'. I wonder whar

Royd is? Someone'll 'ave to ride to Melbourne Town—or Gundagai, an' tell the police. I'd rather *they* shot 'im than any of us Treggs. Let's go to 'Lijah. C'm on."

At dusk a wind rose in the valley. High on the bluff Royd was still flat on his stomach, his uncovered red head out over the edge of the cliff, his pale unwinking eyes staring at the slowly darkening Oliver house, his mighty hands, like monstrous red claws, gripping the edge of the rock. The broken chain curled away from his thick body, and every time he moved its rattle set his fingers clawing. Only once did his eyes shift: when a dingo howled in the far hills across the valley. Cunning urged him to be still, to remain hidden, and in a mind now for ever ruined was no sense of hunger or thirst or fatigue. If the steady watchfulness of his eyes indicated any thought at all it pointed to a lingering remembrance of the reason why he had sought this pinnacle in the first place: to look down and watch for the moving figure of Jane Oliver. The sighing wind touched him. He lifted his head and began wriggling backwards. He stood up, snarled as he felt the drag of the chain, gathered it up in his right hand, and then turned and ran down the slope. It was dark in the valley when he left the bluff.

The lamp was lit in the Oliver's living-room, but they were all out on the veranda looking at a red glow up the valley. For a long time they watched it, until gradually it faded and all was dark.

"They've burned their hut," said Jane.

"What else could they do?" asked Everitt. "They couldn't possibly use it again. Let's go in and have supper. Take up your guns—better not move anywhere now without them."

"What about Royd?" asked Conway as they went inside.

"Well, what about him?" asked Henry sourly. "He is no concern of ours. We're not going to chase all over the valley after him."

They sat down at the table. Henry's chair creaked as it took his weight.

"He's loose, isn't he?" said Conway. "And likely to kill someone again?"

"He won't come here," said Henry. "Anyway we have our pistols and guns. We're ready for him if he does come."

Elliott said thoughtfully, "Supposing—he comes when we are asleep."

Jane looked startled. "That is a thought,"

235

she said. Her gaze went from one to the other. "Perhaps someone should remain awake——"

"You, for instance?" drawled Everitt.

"Oh, for heaven's sake, Everitt," she snapped back. "This is not a matter to be taken lightly."

He shrugged.

"From the way we've been talking I thought it was—the fact that a homicidal maniac was loose in the valley was something that couldn't possibly concern the Olivers——"

Henry waved a hand impatiently.

"I won't have you spitting my words back at me, Everitt. This red devil is the responsibility of the Treggs."

"I know," retorted Everitt. "And until Jane whispered in your ear this morning the Treggs were *our* responsibility."

"Well, they're not now," said Jane sharply. "And it is high time we got rid of them. The men are shiftless, the girls mere sluts. The men will probably take to the roads and turn bushrangers—their kind often do. They'll never work."

"I agree," said Everitt with a little laugh. "But it might have been more sensible to have shed them after this madman had been caught or killed."

"Why so?" asked Elliott.

"*They* could have taken the night watch, and *we* could have slept. But our dear Jane always lets her feelings outrun her judgment. Now we must keep a night watch."

"You think so?" asked Conway.

"Old Sarah would agree with me, I'm sure," was the reply.

Jane shuddered.

"Oh, let us eat," she said. "It's a pity we ever brought them from Port Phillip. And speaking of Port Phillip—next time someone goes there I'm going too. I'm getting all mossy in this valley——"

Conway interrupted her.

"The trouble here is there are no men for the women—*such* as there are, and no women for the men——"

"*Such* men as there are," retorted Jane. "Why papa didn't go west into Australia Felix from Port Phillip I don't know. It's closer to the coast, not hemmed in by mountains. This place is as lonely as the moon. I have three new Shilley dresses, a Thibet shawl, French kid gloves—but when can I wear them? My silk parasol and sable furs would look foolish in the kitchen. I want, as you all want, the Olivers to be important people in this country. Now so much of the valley has been stolen from us, who can say what we'll be? Robert Campbell, the Sydney merchant, has fifty thousand acres across the range near that place called Tumbarumba, as well as what he owns on Limestone Plains. Your neglect has brought us down to the level—of struggling immigrants. Mama would turn in her grave if she knew—no one looked over the Olivers' heads while *she* was alive——"

"She keeps on and on," said Everitt cynically.

"Some one had better say it," said Jane hotly. "How can we become great landholders as are others who are following the line from Port Phillip through Wodonga and Mungabareena, belonging to the Mitchell family, on both sides of the Murray near the village of Albury? Yes; right up to the Darling Downs. And look at Terence Aubrey Murray, on Jingellic, not far from here—he's got Jingellic South across the river also. And look at us. Us! All this valley should have been ours—and would have been if father hadn't been asleep, and you men also. The best thing we can do is sell out and go where we can get enough land to make the name of Oliver a big name in this colony. Anyway, next time we go to Melbourne we'll have to take the covered dray—we need supplies, and we'll certainly need more servants now we've got rid of the Treggs."

"I don't think you should be too severe, Jane," said Henry placatingly. "I admit we—well, I—was lax in not securing title to all the valley. My God—when I think of that Gubby woman I shudder—I shudder! And that little runt of a fellow who peeps round from behind her great bottom! I could screw his skinny little neck. Who ever would have thought *she'd* interfere? It's amazing how we've been balked. But I suppose men are making the same mistakes elsewhere. As for bringing the Treggs here, *that* was a mistake. They had served their purpose. We'll get bounty immigrants; they're cheap; and you shall have your servants, Jane, as befitting an Oliver."

"What about blacks?" asked Conway. "The young gins could help in the house, the bucks with the outside jobs."

"Blacks?" scoffed Elliott.

"Why not?" argued Conway. "Others are

using them, and *they* cost practically nothing to keep."

"I won't have gins in my house—young or old," said Jane emphatically. "I can't stand the smell of them."

"Well, what's to eat?" demanded Elliott.

"Cold mutton—everything's cold. I couldn't bring myself to bother about cooking."

Conway looked at his father.

"You said something about bounty immigrants, papa," he said.

"I did," said Henry.

"What had you in mind?"

"A family, I suppose. Dungaree settlers. The poorer the better."

"I need a woman—two women," said Jane. "A cook and a general servant. I don't care how many men you have for the outside work—I'm sick of being a servant in my own house. Even that impudent Martin girl asked me if I were an Oliver—or a servant. Insolence!"

"Your husband will adore you," murmured Everitt.

Jane flushed. Her eyes glinted angrily.

"At least he will be my husband——"

"Leave Jane alone, Everitt," said Henry sternly.

"Willingly."

"Turn up the lamp," said Elliott.

Conway, who was nearest, turned up the wick. For a little while everyone ate in silence. Jane was about to speak when all at once she sat upright, mouth open, dark eyes staring through the door.

"What's the matter?" asked Conway.

"I—I heard something," she said in a low tone.

"Heard what?" asked Elliott.

"I thought . . . I heard the rattle of a chain. Yes! I did! There it is again—listen!"

No one moved. All sat as if frozen while they listened. From outside came the rattling cough of an opossum.

"There's your chain——" sneered Everitt. "Opossum."

"Don't be a fool, Everitt," Jane hissed. "I've heard opossums before. What I heard just now was a *chain*, I tell you——"

They listened again, but no metallic sound came to their ears.

"I'll see," said Everitt.

"I'll come with you—better make sure," said Conway.

"Don't go out in the dark," said Jane quickly. "Your eyes will be useless after being in here in the light. He could kill you before you ever saw him."

"Turn out the light," suggested Henry.

"No—no!" Jane gasped. "Let us have the light for heaven's sake. I couldn't stand being in the dark just now. I wouldn't know who moved—in the darkness."

"She's right," said Elliott. "Better leave the light, papa."

"Are you certain it was a chain you heard, Jane?" Conway asked.

"Yes. Royd's out there somewhere. It was a chain—a faint rattle, then a dragging sound, then again a faint rattle. It *was* a chain——"

"Oh, it's no concern of ours," said Everitt sarcastically.

Henry's voice was explosive.

"Enough of that, Everitt," he rasped. "I won't have it, boy! This isn't the time for levity."

"And that is the truth, sir," Everitt retorted. "If anyone thinks I'm taking this affair lightly he's a fool. The Treggs haven't burnt their hut for nothing."

"Well, what's to do?" asked Elliott.

"There's no chance of seeing him out there in *that* darkness."

Jane was pale and agitated.

"Perhaps he's gone round the back," she suggested. "Oh, I'll never sleep tonight——"

"No," said Conway grimly. "And it looks as if none of us will sleep tonight. We're just beginning to realize what this can mean."

They sat listening again. There was no sound. No one bothered to eat any more; they just sat listening. The wind had more force in it now; it set the trees near by rustling. But that was not what they were waiting to hear. Their ears were strained to catch a faint metallic rattling. So they sat silent, tense, listening, as the Treggs and the Martins sat listening, aware now that Death walked in the dark valley. Death holding a chain in his hand.

15

IN spite of the threat of Royd the Martins finished their house on the afternoon of Christmas Eve. They stood, Annie with them, watching Tom on the roof fasten the pole holding down the last broad sheet of stringybark. The roof was finished. When the boy waved cheerfully to them John turned with a smile to Hetty.

"There it is, mother," he said. "It isn't much—just a beginning—but we'll have better later. I'm glad it's finished before I journey to Sydney Town in a few days to see Martha Gubby. What think you of it?"

Hetty's eyes were shining. It was different, very different, from the solid, old, red-brick farmhouse in Kent, the house where her children were born, that thatched house where vine and fruit-tree clung to the very bricks themselves. Yes; it was different. Crude. Raw. Just split slabs for walls, thick bark for a roof; but it was the beginning. When smoke began curling up through the wide slab and bark chimney the valley would be transformed. It was home.

"Oh, John—you have all worked so hard. I think it is splendid, and the girls and I will make it very comfortable——"

With a laugh he picked her up in his arms and carried her into the house. The others followed, laughing at her mingled delight and embarrassment. Annie hung back a little, but Hetty saw her hesitation and said:

"Come in, Annie—come in, my dear. You are very welcome, child. While you are with us you are one of us, you know."

"Thenk you, Mrs. Martin . . . it be a wunnerful 'ouse."

The wonderful house had a living-room kitchen with a long slab table in it, a hearth that could take logs enclosed by a wide chimney where before long flitches would hang in the smoke. There were three bedrooms, and a store-room running off the living-room on one side of the chimney. The windows were square openings with canvas drops. Outside, a few paces from the back door, was a shed covering a bench supporting washtubs. There were no tanks, water for all purposes being drawn from the creek by sledge and left in the big cask beside the back door.

Hetty went to Tom and Mark and kissed them both.

"You are good boys," she said. "Now we have a roof over our heads I feel the Martins are at home. We'll be snug here when winter comes. God is good to us——"

Mark knew that Annie was watching him, but he would not look at her. She had no home. From what she had said her unfortunate mother had never shown her any affection, and he wondered what her thoughts were as she stood shy and withdrawn just a little away from his sisters. No doubt her mind was troubled and sad. She had walked into the ghastly horror of a terrible thing. She had scarcely spoken to anyone during the time she had been with them, but she had made herself useful, not hanging back when anything had to be done. When Elijah, the day before, rode away on the borrowed grey horse to inform the police at Gundagai, and to pick up any mail that might be there, she watched him go. She did not speak to him; nor did he speak to her. It seemed that she stood alone, and that, perhaps, was the truth of it; her people, it could be sensed, were nothing to her; and the Martins felt she could not bring herself close to them. She could not forget she was the daughter of a convict.

No time was lost in getting furniture, stores and personal belongings out of the big wagon and drays and into the house. There were no coverings except sheep and kangaroo skins for the floors, but the living-room soon boasted a small oak sideboard proudly supporting bits of silver and china-ware. There was a wall-rack for guns, and John had made a wall-shelf for the precious, striking Dutch clock. From a pole rafter an oil lamp hung directly over the slab table. A shelf of books was above the sideboard, while on the slab wall beside the hearth bright copper utensils winked cheerfully in the afternoon light. The cree was fixed and could swing pots or a kettle over the flames. The bedrooms each held skin rugs, solid pole beds John had put together, large oak chests holding clothes. The storeroom was soon in use, the shelves filled, and casks with lids held stores of lamp-oil, flour, sugar, corn and wheat. Annie's eyes were wide and admiring. Compared with the Tregg hut this simple house was a palace.

All wanted to sit at the long slab table for the evening meal prepared in anticipation over the outside fire. There was no chance of Royd bursting in on them except at night time, nevertheless the guns were always handy and charged with heavy shot. In the excitement of moving into the new house little thought was given to the madman, or to the rest of the Treggs who had camped some distance away on a rich little elbow of the creek, where they intended to build and farm, or to the Olivers at the other end of the valley. Tomorrow would be Christmas Day, and Tom and Mark wanted to cut bushy saplings before dark and decorate the house. They had seen, the previous Christmas, the shops and dwellings of Sydney Town, the veranda posts, and even the coaches and carriages, all embowered in gum-leaves, and they thought it a fine idea for their valley home.

And the girls were going to "dress-up" for the first meal—not Annie, of course, she was always dressed for all occasions. Her brown eyes were still and envious when Tilly, Jeanette and Nan began taking their clothes out of the chests. Actually the three girls had a limited wardrobe, but to Annie the garments displayed were endless and fascinating. Hetty, coming into the girls' room, saw Annie staring at the clothes, and realization came to her of the longing and frustration in this girl's heart. She called Nan out of the room, and spoke to her, then Tilly, then Jeanette.

"My dears," she said to each. "This poor child is in rags. See if there is anything you can spare. I'll do the same, and then talk to her. I don't know if she will accept anything, but her eyes tell her thoughts."

In a little while Hetty called Annie into her bedroom.

"Annie——" she said gently. "The girls' room isn't big enough for four to sleep in, but you will be all right near the hearth, won't you?"

"Oh, yus, Mrs. Martin. I could sleep outside if you wants me to. I s'pose I'm a lot of trouble——"

"Oh, no. You are no trouble, Annie. And you certainly won't sleep outside, my dear. We are glad for you to be here. And—and as it's Christmas Eve the girls and I would like you to have a few things. Here's a shift and a dark, twilled dress of Nan's; a split-straw bonnet, and comb of Tilly's; a pair of shoes and stockings that are too small for Jeanette; and I don't need this shawl—I have two others——"

Annie flushed deeply.

"Oh, no, Mrs. Martin—I couldn't ever do *thet*—I couldn't take *them* things."

Hetty smiled at her.

"Why not, child? You are not depriving any of us of them, and the girls and I would like you to have them. It would please us very much."

Annie looked at her.

"Oh!" she said very softly. "Thenk you, Mrs. Martin . . . but I . . ."

"The girls are going to put on their dresses for supper, my dear. You do the same. They are yours now—your own. I'm sure Tom and Mark will think you a pretty little thing in that twilled dress."

Tom and Mark. Mark! Would *he* think she was pretty? Annie could feel her cheeks burning. She looked at the clothes spread on the bed. She wanted them so much. A real dress! And a pretty bonnet! And shoes and stockings! And that fine, coloured shawl! Oh, how she wanted them. Such things she had never had. Shoes and stockings! Hetty saw the hunger for them in the girl's eyes.

"Take them, Annie, and put them on when Nan is dressing. Tilly and Jeanette will get dressed first. There, child—take them."

Annie's voice was a mere whisper.

"Thenk you, Mrs. Martin. Gawd—you Martins is kind people——"

Hetty turned away quickly. What a hard and empty life this girl—indeed all the Treggs—must have had. But Hetty knew that thousands still in England were no better off than the Treggs. Thousands were in workhouses all over the country, as they were in Ireland, too. And tens of thousands, especially in London, lived in indescribable hovels in narrow lanes and alley-ways where the very gutters stank of the filth they carried away to the Thames. Terrible Jacob's Isle, even more terrible St. Giles, were but two of these festering centres of poverty, lust and violent crime, the spawning areas of criminals who had crowded the convict transports that had first peopled this land. Under the pomp and glitter of London's upper levels were quicksands of poverty and frustration that engulfed the common man and woman, and transformed them when in the depths into thieves, murderers, outcasts, and gin-sodden harlots. Hetty realized now that she could not look back dispassionately at the Homeland, that England had never been kind to her common people, although it was upon them and not

251

upon the peacocks of her aristocracy that her true greatness rested.

Hetty knew all this, and never ceased to thank God that the Martins had by their industry been able to live decently, had been able to school and clothe their children, and now, in this far valley, in New South Wales, had been able to begin a new way of life that in time would bring recompense for this courageous beginning again. But in one swift glance she had seen the quivering eagerness, the terrible joy of this girl on being given these few and simple clothes. And she was troubled. It was as if Annie, all unwittingly as her eyes shone, had drawn aside the dark curtain of her own life to reveal the want, the helplessness and poverty behind it, the harsh indifference and cruelty of the people of New South Wales to such as the Treggs, the assumption that the convict, and the convict's children, themselves innocent, must for ever be outcasts, and like the leper of old cry "Unclean—unclean" as they approached.

As she came into the living-room Tom called from outside:

"We're going for the bushes, mother—any of the girls coming?"

"No, dear—I want them all here. Don't be

too long—and do be careful—you know what I mean."

"We have guns. Make it a grand supper, mother——"

She laughed.

"I will, son—a grand supper," she said. And then a thought came to her. She called: "Tom—Mark! Wait! Tom, come here——"

He stepped off the slide and came to her. "Yes?"

"Tom, tomorrow is Christmas Day. Tregg told us his family is not far from here. I want you to take food to them. Annie will be with us. I would not feel happy if we all sat down to a feast knowing they had nothing. Will you do that for me?"

Tom laughed and put an arm round her.

"Of course I will," he said heartily. "Mark and I were only talking about it a moment ago. But we knew father's views on—on such as the Treggs."

Hetty said quietly. "I think your father, like myself, is more understanding now. This horrible tragedy has shown us these people are human like ourselves, people with their own sorrows and burdens. We must try to lighten them, not add to them. I'll make up the food."

He followed her into the store-room. Tilly came in.

"What are you doing?" she asked.

"Mother's sending food to the Treggs," said Tom. "It's Christmas Day tomorrow."

"H'm," said Tilly non-committally. "I hope they will appreciate it. And while I think of it—how long is this Tregg girl going to be with us? Why isn't she with her own people? The—the other one is."

"The other one didn't care for our company, my dear," said Hetty dryly. "Annie evidently is different. Now don't you upset the girl, Tilly—she's been through a bad time."

Tilly shrugged as she turned away. When she disappeared Hetty said, "There are times when I don't understand Tilly."

Tom laughed. "Oh, bother Tilly," he said lightly. "Tilly has always had her nose in the air. She's all right once she gets her own way—which is most times."

"Well, she seems to be a little more contented lately," said Hetty. "Let me see—flour, tea, sugar. They can shoot ducks and a goose as we have done. Salt, tobacco, and here's a dudeen to smoke it in. Get a round of that salted veal out of the cask, Tom, and a flap of that salted pork. I doubt if they have eaten such meat for a long time. I think that will keep them going for a while——"

"They'll have a good Christmas dinner at any rate," said Tom. "I suppose Tregg himself will get something in Gundagai."

"As a matter of fact, my boy," whispered Hetty. "Your father gave him a little money for that purpose."

Tom showed his surprise. "He did? Father?"

"Hush! He'd be cross if he knew I'd told you. I think he wants to make amends for his former harshness to these people."

"He certainly had plenty to say about them——"

"There, there, dear. Tregg also took a letter your father wrote to Mrs. Gubby. She should get it in a fortnight. He will be going to see her soon. We must know how we stand about the land here."

"Yes, of course. But I don't think we need worry, mother."

"Neither do I, son. Now run along—and do watch out for that terrible man."

Tom grunted with the weight of the sackful.

"I can't understand where the fellow is—or how he is living. It's several days now since he broke loose. Perhaps he has gone out of the valley."

"I do hope so. Hurry along and bring back the gum-bushes—it will be exciting tying them to doors and windows—a real colonial Christmas. And roasting hot. In England it will be freezing cold. Hey, ho! What an upside-down world it is."

Mark stared as Tom placed the sack on the sledge.

"For the Treggs," said Tom. "Mother."

Mark smiled a little. "She thinks of . . . everybody."

Meg, standing with arms akimbo, bare legs apart, saw them coming. She called to Johnnie, Rock and Dick who were cutting poles near by. They came slowly forward to meet Tom and Mark. As the slide stopped the young men eyed each other curiously. Meg flicked the Martin boys with a contemptuous glance, then looked down at the sackful of food. Tom spoke.

"We're the Martins. But I suppose you know that."

Meg looked at him with unfriendly eyes.

"Yus. We knows thet," she replied.

Tom went on: "Mother sent this food, if you will accept it," he said.

Johnnie, Rock and Dick looked at one another. This was surprising and unexpected. But Meg suddenly stiffened, and her face flushed angrily. Because of Tilly, resentment for all the Martins rose in her. Her eyes were narrowed and hostile. She recalled in a flash the scene at the Olivers' house: Tilly on the horse looking down at her; Everitt riding after Tilly—yes; riding after the Martin girl; Oliver scorning her as she stood near the veranda; the Martins and the Olivers giving her dirt. Jealousy, suspicion and a crude pride surged in her.

"We don' want your food, Martins," she said harshly. "Us Treggs can live. I won' eat none of it—an' I'll make sure no other Tregg does——"

She bent and seized the sack, and was lifting it to empty it out on to the ground when Dick hurled her back.

"You crazy bitch!" he growled. "You let alone. You ain't *all* the Treggs, an' you don' *speak* for all the Treggs." He turned to the astonished Tom and Mark. "Us Treggs thenks you," he said evenly. "We ain't got wuds to say much, but we thenks you——"

"I don't!" shrilled Meg. "I want no truck with the Martins or anythin' they've got——"

257

Dick looked at her, his eyes calm in a broad expressionless face.

" 'Course you don't," he said. "But this time it don' matter what *you* thinks or wants."

Tom said rather lamely, "We hope you enjoy the food. Good day . . . and a merry Christmas. . . ."

He knew as he said it he had spoken thoughtlessly. He reddened a little.

"A Merry Christmas—you bleddy fool!" Meg sneered at him.

"Good Day——" he said hurriedly.

He drove the slide away. Dick turned to Meg.

"You——" he said deeply. "You ain't got no more brains in your 'ead than you 'ave in your backside—fac' thet's all you 'ave got—a backside. You spoil thet food an' I'll flatten you so's you won't walk for a week to go aseein' thet bleddy Ev'ritt."

"Same 'ere," said Johnnie.

"Same 'ere," said Rock. "You got some sense, Dick."

Dick spoke slowly.

"Did y'ear what 'e said? A merry Christmas. We could see 'e f'got for a moment

258

what's bin, but I don' remember *anyone* ever sayin' thet to us afore."

Rock looked at the sack.

"Christmas——" he muttered. "Well, strike me dead—Christmas! It never struck me 'twas Christmas——"

"Me neither," said Johnnie. "Why should it? What d'you do at Christmas, anyways?"

"Eat," said Dick. "When y'got it. Well, we's got it. You fix it, Meg—an' no tricks—or it'll be Gawd 'elp you——"

"Ar——" she sneered. "Trucklin' to them Martins——"

Dick looked at her for a long moment.

"You does plenty o' thet somewhars else," he said. "Mebbe you thinks no one knows 'bout it. Mebbe they does. You watch y'self, Meg—you bleddy well watch y'self. 'Lijah'd kill both 'im an' you if ever 'e found out."

Meg paled.

"Found—found out what?" she asked quickly.

Dick turned away from her.

"Fix thet food," he grunted.

16

THE girls had dressed, Tilly and Jeanette first, then Nan and Annie. Tilly's red dress and Jeanette's white muslin were sheer enchantment for Annie. Nan was pretty in a blue, flowered print dress, and Annie trembled as she put the twilled dressed on over the shift.

"Don't forget your shoes and stockings, Annie," said Nan with a smile.

"Oh, lawks, Nan . . . oh, lawks," the girl panted. "I don't rightly know where I be . . . shoes an' stockin's. . . ."

It was an exciting experience to pull the black stockings up over her slim legs and tie them with ribbon garters, but when the shoes were on, and she stood up, dismay showed in her face.

"Ar——" she said in great disappointment. "I can't wear 'em, Nan—ain't ever 'ad shoes on me feet—they pinch like 'ell——"

"Walk round in them to get used to them, Annie. They should fit—you and Jeanette have the same size feet."

260

"Yus—'bout the same, I s'pose," Annie agreed.

She hobbled round the room, and then Nan burst out laughing.

"Oh, lawks, Annie! You've got them on the wrong feet—no wonder they hurt you!"

"Ar—thet mus' be it, Nan——"

She changed the shoes.

"I got no sense—no sense more'n a daffy duck. Yus. Thet's wunnerful. But they do feel bleddy quar——"

Nan's eyes were merry. "You really mustn't swear, Annie."

"Ar—I f'git," said Annie apologetically.

She combed her fair hair and tied it. Nan stared at her. The dark dress with its green piping fitted her slender form perfectly.

"I declare," said Nan, "no one would know you, Annie. Look at yourself in the looking-glass."

Annie did so. Her brown eyes were wide as she looked at her reflection.

"Gawd!" she breathed. "Be thet me? Be *thet* Annie Tregg? It-bleddy-well-can't-be——"

Nan laughed heartily.

"It's you all right, Annie. I'm waiting to

see Tom's and Mark's eyes pop out when they see you. And Annie——"

"Yus, Nan?"

"You won't swear in front of father, will you—I mean at the table?"

"No, Nan. I'll remember. But I dunno—this ain't me, Nan——" she turned and looked at the tattered print dress and the kangaroo-skin jacket. "Thet's me—*thet* be the real Annie Tregg——"

"That was Annie Tregg," said Nan gently. "They're your everyday clothes now—these are your new Sunday-go-meeting ones."

"Sunday-go-meetin'," muttered Annie. "Ar well, Nan—it's jus' wunnerful to 'ave 'em for onct. You look good."

"Do I, Annie?"

"Yus—bl——"

"Annie!"

"I ought to be out with the dawgs——"

"Oh, no. Now fasten your hair up in a bun."

"A bun? What for a bun—can't I 'ave it 'angin' loose like this?"

"You've got so much of it, Annie—it's like a cape round your shoulders. See—mine's in a bun—so's Tilly's and Jeanette's. It's supposed to be proper."

"Yus? All right. I wants to be proper, Nan. I don' want to do nothin' wrong."

"You certainly have a lot of it, Annie——"

"I s'pose. So's Meg. We chops a bit off each other's now'n then——"

"Here—let me do it for you——"

There was a silence for a few moments while Nan coiled the thick straw-coloured mass into a huge bun.

"There. That'll do, Annie. Now, your nails——"

"Them?" asked the mystified girl. "What's wrong with 'em?"

"You watch me," said Nan.

She cleaned her nails. Annie nodded.

"I sees. Gimme thet splinter. Anythin' else?"

Nan smiled. "You'll do. Annie, you're a bit startling. And you're very pretty. But I shouldn't be saying such things."

Annie looked solemnly at her. "Pretty? Me? How pretty?" she asked.

Nan walked round her critically. "In your old clothes, with that kangaroo-skin jacket and opossum cap on, you look a wild creature, Annie. You can't be seen in them——"

"You can't see me——"

263

Nan laughed again.

"I can't see what I can see now—what all the others will see. You'll surprise them. I'm waiting to see Tilly's face—Tilly prides herself on her looks."

"She looks all right."

Nan spluttered. "Goodness! My eldest sister thinks she looks better than that, and she does, really. Tilly's a handsome girl."

"Yus—I s'pose."

"It's going to be fun watching them looking at you—and it's good to be in our own house at last."

"Yus, mus' be," said Annie quietly. "I never lived in a 'ouse like this. On the Tamar we 'ad a sod-earth 'ut—jist the one room. Same at Port Phillip. The Olivers allus 'ad a timber 'ouse—not the Treggs. When we come 'ere 'Lijah put up thet slab place . . . as was jist burnt down."

"I don't know how you all managed in one room——"

"Easy. We-all ate together—we-all slep' together."

"All slept together? You mean—all in one bed?" asked the astonished Nan.

"Yus. Allus did since we was little 'uns. Folks like us Treggs all do the same. As we growed up 'Lijah made the bed wider."

"But—you two girls?" said the perplexed Nan.

"Ar—we gets cunnin'. Got to."

"Well——" breathed Nan. "I should think so. But now we're dressed let's go and help mother. The boys'll have all the bushes tied up by this and are probably dressing. There's the clock striking seven, and it's still bright daylight."

As the girls walked to the hearth Hetty turned and looked at Annie in astonishment.

"Why, Annie——" she muttered.

"Yus, Mrs. Martin?"

"Child, I can scarcely believe it's you!"

Annie felt the colour coming into her face.

"I dunno, Mrs. Martin—I s'pose it be me——"

"Well," said Hetty. "I *am* pleased, my dear. Why, Nan—she's a beautiful girl."

"Yes," said Nan. "She is. Here's Tilly and Jeanette——"

The two girls came out of the store-room. Their eyes opened wide as they looked at Annie. Then Tilly's narrowed, and her mouth thinned a little.

"If it isn't Cinderella," she purred. "Or was it Robinson Crusoe's daughter?"

"Tilly!" said Hetty sharply.

Jeanette said quietly as Annie gave Tilly a sharp look, "How nice you look, Annie. Do the shoes fit you?"

"Yus, Jeanette. I put 'em on wrong fust time——"

Tilly sniggered, but stopped when she saw the warning light in her mother's eyes.

Annie went on, "You look good, Jeanette."

Jeanette was pleased. It was usually Tilly who got all the compliments.

"Do I Annie?"

"And don't I look 'good', Annie?" Tilly asked sarcastically.

"You knows what you look—an' what you are," said Annie evenly. "Can I 'elp you, Mrs. Martin?"

Tilly flushed angrily at the retort, but passed it off with a hard little laugh. Jeanette and Nan gave one another a quick glance. Each seemed to tell the other that Tilly had better not provoke Annie too far.

"Yes, Annie," said Hetty. "I want a few things sorted out in the store-room. Come along."

When Hetty came back she said in a low tone to Tilly, "Tilly, no more of that to Annie. She's a guest in your father's house, and if she is good enough for him, and for me, she is good enough for you."

Tilly shrugged. "She's a saucy chit, all the same," she retorted.

"You provoked her."

"Really, mother! That kind of creature isn't provoked—she's just being herself."

"Perhaps you are, too, my dear," said Hetty. "And it isn't pleasing to see. Perhaps if you had lived as she has had to live, you, too, would be that kind of a creature. But you are wrong about Annie, my dear. Don't be."

Tilly frowned. Nan and Jeanette began setting the table.

"I don't understand this sudden tenderness for convicts," said Tilly. "When we came to the valley father was adamant about our associating with them—and here, within a few weeks, one of them is actually staying in our house with us."

"But, Tilly——" began Hetty patiently.

"Oh, yes, mother! I know what's happened at their hut, but I don't think this girl—or any of them—feels any sorrow or regret."

"You never know what people feel, my dear. Nearly everyone wears a mask—even you."

"Oh, mother!" and Tilly pouted as if she were hurt.

"Don't let us talk any more about it, Tilly. Be kind to the girl. She has never hurt you. Now look after things while I dress. Here's your father."

John, dressed in a long black coat and grey trousers, and with a black stock between the wings of a wide collar, came into the living-room. He looked about him, satisfaction stamped upon him, his blue eyes merry, his round face ruddy and smiling in its frame of white whiskers.

"The boys have done well," he said to Nan and Jeanette. "The gum-branches lend quite a festive air to the new house."

"It's grand," said Nan happily.

"Where's the—where's Annie?" John asked.

"In the store-room," said Jeanette.

"I hope she puts on the clothes you gave her——"

Nan and Jeanette smiled.

"Oh, yes, father—she did," said Nan. "Do you want to see her?"

"Oh, no, no, no. I'll stroll outside and smoke a pipe. I do hope she won't swear during supper—it's like having a stone

268

dropped on one's head when she uses those words."

Tom and Mark came noisily out of their room. Both were in high spirits: the work was done; tomorrow would be Christmas Day; there was a good supper ready; and they were dressed in their best jackets, shirts and trousers. The girls laughed as the boys whooped, ran to them, hugged them, and whirled them round.

"Where's Annie?" Mark asked loudly.

Annie thrilled when she heard him ask for her. Tilly said coldly, "In the store-room. Don't bother her, she's doing something for mother. As soon as mother's dressed we'll have supper."

"A wonderful supper," said Nan.

"Our first meal in our new house," said Jeanette. "Goodness, I feel excited. I feel this part of the valley really belongs to us now."

"You've got to play the fiddle for us afterwards, Jeanette," said Mark.

"I'll sing," said Tom.

"No!" yelled everybody.

Tom laughed. "Hurry, mother," he called. "The Martins are hungry!"

"Coming dear—coming. We'll soon have supper."

"And what a supper?" said Jeanette.

And what a supper it was. The fragrance of the gum-leaves seemed to give the benediction of the Australian bush to the new house, to this family that had come from a far country to live on Australian soil. John, seated on a rustic bench-seat outside under the bark-roofed earth-floored veranda, knocked the ashes out of his pipe when he heard the laughter and happy voices. He looked up and down the valley before going inside, and within him was a profound contentment. This valley, this long, wide, verdant valley, right down to the Olivers' fence, was all his. For this he had sold the Kentish farm, for this he had transported his family to this new world. This valley, and perhaps even lands beyond it, would now be their world. He had no fear for his title. Martha's inexplicable action perplexed him, but for some reason she had come to his aid, and he knew her well enough to know that had she not trusted him and his she would not have moved in the matter. Martha Gubby. Thanks to her their labours were not wasted; thanks to her impulsive generosity and dislike of the mean and the underhand their small capital, their land, their very future, were preserved. It was a wonderful gesture, but typical of the warm-hearted woman who herself had had to rise up from the gutters by sheer courage and the will to make a place in society for herself and her family. But he still must learn just *why* she had helped them. He would have to go to Sydney in a few days even if that dangerous fellow, Tregg, remained at large. Tom and Mark were a match for Royd Tregg; his family would be safe enough. And the girl Annie? Well, the Martins had been helped when they might have been driven from their land, so the Martins would help these others, would not drive them from the valley so long as they proved themselves capable of industry and decency.

They were all at the table when Annie came out of the store-room. It was almost dark outside. The hanging lamp gave a good light. Hetty called, "Come along, Annie—supper's ready."

As the girl came into the living-room the laughter and talk died away. Tom's dark eyes were wide with astonishment as he looked at her; Mark stared; John's white eyebrows went up and came slowly down. The three men, who could visualize her only as a ragged, bare-footed girl in a stained and dirty kangaroo-skin jacket and old print dress, were taken aback as she came towards them. For a moment they stared unbelievingly. Annie? Annie Tregg? This handsome youngster looking shyly at them. What a trans-formation. The girl was beautiful, her lines perfect.

"Well . . . I'll be damned," said Tom softly.

"Tom!" said his father, but without his usual sternness.

"Why, Annie——" said Mark. "You look . . . fine."

"Indeed you do, Annie," said John. "You don't seem to be the same girl."

Annie was breathing a little quickly. This was a tremendous experience for her.

"Thenk you, Mr. Martin. Tilly, Jeanette, Nan an' Mrs. Martin all guv me these things to put on. Thenk you—thenk you-all," she said.

Then she looked at Mark, but did not speak to him.

Hetty said, "Sit next to Mark, Annie—after all, you're his dis-discovery. Nan, you move round to Annie's other side."

"That isn't fair!" said Tom in mock disappointment. "If she has Mark on one side of her she should have *me* on the other——"

"Oh, you, Tom!" said his mother as the others laughed. "You never look at anybody once you start eating. Now what will everybody have?"

"What have we, mother?" asked John. "The board's laden with good things."

Hetty was smiling as she spoke.

"A cod from the pool near the waterfall; pickled veal and pork; a pigeon pie; a saddle of mutton; home-made bread and cream and butter; cold roast ducks and a wild goose; a dish of boiled potatoes and onions boiled whole; scones Jeanette made; some young greens and lots of hard-boiled eggs. How's that, my dears, for our first Christmas Eve supper in our new home?"

John looked at her and smiled.

"Annie," said Tom with a grin, "I believe I *am* going to forget you for a little while."

"Yus, Tom—you tuck in, boy."

A roar of laughter went up at the girl's naïve remark. Annie blushed, wondering what she had said to make them laugh.

In a moment Hetty said, "Give us the grace, John—ask for a blessing on us and these good things."

The laughter faded. Heads were bowed as John rose. He spoke simply and earnestly. Annie, aware now of what was expected of her, inclined her head. Her hands, clasped together on her lap, were shaking a little. She had never, *never* seen such food in all her life; she had never, *never* worn such clothes; and never, *never* before had she seen men look at her as Tom and Mark had looked. And she was pleasantly aware that the stern Mr. Martin was pleased with her. She wanted to please them all so much—not Tilly—Tilly, she sensed, disliked her. Tilly could go to hell. And Mark? She could feel him next to her. What did he *really* think of her? Every time he moved and touched her something seemed to burn inside her. She scarcely heard John say:

"We give thanks, O Lord, for these bounties. Our hearts are grateful and humble in Thy presence. Preserve us now, and in our years to come, and give us understanding, strength and health to go forward. Let us, O Lord, remain united as a family, kindly and forgiving and helpful one to the other. We thank Thee, O Lord, we humbly thank Thee. Amen.

As they lifted their heads John looked at Annie.

"Annie, that means you also—you and yours."

Annie's lips were quivering, her eyes moist. It seemed so strange to her to be in a house such as this, at a table such as this, with a kindly and gracious family such as this.

"Mr. Martin——" she said in a tremulous voice. "I—I ain't got no wuds to tell you what I thinks . . . not a *bleddy* wud. . . ."

17

THE afternoon of Christmas Day saw Royd Tregg roasting in the sun on the rocky ledge of the high bluff, his eyes straining in the shimmering heat to catch a glimpse of Jane Oliver whenever she came on to the veranda of the house. With the chain still round his waist he was panting as he lay there. Animal instinct told him how to live: he had killed several of Oliver's sheep with the heavy chain, just as he had killed Sarah; his powerful hands had torn them apart; his ravenous mouth had feasted on the uncooked meat. Streaked with blood and dust, he was a hellish sight. But there he lay under the fierce rays of the sun, his wild pale eyes often filled with sweat, his long red hair damp with it, watching for the slender figure of Jane Oliver. Only once had he gone back to the Tregg hut. He had stood looking at its ashes uncomprehendingly: the charred remnants, the fresh mound beside the tree conveyed nothing to him. Rock had seen him then, had seen him swaying from side to side like a giant ape as he stood, had himself turned and run for his brothers. But when they all came Royd had gone. They followed his tracks a little way, then lost them.

The valley was hot under the midsummer's sun, and sheep and cattle sought shade, and heat-scents drawn from sap-filled grasses and trees were fragrant across the flats and slopes. The Olivers were lounging on their veranda, the men with guns ready to hand. They were silent, staring along the valley, but all moved with a quick interest when a gunshot sent rolling echoes round the hills.

"Royd?" jerked out Elliott.

"God—I hope so," said Jane as she sat fanning herself. "Christmas Day! With that beast somewhere in the valley. I'm just a mass of nerves, I jump at every little sound."

"A 'roo, more likely," said Conway.

Conway's suggestion was correct. Johnnie Tregg had just shot a boomer. Royd's massive head jerked up as he heard the report, but his eyes soon went back to stare at the Olivers' house. He could see Jane and the others but he had eyes only for her. He wanted Jane. He craved for her. Even in his madness he was obsessed by her. And even in his madness he was cunning enough to wait.

But he would get her, and take her somewhere into the hills where no one would ever find her. That was as firmly fixed in his ruined mind as is a stubborn rock in the broken hulk of a shipwrecked vessel. Yes; he had waited. But he would take her soon, and his laughter would wake the mountains—those mountains where no other white man walked, and from which she would never return. Yes; he would take her soon.

In the living-room of the Martins' house Mark was showing Annie some books, telling her how words were formed by the combination of letters. Annie did not know even the alphabet, but her eyes were hungry, her ears intent as she listened.

"You mus' be clever, boy," she said. "Dunno 'ow you gits all thet larnin' in your 'ead. I didn't know farmin' folks got larnin'."

"It depends on the farming folks, Annie. And a little learning is not got all at once," Mark assured her. "Would you really like to learn to read and write?"

"Oh, yus——" the girl breathed. "I wants to be more'n jist a stoopid thing like a cockatoo in a tree."

"You haven't had a chance," said Mark

278

quietly. "If you'll let me, I'll try to teach you. Yes, I'll try——"

She turned to him, her face flushed and eager.

"You will, Mark?" she asked earnestly. "You *will* do thet?"

"Yes, Annie."

"Lawks!" she whispered. "An' I'll try to larn, Mark . . . by Gawd, I'll try. . . ."

Tilly heard what was said as she came close to them.

"That's noble of you, Mark," she said sweetly. "I'm sure Annie has a high intelligence."

Annie raised slow brown eyes to hers. Annie had never known how to use a verbal rapier so she came back with a club.

"An' I be sure," she said slowly, "thet you be as silly as a bleddy duck."

Tilly's blue eyes flashed angrily. "I suppose you can't help being what you are," she said curtly.

Mark said quietly, "Leave Annie alone, Tilly."

Tilly said significantly, "You'd better take your own advice, brother Mark."

Annie's words were slow and cutting. "An' thar be things in this valley, Tilly

Martin—*you* better leave alone. An' you knows well 'nough what I means. If you don't—I'll tell you——"

Before Tilly could reply Mark cried impatiently:

"For goodness' sake, you two girls—it's Christmas Day. Now go on, Tilly! I'm surprised at you. Let us alone, do."

Tilly shrugged as she walked away. Annie turned to Mark.

"Ar—I ought to be swingin' be me tail like a 'possum—I jist ain't got no sense," she said contritely. "But I ain't takin' no dirt from Tilly. Now tell me more, boy."

Mark's voice droned on. No other voices were heard in the Martin house, or in that of the Olivers. And where the Treggs camped there was a drowsy silence. The whole valley was quiet under the hot sun, and on the great mountains there was no sign of snow, the crests were dark masses, distant, high in the sky.

In Sydney Town Caroline Chisholm's work was progressing in spite of suspicion and intolerance in social and religious circles. By Christmas she had depots for her immigrants at Liverpool, Parramatta and Campbelltown. From these centres the girls, and some married immigrants, marched farther inland to positions found for them. Caroline herself had made several journeys, and now had a white horse which she rode in front of the drays as they went along the dusty roads. Public interest in her unique experiment was quickening, and Christmas Day saw extra rations, donated by the government and by public generosity, distributed to those in the tents near the Barracks. Caroline was indefatigable both on the roads and in her office. Her contracts of work, which employers and employees both had to sign, were models of legal precision and clarity, and were drawn up entirely by herself and written with her own pen. But on this Christmas Day she was with her own little family in Windsor.

But if on this day Sydney Town did not see Caroline Chisholm, it saw Martha and Henry Gubby, in their carriage, driven by the faithful Sam Pink, turn out of York Street and make towards the Government Domain. There they would listen to the military band, watch Sydney Town's citizens displaying their manners and fashions, and later observe on the crowded harbour the exciting regatta that swept under white sails from Sydney

Cove to Watson's Bay and back. Sam Pink was resplendent in livery of scarlet and green; Martha was immense in her flowered bonnet and billowing yellow gown; Henry, as usual, in spite of the stove-pipe hat to give him height, was scarcely noticed by her side. But it was seen by amused observers that Martha's side of the four-wheeled carriage was weighed down by her bulk, and that the vehicle slanted steeply as it rattled along behind the two trotting bays.

Martha was in high spirits.

"That was a proper dinner, Mr. Gubby," she said happily. "The bes' Christmas the Gubbys 'ave ever 'ad. I do wish the gels 'ad bin with us, but I s'pose they done all right."

"I'm sure they have, my dear," said Henry.

"Christmas Day!" said Martha. "Another one. A bit different from them cold an' 'ungry ones we knowed in Lunnon, 'Arry boy."

"Yes, my dear."

"Cold! Lassy me—I shivers when I thinks 'ow we used to wrap straw roun' us 'cause we 'ad no food to warm us."

"Yes—yes, my dear."

"I wonder if them Martins got my letter

282

yet—th' one you wrote for me? I sent it by way o' Gundagai."

"I don't know, my dear."

"Oh, well—I s'pose they'll get it. Fancy thet Mrs. Juleff dyin' las' week—you know, they looked after thet 'Liz'beth 'Olley when she fust come to Sydney Town."

"Juleff will miss her—yes; he'll miss her."

Martha's voice was suddenly strangely husky: "Would—would you miss me, 'Arry boy, if I—if I——"

Henry gave a start. He looked up at her in something like consternation.

"Martha!" he exclaimed. "You mustn't say things like that. Why I—I couldn't imagine what I'd do—I'd be lost—I'd be—oh, dear—please don't say things like that——"

"Ah, you's a good little man, Mr. Gubby," came softly. "I dunno why I said that. Mebbe I ate too much dinner. It's guv me the dratted wind again—I be ready to blow off or blow hup any time. Mus' be the plum puddin'. But does you realize we's becomin' prosperous, Mr. Gubby? This be the bes' day we ever 'ad? It be ten years since we stepped on that hempty beach at Fremantle, more'n five since we come to Sydney Town. I was almos' down to me las' penny—although I didn't tell *you* that—when I bought into the Cock an' Fevvers down in Campbell Street. But she went good. An' now look at us, 'Arry boy! A slap-up 'otel in York Street, an' ridin' in our very own kerridge like a couple o' Tiddley-poms. But we's gettin' a bit old, too. Me teeth ain't as good as they was, an' you got a bit o' grey roun' your ears now."

"Yes, I suppose we are, Martha. But we have a long way to go yet, my dear."

She gave his hand a gentle squeeze that almost crushed it.

" 'Course we 'ave, 'Arry boy. Fancy Sally Fulton, over in Fremantle, 'avin two young 'uns now—I knowed that Nannygai 'Ogg wouldn't let 'er be—but Sally was alwus a bit warm 'erself. Oh, well—sich things do 'appen."

"She was very lonely after her husband died."

"I s'pose—an' there ain't much else to do in Fremantle, anyways."

"Governor Hutt seems to be improving the colony."

"I alwus knowed 'e would, Mr. Gubby. It be a fine colony, fine folks there to make it so. 'Twill be all right. But I dunno 'bout that there Province o' South Hostralia. They's 'ad a bad time——"

"But so did the West, my dear."

"Lawks, yus! Don' hus Gubbys know it? But 'ow many folks be in South Hostralia now?"

"About fourteen thousand."

"There! They's comin' in spite o' hard times. An' Van Diemen's Land?"

"I think just over fifty thousand."

"Well, 'tis near as old as New South Wales. 'Ow many in *this* colony?"

"One hundred and thirty thousand with twenty thousand more down in the Port Phillip district."

"An' there be no convic's now in Port Phillip, South Hostralia an' Western Hostralia?"

"That's right, Martha. New South Wales and Van Diemen's Land are the only colonies now with convicts. They are still being transported from England to Van Diemen's Land, but they're not coming here any more."

"Well, well! What a lot's 'appened lately. No more convic's comin' in! That Mr. Eyre's tramped hall the way from South Hostralia to Western Hostralia! Angus McMillan's discovered Gippsland! Them hexplorers do

285

hopen up a country; I remembers 'earin 'bout 'em. Capting Sturt along the Darlin' an' the Murray; Alan Cunningham found that fine New Hingland; Oxley went hout to the Darlin' River; Mitchell down across the Murray into Hostralia Felix, which 'e discovered an' named; Gray from Fremantle right up to the Gascoyne River; Bonney across the Goulburn River to Adelaide; that Count Strzelecki las' year from Melbourne right hup into them great mountings in the south-east—thet Kosciusko; Patrick Leslie—'im that was out Cassilis way—found the Darlin' Downs right up near Brisbane Town—Mrs. Leslie was the fust white woman to go there. Them fine pioneer folks jus' don' know fear, Mr. Gubby. The New Hingland district be settled. We might 'ave a look at it some day. The Big River—the Clarence, some calls it—an' all the others north an' south 'ave settlers along 'em cultivatin' an' cuttin' cedar an' other timbers. Lawks! I can see them axes flashin' an' th' big trees crashin' down. The Port Phillip district be jus' shootin' ahead—that Hostralia Felix west o' Melbourne be attractin' squatters an' settlers. Folks is all along the Murray, the Murrumbidgee, the Lachlan, the Macquarie, the Bogan, an' there be squatters right out on the Darlin' 'bout five 'undred miles hinland. But it mus' be lonely right out there. An' the drays an' wagons never stops goin' in an' spreading out. Lawks! I wunner what it'll be like in a 'undred years' time, 'Arry boy?"

"Nobody can imagine that, my dear—but probably not much different from what it is now."

Martha's eyes were thoughtful, and they missed nothing as the carriage went along.

"Oh, I dunno, 'Arry. There be a lot of Hostralia no one's seen yet. Nobody knows what's in the middle o' Western Hostralia— or South Hostralia—or north o' Brisbane Town much. No one's bin west o' the Darlin' River—there could be a wunnerful place in there, or nothin' at all. Mr. Eyre didn't think much of the country north o' Adelaide a few 'undred miles. Mount 'Opeless, 'e called one place. Must 'ave bin. But we don' know *what's* in there——"

"And probably never shall, my dear," said Henry. "What would take people into such vast distances? There are no markets, no ports, and wagons would take years to come from and go to such places——"

She looked down at him for a moment.

"I dunno, Mr. Gubby. You never does look on the bright side o' things. If anythin', or any place, ain't jus' within reach of your 'and you gives up. Hif all them hexplorers was like you, Mr. Gubby, the whole world'd be the size of a turnip."

"But—but I'm not an explorer, Martha!" he protested.

She laughed.

"Fancy *you* tellin' me that, Mr. Gubby. An' look at Sydney Town! Would you b'lieve 'ow it's goin' ahead! Thirty thousan' people—an' Parramatta, an' Wollongong, an' Windsor, an' Gosford, an' Newcastle, an' Maitland, an' Scone, an' Tamworth, an' Armidale, an' Liverpool, an' Bathurst, an' Goulburn, an' Yass, an' Bong Bong, an' Berrima—lawks! An' lots o' places! The coaches an' drays be crammed with folks—all rumblin' over mountings an' plains an' sloshin' through rivers to get to some 'omestead or village or town. Bullock-wagons be piled 'igh with wool an' timber an' great piles for th' wharves; farm stuffs and mobs o' sheep an' cattle be comin' in to Sydney Town every day. Lawks! They tol' me in Melbourne two 'undred an' fifty ships come into Port Phillip *this* year, an' Sydney 'arbour be a forest o' masts. We won't see what's 'ere in a 'undred years' time, but I do declare, Mr. Gubby, you an' me'll see wunnerful things in this Hostralia afore we's finished. But I be all out o' breath again——"

He said slowly, "Yes, my dear. You did right to bring us out to this country ten years ago."

" 'Course I did, 'Arry boy! What would hus Gubbys 'ave bin in Hingland? Jus' penniless paupers like a lot o' others—jus' muck. Well, we ain't muck 'ere—we's the Gubbys, we's *somebody*. We ain't nobs, but we's somebody. We can stand hup straight an' spit in th' heye of any who hinsults us—no knucklin' to any nobs, no bobbin' th' ol' noddle an' backside an' scrapin' to the Quality. Th' only real quality in this world be the quality of hachievement, 'Arry boy. But, there y'are! Some folks likes bright colours an' gets all dazzled by 'em, likes to see the silly peacock's fevvers, gets hall himpressed, forgettin' their own hordinary brown fevvers be the fevvers of eagles as well as sparrers. Folks can look at us now in our kerridge an' say *them's* the Gubbys. An' that be somethin', Mr. Gubby, when you looks back to what we *didn't* 'ave, an' *couldn't* get, in Lunnon."

Henry was very quiet. He had not done anything for the family; he had not wanted to come to Australia, had dreaded the thought of the long voyage and the uncertainty in an unknown country right away on the other side of the world. He knew that all that had been done, that their success and increasing prosperity, were due to Martha.

He said very slowly, "Yes . . . Martha."

The lugubrious and ageing Sam Pink turned and looked sorrowfully down at them. Sam had been a convict, then a ticket-of-leave man, but now he was free. He had been with the Gubbys for five years as yardman, groom, and now as an ornate coachman.

"Whar to, Mrs. Gubby?" he inquired dolefully.

"Hover to the military band, Sam Pink. There they be near where th' ol' windmill was——"

"Yus, Mrs. Gubby. Stayin' thar?"

"No, Sam Pink. We'll listen for a while an' then go to where that Mrs. Macquarie used to set on them stones made into a seat."

"The blacks be throwin' boomerangs, Mrs. Gubby——"

"Drat the blacks—an' the boomerangs, Sam Pink! That's all blacks can do—an' I don' believe it's real. It be a trick o' some sort—a piece o' wood flyin' round the sky like a bird an' comin' back to perch on a blackfeller's 'and! Rubbish! It mus' be a trick."

"No, no, my dear," said Henry. "It's genuine——"

"Now, Mr. Gubby—I got eyes, ain't I?"

"Yes, my dear. But the blacks actually make the boomerangs come back to them."

"Does you believe that 'ocus-pocus, Mr. Gubby?"

"Why, of course. It's a very wonderful thing."

Martha moved impatiently.

"Don't be a hidiot, Mr. Gubby. Sticks can't fly. I'm s'prised at your higgerance, me man—a flyin' stick, me backside. 'Twould be jus' as easy for me to go twirlin' round through th' air as one o' them sticks. It be a trick o' some sort same's them mountebanks an' gypsies do at the fairs when they pulls rabbits that ain't there out of 'ats, an' takes gold sovereigns out of your ear-'ole. Rabbits! Sovereigns! Flyin' sticks! Pickles!"

"Oh, very well, my dear," said Henry resignedly. He knew it was useless to argue with the strong-minded Martha.

The carriage pulled in among others close

to the scarlet-coated band, and Martha put up a blue silk parasol to shield her from the hot afternoon sun. People were gathering, young and old. Children, filled with an energy that only children possess, romped and ran here and there. Leather-lunged vendors of sweets; piemen; beggars; sly-grog sellers; touts for the brothels; keen-eyed wantons; constables; officers in colourful military and naval uniforms; ladies in coloured high-waisted silk gowns, with elaborate silk parasols, and with curls peeping from under bonnets or befeathered beavers; clergymen in long coats and gaiters; gentlemen in tall hats, coloured long coats, fancy waistcoats, and elegant trousers buckling under shining boots; artisans in check shirts, beaver hats and moleskin trousers, their wives in sober dresses and bonnets; a few good-conduct convicts with H.P.B. (Hyde Park Barracks) on their shirts; ear-ringed seamen clad in striped jerseys, glazed straw hats and canvas trousers; countrymen in cabbage-tree hats, coloured shirts and moleskins; drovers and teamsters on horse-back similarly attired but flaunting coloured neckerchiefs and huge spurs; bonnetted nursemaids, prim and soberly dressed; bonnetted governesses also prim and soberly dressed; business men and their wives; ragged urchins of both sexes; all were in holiday mood. And weaving in and out among the gathering carriages and throng were natives in nondescript attire, the gins carrying solemn piccaninnies on their backs.

Martha's attention was caught by a "crocodile" of schoolgirls undulating towards the band.

"I dunno, 'Arry boy," she said reflectively. "Some'ow I feels sorry for them schoolgels."

"Sorry? Good heavens! Why? They come from good homes, their people have money——"

" 'Taint that, Mr. Gubby. Boardin' schools mebbe all right for young'uns that 'as no 'omes, or whose folks be queer, or somethin', but I don't see 'ow children can know their parents—or their parents know *them*—when they only meets each other a few weeks hevery year."

"Oh, really, Martha. In England all the best people send their children to boarding schools. It's—it's a tradition——"

"H'm. Mebbe that's what's *wrong* with Hingland, Mr. Gubby. Too much dratted tradition an' not enough knowin' one another. But mebbe I be wrong. Mebbe—mebbe not."

"There's nothing wrong with England, Martha," said Henry testily. "It's a great country."

"Yus," said Martha dryly. "For the peacocks. I knows plenty it ain't great for—an' we was some of 'em."

"It takes all sorts to make a country, my dear."

"Yus, but all sorts don' get the bacon, Mr. Gubby. I be as Hinglish as you, Mr. Gubby, an' as proud of Hingland as you, Mr. Gubby, but that don' stop me seein' the mud in 'er eye. But we's not in Hingland now, so let's look about us."

Some people ignored the band and walked on down to the waterfront where the public baths were close to the fort, and where the headland sloped up to Mrs. Macquarie's chair. From Fort Macquarie right round Farm Cove the foreshore was animated and bright with colour. Others, across the Domain, were watching the blacks throw boomerangs and spears. Others, singly and in groups, were watching the start of a cricket match, the players all wearing top hats, the pitch being in the valley of the Domain. It was Christmas Day; it was holiday; and blue skies and sunshine brought most of Sydney out of doors to revel and, later, when the stars shone, to enjoy fireworks, to feast again, to dance, to romance.

But gone were the kangaroo-skin caps and parrots' feathers of the Currency lasses; gone the barefooted goose-girl with her crook; gone the grim convict transport with its sallow-faced cargo of chained felons. Right down the harbour, on the south side, were stately, tree-sheltered houses on headlands and back beyond the bays. Houses were also to be seen now on the winding northern heights. Sydney was growing fast. The harbour held the tall ships of the seven seas, but the beaches beyond Manly, and south of the Macquarie light, were deserted. No one bathed; no one was there; no houses on the coast looked out across the sea; and no one ever expected dwellings to fringe those lonely, wind-swept beaches where the only sounds to be heard were the wash of waves and the cries of sea-birds.

Martha listened to the band. She watched the gentlemen bowing to the ladies, the ladies curtsying to the gentlemen. She wondered what the first Governor, and all those who camped with him beside the Tank Stream, would think if they could see this scene.

Martha felt a great sense of contentment, and that feeling prompted thought for others.

"Mr. Gubby—I do 'ope them good folks, the Martins, will unnerstan' why I did it. As you know, I thought they was goin' to squat somewhere near those Limestone Plains not far from Yass, them plains near the Molonglo, I think they calls the river there, an' where that Governor's man——"

"I recall his name—Joshua John Moore."

"Yus. 'Im. Where 'e was the fust squatter, an' where the gov'ment also guv about the same time five thousan' acres to Robert Campbell, the merchant an' ship-owner who come from Calcutta in 1798. Campbell's buildin' a church there now. 'E's got a lot o' land somewhere's else, too."

"But the Martins must have gone right in towards the southwest somewhere, they probably turned in from the village of Gundagai that is built on the Murrumbidgee River flats——"

"That's right, Mr. Gubby. I've 'eard folks say the place'll be swep' away in a big flood some day. I 'opes not. But the Martins mus' be south o' Gundagai—well south of it from what you says that ol' Holiver said. They's honest folks an' deserves to get along."

"Yes, Martha. I'm sure they will understand. Perhaps they, too, are enjoying this Christmas Day."

Martha gave him a side glance. She seemed to chuckle deep within her.

"Folks in all th' Hostralian col'nies be celebratin' Christmas," she replied. "Every 'omestead an' grog-shanty outback, every lonely shepherd's 'ut, every shop in the towns, every mansion where the rich folks lives, every roadside inn, every farm-'ouse, all the ships, the barges an' cedar ketches, all be makin' good cheer no doubt. There'll be prayin' an' solemn worship in the churches, an' in many a private 'ouse. There'll be 'orse-races for the grown-ups an' billy-goat races for the young-uns. There'll be coach races, kerridge races, races on foot for heverybody. There'll be bull-baitin', dog-fights, bare knuckle fights, cock-fights an' rough-ridin' of wild 'orses. At night there'll be balls for the nobs, an' farm-'ouse dancin', bonfires an' crackers. Yus, all the col'ny'll be makin' merry this Christmas Day. An' as for the Martins—well, 'Arry boy, you'll be able to find that out when you gets there in a few days' time——"

Mr. Gubby started, stiffened, blanched and

then gasped: "Me? *Me?* Martha! What—what do you mean?"

"Jus' that you be agoin' there, Mr. Gubby, to fix up this land with the Martins. I'll get the dockyments all drawed up afore you goes."

Mr. Gubby's voice cracked, it was a mere squeak when he said, "Me? Go *there?* Out into those dreadful wilds? Oh, no, Martha—I'd be no use out there."

"Mr. Gubby," came evenly. "You ain't much use 'ere—an' you be agoin'. I can't go, an' if I remembers right you *wanted* to travel hoverland not so long ago. You can take all the papers an' get everythin' straightened out."

"But, Martha—how—how will I—? Oh, really, my dear, I'm not strong enough to endure such a journey."

"Mr. Gubby—Hi knows 'ow strong you be," was said deeply. "You—goes! Now, no more hargufyin'—it be a lovely Christmas Day. You—*goes!*"

Mr. Gubby seemed to shrink to an even smaller stature. He had wondered if she would propose such a thing as this. It had now been proposed—nay, commanded. It was no use wriggling, no use making excuses to the adamant Martha, no use telling her he was terrified at the prospect of such a journey. There was nothing he could say or do to extricate himself. He was trapped—*trapped*! She had him. He would have to travel alone, depend upon himself, face unknown perils. His mouth was suddenly dry; his throat seemed to have closed and he breathed with difficulty. Days and nights in a rocking, smelly coach! Blacks! Bushrangers! Wayside inns full of doubtful characters. Heat! Fatigue—dreadful fatigue! And supposing he met the Olivers? What would *they* do to him? He shivered as his mind raced; he was cold even in the hot sunshine. But there was no escape. She meant it. When her voice got down to that deep inexorable note—she *meant* it.

"Yes——" he croaked. "Yes, my dear. Of course . . . I go willingly, my dear. I would do anything for you . . . my dear."

"Mr. Gubby, I be proud of you," said Martha feelingly. "I alwus knowed you to be a man, Mr. Gubby. You used to be a drefful little weasel, but now I be proud of you—but you still *goes*!"

"Yes, my dear."

"Sam Pink——"

"Yus?" came mournfully.

"Drive us to where that Mrs. Macquarie used to set—an' don' forget to *crack* that whip so folks'll see us go by. I likes to see 'em nudge one another, an' 'ear 'em say, '*Them's* th' Gubbys!'"

18

IT was the second day in January when Elijah Tregg returned from Gundagai to the valley. He brought the mail. Martha's letter to John, and some English and Sydney papers Henry had thoughtfully sent, and also the information that the mounted police had gone to the Lake George district and would not return for some days. He was not surprised when he learnt that Royd was still at large.

"Allus was cunnin'," he said gruffly. "I don' want to talk 'bout 'im."

"Any other news?" John asked.

"Not much, Mr. Martin. Folks passin' through Gundagai tell of fallin' prices for everythin'. They be wearin' long faces now Christmas be over."

"Stock?"

"Goin' dirt cheap, Mr. Martin. Some men's bilin' down cattle an' sheep for taller—fust time I ever seed it done in a big way in the col'ny. It ain't good to see."

"That sounds serious, Tregg."

"Yus, Mr. Martin . . . but mebbe they's worser things . . . for some folks."

"Yes, I suppose so, Tregg," John said quietly.

Elijah asked slowly, "Be my gel any trouble, Mr. Martin?"

John answered instantly.

"No, Tregg. Do you want to take her back with you?"

Elijah looked at him.

"No, Mr. Martin—not if she be no trouble. If y' don' mind—I'd be gled for Annie to be 'ere awhiles yet. If you could use 'er as a sarvint I'd be gled for 'er to stay. Thar's . . . summat yet to be done . . . an' I'd rather she wasn't thar . . . when it be done."

John looked at the lined and dirty face of Elijah Tregg. But it was neither the deep lines nor the grimed-in dirt that he saw. Behind that grey face was the soul of a man in torment.

He said gently, "We like to have Annie with us, Tregg."

He watched Tregg walk away, stood watching until the man was out of sight. He sighed as he turned away. There was nothing more he could do. From the corn paddock, where the green stalks were now head high, Annie also saw her father come and go.

" 'Lijah's back," she said to Mark, who was hoeing the row next to hers.

"I saw him," said Mark without pausing in his work.

"Didn't bring no police."

"No."

Jeanette, who was hoeing on the other side of Annie, said, "I wonder if they'll come— but I suppose they must. Heavens, it's hot in this corn, but here comes Nan with some tea and damper. I'm wet through——"

"Me, too," said Annie. "Wish it was sundown, an' I was unner thet watterfall in the crick. Why don' Tilly do this work too?"

"She helps mother," said Jeanette. She hesitated a moment then asked, "Why is it you and Tilly don't like each other, Annie?"

" 'Tain't me, Jeanette," Annie said quickly. "I allus wanted to be frien's, but—but Tilly—well, she don' like me."

"I think you're holding something back——"

"I ain't sayin' nothin' 'bout Tilly, Jeanette," Annie said evenly. "Tilly be your sister. If she don' like me—she don' 'ave to. I can look after m'self—allus 'ave."

Nan came along the row, her face under her bonnet flushed with the heat.

"Goodness—it's hot!" she panted as she put down the can of tea and the knotted cloth holding the buttered damper. "Your father's been here, Annie."

"Seed 'im. What's adoin' of, Nan?"

"I don't really know, Annie. But I heard father tell mother you were to stay with us."

Mark, with a gun in his hands, came through the corn. Jeanette also brushed aside the leafy stalks and stepped through, her dark hair damp with perspiration, her olive skin gleaming with it.

"Another acre to do," said Mark as he sat down. "We'll have a fine crop."

"Here's your tea," said Nan.

The girls sat down, the corn giving a stifling shade. The heat and the hot tea brought the sweat trickling out of them.

"It's hot work," said Mark, wiping his face on his arm. "But I daresay in a few months the wind will come out of those mountains and freeze us."

"It's dem cold," said Annie. "So cold it burns——"

"Burns?" said Nan with a laugh.

"Yus, Nan—burns. Like a fire only

diff'rent. Can't tell it no other way. Watter all be's ice, but flesh burns. Jesus! It be terrible cold."

"Annie, really!" said Jeanette severely.

"Ar—yus! I didn't mean nothin', Jeanette. I was just thinkin' of the cold. When y' on'y got a thin dress an' nothin' unner it, it makes y' say things. Gawd—I bin blue all over—an' time was I couldn't——"

"Annie!" exclaimed Nan and Jeanette.

Annie sighed.'

"Well, never mind. Ain't the police comin', Nan?"

"Father didn't say. I suppose he'll tell us the news at supper. He got a letter and some papers from England——"

"From England?" came excitedly from Mark and Jeanette.

"They're last June's papers so we'll get the latest news from home."

"I wonder if there'll be any news from Kent," said Mark. "Doesn't it seem an age since we left?"

"Goodness, yes," said Nan. "More tea, Annie?"

"Yus, Nan—I c'd do another swaller. But it makes y' sweat—I can feel it runnin' down atween me——"

"Annie!" came sharply from the two girls.

"Me eyes," said Annie with a faint smile. "An' you two needn't pick me up so quick—I won' say the wrong things in front o' Mark. I never 'ave—'ave I, boy?"

"Of course not, Annie. Where's Tom, Nan?"

"He and father are doing something to some of the calves——"

"Takin' 'em out, eh?" said Annie unconcernedly. "I seed 'Lijah do thet to one of Oliver's bulls—to make beef later on——"

Jeanette gulped and spluttered as she tried to swallow her tea. Mark rolled over and buried his face in his hands. Nan gasped and made a great show of pouring tea. Annie eyed them suspiciously.

"Ar—well," she said. "No more tea for me, Nan——"

As she stood up she gave a sharp exclamation and pointed.

"Blacks! Ain't seed any for a long time now. An' naked. Every mother's son of 'em."

Mark took one look, then said as he started to walk away:

"Come on! They might get cheeky with only mother and Tilly in the house."

"Oh, I—I couldn't go while they're—they're like *that*!" panted Jeanette.

Annie stared at her. "They won't 'urt you, Jeanette. They used to come to our 'ut sometimes. But we never 'ad nothin' to give 'em, so they didn't come much——"

"Perhaps they *won't* hurt me, Annie," said the slightly exasperated Jeanette. "But the men are naked. We can't go while they are there."

"What 'bout your mother an' Tilly?" Annie asked dryly. "Ain't they thar?"

"Tilly'll scream and run into her room—she'll be terrified," said Jeanette. "So would I be."

"Yus," said Annie. "I knows what Tilly'll do. Them blacks be 'armless—'less you injures one of 'em. Ar—come on! This ain't no time to be as silly as a duck."

"No! I'm not going!" said Jeanette firmly.

"Nor I," panted Nan. "And I don't think you ought to, Annie. It isn't decent——"

"Lawks! 'Lijah says they bin like thet since the stars was made——"

"Well, I don't have to look at them," said Jeanette flatly.

"No. Mark will call father and Tom," said Nan. "They're savages—beasts. The impudence of them to come to our house like—like that——"

"You got their land, ain't you?" asked Annie.

"You do have quaint ideas, Annie," said Jeanette. "It's *not* their land. That's a lot of nonsense. All they've ever done is roam over it—little better than the animals they hunt. Even if they have been here since the stars were made they've done nothing with it—they've made nothing, done nothing, not even to one acre of all this vast country. They are no more good to the land than those cockatoos up in that tree over there——"

"Ar—you's judgin' 'em by y'selves, Jeanette," said Annie quietly. "It's only folks as don' unnerstan' 'em as talks like you does. I seed a lot o' blacks in Van Diemen's Land, Port Phillip, an' 'ere. They can be good frien's, sometimes they's bin th' only ones I ever 'ad——"

"You've been *friends* with blacks?" asked the wide-eyed Jeanette.

"Yus. I've played with the piccaninnies an' talked with the gins. You treat 'em proper 'an you'll 'ave good frien's in the bush. But treat 'em bad—an' mebbe they'll spear you—an' sarve you right."

The two girls stared at her.

"I don't understand you, Annie," said Jeanette.

"Mebbe, Jeanette. I've 'ad to live different to yous. I was borned out 'ere—you wasn't. When white folks wouldn't talk to me—the blacks would. See? You can go to th' 'ouse—they won' 'urt you?"

"No!" from Jeanette and Nan.

"S'posin' they come walkabout into this 'ere corn—what you goin' to do? Shoo 'em away like they was a lot o' black roosters? You try *thet* an' you'll see somethin' thet'll make your eyes pop out."

"Mark knows we are here—he wouldn't let them come here," said Jeanette.

Annie looked at her for a moment.

"I 'opes you Martins don' do nothin' stoopid. Mebbe you thinks I got a lot to larn—the ways you-all looks at things—but *you* got to larn to know the bush, an' all thet be's in it—an' thet means the blacks, too. I be's agoin' to the 'ouse to see yous don' do somethin' foolish. The blacks'll know me, an' I can talk to 'em——"

The girls looked at her in astonishment.

"Can you speak their language?" asked Nan in great surprise.

"Yus—not bad. I picked up some o' th' Wurindjeri jus' north o' Melbourne. But these blacks be the Wongals. I don' know all their wuds, but I can yabber pretty well to 'em. I'll be back—if you're goin' to be daffy an' stop 'ere."

They watched her run through the corn rows and make for the house.

"She's a strange girl," said Jeanette.

"Yes. But—but somehow I think she was the only one of us who talked sense," said Nan thoughtfully.

"Nan!"

"I'm beginning to think so, Jeanette, although like you, I couldn't bring myself to go to the house. She knows this valley and its native people—we don't. I called them savages, beasts. For a moment I thought she had nothing but—but——"

"But what?" Jeanette demanded.

"Contempt for me," said Nan. "We've all looked down on Annie, but a moment ago she showed us something——"

"What in all the world did she show us?"

"That she had common sense—wisdom, even. I don't think I'll be so superior in future. After all, I can't speak any other language. She may be a great help to us in this valley."

Jeanette pursed her lips thoughtfully.

"Perhaps," she said at last. "I like Annie. I think she's honest—especially with herself. But those blacks—oh, lawks, Nan! I—I just couldn't——"

All at once Nan gave a little giggle.

"No——" she choked. "Neither could I, Jeanette——"

"Oh, Nan!"

"Oh, well, I—I—Jeanette! Jeanette!" Nan's expression had altered.

"What is it?"

"*Royd Tregg*! We're here alone in this tall corn—he could creep up on us—we'd never see him——"

Jeanette began to breathe quickly.

"Heavens——" she muttered. "I forgot about him. Perhaps we'd better follow Annie. Oh, this is dreadful—degrading——"

"If it's the blacks—or Tregg—I'm going," said Nan. "We—we can shut our eyes——"

"Yes! Run! We can't stay here alone. Run, Nan——"

The two girls ran like hares to the house, burst in through the back door and into their room. Tilly was there, white-faced and shaken.

"Don't go outside——" she hissed. "Blacks!"

"We saw them—where's mother?"

"In her room. Mother nearly collapsed——"

"Who's with them?" asked Nan.

"That little slut, Annie. She has no sense of decency——"

"Aren't father and Tom and Mark there, too?" asked Jeanette.

"I think so—I can hear voices——"

"Is Annie talking to them."

"How do I know? I flew in here. My goodness what a shock! I heard strange voices outside. I went to the foor. There were seven tall blackfellows—and nothing else. I—I think I screamed. Mother came running, then she screamed. Jeanette, Nan—they hadn't a *stitch* on them. Oh, my! I heard Mark's voice, then Annie's. Listen——"

They listened and heard a confused sound of voices. Sometimes John's, sometimes Mark's, but mostly Annie's followed by an excited babble in some aboriginal language. She was evidently talking to the natives.

"She can speak their language," said Nan.

Tilly sneered. "I'm not surprised."

"Perhaps it's fortunate for us she can," said Jeanette.

"Why?" Tilly wanted to know.

"Well, *we* can't talk to them——"

"In heaven's name who wants to?" cried Tilly. "Surely we didn't come to New South Wales to—to talk to blackfellows."

"They had no spears, Annie said. Listen——"

They heard someone go into the storeroom. Outside the black men were laughing. Annie was laughing.

"I wonder what she's saying to them," said Nan.

"I wish she'd go back where she belongs," said Tilly. "Someone's in the storeroom——"

"Tom," said Jeanette. "I can tell his walk——"

Cries, laughter and quick-fire talk came to them. They heard Tom go out. Then more yells of laughter, then, after a while, the voices of the blacks began to fade.

"They're going," said Jeanette.

"Thank God," said Tilly. "I never want to see *them* again——"

The three girls went cautiously to the front

door. Hetty, pale-faced and trembling, joined them.

"Are they gone, John?" she asked.

"Yes, wife. Don't be frightened. We'll have nothing to fear from these natives—thanks to Annie."

"Annie?" asked Hetty wonderingly.

"Yes," said Tom laughingly. "I believe she actually *scolded* them."

"Yus, I did," said Annie. "I tol' 'em never to come 'ere like they was—they mustn't be cheeky. I tol' 'em you was their frien's. I tol' 'em to leave your stock an' belongin's alone, an' they'd be treated well. An' they wasn't to bring all the tribe to squat 'ere. I tol' 'em 'bout Royd, an' they'll watch for 'im—they'll soon find 'im—y'can't 'ide from a blackfeller in the bush. They bin out o' the valley awhiles—down in the lower river country. Don' you worrit, Mrs. Martin—them Wongals'll never 'urt you so long's you don' 'urt 'em."

Hetty was amazed.

"Well, I do declare!" she exclaimed. "That is . . . remarkable."

"Indeed it is," said John. "Although not armed their eyes were distrustful and fierce. But when Annie came their faces lit up. I could see they knew her. I couldn't believe my ears when she began talking to them. Well done, Annie. You have well repaid anything we have done for you."

"Thet wasn't much, Mr. Martin. But you was wrong when you said they wasn't armed——"

"Wrong? I saw no weapons, Annie."

The girl smiled.

"The grass be long whar they stood, Mr. Martin. They 'ad spears, all right."

"But, where?" asked Mark. "I couldn't see any——"

"Nor I," said Tom.

"They drag 'em through the grass with their toes—they can use them toes like fingers. I knowed they 'ad 'em, an' they knowed I knowed. I tol' 'em so, an' they bust out laffin'. They likes a joke so long's it be a frien'ly joke. An' they can laugh at themselves, which be more'n a lot of white folks can do. I can drag them spears, too, but nothin' as good as them. They bin doin' it all their lives."

John's face was serious.

"I am glad you were here, Annie," he said soberly. "But I am astonished, very astonished. I've certainly learnt a lesson today."

"So have I," said Tilly coldly. "I can't imagine how a white girl can confront such—such men. And to speak their language, and know their clever tricks, hints at a rather close association with them, I should think."

Annie's eyes glinted as she turned and faced Tilly.

"Yus—you *should* think, but you never does. Your haid be as empty as a cracked aig. If you 'ad fevvers on you'd be even too silly for the ducks—an' Gawd knows all they can do is quack——"

"Now, my dears," said Hetty hastily. "I think Annie has helped us very much. Thank you, Annie. Tilly just doesn't understand."

"Oh, she unnerstan's, Mrs. Martin," said Annie evenly. "An' so does I, an' *thet's* what's gettin' 'unner 'er skin. But if she *won't* 'ave no more sense than a 'airy goat——"

Tilly was white with anger, and her mouth was thin and ugly.

"I won't be spoken to like this," she said shrilly. "She does nothing but insult me whenever she can. Do we *have* to have her here?"

Annie gave her look for look.

"You's a dem liar, Tilly Martin," she flung at her. "An' I says thet in front of your folks

316

to you. You guv me dirt when you tried to make out jist now I was no better'n a black-feller's moll. But when it comes to molls—you watch y' tongue—or mebbe I'll loose mine. I ain't takin' your bleddy sauce no more, Tilly Martin, an' you better knows it——"

"Enough!" cried John sternly. "Tilly, you started this. Go inside. I want to talk to you. You go with Annie, Mark. Nan and Jeanette—I want you also in the house. Tom, I'll join you presently——"

As Annie and Mark walked back to the corn Mark said with a smile, "My! You can be a spitfire, Annie."

She turned anxious brown eyes to him.

"Can I, boy? I don' want to do nothin' you wouldn't like me to."

"You haven't. As father said, Tilly started it. It's about time she came to her senses. I'd like to hear what he says to her—it'll sting. He's stern, but fair. I think you taught all the Martins a lesson today when you talked to the blacks as you did."

"You liked—what I did?" she asked a little breathlessly.

"Yes. And I know you did it for us."

She watched him obliquely, very intently.

"Does you like me, boy?" she asked, her voice not quite steady.

"Yes," Mark jerked out. "I do."

They went into the corn. The long green leaves brushed them as they walked along a row. Annie faced him when they came to where the hoes had been dropped.

"Boy—Mark! You *does* like me—different like?"

Mark was trembling.

"I said I do, Annie."

He could hear her quick breathing. She watched him. There was something she had to find out.

" 'Nough for me . . . to be your gel?" she asked direct. "I mus' know—it be knockin' at me. I mus' know, Mark."

He nodded as he said awkwardly:

"Yes . . . enough for that, Annie. Only——"

Her eyes searched his. She knew what was in his mind.

"Only I be a convic's gel—eh?"

"I told you," Mark said almost fiercely. "I don't hold that against you."

"Your ol' man?" she insisted.

"Yes——" came honestly. "Father."

" 'E wouldn't like me bein' your gel?"

"No, Annie . . . he wouldn't," he admitted.

318

"No—'e couldn't," she said haltingly. "You be only a young boy, yet. Ar—I better go 'way, Mark——"

"No!" the word came sharply. "I don't want you to go away. There's no need to talk about ourselves to anyone—yet. Sit down, Annie——"

They sat down on the warm earth, and were screened by the tall corn. So they sat looking at each other, a boy and a girl, both very young, both very conscious of the other, aware of this moment of drawing together. Mark said hesitantly:

"Annie . . . Annie . . ."

She watched him as he leant towards her. "Yus . . . I be waitin', Mark . . ."

He took her in his arms and pressed her back. She lay still while his arms held her so that she could scarcely breathe, while his lips were on hers. Her arms went round him and held him to her. Wildly she kissed him.

"Mark—from thet very fust night—in the firelight——"

"I saw you, too. I wanted to see you again——"

Fiercely she held him to her.

"Boy—boy——"

In a little while she said, "I dunno what

319

you'll think of me, mebbe, Mark. Not for anythin' in all the world would I 'urt you or bring 'arm to you——"

He looked down at her.

"Annie—you stay. You *must* stay."

"Yus——" she said very softly. "I'll stay, boy, so long's I'm let."

Mark stood up. Annie sat looking up at him.

"You got a good mind, boy, Mark," she said. "You didn't try to paw me. I wanted to know whether you wanted me right. I would 'ave gone all cold if you'd wanted jist—thet. You don' think I'm what Tilly tried to make out, does you?"

"Tilly's spiteful sometimes. Of course I don't."

She stood up. Then she smiled at him.

"Will you larn me more letters, Mark?" she asked.

He laughed.

"Yes, Annie. Tonight. Here comes Jeanette. We'd better be busy——"

"Yus," breathed Annie, "we better. Ain't it a *wunnerful* day. Mark?"

He nodded.

"Wonderful," he said quietly.

He laughed a little again. He was still

320

emotionally shaken by his physical contact with her.

"It takes time, Annie, to learn . . . well, to learn anything," he said.

"Yus—it do. I'm gled it do. I'll never f'git what you be doin' for me, Mark, or what you jist said——"

He looked at her.

"I don't want you to forget it. I meant it."

"Ah——" she said very softly. "But be you sure what you jist said an' done—thet way you 'eld me, thet way you kissed me—ain't jist this dem valley amakin' you like this? Places like this makes some men want a gel—even the gins—lonely men. I've 'eard folks atalkin'—an' I've seen—what I've seen m'self—yus; in this 'ere valley——"

Mark shook his head.

"What I said—was said to you, Annie. The valley has nothing to do with it."

Annie was smiling as she bent to pick up the hoe.

"I won' 'urt you none, boy, Mark— *never*!" she said gently. "No, never!"

19

THE night held just enough moonlight to enable anyone to see a moving object. The enclosing hills were high walls of darkness. It was a hot night, with a resounding frog-chorus echoing rhythmically from the dark fringes of creek and pool. In the wan light the trees were ghostly, very still, touched with moonlight yet brushed with darkness. And now and then there would be a sudden whirring of unseen wings, a screech, a fluttering down of feathers as predatory owl or night-hawk seized its prey. And where the sheep were bunched on Oliver's property the dingo killed.

Elijah carried his long rifle, heavily charged with powder and ball as he walked through the shadows towards the Olivers' house. He also carried sombre thoughts. His heavy face was creased and weary whenever the faint light revealed it; his powerful, barrel-like body swayed from side to side as soundless bare feet took him on his way. He realized now he had lived his life, a poor life, a useless life. A world he did not know was rising all round him; he and his children were not a part of it; they were cast-offs from departed years. When he was pardoned, and when Sarah was pardoned, there seemed to be a light in the sky, a promise of better and happier days to come. But that was a long time ago. Royd would be twenty-six now.

What years! The pardons? A mockery for Sarah and for him. Yes; they were free, but the irons he had once worn were mere cotton threads compared with the invisible bonds of prejudice and hatred and open contempt he and his had been fettered with ever since. Unwanted. Despised. Avoided. Scorned. That had been the story of the Treggs, of many like the Treggs. There was no real forgiveness in the hearts of men: once the brand was fixed it burned in through the cloth to the flesh, and through the flesh to the soul.

Convict!

Within view of England's greatest church, St. Paul's, he had stolen bread so that he might live. Yes; he had lived since then—like a dog. Only the Olivers had helped. Helped? Elijah thought back over it. They had not helped—they had *used*. Royd's madness,

Sarah's death, his poverty-ridden, ignorant family, the seeds of all these things and more were sown the day he was brought before the scarlet-robed judge, and was sentenced to transportation to Van Diemen's Land. Seven years in irons. Seven *years*—in irons! Royd was not right when born. He knew Sarah's fierce love for the afflicted child; he did not understand it through any explanation by mere words, but by a deep, wordless feeling and instinct.

Sarah! She had been a good-looker when she first came from the Factory to the Olivers—tall, fair, and she could still smile. He remembered that smile. But it faded, as did the corn-ripe hair, with the futility of frustrated age. He had never had anything to give Sarah—only want and whatever bones the Olivers threw to him. But through it all she had stuck to him, especially to Royd. Strangely enough, now she was gone from him, he saw it all so plainly. In constant association, day by day, the usual routine of merely keeping alive had not brought any deep reflection. Of what use would reflection have been? Nothing could have been altered, nothing more done. Now she was gone, beaten down to a bloody death by the son she had served so long, so well.

Royd. Johnnie. Rock. Dick. Meg. Annie. They had come in that order. Of all of them only Dick and Annie had the wish or will to rise out of poverty and ignorance. Broad-faced, lumbering Dick, a quiet fellow, seemed to sense the need to get above the life that bound him. His quick acceptance of John Martin's offer to farm showed that. Johnnie, Rock and Meg had no desire to alter their wild and useless way of life. Annie? She was different from all of them. There were depths in Annie entirely lacking in the fierce, impulsive Meg. Her words on the morning of Sarah's death had startled him, had, in a way, shamed him, too. But what could he do? He was nothing, he had nothing, at least not until John Martin made his offer. No other man had ever done that for the Treggs. Elijah hoped Annie would stay with the Martins; they might make something of her, give her vision, and decency, and self-respect—if that could ever be.

And Royd?

Elijah's eyes were watchful as he went along. The mounted police would come in a few days. He knew their kind, that many of them were old lags, vicious, bitter, cruel. They would kill Royd—shoot him like a dog. And they would be justified. Royd had turned killer, and would kill again if his maddened mind impelled him. The Olivers, too, would shoot Royd, because of their fear. And for that they could not be blamed. And the Martins? Perhaps they, too, might have to kill him. But no one knew where Royd was. Evidently he moved about only at night, some deep cunning telling him there was menace for him in the valley in daylight. Yes; he would move at night, getting what food he could, wandering, mad, and filled with all the awful images and obsessions of that madness. Elijah was satisfied Royd was still in the valley; he knew something—*something*—would keep his son in the valley, an impression, perhaps, that it was still his home, a blurred familiarity with his surroundings, a distorted awareness that his people were here.

It was no more than nine o'clock as Elijah walked along the valley. He had papers and some letters for the Olivers sent by way of Gundagai. Meg had offered to take them, but he could not allow the girl to risk the lonely walk. He was not concerned about the Wongals; like Annie and Meg, he could talk to them. Royd, in his sane moments, had been bitterly resentful of Meg, hating her because of her fierce arguments with Sarah. And Meg had ever been jealous of Royd and had no sympathy for him, often mocking him, and taunting him simply to revenge herself on Sarah. It would not do for Royd and Meg to meet. In all the long stretch of the valley, and for miles and miles around it, only three lights showed—the lamp of the Olivers, now that of the Martins, and the fire-glow of the Treggs. Yes; it was lonely; it would never do for Royd and Meg to meet. Thoughtful, watchful, Elijah plodded on.

In the Olivers' house Jane took up her candle and said good night to the others. Tomorrow would see her and Conway on their way to Melbourne in the big, covered dray. She was sensible of excitement at the prospect of going again to the town. People. Shops. Dresses. A day on the bay. Gentlemen. Conversation. Entertainment. And somebody else to do the cooking. And, on her own responsibility, she would make inquiries, unknown to her father, about selling this valley property and buying land in some other part of the colony. She had not mentioned her intention of doing this, but she was determined upon it. This was no place for her. She would be old, withered and grey before any suitable man's eyes rested on her. And she had a right to think of herself, for herself. If she could get a good offer for the property, and her father refused to consider it, she would raise hell itself until he saw reason. Oh, yes, she would. She would *not* be buried alive among these frowning, empty hills, with no other white woman of her own class to talk to, with nothing before her but monotonous days and still more monotonous nights.

In her room, with the door shut, she raised the candle and looked long at her reflection in the looking-glass. She was twenty-five years of age, not pretty, perhaps, but her face had character. Dark hair, dark eyes, perhaps a little close together like those of all the Olivers, a straight nose and firm mouth. She looked at her image intently. Her figure was slender, not tall, but well enough proportioned to be attractive. Nodding to herself, she considered she was still presentable, still firm and young enough to be desired by someone—someone of standing and substance, of course. But the years were passing. She was facing time now, and was aware of it, time that would bring those tiny lines, those tell-tale little lines, to brow and throat, those inexorable warning lines that gave their hateful signals to the observant eyes of men. But they had yet to come; there was still time providing she got out of this valley before it was too late—yes; before it was too late.

She undressed. She placed the lighted candle on the small chest beside her bed. She could hear, faintly, the droning voices of her father and brothers out in the living-room. It was hot. She lay on top of the sheet, clad in a thin cotton night-dress. It had been a torrid day, the heat beating down through unmoving air. At sunset there had been a low rumble of thunder over the west hills, but the storm was far away. As she lay thinking, she could hear the usual night sounds without: the scuffle and bark of opossums in the nearby trees; the stamp of a horse's hoof; the bawling of a calf; the soft bleat of sheep on the hillside. Insects flew in a little cloud round the candle-flame, died in it, and covered the base of the candle-stick. Mosquitoes sang in the shadowed corners waiting for the light to go out before swooping, and hearing them she decided that although it would be stifling she would drop the net to keep them away. Anxiously she examined the walls for the large, creeping tarantulas; she hated them, but none was to be seen. She blew out the light. Presently she heard the scrape of chairs as her brothers rose to go to bed. She listened to their footsteps. Then her father rose and went out through the back door. She waited for his returning footsteps, and after a while she heard them. He went back into the living-room, and she heard the creak of his high chair. It was yet early, just going on for ten, and he did not usually retire until later. She would not drop the net yet.

Jane had had enough of the company of her brothers. She wanted to be by herself so that her mind could anticipate the delights of being once again in a town where people moved and laughed and spoke to one another. She would like to go to Sydney Town, but it was much farther away. In the next room she heard her brothers talking, heard boots being dropped on the boards, the creak of a bed. Conway's and Elliott's voices mounted a little, but presently they stopped talking and were quiet. The heat held, the house would not cool. Jane lay damp and uncomfortable, tossing from side to side to get brief respite from the heated clothes. Thought held her. Twenty-five! Soon she would be thirty. She would not hurry back from Melbourne; the men could look after themselves here. She would have a good look at Melbourne Town, and allow it to have a similar appraisal of her. Twenty-five! Her hands were critical as they felt the contours of body and limbs. But she was not yet old, thank God. Would she ever marry? She lay unmoving at the thought. Not that she wanted marriage for its own sake, or any man for the mere transient pleasure of his company. Oh, no! Jane knew why she desired marriage: she wanted to be a name in the colony, desired her house to be acclaimed, her lands and wealth envied. For those things she would suffer the nuisance of physical surrender, would tolerate some gentleman in his crude moments of possession. But he *must* be a gentleman—at least during daylight hours. And she would soon break him in to the strong curb of her own will. It might be her husband's voice others heard, but it would be Jane Oliver's mind in matters of moment.

And if she did not marry? The thought set her moving restlessly again. Good God! Would she have to live out her life in this valley? Growing old, bitter, a tottering frustrate hating her own flesh and blood, hating everybody, hating herself most of all? She could imagine herself in another thirty years—thin, grey, silent, looking back upon nothing, looking forward to . . . nothing.

But it was not the impact of that thought that chilled her all at once. It was a sound. A sound in her room. A slight sound. As if a board had creaked under a heavy foot. But there was no sound of a footstep. But a board *had* creaked. She knew the very board; it often did so under her own tread. Wide-eyed, mouth open, her breathing almost stilled, she listened. There was no sound. The board did not creak again. But she could not be mistaken. And then she heard him breathing. A silly prank? Everitt? Conway? Elliott? Her father? No. *No! Royd Tregg!* He must have slipped in through the back door when her father went out. Royd! And he was between her and the door. If she screamed she would feel the awful stroke of that merciless chain. She had not heard the chain, but he must still have it with him. She felt as though her heart would burst with its wild pumping; her limbs were lifeless; but slowly she sat up, very slowly, and then she screamed, but only a faint muffled sound came from her lips. A rough hand had clamped itself over her mouth, and she felt herself hurled back. Little bubbling noises came as she writhed, but another hand held her, pinning her down, a hand that gripped her throat and set her brain spinning. She was stiff and helpless with horror. She knew the purpose of this madman: she would be taken until he was sated and then killed as old Sarah had been killed. She tried desperately to struggle, tried to summon enough effort to break away, but terror swept all strength from her, and just before her senses left her she felt herself being lifted up in huge arms. He was taking her out of the room, taking her away to where he could rape her—where none would ever find her. But even as the knowledge roared in her mind all thought snapped and her feeble struggling ceased.

And then she knew she was screaming, and that there was a bright light in her eyes. She heard someone saying over and over "Jane— Jane—Jane! Jane—Jane—Jane!" It was her father's voice. Out of the blurred images all round her the faces of her father, of Everitt, Conway and Elliott, came slowly into focus. Someone poured brandy into her mouth. She spluttered as she screamed and spluttering, swallowed the brandy. Her mind cleared. She looked about her. She was in her room, her father and brothers were beside her bed, all looking down at her.

"She's all right," Conway said.

Jane blinked at the lamp, and memory surged back.

"Royd——" she shrieked. "Royd—he came——"

"Yes," said Henry Oliver. "He came. But calm yourself, Jane. He'll never come here again."

She tried to sit up, but Conway gently restrained her.

"Where is he?" she choked. "Where is he——?"

"With the devil," said Conway harshly. "Elijah shot him as he was carrying you out of the house."

Her dark eyes were wide, uncomprehending.

"Elijah—shot Royd? I—I don't understand——" she panted.

"Yes—shot him," said Henry. His voice sounded thin and old, lacking its usual snap and authority, a voice drained of its arrogance, having a sound like the rustling of dry leaves. "I heard some slight noise, and brought out the lamp to see what it was. I almost collapsed when I saw Royd standing just outside the back door with you in his arms. He had the chain wound round his middle, the end tucked in. Elijah, who was bringing some letters and papers mailed from Sydney, also saw him. God! I can hear Tregg's voice now. I'll hear it to the end of my days. 'Royd——' he said. I can't describe how he said it—it seemed to rip, yes, *rip* through the air. 'Royd—stand still!' And Royd stood still. 'Royd—put Miss Oliver down!' And Royd let you slide to the ground. 'Royd—step forward!' And Royd did so. I stood, unable to move. The moon was down. The rays of the lamp shone upon it all. 'Royd—one more step!' Royd took the step. God! It seemed as if he knew Elijah's voice. Then Elijah shot him. That was something I shall never forget. Royd lurched, the ball must have been already in his heart, but as he sank his eyes were wide, his great head back, his mouth all froth and blood. And I heard him say, ' 'Lijah! 'Lijah! 'Lijah!' It was a weak cry, and pitiful. Elijah stood like a stone man, the smoking gun in his hands. His eyes seemed as lightless, as lifeless as Royd's, but from them tears were falling. Tears. Such tears. His face was as old and sad as time itself. He had executed his own son. Few men are called upon ever to do that. They're out there now, Elijah crouched beside him, holding him in his arms. He did not speak again as he sat with his dead son. Presently he will take Royd away. But not yet . . . not yet . . ."

20

ELIJAH TREGG had gone under arrest to Melbourne Town. Jane, Conway and Henry Oliver had followed the mounted police and their prisoner, Jane and Henry being the principal witnesses. Elijah would have to answer for the killing of his son. He trudged along beside the trooper's horse, a long, thin chain fastened round his neck. At night he was chained to a convenient tree, as Royd had been. He spoke to no one. He seemed to be without realization, without feeling, and his eyes appeared to be staring always at something, or someone, no one else could see. There were two graves now under Royd's tree.

The day after he was taken away John made ready to leave for Sydney. He would take the coach for Sydney Town at Yass. Early in the morning, as he sat in the saddle, he looked down at his family. Annie was inside the house.

"You will be all right, wife," he said. "There is no more trouble in the valley. The blacks are friendly, and that terrible thing is ended. The constable took statements from myself and Annie about Sarah Tregg's death, and no doubt there will be an inquiry sometime in the future. What will happen to Tregg we don't yet know. But I'll be all right, I have a good horse, and I have my pistols."

"And we'll be all right, John," said Hetty. "Come back as soon as you can, my dear, for we shall miss you. And do remember us all to Marth Gubby."

"I shall."

Hetty's face was anxious.

"And *do* watch for bushrangers and other evil-doers, John. Trust no one, my dear——"

"I'll watch. Tom and Mark should have the timber for the new barn felled before I get back. We'll need it to hold the corn and potatoes, to say nothing of an acre of turnips."

"Yes, dear. And *do* mind your horse doesn't stumble and throw you—it's such lonely country, no one would ever know——"

"He won't. Now, now, no tears, Hetty. Tom—Mark!"

"Yes, father——"

"Cut enough for the woolshed and runs we planned. We'll be washing and shearing when I get back. There aren't many sheep, but they have to be done—and Nan!"

"Yes, father?"

"Keep the pigs penned. They'll ruin the corn and potatoes if let out now. There is plenty of milk and green corn for them. And a word more to all of you——" and he looked at Tilly as he spoke. "Be kind to Annie Tregg, and to the others if they come here. Well, I must be off. I have three hundred miles to go. It's a long journey, and no doubt I shall be away for some weeks. Good-bye, and God keep you all——"

"Good-bye, father. A safe journey——"

"Good-bye, John . . . good-bye, my dear. God keep you . . . and send you back to us. . . ."

Hetty blinked back her tears as John turned the grey and rode away. Although she would have her family she would be lonely without him, counting the days until she heard his voice calling as he rode back down the valley. They all stood together until he reached a bend where he reined in and looked back. There they were, all he had in the world, all that mattered and was precious to him—his family and his home. He saw them wave to him; he waved back, and then went on.

Gradually, as the horse loped along, his thoughts turned to the journey and the business before him. If Martha did not press for heavy and quick repayments all would be well, and he felt sure she would not do that. He would need returns from more stock to make satisfactory repayments, and would have to improve the valley's natural pastures if he wished to run several large flocks. Good English grasses—rib and burnett—with fields of rye and oats and wheat for stacks would allow him to graze heavily. He would have to explain all that to Martha. And perhaps he would purchase some young Neapolitan boars to cross with his British Blacks, and a good Saxon-Merino ram or two from the famous Macarthur flocks at Camden, although he wondered if his own run was a little too far south for fine-woolled sheep.

He wished he had a dray full of salted butter, cheese and bacon to take to Sydney with him, although, normally, Melbourne Town, being a good hundred miles closer, would be his market. He knew that settlers on the Yass plains, the Goulburn plains, the Lake George country, the Limestone plains, and down the long road through Berrima, Bargo and Liverpool, all sent fat cattle and sheep to Sydney every half year, as well as carts laden with wheat, wool and dairy produce. But it would be some time before he could do that.

The journey itself would be tiresome; he would not have time to visit the established homesteads along the route. The mail coach wasted no time, and on the long stretches, after changing horses and drivers, it would rattle on through the night, bumping over the rough tracks, its lamps lighting fitfully the bobbing backs of the horses, and the dark bordering trees as they passed by. After passing through Jugiong, Breadalbane and Baw Baw, it would stop briefly at Goulburn Town—not the old village, but the new township near by—after rolling across the splendid Goulburn plains where swans, ducks and teal ignored fat cattle and sheep at the ponds. Then rough country, hilly and harsh with gnarled trees and rocky spurs, then Berrima village that had ousted Bong Bong, then the hospitable Cutter's Inn at Old Mittagong, then Lupton's Inn at Bargo, then the restful Traveller's Inn at Myrtle Creek. Then, with the dome of Liverpool's hospital in sight, there would be little more than twenty miles to go to Sydney Town, the end of the long journey by horseback and jolting coach.

And a little over twenty years before there had scarcely been a settler or squatter in all the sweep of country through which he would pass. In that short time the plains, the valleys, the forest areas, the river frontages, had been widely selected to confirm grants, or taken up under a "ticket of occupation". But, even so, the homesteads were far apart; shepherds' slab huts and stockmen's sod dwellings were miles from each other. Men and women whose names today are history rode or went in slow bullock-drawn drays over the trackless places seeking land for their homes and their flocks; Joshua John Moore, the pioneer of the present Canberra Territory, and also squatter of Baw Baw; Robert Campbell, Sydney's first ship merchant, who took up land near Moore's, and also near Tumbarumba; Alexander McLeay and his sons, of the Cowpastures; the Macarthurs of Parramatta and Camden fame; the Coxes of Lovely Mulgoa; Hamilton Hume and his brother, J. K. Hume, who pioneered the Yass district; Andrew Gibson of Tirrana; Broughton and Kennedy of Appin; the Bradleys of Goulburn; Antill and Cowper of

Picton; Coghill of Oxley's "Kirkham"; Lockyer of "Ermington"; Nicholson of "Newbury"; Edward and George Riley of Mittagong; Hutchinson of "Throsby Park"; Hannibal Macarthur of "Arthursleigh"; James Rose of Goulburn plains; Henry O'Brien of the Yass plains; John Manton of Yass River; William Lithgow of Goulburn; William Macarthur, son of the famous John, who selected near Goulburn; Allen of Lake George; Balcombe of the Molonglo plains: These are but a few of the pioneers who went, or sent their representatives, into the south-west, and set English speech drifting on the inland winds; who raised their families and their flocks, and in time caused settlements to rise and become towns; who set church bells ringing to perpetuate the faith of their fathers.

John, on the long trek by wagon and dray from Sydney, a few months before, had followed the track of earlier men; had seen the isolated homesteads on the hillsides; had seen the lonely folds where shepherds folded their masters' sheep at night; had seen stockmen rounding up cattle; had looked at wheat fields, corn fields, and dairy cattle; and had observed how different was this wide country, and the methods of these settlers and squatters, from the small farms of England that had been producing for a thousand years, farms on which some families had lived for centuries. Here were problems of soil and climate entirely new to be mastered, altogether different from those of the homeland. Here were miles and miles that went on and on from horizon to horizon, from mountain to plain, from range to river. Few men knew what the colony was like beyond the limits of their own part of it. Settlers were mainly in three groups: the coastal men who got the cedar and cultivated the rich river flats; the tableland men of the pine-dotted north, centre and south; and still farther inland the plainsmen of the illimitable plains in the land of the mulga, the saltbush and the mirage. John had no idea what kind of country it was away from what he had seen himself. And in that he was not alone. To read about it, to study reports and maps, is one thing; to go into the country and see it with one's own eyes is another, the only true way to know any country. So he rode on, with the lofty massif of the "Murrumbidgee Ranges", as they were called in his day, always on his right hand, and late the next morning he crossed the first river, where the progressive and picturesque town of Tumut stands today.

The departure of Elijah and John from the valley seemed to be a signal to the Fates to juggle again with human destinies. An hour after John rode away Tilly announced she was going to saddle the bay mare. Hetty looked surprised.

"But, why, Tilly?" she asked. "There's no call for you to go riding."

Tilly's mouth hardened a little. She was impatient to meet Everitt again. The days of enforced separation from him had intensified the urge to be with him. Everitt! Again she would listen to his voice, see admiration for her plainly in his direct dark eyes. She *must* see him; must feel the thrill of his touch as he helped her down from the saddle; the pressure of his hand as it gripped her arm or rested lightly on her shoulder. She could easily handle her mother—Hetty knew nothing about these meetings with Everitt. And why should she not meet him? She was a woman, a woman aware and desiring, not a mere automaton ignoring life and content to move about endless domestic occasions as Jeanette was.

She replied easily, "I feel I must go for a ride, mother. I have missed my riding so much—I seem to have been padlocked since Sarah Tregg's death. A gallop will do me good."

"Very well, Tilly," Hetty said quietly. "But take the mare easily—she foaled only a few weeks ago."

Tilly almost purred as she said, "I'll be gentle with her. Goodness! How I am looking forward to seeing the valley again. I won't go too far——"

"Very well, dear."

On the elbow of the creek where the Treggs were, Meg finished cleaning the breakfast bowls. Near by, Johnnie, Rock and Dick squatted on their bare heels and talked together. It was a fine morning, cloudless with the promise of heat. Meg teased her hair and tossed the red mass over her shoulders. It was now too hot for the kangaroo-skin jacket and opossum cap, and she wore a faded print dress that had been Jane Oliver's. She stood looking about her, up the valley, down the valley. The partly finished log hut was between her and the creek, and in front of her were the brown furrows of some ground Dick had broken with John Martin's plough. But

Meg was not thinking of either the hut or the ploughed ground. She knew, as Tilly Martin knew, that Jane, Conway and Henry Oliver had gone to Melbourne Town, and that Everitt and Elliott were still in the valley. Presently she turned to her brothers.

"I be sick of 'angin' round 'ere," she said. "I be goin' along the valley a-ways——"

"Please y'self," Johnnie grunted. "Think we'll stop 'ere now they's took 'Lijah?"

Meg shrugged.

"Dunno. Dunno nothin'."

The men stood up.

"We'll stop," said Dick. "We got land, ain't we?"

"Think Jack Ketch'll git 'Lijah?" Rock asked.

"Mebbe," said Meg. "Thar be some folks'd 'ang anybody—jist for the fun of it. I'll be back later—dunno when."

Dick said casually:

"Ev'ritt Oliver? *Thet's* who th' ol' man ought to 'ave shot."

Meg's eyes narrowed. Her hands came slowly up to rest on her hips.

"Meanin'?" she asked sharply.

"Jist-meanin'," said the laconic Dick.

"Ar—go talk to a duck!" she spat at him.

347

With that she turned and walked away. Dick's quiet voice followed her.

"I don't think you be any more right in th' haid than Royd was."

She affected not to hear. Dick gazed solemnly after her.

"Yus——" he said. "I reckon someone ought——"

"Ought what?" asked Rock impatiently.

"Put a bullet in thet Ev'ritt Oliver."

"Well, 'twon't be any of us," said Johnnie. "If Meg wants it thet a-ways I ain't shootin' no one acause of it."

"Me neither," said Rock. "Anyways—y' can't stop Meg adoin' what she wants—y' can't chain 'er up like Royd."

Dick nodded slowly.

"Thar be somethin' in thet," he conceded. "But if Oliver gits 'er it'll be *us* thet'll feed the brat. Ar-well! Mebbe 'e won't. I'll do the ploughin'—you both git an' fell timber."

"Ar——" growled Johnnie.

Dick looked at him.

"We got to finish th' 'ut, ain't we? Thar'll be no sleepin' in the open when the snow comes again—an' I might still git a crop."

"Ar——" said the disgruntled Johnnie. "Everythin's changed. Nothin' the same now. Farmin'! An' I c'd do a fill o' beef—fresh beef! Oliver's got plenty——"

"No!" said Dick shortly. "No more o' thet. We aim to stop in this valley. Git *some* sense, Johnnie."

Johnnie scowled.

"Farmin'! I've a bleddy good min' to take to the roads——"

"Yus?" said Dick quietly. "Well, take to 'em, Johnnie—an' see 'ow long you lasts. You'd soon 'ear the bolt click—th' one they pulls on the drop. An' thet'd be all you'd 'ear—ever."

"I be no farmer. I don' like kickin' up dirt all day long—ploughin', plantin', threshin', stackin' dung, tendin' cattle an' pigs till you grunts like pigs. Up afore the sun comes up, agoin' after it drops. An' what for? Nothin'! Nothin' a-tall! Hell! Thet's what farmin' be. If only I 'ad a good 'orse—mebbe, mebbe I *would* clear out——"

"Well," said Rock thoughtfully, "don' 'elp y'self to none. They still wears irons in them road-gangs—an' 'orse-stealin' can git you fourteen years. 'Lijah said so. 'Ere, greb thet axe! I don' like farmin' neither—but I don' like irons roun' me ankles—neither! An'

349

goddlemighty we got to live some'ow. I ain't clearin' out—nowhars to go."

"You ain't game——" jeered Johnnie.

"I ain't a fool," retorted Rock. "I jist see 'Lijah took away with a chain roun' 'is neck—an' thet for doin' somethin' 'e 'ad to do. When you sees *thet*—you thinks. Let's git at it. Sittin' on your 'ocks won' grow corn—or put up th' 'ut."

Johnnie reached a long arm reluctantly for an axe.

"I've a good min' to go bush with the Wongals. Farmin'!"

He spat on the axe handle. Dick shrugged. Rock laughed. Then they stood still, not speaking until Rock said:

"Hey! Thar goes the Martin gel—she be ridin' towards th' Olivers—an' ain't she flash with 'er beaver 'at, ridin' dress an' ridin' whip. Hey, hey! Mebbe Oliver'll git 'er, too."

Johnnie stared after Tilly with low-lidded lustful eyes.

"I'd 'ave no objections, m'self," he growled.

Rock laughed again.

"You? You f'gits somethin'."

"What?" Johnnie demanded.

"You're a Tregg. Thet sort o' moll don't look at the likes of us."

"The likes o' us!" snarled Johnnie. "Gawd—I wish I 'ad a good 'orse. Mebbe I will some day. I'd git some money then——"

Dick said slowly, "Thar's allus somebody got a good rope, too. But, I dunno. Meg won' like thet Martin gel buttin' in—she won' like it a-tall. An' our Meg's got claws, an' can use 'em right wicked if she wants to."

"Them Martin gels be stuck-up," Rock said. "They didn't start as gully-rakers sneakin' unbranded cattle out o' the gullies—they come with money an' wagons. Us Tregg fellers be muck to 'em. Dunno 'ow Annie sticks it thar——"

"Thar's Martin boys, ain't thar?" sneered Johnnie.

Rock shook his head.

"Not thet a-way for Annie—she ain't like Meg. *You* ought to know——"

"Ar——" snarled Johnnie. "You got a big mouth, Rock. Shut it!"

Rock glared at him.

"You ain't so good——" he retorted.

"Box it up! Box it up!" said Dick impatiently.

Rock and Johnnie glared at each other, but

351

did not speak again. They all stood watching Tilly until she rode out of sight.

"I still say I'd 'ave no objections," said Johnnie.

"Ar—sweat it out," grunted Rock. "Let's go——"

The moment Meg heard the horse she whirled and stood staring, fury in her eyes, her mouth pressed to a thin line.

"Tilly Martin——" she breathed. "An' goin' to—Ev'ritt."

She watched the bay cantering towards her, its rider swaying easily in the saddle. Her quick eyes took in at once the wide-brimmed black beaver with its long, drooping white feather, the trim-waisted red riding habit. Meg could ride, but only in the forbidden male fashion; she had never ridden side-saddle; and it was considered coarse and in-delicate for women to straddle a horse, unless in lonely country where necessity demanded it and no one cared.

Tilly saw Meg, and swerved the bay to avoid her. She frowned and bit her lip. So this red-haired trash was abroad this morn-ing. Why? And she had been walking towards the turnstile before stopping and turning round. Tilly did not want to talk to Meg; she loathed her; despised and disliked all the Treggs. So she touched a rein to avoid her, but at the right moment Meg leapt like a tigress for the bridle and brought the horse to a standstill. Tilly went white with anger.

"How dare you touch my horse," she snapped out. "Let go that bridle——"

Meg's eyes were baleful.

"I ain't lettin' go till you an' me unnerstan's each other," she snapped back. "Whar you goin'?"

Tilly's eyes showed the fury mounting in her.

"You impudent creature—that is my business——"

"An' mebbe mine," said Meg harshly. "I wants to tell you somethin', Tilly Martin. I ain't blind. I seed you asettin' your cap at Ev'ritt Oliver. Well, Ev'ritt be *my* man! Mine! Unnerstan'? I'll tell you why——"

Tilly's voice was icy with contempt.

"Don't bother. I refuse to listen to your stupid lies. And I refuse to discuss Everitt Oliver, or anyone else, with you. I have no wish to speak to you now, or at any other time. Let go that bridle!"

Meg's expression was ugly.

"Ain't lettin' it go. Not me. An' you'll

listen! Ev'ritt said I was 'is gel—tol' me so—'cause why? 'Cause Ev'ritt's my lover—see? Thar! dem you, Tilly Martin! Now you knows. But you won' talk—'cause you'd be talkin' 'bout 'im if you did."

"You wretched little beast——" Tilly panted. "Everitt Oliver is a gentleman——"

"Not on the grass 'e ain't——"

"You miserable tramp—I *won't* listen to you! Let go that bridle!"

"Not yet——" came with a hiss. "I ain't finished talkin'. An' don't call me no tramp—you flash bastud! I tell you I be Ev'ritts woman—an' thar ain't goin' to be no other—not in this valley—nohow! I be tellin' you, Tilly Martin, I'll splash you all over this 'ere valley if you gits makin' up to Ev'ritt. Y' yaller bitch! Thet puts y'long ears back. You *better* listen!"

Tilly gasped. She was unused to such stark and uninhibited revelation.

"I still don't believe your tawdry lies," she ground out. "Mr. Oliver would not lower himself to associate with you—you unclean little wild-cat. That's what you look like—and it's obviously what you are! Now you listen to me and I'll tell *you* something! Some time ago I did ask him if he were amusing himself with you, and his answer was 'I? A Tregg girl? The daughter of an old *lag*? You can't think me as stupid, and as having such poor taste as *that*, surely?' Those were his words about you, so naturally I don't believe what you are saying now. Let go that bridle—I warn you!"

"Dem you, no, Tilly Martin——" was screamed back. "I'm goin' to pull you out o' thet saddle——"

Tilly's voice was vibrant with anger.

"I say again—*let go that bridle!*"

Meg's face was hideous with rage.

"I'll let go when I've fixed you——" she gasped.

Tilly's arm went up, and the heavy crop she carried came down across Meg's wrist with a vicious stroke. With a startled cry of pain the girl released the bridle, and in that moment Tilly sent the mare away with a quick touch of the spur. She rode on, not looking back, cleared the fence at the rise, and cantered down the slope towards the Olivers' house. Meg stood as if uncomprehending what had happened; her eyes were filled with tears of pain and fury. The Martin girl had struck her—struck her with a *whip*! By God—she had been slashed as if she were a slut. With a whip—a *whip*! Presently a cry shrill and high broke from her white lips. It carried along the valley, but Tilly did not hear it.

"Tilly Martin—I'll git you for thet. If ever I gits me 'ands on you I'll *blind* you—I will, I will, I *will*! So 'elp me—Gawd!"

She stood swaying with ungovernable yet futile fury, then she turned and ran back the way she had come. Dick, who was ploughing, saw her coming. Johnnie and Rock also saw her, and her haste and wild demeanour told them something had happened. Dropping their axes they came to the hut. Dick spoke first as the panting girl raced up to them.

"What's to do, Meg?" he asked in his curiously level voice.

Her voice came with a thin, vicious sound.

"I bin whipped——" she snarled at her staring brothers. "*Whipped*! Thet Martin—thet flash Tilly Martin whipped me——"

"Whipped you?" asked Johnnie deeply. "Why?"

Meg's words came pouring out.

" 'Cause I grebbed 'er bridle——"

" 'Tain't enough—why?" demanded Rock.

Meg's eyes had an animal glare in them.

"I 'ad somethin' to tell 'er——"

" 'Bout Ev'ritt?" asked Dick.

"Yus——" came defiantly. "If you mus' know—yus! She wouldn't listen—tol' me to let go the bridle——"

"An' you wouldn't?" said Johnnie.

"No! Then she swung th' whip an' cut me over the wrist. I ain't takin' it—I ain't *takin'* it! Whar's your gun, Johnnie?"

The three men exchanged glances.

"You gits no gun," said Dick. "Thar's bin 'nough o' thet already."

"Whar's a *gun*!" Meg raved. "I'll fix 'er so's she'll be no good to Ev'ritt or no other man. Rock——"

"No. We ain't goin' to see you led away with a chain roun' your neck. You gits no gun."

Dick spoke.

"An' you better git sense. You don' own this valley, Meg Tregg—you don' own Ev'ritt Oliver——"

"You mis'able bastud!" she shrieked at him. "All of yous. You ain't no brothers—you's bastuds——"

"Mebbe," said Dick coolly. "But we ain't stoopid bastuds."

Meg was almost choking with resentment and wild rage.

"You'd let 'er *lash* me? Lash me—y' own

sister—would you? An' you calls y'self a Tregg——"

"I be a Tregg," said Dick. "Same's all of us. It be somethin' we can't f'git. An' it's 'cause *you* be a Tregg you got to steady up. I ain't pleased 'bout 'er lashin' you, but seems you grebbed the bridle an' wouldn't let go. Unner the law she can strike in defence. Everybody knows thet, y' fool."

"The law—the law!" panted Meg. "I'll give 'er the law—the law thet says no woman can cut in on another——"

"What d'ye mean—cut in?" growled Rock. "How cut in—you mean Oliver?"

Meg's lips were white and working. She was still panting heavily. She held her swelling right wrist in her left hand. Wildly her eyes went from one brother to the other. Their faces were grim, but it came to her that their sternness was concerned with what she might be to Everitt Oliver rather than with the mere sting of a whip. Warned by the quick impression she said bitterly:

"Never mind Oliver—never mind 'im. Anyone can thrash a Tregg, an' the Treggs crawl unner the whip like cringin' dawgs. Allus 'ave! Allus will, I s'pose. The gutless Tregg *men*, I means."

Johnnie and Rock moved uneasily. Dick's expression did not alter.

"Seems the Martin gel's got claws, too," he said in his slow way. He looked at his brothers. "It don' be a man's consarn—it be a woman's. We better let alone, Johnnie—Rock." He turned his eyes to Meg. "An' *you* better let alone. You ought to 'ave more sense tryin' to *claim* Oliver—from 'er. If you *mus'* claim 'im—claim 'im from 'imself."

"Yus," said Johnnie. "Thet's sense."

"Yus," said Rock. " 'Tis sense."

Meg looked at them scornfully. Then she spat at them.

"Muck! All of you," she said contemptuously. "I'll fix this in me own way—ho, yus! Thet I will——"

"You watch y'self, Meg," said Rock as she walked towards the hut. "Dick's right. No more trouble like we 'ad with Royd. But us men'll deal with Oliver—if you wants us to."

She half turned.

"You let Ev'ritt alone," she shrilled back. "I won' 'ave you touchin' 'im——"

"An' you better let the Martin gel alone—or you'll git more'n you're lookin' for," Johnnie told her. "Mebbe it'll larn you somethin'—you allus was a bad-tempered bitch.

Sarves you right—for gettin' tangled with Oliver."

Meg swung furiously into the hut without replying. Rock looked at his brothers as he said, "Mebbe we ought to git Annie away from them Martins."

Dick turned stolidly towards the plough.

"No. 'Lijah said let 'er stop thar," he said. "Meg's no good for Annie. Let Annie be. 'Lijah wants it thet way."

Johnnie's eyes were thoughtful.

"Yus——" he said at last. "It be better thet way. Hey! Lookit thar! Thar's the Martin gel comin' back——"

They looked at Tilly. So did Meg.

"She ain't bin with Oliver," said Dick. "Never 'ad no time——"

"No," said Johnnie. "Gawd, I could——"

"Ar——" said Rock. "Shut up."

The disappointed Tilly could have told them she had seen no sign of either Everitt or Elliott although she had ridden a mile or so beyond their house. She did not look at the Treggs as she cantered past.

21

ANNIE was helping Nan feed the pigs when Tom and Mark came to the pens. They had finished work on the barn for the day. It was now the third week in January, and an evening when the westering sun flushed the valley with gold and set the eastern hills aflame with orange light. High in the sky black swans and wild geese were honking and homing to the long lagoon beyond the Martins' house.

"Coming, Annie?" asked Mark as Tom and Nan began walking away. "Soon be supper-time."

"I be in no 'urry, Mark—it be so 'ot," she replied. "You go if you wants to—I'll wait awhiles."

He looked at her intently.

"Oh, come on, Annie," he said gently. "I know . . . how you feel about everything. I'm sure they will let your father go——"

Annie's voice was quiet.

"Yus. Mebbe, boy, Mark. Now Johnnie

an' Rock 'ave finished the new 'ut I shouldn't be 'ere."

"But your father wanted you to stay with us——"

"Yus."

"Don't you want to stay?"

She looked at him.

"For m'self—yus."

"Then why do you think you should go?"

" 'Cause . . . I be's a Tregg. Every time I comes into your 'ouse . . . I feels jist thet."

"But, Annie——" Mark began in protest.

"Yus. An' I thinks I be somethin' of a worrit to your mother. I seed 'er lookin' close at me moren't onct, Mark. She *knows* I likes you. She can see it. I try not to show it in front of the others—but she can see it. I said I'd never 'urt you, boy, Mark. I thinks . . . I should go."

Mark's face was flushed and concerned.

"But you *mustn't* go. I—I can't teach you to read and write if you go back to your family. I—I'd never see you——"

"No——" was said slowly. "Not much, anyways——"

"Has mother said anything to you, Annie?"

The girl shook her head.

"No. She couldn't. I ain't done nothin'.

But she can see everythin' I could tell 'er m'self. She be kind—yus, kind an' gentle— But she'd think I was askin' too much—she wouldn't want a Tregg gel for you. I got nothin' but a bad name to give you. Nothin'. She won't want *your* young-uns—if I ain't bein' bold—to 'ave convic' blood in 'em—sich blood—murder an' madness—an' other things——"

Mark was trembling.

"But—but *you* can't help those things—and I know about them——"

Annie looked at him for a long moment.

"Yus, boy, Mark. But your young-uns don' know 'bout 'em—yet."

Mark was distressed.

"You mustn't go, Annie. Never mind about me. We want you to stay—for your own sake. Your father wants you to stay for that reason. Never mind about us. You *do* want to stay, don't you?"

She nodded.

"Yus. But not to make trouble for your folks, Mark."

He drew in a breath.

"You won't, Annie. You're different. You're not a Tregg——"

"Oh, yes——" she interrupted quietly, "I be's a Tregg, Mark."

"Well—well—I meant—oh, *damn* it, Annie——"

She smiled faintly.

"You mus' not swear, boy, Mark."

He went on breathlessly.

"I'm *not* swearing. I won't let you go, Annie . . . even if I have to tell you . . . you don't mean anything to me any more. . . ."

Annie's voice was a whisper.

"Sooner than 'ear you say *thet*, Mark, I'd walk away now——"

"You know I won't say it," he assured her earnestly.

"Yus—I knows. Well, mebbe I won't make no trouble. I wouldn't want to pay you-all back with trouble."

"Of course you won't. Let's go to the house. There's Tilly watching us from the door."

"Yus. Tilly. But mebbe someone's watchin' Tilly. All right. I'll git me towel an' soap an' git unner thet watterfall afore supper. Thar'll be time——"

Annie was soon running to where the girls bathed in the rock-pool. She knew no one would follow her. Quickly she slipped off her clothes and threw them over a branch, and then waded to the hanging rock from which fell a gentle waterfall. After the heat of the day it was good to feel the cool water running over body and limbs. There was still plenty of light, and as she stood under the crystal shower she thought of her talk with Mark. She had not realized until then that although he was as old as she was, in years, he was younger in mind. She recalled his flush when she spoke of the children he would one day have; but she had to say it; he had to know what was in her mind. He was a fine lad, clean-minded, wholesome, sincere. That he was fond of her she knew, but she wondered if deep down in him were secret thoughts about her, perhaps some doubt he would not allow to rise to full thought. And being a woman she also wondered if his fondness for her was not prompted by the fact that she was the only girl of his age in the valley. But those were matters only the time ahead could answer.

Yes; she would stay with the Martins. She was happy with them; she had never been so happy. The tragedies of her own family were cruel burdens, impelling for her a withdrawing to a great extent from these kindly people.

She found she could not laugh when they did; that their own laughter was checked when their eyes turned to her. Between her and them was the impassable barrier of the Tregg name and blood. She had seen what industry could do for a family, even in a few short months, and it was what she wanted for herself. But what hope had she? Mark? How could a boy know the mind of a man? But she would stay; she did not want to go back to the squalor of a Tregg hut; she did not want, ever again, to lie in a wide bed that held them all; she did not want the dull minds of Johnnie and Rock mocking her for having "notions"; she did not want Meg's way of life.

Meg!

Annie frowned as she thought of her sister. She had never been close to Meg, to any of them, for that matter. Dick, quiet and usually wordless, was the only one who seemed to see things as she saw them. Meg never had, never would. There was nothing quiet in Meg; she had never been tamed, never would be tamed. She gave herself to Everitt Oliver, not because of any love for him, but merely to gratify her own craving flesh. Consequences? As if Meg would care.

In her own way Annie made shrewd comparisons. She was young, only seventeen, wholly untutored and illiterate, but she had seen settlement in three widely separated places, and she knew there were different types of settlers just as there were different kinds of country on which they could settle. She had seen the Oliver type many times—the rich speculator and the grantee; her own kind only too often; but the free settlers who had background and some money, who had some learning, good characters, and firm industry, were not so plentiful. The Martins were like that, and deep in her heart she wanted, wanted fiercely, to be as they were. As she stepped from under the waterfall the voice called:

"Annie—Annie!"

Meg was on the bank. Annie stared at her sister.

"What *you* want?" she asked as she left the pool. "Any more trouble?"

Meg watched Annie dry herself.

"Mebbe. Thet's why I come."

"Well?"

Meg looked keenly at her sister.

"You like bein' with the Martins?" she asked.

Annie put on her clothes before replying. Then:

"Yus. You knows thet—or I wouldn't be 'ere."

"Mebbe y' won't want to be 'ere when I tells you somethin'."

Annie watched her closely.

"What?"

"Thet 'igh an' mighty Tilly Martin——"

Annie's eyes narrowed.

"Yus? What 'bout 'er?"

Meg's voice trembled.

"She whipped me."

Annie's mouth opened in quick astonishment. Tilly Martin whip Meg? *Meg?*

"How?" she asked when she recovered herself.

Meg's voice was bitter and vicious as she told of the incident.

"Thet's what the yaller bitch did to me—an' if ever I catches 'er alone—she'll be sorry. I'll mark 'er so's she'll never f'git it——"

"What's Johnnie an' Rock an' Dick say?" Annie asked.

Meg spat into the pool.

"Them!" she said scornfully. "Them! They got watter 'stead of blood in 'em. Tol' me 'twas me own fault. But I don' aim to 'ave a sister o' mine livin' with sich as 'er. You got to come beck, Annie."

Annie's lip curled.

"You be mighty consid'rate 'bout your sister all at onct," she said quietly.

"You ain't takin' 'er part agen me, are you?" Meg asked angrily.

Annie shook her head.

"No. I ain't. I don' like Tilly Martin no more'n you does. She don' think o' no one but Tilly Martin, an' I think she be pretty much like you only she ain't so dem silly as to let a man——"

"Never min' preachin' at me, Annie Tregg," Meg said harshly. "I knows what I wants—an' I 'as what I wants. Why shouldn't I? What else 'ave I—or you—or any of us got in this world but what we gets for ourselves?"

"S'pose you 'as a babby by 'im? What then?"

Meg sneered.

"Well—what then?" she retorted. "Y' don' think anybody'd ever want to marry me—a *Tregg*, do you? Or you? But thar won' be no babby. An' I ain't goin' to spen' all me life jist clingin' to a tree like a stoopid goanna. I *ain't* no goanna. I ain't goin' to *be* no bleddy goanna! Don' give me thet talk, Annie Tregg."

The ghost of a smile touched Annie's lips.

"You shouldn't swear like thet," she said.

Meg looked startled. Her eyes opened wide. Then she said:

"I thinks these 'ere Martins 'ave made you a bit soft in th' haid. The Martins! Gawd—thet Tilly Martin called me a tramp—an' somethin' else—but since 'er ol' man's bin away she's bin ridin' reg'lar to see Ev'ritt, an' only yisterday I tracked 'er an' 'im. An' I saw. I *saw*!"

"What?"

"They was in thet narrer gully whar the rock walls go up——"

"I knows it. Jist wide 'nough to git a wagon through."

"Yus. Thar. She was lyin' in 'is arms——"

Annie's brown eyes showed astonishment.

"Meg! You don' mean——"

"No!" snarled Meg. "She's bein' smart yet awhiles. But I knows Ev'ritt. An' she'll find out. She was only ateasin' 'im—you know—lookin' up into 'is eyes, kissin' 'im, strokin' 'is 'air—the bitch! This mornin' I went to Ev'ritt——" Meg's voice deepened to a husky, trembling tone. "I tol' 'im what I thought of 'im——"

"What did 'e say?"

Meg's lips were pale, her eyes blue slits.

" 'E tol' me 'e never wanted to see me again—calm like—cold like—jist like thet—jist like I was a dead duck—which I was—an' if I made trouble—if any of us made trouble 'bout it—'e'd swear a information an' git us put whar we wouldn't make trouble for a long time. Said 'e knowed, an' 'ad proof, Johnnie an' Rock was cattle-thievin' gully-rakers—thet 'e an' Conway an' Elliott saw 'em kill an' take a Oliver bullock—more'n one—an' they'd swear to it. *Thet's* why I won' 'ave no babby. But 'e ain't th' only man in this world be no means. Yus—thet's what Tilly Martin's done to me. She be Ev'ritt's woman now, but 'e wouldn't marry 'er any more'n 'e would me. Them fellers don' marry their molls. I allus knowed thet. I didn't care. I ain't nothin'—no better'n a gin, mebbe, 'cept I be white. I knowed *thet*, too. I be a Tregg. But I ain't finished with Tilly Martin—ho, no! Not me."

"P'raps you be wrong. P'raps she will marry 'im——"

"Thet's what she wants. She thinks she's

got 'im. She'll find out when she wakes up one mornin' sick an' shakin' with fear. An' wouldn't I like to be thar when 'e tells 'er 'e's finished with *'er*—which 'e will. Ho, yus—'e will. If we be's muck to the Martins—the Martins be muck to the Olivers. You better come beck with me."

Annie sat down, and ran slow fingers through her fair hair. The pool was dusky-dark now, but she did not see the dull sheen of the water. The little waterfall gave its low note to the soft sounds of the summer evening, but she did not hear it. She heard only Meg's harsh, vituperative voice. Presently she answered.

"Yus—I would," she said slowly. "Only for one thing——"

"What thing?" Meg asked sourly.

"I promised 'Lijah I'd stay . . . an' someone else . . ."

"Not—not a Martin feller?" rasped Meg.

"Yus . . . a Martin feller."

Meg's voice was choked and breathless with a surge of bitter anger. Her staring eyes seemed to be green rather than blue in the dying light. She swung a vicious hand and brought it hard across Annie's face. Annie's head jerked back with the force of the blow.

"You little—rat!" Meg shrilled. "You'd sell me out—y' own sister—to Tilly Martin—acause of a *Martin* feller! Well, stay! Stay an' rot with 'em! An' if ever you sees *me* again—you jist watch me spit——"

Annie heard Meg running away, but she did not turn her head.

22

WIDESPREAD rain came during the third week in February. As the corn was cobbing heavily the Martins were glad. The dry valley, as well as the cultivation, needed rain after the parching December and January sun. Bushfires were inland and along the ranges, and this welcome rain would wash them out. Some settlers in the south, whose wheat had not been harvested, hoped it would pass in the night, but its steady drumming told that the clouds from the Tasman Sea would drench the countryside for days to come. Nor did the drivers and guards of mail and passenger coaches welcome it; for it meant impassable roads, bogged vehicles, wet and uncomfortable journeys, saddle and collar sores for the teams, and irritable and complaining passengers and innkeepers.

In the south the veil of the rain falling over the vivid summer colours of mountain, plain and valley, the lilac blue of distant hills, the reds and browns of lofty escarpments, the variegated greens of forest, ferny dell and tree-lined watercourse, seemed to deepen the gloom that had recently settled on Melbourne Town and the Province of Port Phillip. All at once, it seemed, the pastoral industry had collapsed. Squatters had bought to the limits of their cash and credit, and were caught on a falling market. Already sheep were selling for sixpence a head. Panic was spreading. William Verner was sworn in by the eccentric Judge Willis as chief commissioner of insolvent estates, and many firms and individuals were passing through the insolvency court. The outlook was black. And the rest of New South Wales was being gripped by this sudden depression. Costs of production were high, flocks and herds were everywhere held in as large numbers as the runs would carry, and there was no market anywhere for the natural increase, or, indeed, for the sheep and cattle on hand. So began the great experiment in boiling-down. Thousands of cattle and sheep were slaughtered for their fat. Tallow became an exportable commodity. But daily men were ruined, families saw their work, their money and their dreams, swept away.

Nevertheless, faith in the colony was still strong. It was realized that although the incautious and overstocked grazier would suffer, and, naturally, others with him, all the future and enterprise of Australia was not bound up in sheep and cattle alone. At Geelong, early in February, the first Mechanics' Institute was formed, proving that there were others than graziers in this expanding colony; and about the same time Melbourne's first dramatic performance was held in the newly named Theatre Royal, formerly the Pavilion, in Bourke Street. Here, before an enthusiastic audience determined to forget, at least for that night, the financial ruin spreading about them, were played *The Widow's Victim* and *The Lottery Ticket.*

Jane Oliver, with her father and Conway, had been to the theatre. Afterwards, in the comfortable inner parlour of the Lamb Inn, in Collins Street, where they were staying, Jane said thoughtfully, "Papa, are you still willing to sell the valley property?"

Henry pursed his lips. His white hair trembled on his shoulders as he moved. Beside him on the table was a steaming whisky, his usual night-cap. Coming down in the dray he had agreed to Jane's proposal to sell out and take up land elsewhere—much to her astonishment—but none of them had at that time realized the developing crisis in the affairs of the colony.

"Yes, I am willing," he said. "We have yet to get our wool down here to Melbourne, and have it shipped to Garraway's, in London, but I'll see to that. If I do make a sale shortly none of us will go back. I'll sell everything as it stands—including the wool, if the buyer will take it. Everitt and Elliott can join us here when the purchaser takes possession." He paused for a moment to sip his whisky. His close-set blue eyes looked down at the plush-covered table. Then he went on slowly, "I agree the valley is no place for us. I, personally, could not live in that house again. Every time I opened the back door I'd see Tregg kill his son. Somehow . . . I can't get that night out of my mind. A man could not see a more terrible thing. No; there is nothing more terrible, more tragic than that. And I have the uneasy feeling the Olivers are partly responsible for that awful moment."

Jane and Conway looked at him in surprise. Such talk was unlike the unbending Henry Oliver. It seemed to indicate his character was softening with age—or with conscience. But they were silent as he went on.

"I have no time for such trash as the Treggs, but they were our servants, and it may well be asked in court what we, the Olivers, had done for them. They probe like the very devil, these lawyers——"

So it was only conscience, after all. Jane shrugged. In a tight-waisted corsage, a puffed-sleeved gown of grey satin, and with a froth of lace at her throat, she sat severely upright in her chair, her dark, implacable eyes shrewdly appraising her father.

As he finished speaking she said, "It is agreed we must get away from there—whether the court asks questions or not. The Treggs do not trouble me——"

Conway spoke.

"One of them did—on a certain night," he reminded her. "But for old Tregg——"

"I don't want to hear any more about it," said Jane sharply.

"Well, you do owe Elijah something," Conway persisted.

"I do not!" Jane snapped. "If he couldn't look after his crazy lout of a son, the best thing he could do——"

"Well?" asked Henry slowly.

"Was what he did do. No one was safe with that beast about."

"And what would *you* have done—had Royd taken you?" asked Conway. "And you know what I mean."

Jane flushed. "Really, Conway—must you be so crude?" she retorted.

Conway laughed. "I? Oh, well—let it pass. But I agree with papa that we owe Tregg something for preserving your precious chastity if not your life. There'd have been no marriage market for you, dear sister, if Elijah hadn't come along just then."

"You're a beast, Conway——"

"Conway!" said Henry reprovingly. "You are speaking to your sister, not to some town wench."

"I know, papa—how well I know," said Conway. "But my dear sister has the soul of an old boot, and a selfishness as sure and cold as death itself."

Jane went pale with anger. "I won't have you speak about me like that, Conway——"

"Oh, go to the devil. If papa can't see through you—I can. God help the man who gets you. You have no more feeling for others than a coiled snake."

"Conway—apologize to Jane. I'm surprised at you, boy——"

"Oh, all right, all right. Let it go."

"I shall go to bed," said Jane harshly. "But I'm glad we are not returning to the valley—I'm not, sale or *no* sale. The rain will be streaming along it tonight. I can hear the trees sighing in the wind, wet and lonely, and the rain thrashing against the house. Ugh! A black valley lost in the heart of black mountains. We were fools to go there—fools!"

"It's like a thousand other valleys," said Conway.

"Perhaps, but not to me. Nothing could be as wretched as that place to me. I am never going back there. And thank you, my dear brother, for your good opinion of me."

Conway looked at her as she walked to the door.

"Some day I'll tell you the rest of it," he retorted. "I knew you were many things—but I didn't know until tonight you were an ingrate."

Jane's eyes were black discs of anger in a white face as she turned to her father.

"Good night, papa. Kick some sense into Conway, will you? He'll be weeping tears at the death of a he-goat next. Good night."

Five hundred miles away, in Sydney Town, Martha and Henry Gubby were preparing to retire for the night. The night lamps burned low in the passage-ways of the York inn. Out in the rain-swept yard Sam Pink went sorrowfully about his duties of seeing all was well with horses, gigs and carriages. In the large kitchen Polly Wedge and Mary Kissane sat over a hot toddy waiting for Sam to come in for the nightly chat. In their rooms the guests listened to the rain and were thankful to be in this comfortable and friendly house.

Martha sighed with relief as she took off her stays. She stood rubbing herself as she said, "Them dratted stays gives me th' 'itch, 'Arry boy. But I dunno what I'd do without 'em. Lawks, I'd bulge! Look at me! I mus' do somethin'—I mus'!"

"Yes, dear," said Henry.

"Does you remember when I was different? When you fust knowed me?"

He nodded as he took off a boot.

"Of course, my dear. You were the prettiest girl in London."

Martha smiled slowly.

" 'Arry boy—sometimes I believes you be still human. Yus, I *was* a good-looker—a fair smasher. So's Mary Ann now—an' Pagan. But, lassy me—I be's the size o' a helephant. Jus' look a this 'ere stummick!"

"Yes, dear."

Martha put on her night-dress.

"I s'pose Mr. Martin be gettin' near 'ome now," she said.

The bed sagged and creaked as she got into it; the four tall posts shook.

"Oh, he must be," said Henry.

Martha laughed. "Saved you a journey—eh, 'Arry boy?"

"Yes—yes! But I was perfectly willing to go, my dear——"

Martha's eyes twinkled. "Yus? Oh, well, 'twasn't necessary. An' mebbe I'm glad. Some'ow the place wouldn't be the same without you settin' about doin' nothin'. Anyway, we fixed up 'bout the land—heverythin' legal an' sat'sfact'ry. Lawks! 'E was glad. So was I. That ol' Holiver! What be you thinkin' of, 'Arry boy?"

Mr. Gubby put on his night-shirt.

"Oh, I—I was just hoping everything is all right, Martha. It seems from the talk, and the newspapers, the colony is in for a bad time."

"Mebbe. Go hon."

"And if trade falls off here——"

"Yus? Go hon."

"And the Martins can't find any money——"

"Yus? Do go hon, Mr. Gubby."

"We—I mean you, my dear, may find it difficult to—to meet your liabilities, and, well——"

"Ain't I alwus met 'em, Mr. Gubby?"

"Yes, I know. But you've never before committed yourself to anything as big as this."

"Hi knows that," said Martha calmly. "Hif things get *that* bad you can alwus get work o' some kind—you can read an' write."

Henry looked startled, then dismayed. Work. *Work?* Good heavens!

"Oh, perhaps," he said hastily, "I am looking at the dark side of things, my dear."

Martha chuckled softly. "You is, Mr. Gubby. Now turn hout the lamp an' get into bed. An' don' let the dark scare you none—'bout 'ard times, I means, nothin' else. I be glad I got them Martins out o' ol' Holiver's clutches—ol' wolf! Want another blanket?"

"No."

Henry got in beside Martha. There was silence for a little while. Then she asked, "You does think I done right, don' you?"

"Yes, I do." There was a ring of sincerity in Henry's voice.

383

"So does I. You know, 'Arry boy, hus Gubbys 'as bin fort'nate. We's got on a bit. So's a lot of others. But there's plenty ain't. We got a fine inn 'ere, the right kind o' folks. The Cock an' Fevvers, down in Campbell Street, was all right, too, with all them good people—farmers, drovers, sheep an' cattle men, wagoners, teamsters, travellers an' sich like—but as well as gettin' all *them* we now gets business folk, merchants, bankers, folks off the ships when they comes in, folks out o' shops. Lawks, lawks, lawks! I can 'ardly believe it be true. Hevery time I sees them red plush chairs an' sofas, them long silk bell-ropes, them carpets in the parlours an' on the stairs, them big mirrors on the walls, them luvly stuffed birds unner them glass cases, them big coloured pitchers in their gold frames, I says, 'Lassy me! Be *this* the Gubbys?' An' the furniture! Some from Hingland, some from China. The four-poster, canopied beds, an' wunnerful dressin' tables, in the fust class, an' a night-pot in hevery room. Th' hothers be comf'able, too. Yus, I ain't forgot them years when I used to cry at nights, wonderin' 'bout us all—you, me, the two gels. You never knowed what I kep' bottled hup inside me when we 'ad to leave Hingland; when we was comin' out on the *Lunnon Lass*, when Pagan fust met Simon; when we got out of the ship's boat on to that lonely beach at Fremantle over ten year ago. Times I thought I'd break—an' then I'd think of us all again, an' I kep' busy. There's nothin' like keepin' busy, even hif you ain't doin' nothin'. You was no good——"

"I—I know that, Martha," came quietly.

"Now, now, 'Arry boy—I didn't mean that unkind like. But 'twasn't your sort o' life— inn-keepin' never was. You was a clurk, even hif you ain't done no clurkin' for over thirty year. I ain't givin' you a back-'ander. You bin a good 'usband, an' a good little man, an' never caused me no worry."

"I am under no illusions about myself, Martha—and I know you're not."

"Ar—pickles! You be all right, 'Arry boy. You bin a bit o' a weasel sometimes, adodgin' doin' anythin', but the good Lord didn't make you to stan' up to 'ard knocks. That's why 'E guv you to me, I s'pose. But we's walked a long, long way together, 'Arry boy, an' God willin' we'll go a long way together yet."

"Yes . . . God willing," said Henry. "Yes, we'll be all right, my dear, and perhaps we'll

385

both live long enough to see great changes in this country—great changes."

"We seen some already. They's stopped sendin' convic's 'ere. Free folks be comin' in. Settlers be takin' hup lan' heverywhere—like them Martins. Sydney Town's never bin so busy, or 'ad so many ships in th' 'arbour—merchant ships, coastal ships, whalin' ships, warships, little ships, big ships—ships from heverywhere. Wool? Mountings of it! Timber? Forests of it! Sheep an' cattle? Mobs an' mobs of 'em! Farm stuffs? Wagon-loads all day long acomin' in. Shops be filled with goods till they looks like Lunnon shops, an' you can almost buy 'ere what you can get there. Lawks! It do be a lively, bustlin' town! 'Ouses be bein' built all over the place. The streets be full o' coaches, gigs, kerridges. Schools, churches, a theatre—all sorts o' things. An', lassy me! we's close, they says, to self-gov'ment, thanks to that Mr. Wentworth, Dr. Bland, an' others. The day we gets our own parlyment, Mr. Gubby, you can say th' bad ol' days be past. An' th' himmigrants be agoin' hout into the country—why, look what Mrs. Chisholm be adoin'! She be gettin' lots o' single gels settled in good 'omes in the country, an' some fambiles, too. Over

386

fifty famblies, so far. There ain't no young gels sleepin' in parks an' the Domain now—'less they be 'arlots an' wants to. That woman mus' be a hangel to face all them long roads, to suffer all that privation an' discomfort, an' put up with all sorts o' cranky people jus' to 'elp people. She mus' be . . . yus, she mus' be."

"Yes," agreed Henry. "A remarkable woman. But I know of another great woman——"

"You does? Who?"

"You, my dear."

There was silence, then:

"Ah, 'Arry boy—I likes to 'ear you say things like that—but I ain't done nothin' like that—'cept get hus Gubbys up a bit in the world——"

"That isn't all you've done, Martha," said Henry. "Many and many a time you've helped others—as well as the Gubbys. Many and many a time others would have given up but for your help. You've always had courage—a courage you could give to others, even to me at times, and I wasn't born with that quality. You've always had faith in yourself, and in others, and in this strange young country—and it is a strange country.

And you've always had wisdom. I confess, when we came to Western Australia, before coming to New South Wales, my heart was sick with fear and dislike of the place. You have given me a different outlook. I'll never be other than what I was born to be, I suppose—a nobody. I never seemed to be able to do anything. But you never faltered. Look what you've just done for the Martins! You've saved that family—saved them from heartache and ruin——"

"Ah, well—I couldn't see them busted jus' acause ol' Holiver wanted their land. They be good folks, an' they'll do well. But . . . 'twasn't much, anyways."

"That's just you. No one ever appealed to you in vain, if deserving. Your own philosophy of 'Worship God, be up and doing, and help your neighbour' has been the daily practice of your own life. I only wish . . . I'd had strength of body and character to have done likewise. I've had some education. Perhaps that spoilt me—gave me fear instead of courage. I know myself, Martha. I'm for ever running away from myself, from others, and from everything. But as you helped others, and our children, so have you helped and shielded me. You're a wonderful woman, my dear. I'm grateful to you."

Martha was silent. Never in all their married life had Henry Gubby spoken like that. His words "I'm for ever running away from myself, from others, from everything" were a brave confession of his own futility and weakness. She bundled a massive arm under his head and drew him to her.

"You silly little feller," she said gently. "You be my Mr. Gubby. Tomorrer be another day, an' there be plenty to do. An' if 'ard times comes we'll face 'em, 'Arry boy—like we's alwus done. I trusts Mary Ann be safe this night over in them furrin parts, an' Simon and Pagan in that wild New Zealand, an' that Halbert Hernest'll grow hup a good feller. 'E'd better. I 'opes John Martin gets all that long way safely 'ome. It be a long, long way to that there valley . . . a long, long way. Good night, 'Arry boy——"

"Good night, my dear."

23

THE Lower Court in Melbourne Town, the *Little Go*, as it was commonly called, was crowded. The town was agog with the story of the man, Elijah Tregg, the man now standing in chains in the dock. It was a sultry morning with a warm wind whipping the flags on Flagstaff Hill, sending high ripples over the flood-smashed weir at the falls, and putting white caps on the heaving rollers of the great bay.

The people of Melbourne packed into the hot court-house, hundreds more stood outside, at the corner of King and Bourke streets, and not even the heat and a stinging, gritty wind could disperse them. On the outskirts of the restless crowd mounted constables and men on horseback waited, talking and catching the latest news from inside the court-room. Women with baskets on their arms jostled one another in their eagerness to hear what was said. Tongues wagged, hands clawed at wind-blown hats and shawls, at lifting parasols and ballooning

390

dresses. Tregg! Elijah Tregg! The name was hissed from mouth to mouth. The man who had deliberately murdered his own son! Yes, an ex-convict, of course. So important was the matter that the Chief Police Magistrate, Major Frederic Berkeley St. John, calm, tall, with greying hair and deep, penetrating grey eyes, who had lately replaced James Simpson, had taken the bench, and it was whispered the prisoner had no friend, no one to speak for him. A friend? Who would befriend such a creature? The gallows—*that's* where he would go—the rope would be his friend.

"I seen the wretch——" said a woman. "Saw 'im brought 'ere in chains. A dreadful villain! A murderer! He'll go to trial from 'ere an' swing, an' good riddance, good riddance. The col'ny don't want such devils——"

"Mebbe 'e ain't guilty," said a man.

"Ho, ho!" jeered another. "What they got 'im in chains for? The police says 'e *said* 'e done it. 'E'll swing—'e'll swing!"

Everyone seemed to agree. Those in the court-room stared with hostile eyes at the chained man in the dock. They noted his wretched appearance, his uncut hair, his pale and downcast face with its ragged grey whiskers, his trembling hands, his lowered, staring eyes. A monster! A man who had deliberately slain his own son. It was incredible that such as he could exist. But society would soon be rid of him. Just look at him! Dirty, barefooted, ragged—a miserable kangaroo-skin over tattered shirt and moleskins. He would not look at anyone, would not raise his eyes—he dare not raise his eyes and see the horror and hate and loathing for him in the grim faces of all present. And sitting across the court were the people for whom he had worked—the Olivers. There was Henry Oliver, white-haired, well dressed; his daughter, Jane, cool and composed, her dark eyes calmly surveying the scene from under the rim of her bonnet; and his son, Conway, also well-dressed, but looking hot and uncomfortable under the curious eyes of the onlookers.

Elijah did not move, not even when his ears caught the hisses sent at him from accusing lips. Again and again the cry "Silence in the court!" rang above the hum of voices and the hisses cutting sharply through all other sounds. Constables moved here and there; court officials passed to and fro; where the watching people sat was a constant swaying and turning of heads and bodies; but Elijah did not move.

The charge was read, and sonorously it was asked of the prisoner: "How do you plead—guilty or not guilty?"

It seemed an unnecessary question. But there was a loud sound of movement of scraping feet and indrawn breaths, as Elijah spoke slowly:

"Not . . . guilty."

Not guilty? Voices rose in volume. Was the man crazy? But the Crown would get to work on him. The first and only question by the Crown was a terrible one.

"Did you shoot your son, Royd Tregg, to death that night outside the house of Mr. Henry Oliver?"

For a long moment there was no sound in the court-room. Then, almost in a whisper:

"Yus . . . yus . . . I shot Royd . . . yus . . . I shot me son . . . to 'is death that night. Yus."

Someone laughed. And the poor fool had pleaded not guilty! The Crown, shrugging its shoulders, said: "That is all, Your Worship. The accused has admitted killing his son. It is only wasting the time of this court to prolong proceedings here. This murderer must stand trial for his awful crime. That, it is submitted, is irrefutable."

The Crown sat down, heavily complacent, satisfied that the matter, so far as the Lower Court was concerned, was closed. It only needed the direction of the presiding magistrate to commit the prisoner for trial, and everyone could then go home for the midday meal.

But the magistrate was in no hurry to close the matter. His eyes, in which there was neither accusation nor sympathy, looked calmly at Elijah as he said, "I understand Mr. John Segrave Hallett has agreed to appear for you."

Elijah did not answer, but sucked in his breath with a sharp, shuddering sigh. For a moment his eyes turned questioningly towards the Olivers; they did not move, but sat looking straight before them. He looked away, and gave a hesitant glance round the court-room before dropping his eyes to gaze stolidly down at his chains. His hands were shaking a little. As he looked down a man's sharp incisive voice, coming from the back of the court, said curtly:

"I will also speak for the prisoner, Your Worship!"

And then there was uproar in the court. Noise, movement, voices that raised a babble in the room. A little man was striding forward, a man about five feet in height, thin, wiry and active, although he appeared to be about fifty years of age, whose keen blue eyes in a seamed, hawk-like face had in them a frosty gleam as he advanced. Voices gasped:

"It's Fawkner . . . John Pascoe Fawkner! Fawkner——"

Necks were craned, eyes were wide as Fawkner walked to confront the magistrate.

"Up to his old games—getting the lags off——" someone said sarcastically. "I thought he'd left his bush-lawyer tricks behind in Launceston——"

"You shut your mouth," came a deep growl. "John Fawkner wouldn't speak 'less he knowed something!"

"Silence—silence—silence!" bellowed the constables.

But it was some time before the crowd became quiet. John Pascoe Fawkner was going to speak for this fellow Tregg. Fawkner! It was a sensation! The "King of Pascoeville" himself! Now the court would hear something. The Crown had already lost its complacent look; it stared coldly at

Fawkner and braced itself for whatever might come from his sharp and fearless tongue.

Everyone there knew the story and reputation of the fiery founder of Melbourne Town, of whom the *Cornwall Press* the organ of his enemies in Launceston some years before, said scathingly: "Addlepated upstart—a garrulous maligner—five feet two inches and a quarter—whip-deserving impudence—as a moral pestilence, must be checked." They knew how his pen had scratched to some purpose in reply; knew how, in 1803, he had come out as a boy of ten on the *Calcutta* with his father, who had been transported, it was said, for receiving a box of stolen jewellery. They were aware that when Collins's attempt to form a settlement with his convicts at Port Phillip failed he had gone across to Hobart in the transport *Ocean*; that his father had been emancipated; that in his early manhood he had been a sawyer, farmer, baker, and had, in a moment of indiscretion, helped certain prisoners to build a boat and try to escape. Everyone watching him at this moment knew he and they had been captured, and that a harsh and vindictive authority had publicly flogged him in front of his father's house, and then had banished him for a few years to New South Wales. His later years and story were household knowledge. He had settled in Launceston, and had become a hotel-keeper, newspaper proprietor, self-appointed pleader in the Lower Court, pioneer of coach routes, teacher of the French language, and enthusiastic reader and collector of books. Then came his great venture, his feud with John Batman who also claimed to be the rightful founder of the town of Melbourne. Here beside the Yarra he had built the first store and grog-shanty, then a hotel that could accommodate comfortably "the wife of a Lieutenant-Governor". His hotel library—a few books, and English newspapers and magazines—was well-known. He had issued the first hand-written newspaper; he headed his letters "Pascoeville, Fawkner's River, Port Phillip"; he was now the proprietor of the printed and widely read *Port Phillip Patriot*, and had many other interests; and he was now, indubitably, a power in the community, a Justice of the Peace.

The atmosphere in the court-room was tense with expectancy and surprise. Fawkner had always tilted at authority and the squatter class for the comfort of the emancipist and doubtless his own deep feelings. Although now in his fifties, grey, but with the combative light still bright in his blue eyes, the forcefulness of his truculent personality was still manifest to his bearing. He was John Pascoe Fawkner, the *founder* of Melbourne Town, and although not present when his *Enterprise* first put out its plank on the Yarra bank, not present when earlier John Batman walked over the same lush banks, he claimed that he and he alone was the founder because of his money, his enterprise, and his will to make a town where others merely wanted empty miles on which to graze their flocks and herds.

Jane and Conway were both startled; Jane particularly being agitated by this new and unexpected turn. She whispered to her father:

"What is this? Why will Fawkner speak for Tregg? Do you know anything about it?"

Henry nodded slowly. "Naturally. I asked him to speak. I told him the story. It was the least I could do. I don't like this man Hallett very much. I believe he has a merciless way of getting at—at things. But I—I can't see the fellow hang. He served us well that night, even if he has been a shiftless oaf all his life."

Jane gasped.

"But—but—this will bring *us*—*me*—into it——"

Henry sighed. "Do you imagine the Olivers can avoid this? Undoubtedly we shall be asked some very pertinent questions. This is the court of the land, Jane. Here is the Queen's Law, and it is not concerned with the opinions or the feelings of the Olivers. Tregg's life is in jeopardy——"

"I don't care about Tregg's life!" she hissed. "I do care that the Olivers' name be not bandied about——"

Conway whispered harshly, "Here is one place where your wishes will be ignored. I've heard of this Hallett—he must have been somehow interested—Tregg has no money. I am glad father has spoken to Fawkner; he is listened to in Port Phillip. You and Everitt have had your ways in almost all matters so far as yourselves and this family are concerned. This court is the house of the people—not of the Olivers. Damn it—what else could father do?"

Jane was pale. She looked at the crowd. If the story of Royd's attack on her became public it would cause doubt to rise in many minds concerning herself. Royd had been in her room; he had overpowered her; he had lifted her in his arms and was carrying her away when he was shot. Would anyone believe he had not had his way with her before taking her out of the room? Not everyone—not everyone. She was trembling. What a fool her father was to come to Tregg's aid—Tregg did not matter, he was nobody, no one would care a snap of the fingers what happened to him. How dare her father jeopardize her good name and standing in society merely to help this useless and dirty old lag! She sat back on the bench, breathing quickly, dark eyes now wide and very alert. Hallett! He would ask questions. He would ask horrible questions. Had she retired for the night? Was she undressed? Was the room in darkness? Had she cried out for help! God—the fellow could tear her character and reputation to tatters. Had she ever encouraged Royd Tregg? Had she ever before been alone with him? Had he ever before taken any liberty? Oh, her father was mad! *Damn* Elijah Tregg! She might yet walk out of this Court suspected of being a soiled woman. Her head jerked up as Fawkner spoke.

"May it please Your Worship! I crave the Court's permission to make a public statement concerning the matter that is now before the court."

The magistrate nodded.

"You may proceed, Mr. Fawkner," was said in quiet, level tones.

Fawkner looked about him.

"It was only yesterday I came into possession of the true facts of this tragic happening," he said. "I want to preface my public statement, Your Worship, by saying that knowing what I now know, I support the prisoner's plea of 'Not guilty'——"

It was several minutes before the roar of astonished voices died away. Jane's hands were making nervous little movements now; her eyes were neither so cold nor so arrogant; apprehension was in them, and something like a slowly mounting fear. But no one was looking at her: all eyes were upon the diminutive John Fawkner. He went on:

"This story I heard goes back a long way——"

The Crown rose.

"Your Worship, we are not here to listen to any of Mr. Fawkner's stories. The prosecution submits——"

Major St. John held up a hand.

"We are here to determine whether the

prisoner in the dock shall be sent to a higher court to be tried for his life. If the matter is relevant I shall hear it. Proceed, Mr. Fawkner."

"Thank you, Your Worship. I assure the Court that what I have to say is both material and relevant. The story of this man Tregg brings before us once again the heartlessness and cruel attitude of the privileged classes towards those who have at some time in their unfortunate lives transgressed the laws of the land."

The Olivers stared straight before them. There was no sound. But Jane was uncomfortably aware that questioning eyes were slowly turning to her and her father and Conway. Those who regarded Fawkner so steadily wondered if the whip still burned across his back for that impulsive escapade of years before. Every word now uttered was measured and clear.

"The prisoner's son, Royd Tregg, was a madman. At the moment of his deed he was a homicidal maniac, having in his frenzy already slain his own mother—the wife of the man in the dock!"

No one moved. No one spoke. Even the crowd outside seemed to be incapable of sound or movement. Opinions for or against John Fawkner were forgotten; all were intent upon the drama of this moment.

"What I have just said is verified, it is a statement of fact, and is known to the Crown. Being isolated in that far and lonely valley, the man, Royd Tregg, twenty-six years of age, and the eldest son of the prisoner in the dock, had, when madness was on him, to be chained to a tree. Why? That is obvious, and can be understood by anybody; there was nothing else that could be done for him. The family knew he was dangerous, and were ever on the alert to seize and overpower him when these terrible paroxysms gripped him. Very well. One morning, when all except Sarah Tregg, his mother, were away from the crude and squalid hut in which the family lived, he broke his chain, went into the hut, and brutally murdered his own mother. He killed her with the heavy chain that still dangled from his body. Then he vanished. Annie Tregg, younger daughter of the prisoner, came back later and discovered the tragedy. She went to warn the other families in the valley—the Olivers, for whom the Treggs worked, and newly-arrived settlers named Martin. Search was made for the madman, but he could not be found. Elijah Tregg—yes, the man in the dock—rode to Gundagai to inform the police. Let that be remembered. He was told the police at that time were at Lake George. Tregg came back——"

John Fawkner paused. He looked round at the intense faces watching him. Elijah stood with head drooping, looking down at his bare feet. Fawkner drew in a breath and went on:

"No one knew where the madman was, but all knew that the lives of everyone in the valley were now threatened. No member of either family, or the Treggs themselves, knew when from behind a tree, or a rock, or out of the darkness, death would strike. One night after his return, Elijah Tregg, gun in hand for his own protection, went from his new hut to the house of his employers, the Olivers——"

Eyes turned to them. Jane was deathly pale; the scrutiny of those staring eyes was unnerving. Henry's thin face was also pale; he, too, knew that questions would be asked on oath. Conway kept his eyes on John Fawkner.

"What I relate now was told to me by a reputable eye-witness, Mr. Henry Oliver himself. It appears the family, that is, the Olivers, had retired early leaving Mr. Henry

Oliver sitting at the table in the living-room. Presently he got up and went outside, by way of the back door. He saw no one, heard nothing, but in that short time——"

The Crown rose to its feet; its voice boomed in the silent court-house.

"All this, Your Worship, is entirely unsubstantiated. This procedure is contrary to——"

Fawkner interrupted.

"Your Worship, I merely asked the Court's permission to make a statement. Mr. Hallett, I understand, will appear for the accused. The witnesses can and will, if the Crown wishes, give substantiation on oath. I appeal to Your Worship! The prisoner has been charged with murder, the penalty for which is death by hanging——"

"Proceed, Mr. Fawkner——" came tonelessly. "The Court is unlikely to be influenced by mere oratory. As to procedure, that is for me to determine, not the police prosecutor. Proceed, please."

Fawkner's voice rang out.

"I repeat, that in that short time the murderer crept into the house, and into the darkened bedroom of Miss Jane Oliver——"

Somewhere a woman's voice, startled and strained, said "Oh—oh!" and Jane flushed hotly and knew that all eyes were upon her.

"Miss Oliver was aware that someone was in her room, but terror prevented any movement or outcry. And then the madman seized her, and in that moment of horror and ordeal her senses left her——"

Jane was furious. Her hands were opening and shutting, her eyes blazing with anger. What would these listening oafs think now? What could they think? Only that she had been violated, the sport of Royd Tregg. Fawkner's voice cut in on her raging thoughts.

". . . he was cunning enough to wait with his insensible victim until Mr. Henry Oliver went back into the living-room, then, with Miss Oliver in his arms, he crept out into the darkness——"

The shuffling of a foot somewhere sounded like a thunderclap.

"There had been a moon; it was down. Henry Oliver, hearing some slight sound, took up the lamp and went to see what it was. There in its rays, before his horrified eyes, was his daughter in the arms of the madman, Royd Tregg. Henry Oliver could not move or speak, the shock held him rigid and silent. But the lamp also showed another—Elijah

Tregg, who had come to the back of the house at that moment. It was impossible for Elijah Tregg to do other than what he did. On hearing his father's sharp command to put Miss Oliver down Royd Tregg let her fall to the ground, but that he was determined now to kill her could be seen in the stealthy way he began to unwind the long heavy chain coiled round his body. With a madman's cunning he was unloosening it so that at a stroke he could kill Miss Oliver and any other who came to seize him. Had not Elijah Tregg shot his son at that moment Miss Oliver would not be alive and in this court today."

He paused. The court was hushed.

"Is there any man, or woman, who believes that a man, whatever his past, especially a past that has been atoned for, would while of sound mind take the life of his own son if he could avoid in any way, in any possible way, that terrible act? No! Elijah Tregg was faced with a horrible choice—either to destroy his own son, or watch that son mercilessly kill the woman lying helpless at his feet. To say Royd Tregg would not have killed her, or might not have killed her, is nonsense: he had so killed his mother only a little time before. What the thoughts and feelings of Elijah

Tregg were at that moment only the man standing there in the dock can tell. I can imagine no more terrible alternative—or responsibility . . . yes; responsibility . . . for, being armed it was his duty to prevent another murder. That man, Elijah Tregg, is no murderer—indeed, he deserves the pity and gratitude of everyone in this colony. At a cost known only to himself he rendered a public service to this community. He has to live with his thoughts—never forget that. I have spoken for him because these are the true facts. Elijah Tregg has committed no crime—he is not guilty of either murder or manslaughter. It was justifiable homicide, and the tragedy is that it was his own son he had to slay—to preserve the virtue and life of a woman. That is all, Your Worship."

There was a desperate light in Jane's eyes as she watched John Fawkner bow to the bench, ask permission to leave the court, and go strutting purposefully past goggling Melbournians. Those in the body of the court who looked and listened seemed to be stunned by what they had just heard, and the drooping man in the dock had already assumed a different character in their eyes. But Jane knew that she would be questioned, that her father's word in the matter would not be enough. When the Crown was granted an adjournment until the next morning she walked out of the court fearful and uncertain, wishing she could hide from the staring, suspicious eyes that watched her. What were they thinking? What were they *thinking*? Yes, about her. Her cheeks were crimson as she passed through a line of intent people.

"There she is . . . that's her . . . that's Jane Oliver . . . he was in the room with her . . . I wonder what she'll say about *that*. . . ."

Jane heard the remarks as she hurried along. For the first time in her life she could not play the cold and haughty role of Jane Oliver. She was almost choking with chagrin and apprehension as she stepped into the gig that waited to take them back to the Lamb Inn. Tomorrow? Good heavens—she would have to answer the devilish questions of that man Hallett. Tomorrow. . . .

There was only one topic of conversation in the streets, the newspaper offices, the homes, the shops, the Royal Exchange, the Jockey Club, the markets, the hotels, the banks, the trundling carriages, and the ships swinging at their chains in the bay. Elijah Tregg! John Pascoe Fawkner! The madman, Royd Tregg!

Jane Oliver! It seemed to be accepted now that there would be no case against Elijah Tregg. In the light of Fawkner's statement, and doubtless the support it would be given in cross-examination of the principal witnesses, everyone doubted that Elijah Tregg would be sent for trial. And it seemed as though the Crown held the same opinion, for the next day, in the same crowded and breathless room, the prosecutor's examination of Henry and Jane Oliver was a mere formality. But the portly, florid and genial John Segrave Hallett, whose suave tongue had a needle-point to it when he probed a witness, was determined that the bench and the public would be under no misapprehension or doubt as to the innocence of Elijah Tregg.

Henry Oliver was the first witness examined. He answered quietly, flushing slightly when questioned about the living conditions of the Treggs, resentful, but not daring to voice his thoughts as the cross-examination brought out the pitiful dependence and poverty of his servants, his neglect of them, his dismissal of them in the moment of tragedy. Mr. Hallett's voice was silky.

"You are a Christian, I presume, Mr. Oliver?"

"That is my belief, sir," came coldly.

"Are you sure of that?"

Henry flushed again. "I have always believed I am a Christian, sir," he rapped back.

Mr. Hallett smiled. "Are your late servants, the Treggs, also Christians, Mr. Oliver?"

"I cannot answer for the Treggs."

Mr. Hallett was still smiling. "Can you answer for your own family, sir?"

Henry swallowed. "I believe so."

"Have you any reason to doubt it?"

Someone in court sniggered. Henry went a dull red. He did not like this personal kind of questioning.

"I have no reason to doubt it," he said curtly.

"Would you say your sons and your daughter are of good character, Mr. Oliver?"

Henry stared at him. What the devil was all this?

"They are of good character," he almost snarled.

Mr. Hallett's plump white hands came gently together and remained clasped. Those who knew Mr. Hallett knew that when his hands joined one another so caressingly he was about to sting somebody.

"Indeed. Indeed! Did your daughter ever encourage the attention of this madman—amorously, I mean?"

Henry's reply was almost explosive.

"No!"

"How do you know that?"

"I know my daughter."

"Indeed, indeed! Could you furnish any reason why *she* was the one he sought to possess?"

"No."

"Was she kind to him?"

"I—I——"

"You are on oath, Mr. Oliver——"

"I don't know."

"Would he have any reason to hate her, to be revenged on her?"

"Not that I know of."

"Could he have been infatuated with her?"

"It isn't possible——"

"How do you know that?"

"I repeat—I know my daughter. She detested the fellow, never gave him the slightest encouragement."

"Ah——" said Mr. Hallett gently. "She

detested him. Do you know if she ever let him see she detested him?"

"No, I don't know that——"

"But a moment ago you said she *did* detest him."

"I have heard her say so."

"I see—I see. Those far valleys are strange places, they seem to exert a peculiar influence over the emotions of those who dwell in them. Do you think there was any likelihood of any secret intimacy between your daughter and Royd Tregg?"

"Good heavens, no!" panted Henry.

"Can you swear there was not?"

"I can't swear that—I wasn't with my daughter every moment of her existence. But knowing her as I do I know it would be the last thing she would encourage or even contemplate."

"Yes, yes, of course, Mr. Oliver. And you cannot say whether it was love or hate that drew Royd Tregg to your daughter's room that night?"

"I think he was crazy and didn't know what he was doing."

"There's no doubt he was mad. That is agreed to and proved. But there must have been *something* still left in his broken mind that drew him so surely and craftily to your daughter. Was there any other woman in the valley?"

"Yes. Four women in the Martin family."

"He did not go near them?"

"No."

"But he crept stealthily and deliberately to the bedside of Miss Oliver."

"He was there."

"Have any of your family ever wronged any member of the Tregg family?"

"I don't understand."

"Your sons, for instance. I believe there are two girls in the Tregg family——"

"No! Certainly not! The thought even is preposterous——"

"Indeed, indeed? I have talked to the prisoner. He tells me your son, Everitt, is the lover of his daughter, Meg."

Henry gasped. Jane licked dry lips. Conway whispered, "They get right into the bone, these fellows——"

Henry said, "I know nothing whatsoever about it."

"I don't doubt you, sir," was said smoothly. "But if that be true there *is* a member of the Oliver family giving a possible motive for Royd Tregg's attack on *your*

414

daughter. Revenge for the shame put upon his sister might have been flaming in his mad mind."

"I don't know, sir."

"I agree that no man can explain the thoughts in the mind of a lunatic, Mr. Oliver. But it seems much went on in the valley, and in your own family, of which you were blissfully unaware. You could have been unaware of any intimacy between your daughter, if there was any intimacy, and this man?"

"No. Not my daughter." Henry's voice was cold and brittle. "She is a woman of strong, firm and upright character. I believe she would rather be dead than associate with the Treggs."

"There are, indubitably, great differences of characters and opinions and desires in the different members of a family. Nevertheless it is incontestable that Royd Tregg attacked Miss Oliver, and no other woman. Did she scorn him to his face?"

"She regarded him as a servant, nothing more."

"Do you think he resented that?"

"Why should he? He was our servant."

"You knew he was subject to these awful moments of madness?"

"Yes."

"Did you ever do anything to lessen or to relieve his malady—did you ever discuss the wisdom or otherwise, the cruelty or otherwise, the efficacy or otherwise, of chaining him like a beast to a tree?"

"No."

"Why not?"

"It was a purely personal and domestic matter concerning the Tregg family."

"And were not the members of the Tregg family *your* concern?"

"I—I suppose so——"

"You are not sure?"

"I did as much for them as anyone does for such servants."

"But you merely regarded them as human chattels, there to serve you, to do your bidding, just as your dogs would do?"

Henry was white with anger, but he kept his voice under control.

"I rationed them, clothed them——"

Mr. Hallett turned and stared at Elijah for a moment. Everyone looked at Elijah. Someone laughed. Henry's hands clenched into thin fists. Mr. Hallett turned back to him.

"Did you give the prisoner *those* clothes, Mr. Oliver?" he asked.

A number of people laughed.

"Yes—not—not the skin jacket—the shirt and trousers——"

"Has he anything better than that to wear that you know of?"

"I don't know."

"But if you clothe him you ought to know, oughtn't you?"

"These people are lazy and improvident. They take no care of what is given to them."

"I see. Nothing like kicking the dog, Mr. Oliver—or sometimes the servant—who cannot kick back. Is it your opinion that the accused had to shoot his son?"

"Yes——" said Henry sourly. "He had to do so."

"Why?"

"It has been told—to save my daughter's life."

"Did you ever pay wages to the Treggs for working for you?"

"No. They worked only now and then, and for that they drew rations and clothes and other necessities such as guns, powder and ball. Most of their time was spent enjoying themselves roaming and shooting in the valley——"

"The prisoner appears to have had a most enjoyable life under your kindly care."

Mr. Hallett had to wait until the laughter died away. Henry was shaking; so was Jane, who dreaded the ordeal before her. Mr. Hallett looked positively unctuous as he continued. His hands were now extended, the palms together, the fingertips touching, as though he were at prayer, at least inwardly.

"Was there no other way of saving your daughter's life at that moment?" he purred.

"At that moment—no."

"Do you believe Royd Tregg would have killed your daughter?"

"Yes. I believe that."

"Are you quite positive, in your own mind, that the accused *had* to kill his son?"

"Yes. Quite positive."

"Could Royd Tregg have been reasoned with?"

"He was a homicidal maniac. Who can reason with a madman?"

"Could your sons have overpowered him?"

"There wouldn't have been time. They were all asleep in their room."

"Could you and the accused have mastered him?"

"Impossible! He had the strength of ten

men when the fits were on him. And he was even then unwinding the chain for the stroke that would have killed my daughter."

"You have absolutely no doubt in any way that Elijah Tregg had to shoot his son?"

"I have absolutely no doubt."

"Are you grateful to the accused for saving your daughter's life?"

Henry breathed deeply.

"Yes," he said slowly. "He saved my daughter's life. But for his action she would have been murdered. I am grateful to him——"

Mr. Hallett smiled again.

"Thank you, Mr. Oliver, thank you. That is all."

Henry almost crept back to his seat. He would not look at Jane or Conway, but inwardly he was boiling at the knowledge of Everitt's scandalous conduct. He would certainly trim that young cock's feathers so that he would not fly so cunningly in future. Jane heard him grinding his teeth as he sat down, but her thoughts were not concerned with him as she went to the witness stand. Her lips were thin and set; she had listened almost in a panic to the questions asked of her father; and she was also aware of the mounting hostility and contempt in the eyes of the onlookers. It came to her that being Jane Oliver back in the valley was a different matter from being Jane Oliver in this place where one's very thoughts were stripped bare and exposed to the gaze of the crowd. But she would make it clear to all she was a chaste woman, an Oliver, and not one to be pawed verbally by this smooth lawyer. Her face was set and cold as she seated herself, but the urbane Mr. Hallett summed her up at a glance.

"You are Jane Oliver?" he asked in his most friendly manner.

"Yes!" was snapped out.

Still smiling, his next question was quite unexpected.

"Were you raped by Royd Tregg?"

The spectators gaped. Jane's dark eyes glittered with fury.

"Certainly not!" she hissed. "How dare you ask——"

Up came a plump white hand.

"One moment, Miss Oliver—I am asking the questions, not you. And I take it you *want* it established beyond all doubt that you were *not* a victim of such lustful desire. Please confine yourself to answering my questions. Very well."

Jane glared at him, but a retort trembling on her lips was choked back when she saw the glint in Mr. Hallett's watchful eyes. He went on.

"Were you happy in that valley?"

"No!"

"Why not?"

"If you must know——"

"Yes, I must know. I am not asking these questions, Miss Oliver, merely for the sake of asking them. Perhaps it has not yet dawned on you that your ex-servant, Elijah Tregg, the man who shot his son, as your own father avows, to save your life, may yet be tried for his very life. I must ask you, Miss Oliver, not to exhibit your customary hauteur in this court. Here you are a witness—and nothing more. Why were you not happy in the valley where you lived?"

Jane looked as if she could kill him. Such a public rebuke was unbearable. But she controlled her voice.

"It was lonely; we never saw anyone—other than the Treggs; there was no woman of my own class to whom I could talk."

Mr. Hallett nodded.

"I can appreciate that, Miss Oliver. Did the loneliness of the valley induce you to talk with Royd Tregg at any time?"

"Never at any time—or with any of the Treggs."

"I see, I see. Did you know about your brother's affair with Meg Tregg?"

"I did not."

"Did you—suspect it?"

"I—I—perhaps."

"Are you very friendly with all the members of your family?"

"Naturally."

"Please answer my question."

"Yes."

"Did any of them ever tell you about your brother's intimacy with this girl?"

"No."

"Then what made you suspect it?"

"I don't rightly know."

"I see, I see. Before the night of this tragic happening, were you ever alone with Royd Tregg at any time?"

"Never!"

"Do you know why he selected you to be his victim when there were other women in the valley?"

"No."

"Do you think the accused had to kill his son?"

"I don't know——"

"Why don't you know?"

"I was unconscious."

"Why were you unconscious?"

"I had been attacked."

"Will you tell the Court where you were attacked?"

"In my room—my bedroom. I had retired for the night. The room was in darkness. He crept in. I tried to scream . . . but his hands were on my throat. I fainted. I knew no more until my senses came back and I realized I was in my room with my father and brothers bending over me——"

"Do you not remember being lifted up in Royd Tregg's arms and being carried outside?"

"No."

"But it was the madman, Royd Tregg, who came into your room and attacked you?"

"Yes."

"How do you know it was he? Wasn't the room in darkness?"

"He was killed outside where he had carried me. My father saw him. His father shot him."

"Do you think he would have killed you?"

"I have no reason to doubt it—he killed his mother with the chain he still had round him."

"Were you injured in any way?"

"No."

"And you had never encouraged this man in any way whatsoever?"

"Most certainly not!"

"Had killing you been the only thought in his mind he would have killed you there on your bed, but it seems he had another purpose. Do you know why he should have that inclination towards you and towards no one else?"

"No."

"Had you ever hurt him in any way?"

"No."

"Were you ever aware he might have been infatuated by you?"

"No."

"You can give no reason for his attack on you?"

"No."

"And you are completely unaware of any attachment he might have formed in his mind towards you?"

"Completely."

"Do you fully realize what this man, Elijah Tregg, has done for you?"

"I—I realize what he has done."

"For you?"

"Yes . . . for me . . ."

"I trust I mistake your tone to be a grudging one, Miss Oliver. I would not like to form the opinion that you regard these proceedings as being something of a mere necessary nuisance to you. But your demeanour leads me to suspect that you are completely unsympathetic towards the man who saved your life."

"I—I do not wish to convey that impression——"

"I am sure you don't, Miss Oliver—but you *are*. You seem to be more concerned with your small personal feelings than with this unfortunate man's chance of living."

Jane dared not look round her. She could sense the hardening anger and hostility in the people listening. She knew she was trembling; knew she was *not* impressing anyone with her haughty concern for herself and her good name. She blanched as soft hisses followed Mr. Hallett's remarks, but she knew they were not directed at him. Fear was rising fast in her; she felt helpless in this place; she could not loose her tongue, could not give full play to the anger within her. Fear! This Hallett would ridicule her, hold her up as a heartless woman. He may even yet throw doubt on her chastity. Fear! Supposing his clever tongue raised the impression, even just the impression, she had been raped, the imputation would cling to her all her life. Always people would ask themselves if it really happened. She was frightened. Very frightened. Never in all her life had she been so frightened. Her voice was so low and faltering when she replied that many did not hear what she said.

"I am concerned with his chance of living——"

All now could see her shaking hands, her trembling form. To Conway's amazement Jane was breaking; the hard shell of pride and arrogance was cracking; and the smiling Mr. Hallett was quietly watching it crack. Conway stared at his sister. Jane weeping! It was unbelievable!

Hallett said, "I know how distressing this is for you, Miss Oliver, but it is immeasurably more distressing for the man in the dock. You do not stand there. You are not in the public gaze because you have killed your son——"

"No—no! Please—please——" Jane gasped. "I—I know what he has done. I—I——"

"Just take a moment to compose yourself, Miss Oliver," said Mr. Hallett in his most kindly way.

"I—I am all right——"

"Very well then. You do realize what he has done for you?"

"Yes—I do."

"Are you grateful to him?"

A shuddering sigh and the word seemed to combine.

"Yes——"

"Sincerely and deeply grateful to this unfortunate and tormented man?"

Jane's hands came up to cover her face. Hard sobs suddenly shook her; her voice came brokenly.

"Yes—yes! Oh, God . . . I know what he did for me . . . I can't, I can't bring myself . . . to think about that awful night . . . that silent, brutal maniac . . . those choking hands . . . I thought Royd would kill me . . . I knew it was Royd Tregg . . . I tried to scream, I couldn't, I *couldn't*! And then I found . . . I was safe . . . I was alive and unhurt in every way. Yes—yes—I know I owe my life to Elijah Tregg . . . my life . . . my good name . . . I owe to him. Yes, he *had* to shoot his son . . . to save me. I am grateful . . . before God . . . *I am grateful.* . . ."

Mr. Hallett beamed at her.

"Thank you, thank you, Miss Oliver. That will be——"

He did not finish the sentence. Jane had tried to rise, had given a little cry, and then had crumpled senseless to the floor. During the tumult that roared in the court Conway darted forward and picked her up in his arms.

"Well said, Jane——" he muttered huskily as he carried her out of the court-room. "That was well said—well said, indeed. They won't send Tregg to trial now—not now."

24

TILLY'S resentful eyes were on Annie as the girl sat at the lamp-lit table poring over some simple words Mark had set for her to learn. Outside there was a half-moon, and with the passing of the rains creeks and rivers were falling. The Martin family were in the living-room, Hetty, with steel-rimmed spectacles on the end of her nose, dozed by a small fire; Nan and Jeanette were sewing; Tilly was darning some stockings; Tom and Mark were reading over again the English newspapers Henry Gubby had sent. Tomorrow they would all pull corn; enough of the new barn had been slabbed and roofed to hold it; and everyone was excited at the prospect of getting in the first crop. They had talked about it; how Annie and Nan and Mark would be on one side of the dray as it went down the rows, Tilly, Jeanette and Tom on the other. They would husk as they pulled. Five acres would put a mountain of golden cobs in the barn, and they were all eager to see it there.

Tilly was in an irritable mood at the moment, however, and she nudged Jeanette as she whispered, "Look at that little fool trying to get some 'larnin'. I wish mother would send her back to the Tregg kennel."

"Hush, Tilly," whispered Jeanette. "She might hear you."

Tilly sniffed. "Would I care? She hasn't a brain in her stupid head—and might as well know it."

Jeanette frowned. "You are too harsh, Tilly," she said in a low tone. "It says much for her that she wants to better herself."

"Then I wish she'd do it elsewhere——"

Tilly ceased whispering as Hetty opened her eyes and looked at the clock.

"Bed-time, my dears," said Hetty. "I wonder if your father will come tomorrow——"

Annie lifted her head, stared in front of her for a moment, then lowered her head again. For a moment the print in front of her was blurred as her thoughts went to her own father caged in a cell somewhere in Melbourne Town.

"Goodness, mother," said Nan. "Father's been away for weeks now. So have the Olivers, and—and——"

Nan's voice trailed away as she glanced quickly at Annie. There was warning in Hetty's eyes.

"Yes. I do hope he won't be long now. I'm sure nothing has happened to him—but we're into late March now. The weeks do go by."

"It's a long journey, mother," said Tom heartily. "No doubt the coach has been delayed by the rains—some of the rivers would be up, you know, and the coach might have to wait a day here and there before it can cross. I suppose some day there'll be bridges."

"I expect it is that, Tom?"

She looked at Annie. She understood the reason for Nan's momentary confusion, and her eyes were sympathetic. "Can you understand the words, dear?" she asked.

Annie nodded as she looked up.

"Yus, Mrs. Martin, thenk you—on'y some of the little 'uns, though."

"Well, Annie, you do try hard."

"Yus, I does, Mrs. Martin. I wants to larn."

"I know you do, Annie. You will."

Hetty stood up.

"I'm for bed. Don't be long after me,

children. We'll have a long day tomorrow. Good night."

"Good night, mother."

"G'night, Mrs. Martin."

Tilly wrinkled her nose as Hetty's door closed, and malice rose in her eyes.

"You're wasting your time, Annie," she said. "You Treggs are not exactly 'larnin'' people."

"Meanin'?" asked Annie quietly.

Tilly's tone had a sting in it. "What I said. What's the use of your trying to be what you're not?"

Annie's voice was level and slow. "You mean—th' same as you?" she asked.

"The same as I!" came sharply.

"Oh, let Annie alone," said Tom impatiently.

"I'm only offering her good advice," retorted Tilly.

Mark said, "Why don't you take Tom's?"

Annie spoke. "I don't mind what Tilly says, Tom, Mark——"

"That is condescending of you," came with cutting sarcasm. "But isn't it time, Annie, you thought of going back to your own people?"

"Tilly!" said Mark angrily. "Annie is staying with us—you know that."

"She doesn't have to—if she doesn't want to——"

"I does want to," said Annie quietly.

"So it seems," Tilly said pointedly. "Oh, well—you can always be useful as a servant."

"Oh, really, Tilly!" remonstrated Jeanette.

Tilly's eyes seemed to express surprise. "What else can Annie ever be here? And I doubt if, with this thirst for 'larnin'', she wants to be that. You wouldn't like to be our servant, would you Annie?"

Annie's eyes were beginning to glint. Why Tilly wished to be unpleasant at this moment she did not know. But Tilly was always unpleasant.

"Ain't never bin a sarvint—ain't never goin' to be a sarvint," she said slowly.

"Admirable. And so well expressed——"

"What the devil's the matter with you, Tilly?" Tom wanted to know.

"Nothing except that I have the interests of the Martin family at heart, my dear brother," was said smoothly.

Before anyone else could speak Annie said, "I ain't the one thet's agoin' to make trouble for the Martin fambly."

433

"And is anyone—that you know of?" Tilly asked quickly.

"Mebbe."

Tilly's lips tightened. She was not sure how much this girl knew about her affair with Everitt Oliver. She went on.

"Can't you be more definite than that, Annie? This is really interesting. Someone—according to Annie, of course—might bring trouble into this family. Is that what you mean, Annie?"

"Mebbe."

Tilly turned to Mark with a hard little laugh.

"I fear your 'larnin'' hasn't had much effect, Mark——"

"Oh, shut up!" said Mark rudely. "I don't think it's fair of you, Tilly, to make a butt of Annie, to try to make her look small and foolish in front of us all."

"Do I have to *try*?" Tilly purred.

"Don't be a bitch!" said Tom loudly. "Let the girl alone!"

Tilly's eyes blazed. "Don't speak to me like that, Tom! You forget yourself——"

Tom's dark eyes showed his anger. "I like that!" he exclaimed. "You seem to think you're the only one who can say unpleasant things in this house. Let Annie alone——"

"I've said nothing unpleasant—unless the truth be unpleasant——"

Annie interrupted her. She spoke slowly, very slowly.

"S'pose you says the truth—'bout y'self, Tilly Martin—or does you want *me* to say it? I've took your sauce an' dirt for a long time now, an' jist acause I keeps quiet you thinks you can claw me easy. You never made a bigger mistake. Jist acause you slashed me sister, Meg, with your ridin' whip, don' think you can slash me—with a whip, or your tongue, or anythin' else. An' Meg's still waitin' to ketch you for thet, an' I wouldn't like to be you—when she does."

Astonished eyes were turned to Tilly. But before anyone could speak all heard a voice out in the valley calling:

"Hullo, there! Hullo, there! Hullo . . . there!"

Nan gave a shriek. She raced to the door and flung it open.

"It's father——" she screamed. "Here he comes! Father, father——"

All except Annie ran to the door.

"Yes—there he is!" cried Tilly excitedly. "Jeanette, tell mother——"

435

Hetty's voice came from behind her.

"I heard it, Tilly. I would have heard it . . . a hundred miles away."

Jeanette and Nan were dancing with excitement. Tom and Mark were already running to meet their father. Tilly and Hetty were smiling as they stood together.

"He's safe——" said Hetty. "He's home again——"

Annie sat very still. No one at that moment gave her a thought. She could not remember ever being excited about her own father, or seeing her sister and brothers dancing with joy when he returned after some short absence. But he was her father. Something hard rose in her throat as she listened. Here was something the Treggs had never known. Blows, curses, indifference, poverty—yes! But never affection, never such manifest and sincere delight as she now looked upon. And as she realized what was here, what this family meant to each other, she felt her presence to be intolerable, a kindly sufferance. Tilly's words had hurt, but they were true. She was not a Martin; she was an intruder; and her desire to better herself and become as they were was a matter for laughter. She sat staring down at the simple words on the paper before her, and a tear fell, then another, and then her eyes could not see. Quietly she stood up and went out through the back door; they would not want her in the room when their father came in. Slowly she walked towards the corn paddock and, pausing there, wept blinding tears, wept with the understanding of what she was, wept with the knowledge of what she could never be.

Presently she grew calmer. She looked down the slope at the house. There was something there that might have been. The small, bark-roofed dwelling was plain in the moonlight. Excited voices came faintly to her. She rubbed her eyes with shaking hands. She could not go back. She could not live close to Tilly Martin; sooner or later she would be provoked into furious retaliation; her tongue would hurt the rest of the family the moment it lashed Tilly. She could not do that. Never had she known such kindness, such friendliness, such comfort, apart from the spiteful Tilly. But it could not be. Meg and Johnnie and Rock and Dick were not getting these things, and with Elijah standing in the shadow of the gallows she ought to be with them. Meg had been right—so right—but she had clung to this precious thing, this chance, this light that had never shone for her before. All her longings, all her dreams, were but dreams. The reality was she was Annie Tregg, born of convict parents.

She had not changed from her working clothes; she had on the old kangaroo-skin jacket over the tattered print dress. And she was glad of it. She walked slowly along the paddock fence, her ears catching the rustling of dry cornstalks as she passsed them. She did not walk towards the house; she turned and, crying softly again, went south along the moonlit valley.

John was laughing as the boys almost pulled him out of the saddle.

"Hey—it's good to be home, boys," he said. "Take the grey, Mark; look after him; he's had a long day. Is all well?"

"Yes, father."

Nan threw herself into his arms.

"Oh, you *villain* to stay away from us so long——" she panted. "We thought you were never coming back——"

He kissed her, then Jeanette and Tilly. And then Hetty was in his arms.

"John——" she managed to say. "Oh, we've missed you——"

"What are all the packs?" Tom asked as he

staggered under the weight of the laden saddle.

"Something for each of you," said John.

"I'll get a fine supper for you, father," said Jeanette.

"Did you have a good journey, father?" asked Nan.

"Oh, it wasn't so bad, Nan. The coaches nearly shook all the bones out of me. And some of the inns were comfortable, and some were not. We had one or two bad moments crossing rivers, but I'll tell you more about it later—especially about the coach we had to abandon in a quickly rising river. It got bogged, we got the horses away, and the passengers, but we overlooked one man who was drunk and asleep. When we went back for him he was still asleep with the water up to his chin. We got him out——"

"What did he say?"

"He asked for a drink of water," said John amid laughter. "But there were other amusing things—I'll tell you after I've eaten. Hey, hey! It's good to be home."

"Are we all right here, father?" asked Tilly. "I mean—the land?"

He nodded.

"Ay—indeed we are, Tilly."

"Can we manage, John?" Hetty asked as they sat down.

"We can, wife. We need have no fear for our home or our future."

"Thank God," said Hetty softly. "I have been wondering, and wondering. Jeanette—warm up that pie, dear, and make fresh tea."

"Lots of it," cried Nan. "We'll all have another supper. Oh, I couldn't sleep—goodness, no!"

Tom came in with the parcels and placed them on the table.

"Whatever have you here, father?" he asked with a laugh.

"A small present for everybody——"

"Open them now—open them now——" said Nan eagerly.

"Oh, wait for Mark——"

"Mark's coming," said Tilly.

"The grey all right, son?" John asked as Mark came into the room.

"Yes. In fine fettle. Not a bit blown. He's all right."

"You must have spent a lot of money, father," said Jeanette. "Mind, Nan—mind! Goodness you nearly upset the pie."

"Oh, I don't know what I'm doing," said Nan.

"I couldn't go all that way and come back empty-handed," said John. "I felt I was able to spend a little money."

"How are the Gubbys, dear?" asked Hetty.

"They're very well. Hetty, perhaps we don't yet realize what we owe to them. I was fearful, but her first words showed me I had nothing to fear. 'I don't want your land, Mr. Martin,' she said. 'I'm an innkeeper; I wouldn't know what to do with all that land. Mr. Gubby and I wouldn't know the difference between a furrow and a farrow.' And then she left it to me to say what I thought we could do. She told me her own name was Martin before she married Gubby——"

"Well, now! I do declare!" said Hetty.

"Perhaps that had something to do with our good luck. But I'll be talking for days to come——"

"The presents, father," pleaded Nan. "Oh, don't keep us waiting any longer——"

John laughed and turned to the packages.

"Here we are then," he said, opening the first. "The first is for you, wife—gold chain and locket. I felt these little gifts should mark our good fortune, our firm possession of our land and our home."

Hetty could scarcely speak.

"Oh—John! I've always wanted a gold chain and locket. Oh, my dear—it's beautiful——"

He clasped it round her neck, then patted her cheek.

"It's just a little something, Hetty—not anything like what you deserve. Now Tilly—ah! A hand-glass in the wonderful mother-of-pearl, as they call it in Sydney."

Tilly gasped.

"Oh, father—I have never seen anything like it—oh, thank you——"

"Jeanette, my dear, a silver-inlaid ornament comb for that fine black hair."

Jeanette's dark eyes shone.

"It's a lovely comb——" she breathed. "Thank you, father——"

"Nan—oh?" and he looked dismayed. "Oh, don't say I've forgotten Nan's present——"

"Oh, no, father!" Nan wailed. "Don't say that—no, no, no!"

John laughed.

"As if I would. Here, you puss! A broad, filigree, silver bracelet."

"Father!" Nan gasped. "Oh, look at it, mother! Jeanette, Tilly—Tom, Mark, look!"

"That will keep you awake all night," said

442

Tom amid laughter. "Vanity, thy name is Nancy Martin——"

"Oh," gulped Nan. "Oh——"

She threw her arms round John's neck and hugged him.

"Thank you, father. Oh——"

"Tom, you next—here we are——"

"It's a piece of paper?" said Tom inquiringly.

John nodded.

"Open it and read it, son——"

Tom opened it and read:

The bearer of this note will take delivery at the smithy, Gundagai, of a black blood stallion, guaranteed entire and broken to saddle, on the fourteenth day of April, 1842.

Tom stared. He could scarcely believe his eyes.

"A black blood stallion, Father——" he whispered.

"That's for the grand work you've done here, Tom. You've earned him. You and Mark will take the big dray in, and pick up two Neapolitan boars and a Saxon-merino ram. Now, Mark—here's your reminder of my journey and our good fortune, son."

Mark's blue eyes were wide. Out of the package came a pair of swan-neck, solid silver spurs with rowels as big as half-crowns.

"They're fine——" he breathed.

"That's not all. Tom will get a black stallion, I'll keep the bay mare, and I'm giving you, for your own, the grey gelding."

"Thank you, father. That's wonderful——"

John turned to the table. One more package lay on it.

"Why, of course," he cried. "That's for Annie. Where is Annie?"

Annie? It was only then they realized the girl was not in the room.

"Oh, sulking somewhere, I dare say," said Tilly lightly.

"Find her, Mark," said John quietly. "I have something very nice for Annie. I'll have some supper while you look for her."

Mark ran to the back door.

"Annie—Annie——" he called. "Where are you?"

There was no answer. Mark ran out of the house still calling her name.

Hetty asked, "What did you get for yourself, John?"

He looked astonished, and a hand came up to rub his chin.

"Well—upon my soul, wife—I forgot about myself——"

"Oh, John! All these wonderful gifts for us and nothing for yourself?"

He looked round at them all, smiling as he did so. "I had the journey; I have the land; and I have—you. I am content. When Mark comes in with Annie we'll give thanks to God for my safe return, and for the richness of His blessing upon us all——"

John finished his supper before Mark came back. The boy's face showed his concern when he came in.

"Where is she?" asked Nan.

Mark shook his head. They all stared at him.

"She's gone. I called and called." He looked directly at Tilly. "She's . . . gone."

25

TOWARDS the end of April Elijah Tregg walked on bare feet into the new hut Johnnie, Rock and Dick had built. The three men, with Meg and Annie, were having their midday meal when his shadow fell across the doorway. As he entered they looked at him in silence. Then Annie rose.

"I'll git you somethin', 'Lijah," she said. "You don' look too good."

The rest of them seemed incapable of movement or speech; they stared at their father as if he were a ghost. Annie looked over her shoulder at them all, at Elijah standing, his shoulders sagging, at Meg and her brothers sitting motionless at the table. How different was Elijah's homecoming from that of John Martin.

At last he said, "They let me go. I come beck with the Blairs. They's bought out th' Olivers."

He shuffled to the table and sat down. Still no one spoke. It was as if a phantom had entered and sat down with them. Perhaps his physical appearance was itself a shock to them: he seemed a different man from the one they had known. He was thin, almost enfeebled. The flesh of his face had shrunk until his cheeks were grey hollows; his eyes, lustreless and filmed, were far back in dark sockets; his hands were claws of sinew and bone. He was but the husk of the man who had left the valley a little while before. And his speech was slow and slurred, as if he could not frame thought for utterance.

Dick said in his level way, " 'Ow come you got free?"

Elijah did not look at any of them.

"Oliver did it," he said. "Oliver did it."

" 'Ow?" asked Johnnie.

"What 'e said . . . got me free. 'E tol' 'em 'bout me, an' Royd, an' Sarah. They said . . . I couldn't do nothin' else . . . said I saved Jane's life . . . thet I wasn't to blame. They talked a lot, but thet be the guts of it. I come back with the Blairs . . . they's bought out th' Olivers."

"Bought out th' Olivers?" said Meg. "Then all th' Olivers be leavin' the valley?"

He nodded.

"Yus. An' so be we."

447

"Us?" asked Dick. "Goddlemighty—why?"

"They said . . . when they let me go . . . I was to go to 'nother col'ny . . . all us Treggs mus' go . . . to 'nother col'ny."

His words shocked them. Annie swung round, eyes wide, mouth open.

"Whar to?" she asked.

"Van Diemen's Land . . . South 'Stralia . . . the West . . . anywheres but New South Wales. Git out an' stay out . . . they said."

"We got no money," said Dick. " 'Ow can we go?"

Elijah seemed to raise his eyes, but they fell and he continued to look down at the table.

"Oliver guv me . . . fifty poun's," he said.

"Fifty—poun's!" jerked out Meg. "Oliver did? Was 'e drunk?"

"No."

Meg spoke again. "Whar's th' Olivers goin'?"

"Dunno. Somewhar's in Port Phillip, mebbe."

She asked, "What like be these Blairs? 'Ow many of 'em? Tell us."

Annie put some stewed kangaroo flesh and bread in front of him.

"Fill y'self, 'Lijah," she said quietly.

He answered Meg. "The Blairs be good folks—gen'le folks——"

"More bleddy Olivers, I s'pose," sneered Rock.

"No. Not like them. Kindly folks . . . like them Martins." He looked at Annie for a moment. "Why ain't you with the Martins?" he asked.

"I was—I ain't," said Annie shortly.

"Why not?"

" 'Cause I be a Tregg."

He drew in a breath. Meg asked impatiently, " 'Ow many Blairs?"

"Two gels 'bout Annie's age—twins. Five sons an' the two ol' people."

"Did they all come with you?"

"Yus. Brought their wagons an' drays an' everythin'—furniture an' stores."

"Without fust seein' the place?" asked Dick.

"Blair seen it when Oliver come to look at it. Blair nearly settled 'ere then, but didn't. I 'eard 'em say they'd go 'long to meet the Martins today."

"All of 'em?" asked Annie. She was thinking of the two girls of her own age."

"S'pose."

"So thar'll be on'y them Blairs an' the Martins in the valley," said Dick.

"Yus."

" 'Ave we *got* to go?" asked Rock.

"Yus."

" 'Ow old be the Blair fellers?" Meg asked.

"Like Johnnie, Dick an' Rock, mebbe. Mebbe a few years this a-way an' thet a-way."

"An' they ain't bastuds like th' Olivers?" Johnnie asked.

"No. Kindly."

"Eddicated?" asked Annie.

"Yus—all of 'em. They'll do well. They'll be liked. They seems to unnerstan' other folks—an' things."

Dick filled his lungs.

"I ain't goin'. I got somethin' started 'ere—somethin' I'll never git nowhar's else."

Elijah raised slow eyes.

" 'Tain't for you to say. The guv'ment says you goes—so you goes. All the Treggs."

Meg's lip lifted.

"An' all acause *you* killed Royd——"

"Meg!" said Annie sharply.

"Well—ain't it so?" Meg demanded.

Elijah nodded.

"Yus. It be so. I killed Royd. It be so."

Meg's eyes began to gleam.

"I ain't goin' out o' this col'ny for no police," she said harshly. "I didn't kill Royd—I ain't answerin' for *thet*——"

"Shet up, Meg!" said Annie.

"I won' shet up!" said Meg. "I bin kicked roun' all me life—for what I ain't done as well's what I 'ave. No one's goin' to kick me roun' no more."

Elijah sighed. He ate a little, but soon pushed the bowl away.

"But for ol' Oliver, they'd a 'anged me, I s'pose," he said. "I didn't expec' 'im to speak for me—'tain't like 'im—but 'e did. Mebbe 'e thought it'd squar things a bit. Dunno what 'e thought."

"Eat somethin', 'Lijah," said Annie. "You mus' eat——"

"No. Not 'ungry, Annie. I be goin' over to the tree. I don' want no one to come."

They watched him go out of the hut.

"Well, thar we are! Kicked out o' th' col'ny," Johnnie said with a snarl, "An' *thet'll* stick to us all our lives—like we was *all* bleddy murderers——"

"Don' you talk like thet, Johnnie—'e 'ad to do it," said Annie.

"What? To save Jane Oliver's skin?" rasped Johnnie. "What matter if Royd 'ad

451

raped 'er? Sarve 'er right. She was allus ready to spit on us Treggs. 'Er! 'Lijah shouldn't 'ave shot 'im—for 'er! 'Lijah 'ad no right to kill a Tregg."

"No! 'E shouldn't," Meg agreed fiercely. "An' no guv'ment'll ever git me out o' the col'ny 'less I wants to go."

"Me neither," said Rock.

"Me neither," said Dick slowly. " 'Lijah can go by 'isself. No law can transport us—we's done nothin'."

"Mebbe the guv'ment thinks we's all got Royd's madness in us somewhars," said Annie.

"What if we 'ave?" argued Meg. "We still ain't *done* nothin'."

"Can't argufy agen thet," said Dick.

"Dunno——" said Annie thoughtfully. "Guv'ment can do mos' anythin'."

"Then why wasn't 'Lijah stretched?" asked Meg.

"They said 'e 'ad to do it—to save Jane Oliver."

Meg sneered. "D'ye think th' Olivers would 'ave done it to save *you* or *me*? You ain't right in the haid. But you never was—an' I often thinks you never was a Tregg——"

452

"Who cares in 'ell what *you* thinks!" Annie rapped back. "You be savage an' sore 'cause Tilly Martin beat you for Ev'ritt——"

"You——" Meg half rose as she spoke.

Annie watched her.

"You keep your 'ands to y'self, Meg—or I'll claw *you* this time—fierce! I took your slap at the pool thet day 'cause I knowed you was right. But don' git notions I be allus takin' slaps."

"You watch y' tongue!" threatened Meg.

"You watch—somethin' else," said Annie sharply. "If 'Lijah says we goes—we goes. All of us!"

"Not me," said Johnnie, forgetting that a little while ago he was urging them all to leave the valley.

"I'm stayin'," said Dick. "I got a chanct 'ere."

" 'Lijah can go to the devil," said Meg. " 'E shouldn't 'ave come beck 'ere—an' 'e shouldn't 'ave shot Royd."

Annie looked at her.

"What's the use o' *you* stayin'?" she asked. "Ev'ritt won' be 'ere."

Meg sat very still, her fierce blue eyes on Annie.

453

" 'Tain't Ev'ritt I wants to meet—now," she said slowly.

"You better let well alone, Meg," Annie advised. "Or mebbe *you'll* get the rope for killin' someone."

"Mebbe—mebbe. But I still wants to meet someone if I can ketch 'er."

"Annie's right, you fool," said Dick. "You can't no nothin' 'cept git trouble."

"Mebbe——" said Meg tonelessly. "But I still wants thet Tilly Martin."

Annie, who was near the door, said quickly, "Lookit! Thar's the Blairs aridin' towards the Martins—all of 'em—an' Ev'ritt Oliver——"

Meg leapt to the doorway. Everitt, she noticed, did not bother to turn his head. He was laughing and talking with one of the Blair boys, and was evidently in high spirits. Annie glanced sideways at Meg as Johnnie, Rock and Dick came to look at the new people.

"Don' seem to worrit Ev'ritt Oliver none leavin' 'ere," said Annie. " 'E mus' know 'bout it."

Meg's eyes followed Everitt.

"Don' seem to worrit the Martins none *you* leavin' them," she retorted. "You bin gone weeks now, an' no one's come to fetch you

454

beck—not thet Martin feller you was all wet about——"

Annie was silent. What Meg said was true enough. Every time she had heard the hoofbeats of a horse she had waited breathlessly for the sound of Mark's voice. But he had not come. Meg went on.

"As for me? I ain't leavin'—I ain't leavin' nothin'. You'll see——"

Along the valley John Martin looked up in astonishment as he walked from the barn towards the house. Coming round the stripped corn paddock were men and women on horseback. He recognized Everitt Oliver, but the others were strangers. Nan, who at that moment came to the back door, also saw them. She ran back into the living-room.

"Mother, people are coming to visit us. Mr. Oliver's bringing them," she panted. "Oh, dear—there's a lot of them——"

"Visitors?" said the astonished Hetty. "And Mr. Oliver? Are you sure——"

"Of course. I saw them. It looked so odd to see other people here."

"Did you say Mr. Oliver was with them?" Tilly asked.

"Yes. He has a cheek, hasn't he? It's the young Mr. Oliver. There's an elderly couple, both riding, five younger men and two girls about my age——"

"Oh, my goodness!" exclaimed Hetty. "They'll be just in time to join us for a meal. Visitors! I wonder who they can be——"

"Yes," said Tilly. "I wonder why they are here. This is unexpected."

Tom came out of the barn and saw them. He stared, then called to Mark.

"Hey, Mark! Look! We've got company!"

Mark came running.

"Quite a crowd. What's up, I wonder? Better go and see. Come on, we'll have a look at their horses——"

"Horses?" said Tom with a grin.

"The girls don't interest me," said Mark briefly.

"Why don't you go after Annie and bring her back—if you think *that* much of her?" Tom asked.

Mark walked a few paces. "No. She ran away from us. I don't think we deserved that——"

Tom's eyes were on the Blairs. "They've got good horses, anyway. Look at that chestnut mare. A beauty! A foal out of her by my black stallion should be worth having——"

"No doubt," said Mark shortly. "There's Oliver talking to father——"

Everitt was saying, "I've taken the liberty of coming to your house to bring with me Mr. and Mrs. Blair, and their family. They will be your new neighbours."

New neighbours? What was this, John wondered.

"You are welcome, my friends," he said. "But I—I don't understand——"

"The Blairs have bought our property," Everitt went on. "They expressed a wish to meet you."

John was astonished, but managed to conceal his feelings.

"Please get off your horses and come inside," he said. "I am John Martin—we ourselves have been but a few months in this valley."

The Blairs dismounted.

"And I am William Blair . . . my wife, Alice."

John bowed to Alice Blair and shook hands with William Blair. Blair went on:

"My sons—Henry, James, Arnold, George and William. My twin daughters—Mary and Molly. We are pleased to be your neighbours, Mr. Martin."

The two men looked at each other, and liked each other. William Blair, blue-eyed, greying, of medium height and slender, was a little older than John, and a firm character was revealed by his frank and open countenance and direct eyes that seemed always to smile. Alice Blair was a plump little woman whose grey eyes and friendly manner also showed a pleasant nature. The young men were tall and muscular and quiet, but it could be seen they would unbend readily enough with friends. The twins were good-looking, fair girls, and laughter seemed to be trembling on their lips. Hetty made them cordially welcome at once; she and Alice Blair liked each other.

When all the members of the two families were made known to each other Hetty said, "This is a pleasant and welcome surprise. And you are just in time to join us at table. Will you come in, Mr. Oliver?"

Everitt's face was impassive as he bowed slightly.

"Thank you, Mrs. Martin."

Everitt sensed the coolness of the Martins towards him, but he wanted a quick word with Tilly, so he blandly accepted the invitation to enter the Martins' house.

"When are you leaving the valley, Mr. Oliver?" Hetty asked.

Everitt would not look at Tilly.

"Very soon, Mrs. Martin. My sister, Jane, never recovered from the shock of her terrible experience, so my father decided to sell."

John was glad the unfriendly Olivers were leaving the valley, pleased to know such pleasant people as the Blairs would be next to him. As they seated themselves he turned to Blair.

"And what is the news from Melbourne Town?" he asked.

"I suppose, first of all, you should know that the man Tregg has been freed."

"I am glad to hear that," said John quietly. "Where is he?"

"He came back with us. But he and his family have to leave the colony."

"Indeed. Perhaps he won't be sorry. I should think this valley would haunt him if he were to remain."

"Yes—I suppose so," said William Blair. "Well, the news from Melbourne is mixed. Sir George Gipps held Melbourne's first levee in the Customs House, in October last. There's an increasing depression due to the failure of many graziers. The Government

Offices are now in Batman's cottage, on Batman's Hill. The mounted police have been increased at Mitchell's Town, on the Goulburn River, and on the Broken River and the Hume. The first Scots' Church was opened in October. A Savings Bank has opened in Collins Street—a strange time to open such a bank. Also a Chamber of Commerce, last August. Cattle markets have been established at the corner of Elizabeth and Victoria streets. The Reverend Geoghegan laid the foundation stone of St. Francis' Church. A Wesleyan Chapel has been opened in Geelong. Things are certainly moving fast down there, Martin. A fellow named Henry Dana is to form a force of aboriginal police. The first stock and produce show has been held by the Pastoral and Agricultural Society of Australia Felix, and there has been a protest against including the Portland District in South Australia. The desire for separation from New South Wales is more widely supported than ever, and will before long become effective, I believe. After all, Melbourne is a long way from Sydney."

"Yes, indeed it is," said John. "I have just returned from a visit to Sydney Town. I made the journey to arrange for the purchase of my land——"

Everitt pretended not to hear. He was smiling, and talking to young Arnold Blair, but he missed nothing of what John was saying.

"Sydney also is astonishing in its growth. Do you know South Australia at all?"

William Blair nodded.

"I've been there—in fact I was there in '37 and part of '38. Hindmarsh was Governor then. They had their troubles, early settlement always has, as you know. But the colonists did not always wear long faces—they arranged excursions to the ranges and beaches, they had horse-racing, an archery club, and other diversions—the archery club was formed toward the end of '37, and the first race meeting held on New Year's Day, '38. Being a Van Diemenslander, as is Mrs. Blair, I was particularly interested, when I paid another visit to South Australia last year in the stone monument erected in the first year of Captain Grey's governorship to the memory of Matthew Flinders, who first surveyed the gulf and its shores. I assure you, my friend, it was most impressive. The obelisk is on Monument Hill overlooking charming Port Lincoln, and Lady Franklin herself supervised its erection by the express wish of her husband, the donor, Sir John Franklin, the present able Governor of Van Diemen's Land, because he was with Flinders as a midshipman at the time of the survey."

"That is interesting, indeed. How recent everything here in Australia really is. You and I were both alive when Phillip brought civilization to this dark continent. Do you think South Australia will progress?"

"Oh, undoubtedly, Martin. There are fifteen thousand people in the province now. Adelaide itself, delightfully situated on the Torrens—thanks to the foresight of Colonel Light—is growing; settlers are becoming well established and moving ever farther out; vineyards and general farming are spreading; the overland route between Adelaide and Port Phillip is established; villages are rising inland; minerals are being discovered; and religion and learning are the sure foundations of the future. Martin, I believe the Province will go on to great things. Many believe Wakefield's concept of colonization to be sound—although there are plenty who condemn it—and that George Fife Angas, chairman of the South Australian Company, is an admirable man to implement it. But no doubt there will be changes, Martin, many changes. You know, it must have been impressive—that first ship-load of settlers and officials, men, women and children—stepping ashore on the empty beach at Holdfast Bay, and the touching scene of the youngest of them all, a toddler named Beare—'Baby Beare', as it was affectionately called—being carried through the surf to the beach by a stalwart seaman, and given the honour of being the first to land. And then the nailing of the Proclamation to the old gum-tree that bends over and down so that it resembles a horseshoe."

John and William Blair talked on. Hetty and Alice Blair chatted animatedly.

"And you *rode* beside your wagons all the way from Melbourne Town!" exclaimed Hetty. "That was a long ride——"

"Yes, it was. But the wagons were full of stores, and the weather was fine. I've been used to riding ever since I was a girl, in Van Diemen's Land. Nevertheless I confess that once or twice I wished I could have emulated Lady Franklin—the wife of the present Governor of Van Diemen's Land, you know——"

"Why—what did she do?" asked Hetty.

"An adventurous thing, but typical of her. Three years ago, this month, actually, she came to Melbourne Town, determined to visit Sydney, but also not to undertake the long sea voyage. So she brought over her carriage, and in it drove overland, escorted by mounted policemen, and stopping at hospitable stations on the way. But I didn't have any mounted policemen, nor am I a Governor's lady——"

Hetty laughed. She liked Alice Blair. Tom and Mark and the Blair boys were talking horses, sheep and crops. Nan and Jeanette were in lively conversation with Mary and Molly Blair. Nan turned excitedly to her mother, her eyes glowing with delight.

"Mother—mother!" she called.

"Yes, dear?"

"Molly says they have a piano—a *piano*! And she wants Jeanette to take over her fiddle some time—oh, mother!"

"That will be nice. Jeanette plays the fiddle very well."

"And my boys have quite fair voices," said Alice Blair. "Oh, it's good to have the right companions for the young people. I can see they will get on very well together."

"Yes, indeed," said Hetty. "This valley won't be so lonely now."

But Tilly was quiet, very quiet. Hetty turned to her.

"Will you make the tea, Tilly? I see the kettle is boiling."

"Yes, mother."

Everitt stood up.

"May I help you, Miss Martin?" he asked.

"Thank—thank you, Mr. Oliver. If you would care to do so."

He went to the hearth with her, and when he was close to her he said in a whisper, "Meet me at dusk—you know where. You must come. Can you get away?"

He just heard her reply. "Yes—yes. I will meet you. But you shouldn't have come here——"

"I know. I'll make my excuses and leave now. At dusk?"

"At dusk——"

"Tilly—you must come with me to Melbourne Town. Come prepared——"

"Everitt, I could only do that on one condition—you know what that is."

"Marriage. I know. Come, then——"

"You will keep your word . . . and marry me . . . as soon as we get there?"

"Tilly—you are everything to me. Meet me at dusk."

"Yes, Everitt," she whispered slowly. "At dusk."

26

IT was a golden April afternoon, and the valley, green and refreshed after the rains, was warm under the sun. The air was crystal clear, the bordering hills with their colourful scarps and tree-crowned heights, seemed very close, and even the majestic Alps, tremendous in their lofty outlines, seemed not so aloof, so far away, so wrapped in immensity and solitude.

As the sunlight slanted and sent saffron shafts through the trees, Meg, with her kangaroo-skin jacket hiding her rags, sat in the cabin doorway, silent, looking straight before her. She saw no beauty in the peaceful scene; all she saw was the constantly recurring picture of Everitt riding with the Blairs towards the Martin homestead. Thought racked her. He would now be with Tilly Martin—with Tilly Martin! He would soon be gone from the valley—and in a little while the Treggs, too, would leave the valley. The girl's face was a mask, still and expressionless, though emotion blazed as white fire in her brain. Everitt! The man who would not bother to turn his head as he rode past her cabin; the man who had so coldly put her aside for Tilly Martin. Yes. That was Everitt. She knew she still wanted him with all the burning blend of longing and desire, wanted him for herself and for all time. She had realized it the moment Elijah had told them all they were done with the valley. All she had now were empty days and nights because of Tilly Martin. But for that one she would have had Everitt right up to this moment, until the time when he rode out of the valley and out of her life. Tilly Martin!

She could hear the voices of her brothers somewhere at the back of the cabin, voices that were mere sounds without meaning. The cabin had no meaning. The ploughed ground before her had no meaning. Her days in the valley, her passionate hours with Everitt, the murder of Sarah, the killing of Royd, all had no meaning. And she was cast-off and despised. Annie came out of the hut and walked away. Meg watched her; she knew Annie was going to Elijah. Let her go. Annie was not so smart, she had soon found out that she was not wanted. Meg watched her sister walk out of sight. She found herself wondering what would become of them all: no doubt they would have to go. The surge of rebellion was still there, but if they defied authority they would be forcibly taken, or hunted through the hills as outlaws. John Martin would not support them in defiance of the law—or these new Blairs. They would have to go—but where? What would she do? Or Annie? Become domestic scullery-sluts below stairs somewhere? She moved restlessly at the thought. Or bargaining harlots in some town inn or wayside grog-shop or back-street brothel? Or get married? *Married?* Who would marry her or Annie? Only men whose ankles still showed the marks of the irons, or some drunken whaler, or some desperate shepherd living in isolation and loneliness who could not get even a gin. What Annie's thoughts were she did not know. Ever since the girl came back from the Martins she had been tight-lipped, withdrawn into herself. Elijah? Johnnie? Rock? Dick? Annie? Sarah? Royd? Everitt? Tilly Martin? Herself? Why would her hands keep shaking? Why would her lips and limbs keep quivering? Why *was* she always in this torment?

Then she saw Everitt riding back. He was alone. She stood up, hoping he would turn his head, but he did not look at her. Yes; that was Everitt, the man she desired with a blind intensity that mocked at reason. Meg was rigid now, rigid with humiliation and anger that set her body aching. She stood, bare-headed, bare feet apart, hands on hips as she always rested them when some surge of emotion roused her, small chin jutting, eyes mere blue pin-points of lights.

"You cruel bastud! You cruel bastud, Ev'ritt! I wish to Gawd I c'd pay you beck—an' thet Tilly Martin—thet Tilly Martin——"

No doubt the Martin girl would soon follow him. Yes—*that* was it! She would follow him. Meg gave a choked little cry and ran into the hut and snatched up Dick's gun. Quickly she primed and loaded it. She knew where they would meet—oh, yes; she knew! But this time *she* would be there, and there would be a reckoning. She ran out of the hut and along the valley, her hair lifting behind her like a red plume; but there was no sign of Everitt when she paused, panting, at the turnstile. She went through and turned towards the hills on her left. Across on the right was the high bluff; she did not look at it. She walked now for she knew Tilly Martin had not passed her. In a little while she had crossed the flats and was among the low spurs. She went up one of them, looking about her as she walked through the trees, and presently she came to a narrow gully, the sides of which were smooth rock walls for hundreds of yards. On the lip of this cutting she sat down, the long-barrelled gun across her lap, directly above the spot where Everitt and Tilly met. She would wait. She knew they would come.

In the Martin home there was gladness in the hearts of all except Tilly, who kept her thoughts well to herself. The Martins knew they now had friendly neighbours; that the land was theirs; that their house was built; and that with the coming of the Blairs the sense of loneliness had vanished. The going of the Olivers seemed to remove some resentful and malevolent presence from the valley, and the coming departure of the Treggs was as though sad echoes were dying away.

The Blairs, after many expressions of friendliness and goodwill, had left soon after the midday meal. The men were going to muster the Oliver cattle, and wanted them in the yards before dusk. The turnstile had amused Alice Blair, and she was emphatic that it must be removed and a swinging, barred gate put in its place.

"A ridiculous thing!" she exclaimed. "I wonder why Oliver put it there?"

"It might have reminded him of something back in his youthful days," her husband replied. "Of his wife, perhaps, in some way. Who can tell?"

Annie had seen the Blairs ride back as she stood talking to her father. Elijah sat near the two rough crosses beside Royd's tree.

Annie said, "Thar goes the Blairs beck."

He did not look round. "Never mind them," he said. "I was talkin' to you 'bout the Martins. Annie, you mus' go beck——"

The girl shook her head.

"I can't, 'Lijah—I jist can't," she said in a low tone. "I tol' you why. I ain't no Martin. Yus, they was kind—all of 'em 'cept thet Tilly. But I ain't a Martin. An' us Treggs, bein' what we be, an' all thet's 'appened in the valley 'cause of us, don' track along with folks like the Martins."

"I wants to know——" Elijah said slowly. " 'Ave *they* ever said so?"

"It be what I says—what Tilly Martin keeps flingin' at me——"

472

"Did Mr. Martin—or Mrs. Martin—ever give you dirt?" he persisted.

Annie shook her head.

"No. The boys neither—or Nan or Jeanette. Jist thet Tilly."

"Was they real kind to you?"

Annie's lips quivered. "Yus—yus. They was kind, 'Lijah. Mark was larnin' me to read an' write."

Elijah looked up at her, then away again. She went on.

"I ain't never 'ad sich kindness as they give me——"

Elijah sighed. He did not speak.

"An' I don' s'pose I ever will again——"

"Annie——" he said. "I be agoin' to take you beck to them——"

"No!" and her voice rose a little.

He lifted a hand.

"Lis'n, gel! We be goin' away—an' I don' want you to be like Meg—oh, yus—I knows 'bout Meg. I ain't blamin' Meg, but she'll never be any different. Jist as Royd was borned quar—so be Meg borned like she be. Meg'll go down an' down. The boys? Dick'll walk straight, but not Johnnie or Rock. 'Tain't in Meg or Johnnie or Rock to be right. You be different. I've watched you. I knows."

"Why didn't you stop Meg, then?" Annie asked harshly.

He was silent for a moment, then: "Stop Meg? No one c'd stop Meg. She couldn't stop 'erself. Ever since she was a babby she was screechin' wild, an' clawin' wild, an' she growed up as wild as any dingo bitch. Might as well try to stop the wind, might as well talk to the moon 'an tell it to stan' still in the sky. Stop Meg? Don' you know your own sister?"

"Yus——" breathed Annie. "I does——"

"Thet's why I be askin' you to go beck to the Martins, Annie. You be a Tregg, but you be clean. You can walk with the Martins an' not be 'shamed for y'self. They ain't the folks to blame you—for the rest of us. Y' knows, Annie—'tis quar 'ow things turn out. All me life it's bin thet way for me. I knows what Meg an' the boys thinks 'bout me shootin' Royd—they thinks I should 'ave bin 'anged. I wish I 'ad bin. Do *you* think I wanted to kill Royd?"

Annie shook her head.

"No, 'Lijah . . . I don't," she whispered.

"I be gled you say thet. Royd was my son. Mad an' dangerous as 'e was—'e was my son.

As I lifted the gun on 'im thet night I could 'ear Sarah cryin'; 'No, 'Lijah! No, 'Lijah!' I shot 'im. An' I done right. 'Fore Gawd an' man I done right. I guv 'im 'is life—I took it 'way—afore 'e took another life away. I was watchin' 'is eyes, Annie. I don' think 'e knowed me, until th' ball 'it 'im. Thar was a madman's cunnin' astarin' at me, an' 'is 'ands, after 'e dropped Jane Oliver, was unwindin' thet chain from roun' 'is belly. Thar was death an' murder in Royd's eyes as I looked at 'im. 'E was playin' fox till 'e got thet chain loose—then 'e would 'ave swung it on the gel as 'e did on Sarah. I shot 'im. But the ball thet killed Royd . . . killed me. I wanted to tell you, Annie. I wouldn't tell th' others. They wouldn't unnerstan'—or care. I don' want you to leave the valley with us . . . an' I've decided we leaves tonight . . . so no one'll see us go. I wants you to stay with the Martins. I wants you to stay clean all your life . . . the fust o' the Treggs to do thet. Well?"

She was silent. He could see her trembling, her young face working. Presently she said:

"Dunno, 'Lijah—dunno yet. I guv 'em dirt when I run away——"

"Mebbe not. I'll go see John Martin——"

475

"No!" she cried. "Not yet, 'Lijah—not yet! If anyone goes—I goes by m'self."

"You go then, Annie. Git away from Meg an' Johnnie an' Rock. If you goes with 'em—you'll go down. Thar'll be nowhars else for you to go—nowhars."

"S'posin'—s'posin' they don' want me beck?"

Elijah was staring at the mounds.

"No call to s'pose thet till you've spoke to 'em."

"Dunno. I feel 'shamed. I'll go walk a bit—an' think 'bout it——"

He nodded.

"Then think well, gel—think honest—think fair for y'self. What you does now makes or breaks your life. Life's beat me, Annie, beat me right down to the ground. Don' let it do thet to you. Take your walk."

"Yus——" she whispered. "Yus, 'Lijah——"

He watched her walk away, then his eyes turned to the two graves again. And so he sat, not moving, not speaking, not praying while the hours passed. He was a man beaten, beaten right down to the ground.

The Martins were just finishing a late

afternoon tea as Annie stepped into the living-room. They were so surprised that for a moment no one spoke. Then Hetty rose with a smile.

"Why, Annie! Have you come back to us, dear?"

Annie swallowed several times before she could find her voice. Her brown eyes searched each face. Tilly's was the only one in which she saw hostility.

"I come to ask . . . if I could, Mrs. Martin," she manged to say.

"Of course you can, my dear," said Hetty gently. "Come right in. Why did you leave us like that?"

Tom spoke.

"It's time that was asked, mother. We all know why Annie left us. She left us because Tilly kept rasping at her, and never letting her forget she is a Tregg. Isn't that right, Annie?"

"I don' want no one to blame Tilly for what I done, Tom——"

"That *is* kind of you," came sarcastically from Tilly. "And *very* brotherly of you, Tom."

John spoke.

"Let us take this quietly. Why did you come back then, Annie?"

The girl faced him. Her hands were making nervous little movements, and all could see the strain in her young face. She appeared to be groping for words, and seemed about to speak several times before she at last said:

"Mr. Martin . . . 'Lijah asked me to come back to you. 'E said 'e wanted me to stay clean all me life . . . to stay with you if you'd let me. I . . . I s'pose you'll be laffin' at me now. I wants to stay, too."

"We are not laughing at you, Annie," said John quietly. "Are you sure *you* want to stay with us?"

"Yus! I does! I wants thet mos' of all, Mr. Martin. I be sorry I guv you dirt the night you come beck, but I wouldn't like you—any of you—to think I—I wanted to do thet. 'Lijah said they was leavin' the valley tonight. My folks . . . be leavin' . . . tonight. 'E said, 'Don' come with us, Annie. You'll go down—to nowhar.' 'E said, 'Go to Mr. Martin—for what you does now makes or breaks y' life.' I've come. I don' want to go down . . . to nowhar. . . ."

No one spoke. Hetty's eyes were moist. She

478

could see the hope, the longing that had given this trembling girl the courage to face them.

"And neither you shall, child," she said warmly. "You shall stay and be one of us. Sit down and have some tea."

"I'll take a ride," said Tilly shortly. "I need the air."

"Tilly," said her father. "Take the ride, and take the air, my dear, deep down into your lungs. And when you come back let there be no more of what, seemingly, has been plaguing your mind. Annie will stay with us. Will you remember that?"

Tilly was white with suppressed anger at this reprimand. She would not look at Annie as she rose from the table, but she said evenly enough, "Yes, father, I shall remember . . . that." She went into her room.

John turned to Annie. "We shall be happy to have you with us, Annie."

Annie looked at him. "Thenk you, Mr. Martin—an' Mrs. Martin—an' Gawd, too," she said.

"I've something to do," said Tom gruffly. "Coming, Mark?"

"Yes," said Mark. He looked at Annie. "There's a lot of husking from the second paddock, Annie. We'd be glad of your help."

She lifted her eyes to his.

"Yus, Mark. I'd be gled to." She turned to John. "But thar be one thing I wants to do fust—if Mr. Martin'll let me. . . ."

"What is it, Annie?" he asked.

"I wants to say g'bye to my folks, Mr. Martin—to 'Lijah afore 'e goes. Yus, to 'Lijah."

John nodded.

"Of course, Annie," he said. "I understand. In fact I'll come with you myself, and your father will know from me that all will be well with you."

"Yus," she said huskily. "Yus—thet's what 'e wants to know—thet all will be well with me. Yus——"

"We'll go on the sledge to save walking," said John. "Mother—it's a long way out of the valley——"

Hetty nodded.

"I'll put some things together, John. As you say, it's a long way . . . out of the valley."

Almost sundown.

In front of the Olivers' house—the Blairs' house now—Everitt and Elliott sat in their saddles saying good-bye to the new owners. William Blair shook hands with them.

"But why won't you wait until morning?" he asked.

Everitt's cold dark eyes looked down at him.

"We'll be many days and nights on the track, Mr. Blair," he said. "It makes no difference. Thank you for carting our personal things to Melbourne when you go there in a few weeks' time. We'll camp tonight ten miles from here, and be that far on our way when tomorrow comes. We have our guns and blankets and enough food. We hope you have a more pleasant sojourn here than we have had. Good-bye."

The voices of the Blairs wished them safe journey as they rode away and turned to the south. When out of earshot Elliott turned to his brother.

"Why in the devil's name *did* you want to leave tonight?" he asked.

Everitt shrugged. He brought his horse down to a walk. Elliott did likewise.

"I had a very good reason. I had an assignation with a woman at dusk."

"The Martin girl?"

Everitt nodded.

"Yes. The Martin girl. I had no intention of keeping it when I made it."

481

Elliott looked sideways at his brother.

"Why not?"

"Miss Martin has the quaint notion I'm a blockhead," Everitt said harshly. "I have been amused watching her play. She thought to keep me chasing after her. At first I did so. Oh, yes! In the language of our hunting ancestors I could come right up to the quarry—right up to it—but no kill. The dear Miss Martin is a clever and calculating little actress. She wants it her way—marriage—and no other. Amusing, isn't it?"

Elliott laughed.

"Not an unusual price is it?"

Everitt smiled slowly.

"Not in the least. I'll be in Melbourne Town in a few days. By that time I doubt if I shall even remember her name. She is merely one of my few—mistakes."

Elliott chuckled.

"And Meg?"

Everitt's lips thinned.

"A stupid little animal. I can hear her, 'Ev'ritt, Ev'ritt, Ev'ritt—I be's your woman now. I won' let thar be no other.' Little troll."

"Do you think the Martin girl will keep the appointment?" Elliott asked.

"Yes. She knows we are leaving the valley. I could see her thinking, thinking hard. She thinks she is going to Melbourne with me—to be Mrs. Everitt Oliver."

"You have an extraordinary sense of humour, Everitt."

"I need it—with women like Tilly Martin. I wish I could see her waiting for me, gradually realizing her final act is lacking an audience. I can see the flash of her eyes, the hard set of her lips. Miss Martin loves to call the tune and watch others dance. Oh, yes; pretty Miss Martin has the very devil of a temper behind her sweet smile. I saw that quite clearly. She will be furious, but it will be a useful lesson for her. I have no time for women who bargain. Let's push on. Melbourne Town is a long way from here."

"Thank God it is," said Elliott, as the horses went into a canter. "I never want to see this valley again."

Everitt looked about him. Long shadows from the hills were across the flats. His face, with its thin nose and close-set eyes, was dark and sardonic.

"You won't," he said. "Nor will it ever see us again. This valley, the languishing Meg, and the scheming Miss Martin, will know the Olivers no more——"

The two men rode on, and the miles swallowed them. In a little while they were out of the valley, and the sound of the hoofbeats died away. They were gone. The Olivers had departed.

Sundown. And Annie asking Elijah:

"Whar's Meg?"

The Tregg men stood close together in front of the hut. John could see the sullen resignation in their faces. They, too, were ready to go, guns in their hands, bundles on their backs.

"Ain't seed 'er," said Elijah. "We be waitin' for 'er to come so's we can go." He turned to John. "Mr. Martin, thenks for takin' Annie. She be a good gel, an' will give no trouble. I know this be what she wants— an' it be what I wants for 'er. You bin good to us Treggs, an' you bin kind. Thenk you."

"Annie will be all right, Tregg," said John. "She will be well taken care of."

Annie was looking at Dick.

"Whar's *your* gun, Dick?" she asked suddenly.

"Meg took it—to do some shootin', I s'pose. Ain't 'eard no shot yet——"

"Meg——" breathed Annie. "Meg. Johnnie—Rock! Thar's Tilly Martin ridin' past now——"

"I sees 'er," said Johnnie tonelessly.

"Got saddle-begs on the saddle, too," said Rock. "Looks like she be ridin' out o' the valley——"

John looked from one to the other.

"Out of the valley? Oh, that's nonsense. She is probably taking something to the Blairs. She often rides at this time. Why are you so concerned, Annie?"

"Nothin'—nothin', Mr. Martin," the girl panted. "Johnnie—Rock! Drop them bundles an' come with me—an' run as you never run afore——"

"Meg?" jerked out Rock.

"Yus——"

"Hell," whispered Johnnie. "She said she'd do it——"

They ran as fast as they could towards the fence. John turned to Elijah.

"What is this, Tregg? Why is Annie so alarmed?"

"Ain't quite sure, Mr. Martin," was said slowly. "Mebbe if we puts them things on

485

your slide an' goes thet way . . . we'll see."

"Very well. We can follow them, if you wish."

Elijah and Dick exchanged glances.

"I 'opes Annie an' Rock an' Johnnie'll be in time," said Elijah, as the bundles were placed on the slide.

"In time for what?" John demanded.

Elijah raised his eyes.

"In time to stop another killin', Mr. Martin."

John stared at him.

"A killing? But what—but—but I don't understand. Let's hurry——"

The slide pulled away.

"I still don't understand," said John.

Dick's slow voice told him.

"Ev'ritt Oliver. Ain't no need to say more. Meg was Oliver's woman till your darter come into the valley. Your darter took 'er place. Meg's savage. She's jist waitin' 'er chanct—an' she took my gun——"

John went white.

"Ah——" he said. "I understand—a lot of things—now."

Dusk! And Tilly Martin rode into the narrow gully.

She had seen her father and Annie talking to the Treggs, and she seemed to hear her own voice saying, "Stop, Tilly—stop! Don't go on with this thing! Go back—go back while there is time." But she knew she would not go back. She wondered what her family would think of her. It would shock them, stun them, for no hint had been given to them of this affair. But she could not live in the valley without Everitt—she would not. Thought set her trembling. Mrs. Everitt Oliver! She would be that soon, and she would be done with this lonely place. But her people? It would be a terrible blow to them, and her father, stern moralist as he was, unbending where the laws of decency and religion were concerned, would probably forbid her to enter his house ever again.

But she must go on—she *must*! She could not stop herself now. In the saddle-bags, crammed tight, were clothes and personal necessities. She had no money—but she would need none. This was escape! Escape from monotony, from the soul-chilling loneliness, from these eternal, imprisoning hills, from this long, narrow valley that mocked her and would never let her go until she broke from it, and from her own flesh and blood.

How many women, and men, she wondered as she rode along, were prisoners of far valleys; how many, in the long, long sweep of the colony, from Port Phillip right up to Moreton Bay, were hating their existence, hating the heat of the sun, the bite of bitter frosts, the toil, the frustration, the never-changing round of lonely years?

She would get away from that. She could see her family, her mother's face when it was known; she could see her father, and Jeanette and Tom and Mark and Nan. But it was her life, and she must live it as she wished to live it. No one had the right to hold her back, to expect or demand that her years be wasted, that her life be an empty thing merely to subscribe to some convention. She was *not* immoral. She had not surrendered herself! She was not like Meg Tregg. Meg and Everitt? Stupid lies! No wonder he had been amazed that day when her jealousy charged him with deceit. But they would be together soon, and she would not be Tilly Martin any more, but Mrs. Everitt Oliver. No! She could not stay in the valley. She must go on.

She was a little surprised when she rode into the gully and found no one there. It was dusk. She dismounted to rest the horse. She did not look up, did not see Meg rise slowly to her feet, but she whirled, trembling and furious when Meg called down to her:

"I knowed you'd come!"

Tilly's eyes flashed as she looked up.

"You little spy!" she said harshly.

"Ain't no spy!" Meg said shrilly. "I come to settle somethin'—an settle it I will!"

"I don't know what you are talking about."

"Yus, you does!" came fiercely. "I be talkin' 'bout thet cut you guv me with the whip—an' 'bout Ev'ritt."

"I've already told you I won't discuss Mr. Oliver with you——"

"No! Nor with no one else!"

The strange, jeering, threatening note in the girl's voice sent a chill through Tilly.

"What do you mean?" she demanded.

"I can see th' Olivers' 'ouse from up 'ere. I jist seed Ev'ritt an' Elliott ride away—south! With saddle-begs an' rolled blenkets! You ain't agoin' to see Ev'ritt no more—*never* no more——"

Tilly gasped.

"I don't believe you——" she said pantingly. "No! I don't believe you——"

Meg's voice was now level and deadly. The loaded gun was on the ground at her feet. She stood in characteristic attitude—chin jutting, hands on hips, legs apart.

"Ho, no, Tilly Martin? I ain't lyin'. They's gone. 'E's finished with you as 'e's finished with me. But *I* ain't finished with you! You took Ev'ritt from me. I wanted Ev'ritt more'n I wanted anythin' or anybody in this bleddy world—more'n I wants me own life. But you——"

Tilly's voice was bitter. And there was fear in it.

"I won't listen to this nonsense. I told you before not to speak to me, or to come near me. You're wasting your time standing there spitting out venom. You're trash to me, and you were trash to Mr. Oliver——"

Meg's voice was a scream.

"Trash? Trash—eh? You said thet afore, Tilly Martin! But be the livin' Gawd you won' say it never again——" She bent and picked up the gun. Tilly was incapable of movement. She stood, clad in the red dress and bonnet, staring up at the frenzied Meg.

She could see the girl was beside herself, that the loss of Everitt had turned her into an unreasoning little fiend whose only desire now was to hurt or destroy those whom she thought had hurt her. Cold fear gripped

Tilly. She knew now that this obsessed girl, this lusting red-haired girl, had come to kill her—and Everitt, perhaps. But Everitt was gone. Yes; she knew that now. She managed to gasp out:

"You—fool! Put down that gun! Put it down——"

Meg suddenly threw back her head and shrieked with laughter.

"Yus——" came wildly. "When I've blown you to whar you'll never no more cut in on me nor no other woman——"

"I've been nothing to him—nothing, I tell you——"

"Expec' me to b'lieve *thet*? I seed you with 'im Tilly Martin—I seed 'is lips on yours—I seed 'is arms draggin' you close—an' then closer. I ain't no fool! No woman 'lows thet 'less she wants. I'll swing for you, Tilly Martin—an' laugh whiles I be swingin'. I be agoin' to kill you, Tilly Martin—for takin' Ev'ritt from me——"

"Listen to me—listen!" Tilly's voice was frantic.

"No!" and Meg was screaming again. "Trash, be I? You be frightened now, Tilly Martin—you knows what be acomin' to you—you yaller thievin' muck! Don' you

491

move—you can't git away—an' you ain't got no whip to slash down on me. 'Member the whip? I does. You won't whip me no more——"

Tilly was on the point of collapse. She knew Meg would kill her. Her body was wet with a cold sweat; her lips were white with terror. Everything was spinning, becoming blurred, a world of shadows in which the only thing she could see was that screaming girl with the gun. And she knew Meg was right. Everitt had mocked her, had mocked and scorned them both. She felt sick. The fleeting seconds seemed years while she listened to Meg. Mrs. Everitt Oliver? What a fool she had been! Blind! A vain and self-centred woman offering her very soul on the altar of vanity. Now it was too late. This demented creature shrieking at her would end it all. A red mist was filling the world, soon that, too, would be gone. Mrs. Everitt Oliver? She heard someone laughing. Yes; it was her own laughter she heard. Mrs. Everitt Oliver! Meg was screaming words at her, and she was laughing. Or was she sobbing? Mrs. Everitt Oliver! Yes! she was sobbing—sobbing with an awful fear, with helplessness, with humiliation. She heard Meg say:

". . . to the devil . . . thet's whar we both be agoin', Tilly Martin, an' you can give to the devil what you guv to Ev'ritt——"

Neither of them heard the quick patter of bare, running feet. Johnnie and Rock reached Meg as Annie came to Tilly. Johnnie flung himself at his sister and sent her reeling as she pulled the trigger.

"Ar—goddlemighty!" he rasped. "Lookit—lookit what you've done——"

Rock wrenched the smoking gun away from her. She stared down into the gully. So she stood, swaying on her feet, staring, mouthing words.

"Annie——" she heard herself say. "No! No!"

Rock raised the gun-butt to smash her down, but Johnnie stopped him.

" 'Nough——" Johnnie roared. " 'Nough's bin done! Let's git down thar—quick!"

Meg seemed unable to grasp what had happened. Rock thrust the gun-butt into her back and sent her staggering after Johnnie.

"You git down, too——" he snarled. "You done it—you face it——"

"Annie——" Meg whispered. "I—I didn't shoot Annie——"

This time Rock's clenched fist made her

reel. It was a vicious punch, and blood flowed from her broken lips.

"Git——" he hissed. "Git afore I smashes you down——"

Tilly, shaking and dazed, was kneeling beside Annie when John Martin, Elijah and Dick, came to them.

"It's—it's—Annie——" she managed to say. "It should have been me——"

"Bad?" jerked out Elijah.

"She's moving——"

"Lemme see——" said Elijah.

He bent over the girl, turning her head this way and that.

"Cut the skelp—not too deep—jist shock an' blood. Bind it, someone."

Tilly ripped her petticoat and bound the wound.

"I—I felt her push me——" she said. "That ball was meant for me. She got between me and the gun."

John's voice was unsteady with shock.

"Lift her gently—on to the sledge," he panted. "We'll get her back home where my wife can attend to her. Will she be all right, Tregg? Are you sure? There is something fine in this girl of yours—I hope she will be all right——"

Elijah passed a trembling hand over his eyes.

"Yus; she'll be all right. Jist broke the skin an' flesh an' stunned 'er—but 'twas close. She'll be all right soon. Wish I could say the same for the rest of us. But we better go, Mr. Martin—— Yus; thar *do* be somethin' fine in Annie. Tell 'er g'bye from us—from me. Yus—from me. We better go——"

"One moment, Tregg——"

Elijah trembled.

"Yus, Mr. Martin? Be you agoin' to take it out on Meg? I s'pose you will. But Meg can't 'elp 'erself—she never knowed 'ow——"

John shook his head.

"No. We won't speak of that. I know you must go. I deplore what has happened just now. It has shocked me—shown me that I, too, as a father, must have failed somewhere. I can see now why it happened, and the Martins are not blameless——"

Tilly, holding Annie in her arms, was crying quietly. John went on:

"I shall arrange matters with the authorities about Annie. One thing more. I know how life has turned against you, Elijah Tregg. If ever you need a friend—remember me."

Elijah stood looking at him for a long moment. He said simply, "Yus. I'll remember you. Watch over Annie, Mr. Martin. Thet be all I ask of you. You be the fust man thet *ever* said you'd be my friend. Thenk you. G'bye——"

He stood for a moment looking down at Annie. He murmured gently, "G'bye, Annie, gel. Walk straight. Don' do anythin' wrong—ever! It gits you—nowhar!" He nodded his head several times, then he turned away. The others, after looking at Annie, and taking up their bundles, followed him. Meg, still whimpering meaningless words, walked with stumbling, uncertain steps beside Rock. She talked on and on, but no one listened to her. John turned to Tilly and spoke quietly.

"Enough has been said and done. We'll go home, Tilly."

Tilly nodded as she made Annie comfortable on the sledge, and then reached for the bridle.

"Yes, father. Enough has been said—and done. Elijah Tregg spoke the simple truth: doing wrong gets one nowhere. How well I know that—now. But this also is the truth: I was never Everitt Oliver's woman—although my foolishness did this. My vanity—my concern only for myself—my shallow pride—my cheap conceit. We'll go home together . . . Annie and I. Yes; Annie and I. . . ."

John saw something in her face he had never seen before. There was a strange expression of quietude, of gentleness. He was about to speak, but checked himself. In that moment he showed himself to be a wise man a well as a kindly one. It would take time to heal the wound on Annie's head, a longer time to heal the hurt that was Tilly's, but he knew time would do both.

It was almost dark when the sledge, with the grey horse following, made back towards the fence. There was no sign of the Treggs. They, too, had departed, the night and the miles would swallow them, and the valley would know them no more. Only Royd and Sarah remained, quiet under their tree. But this fair valley, and the valleys beyond it, would in time know others. The work of the hardy pioneers, of brave explorers, of such as splendid Caroline Chisholm, and those fighting for justice and self-government, would bring strength and dignity and purpose to the growing colonies, and with the passing of the years the crude beginnings would die away, and a people strong and united would walk freely under their own Australian skies.

THE END

GUIDE
TO THE COLOUR CODING
OF
ULVERSCROFT BOOKS

Many of our readers have written to us expressing their appreciation for the way in which our colour coding has assisted them in selecting the Ulverscroft books of their choice. To remind everyone of our colour coding— this is as follows: .

BLACK COVERS
Mysteries

★

BLUE COVERS
Romances

★

RED COVERS
Adventure Suspense and General Fiction

★

ORANGE COVERS
Westerns

★

GREEN COVERS
Non-Fiction

THE SHADOWS
OF THE CROWN TITLES
in the
Ulverscroft Large Print Series

THE WHITEOAK CHRONICLE SERIES TITLES
in the
Ulverscroft Large Print Series

by Mazo De La Roche

The Building of Jalna
Morning at Jalna
Mary Wakefield
Young Renny
Whiteoak Heritage
The Whiteoak Brothers
Jalna
Whiteoaks
Finch's Fortune
The Master of Jalna
Whiteoak Harvest
Wakefield's Course
Return to Jalna
Renny's Daughter
Variable Winds at Jalna
Centenary at Jalna